TORI CARRINGTON

"Tori Carrington once again scorches the pages as
she creates an unforgettable read with exceptional
characters, outstanding romantic adventure
and emotionally layered conflict."
—*Romantic Times BOOKclub*

"They always deliver a satisfying read but still
leave me wanting more of their stories!"
—*TheBestReviews.com*

Praise for

ANNE McALLISTER

"A brilliant writer who can make one tear after
another roll down your cheeks, Ms. McAllister
brings us both passion and joy."
—*Romantic Times BOOKclub*

"Anne McAllister is a master storyteller…"
—*WordWeaving.com*

Bestselling, RITA® Award-nominated husband-and-wife collaborative team Lori and Tony Karayianni, aka **Tori Carrington,** credit being in love with love for earning them such high regard so early in their career. From the release of their first Harlequin Temptation in January 1999, their books have earned dazzling reviews and numerous finalist spots in national contests, as well as the prestigious RITA® Award for their books *Private Investigations* and *What a Woman Wants*. They speak on various topics in a variety of venues and travel widely.

Award-winning author **Anne McAllister** was once given a blueprint for happiness that included a nice, literate husband, a ramshackle Victorian house, a horde of mischievous children, a bunch of big friendly dogs and a life spent writing stories about tall, dark handsome heroes. "Where do I sign up?" she asked, and promptly did. Lots of years later, she's happy to report, the blueprint was a success. She's always happy to share the latest news with readers at her Web site, www.annemcallister.com and welcomes their letters there or at P.O. Box 3904, Bozeman, Montana 59772 USA (SASE appreciated).

MARRY ME...
Maybe?

TORI CARRINGTON
ANNE McALLISTER

HARLEQUIN®

TORONTO • NEW YORK • LONDON
AMSTERDAM • PARIS • SYDNEY • HAMBURG
STOCKHOLM • ATHENS • TOKYO • MILAN • MADRID
PRAGUE • WARSAW • BUDAPEST • AUCKLAND

ISBN 0-373-23027-3

MARRY ME...MAYBE?

Copyright © 2004 by Harlequin Books S.A.

The publisher acknowledges the copyright holders of the individual
works as follows:

LICENSE TO THRILL
Copyright © 1999 by Lori and Tony Karayianni
I THEE WED
Copyright © 1991 by Barbara Schenck

www.eHarlequin.com

Printed in U.S.A.

CONTENTS

LICENSE TO THRILL

Tori Carrington

1

JUST THINKING about Marc McCoy made Melanie Weber tingle with need. Even now. Especially now.

She slid her palms over the thick silk of the traditional wedding dress she was being fitted for. It was ironic, really. She had never thought of her relationship with Marc in the traditional sense. Still, she had expected they'd always be together. Always be partners. Always be lovers.

But that was three months ago. Before she realized Marc could never love her. Before she was injured in the line of duty. *Before she found out she was pregnant.*

Melanie reluctantly opened her eyes, then tugged her hands away from the wedding dress. A pinpoint of guilt started in her stomach and slowly spread through the rest of her body. The last person she should be thinking about was Marc McCoy. She'd carefully tucked him in the past the day Craig had generously offered to solve both their problems by proposing to her. She owed it to Craig to keep focused on their plans for the future. She owed it to herself to keep her thoughts away from the past and all that could never be.

Still she recognized the churning signs of panic that had been swirling in her since she and Craig had picked up their marriage license that morning. She'd felt the same way the day she had faced her mother to tell her that she wasn't majoring in business, as her mother so wanted. Only now she suspected hormones were more to blame for her anxiety—she hoped.

She turned slightly to view her profile. Funny, her jumbled thoughts didn't keep her from longing to wear a dress with an open décolletage neckline. But that was impossible. The fresh scar just below her left collarbone was difficult to look at, even for her. She could imagine what would happen if she flashed her gunshot wound to one hundred of Bedford, Maryland's, prominent citizens, much less her own mother. She shook her head. The seed-pearl-studded mock turtleneck that covered nearly every inch of her skin would have to do.

Melanie sucked in her stomach. If she didn't have the dress let out just a tad, she would split a seam in front of Craig Gaffney, God and everyone halfway down the aisle two days from now.

"Wouldn't *that* fuel Bedford's gossip hot line for at least a month?" she whispered to her reflection. As it was, she'd already given them enough to talk about. Scary, since they didn't even know the half of it.

"Joanie? Can you come here for a minute?" she called.

Her younger sister, Joanie, owned the Once Upon a Time Bridal Shoppe. It was just before closing, and with June looming but a few days away, Melanie's dress wasn't the only thing bursting at the seams. The shop was filled with stressed-out brides and overbearing mothers. She stuck her head into the hall. In the room opposite hers, Joanie slid a stray pin from the fabric peach forever around her wrist, then blew her hair from her eyes.

"Be with you in a minute, Melanie."

"Hey, be careful!" complained the bride whose dress Joanie skillfully worked on. "If you get so much as one drop of blood on this dress, I won't hesitate to sue."

Melanie ducked into her dressing room. Her sister could probably make a good chunk of change by videotaping some of the more interesting fittings and selling the footage to their grooms. But something like that would never occur to Joanie.

Her sister's generous spirit and endless patience were the main reasons her business had grown so successful. They were also the reason she radiated happiness like a sweet perfume.

Melanie glimpsed her own rare smile in the mirror, then eyed the chair behind her. But no matter how much she wanted to rest her swollen feet, she didn't dare sit down. Not unless she decided to let out the dress herself in a way that would guarantee she couldn't wear it two days from now.

Saturday. Her wedding.

Her throat tightened, choking off her airway. She closed her eyes to ward off the unwanted reaction. Cold feet, that's all it was. A major case of cold feet. What more could it be?

"You can handle this, Mellie. I don't think I've met a braver woman than you. Aside from my Mary, of course."

The words conjured up the image of Sean's kind, time-marked face and sober green eyes.

Sean. Just Sean. She didn't know his last name. But his presence had been the only thing that had kept her sane during that long week in the hospital. Odd, she thought, because he had been little more than a stranger. A visitor, there for another patient, who had entered the wrong room and found her alone and crying. It was the only time she'd been left alone by her mother, Joanie and Craig, who had all meant well but hadn't a clue how to handle an injured secret service agent whose heart was breaking for the only person who hadn't visited.

Sean hadn't pried. He hadn't tried to comfort her. He'd simply handed her a tissue and sat next to her bed as if it had been her he had come to visit all along.

Picking up a bouquet sample, Melanie listlessly straightened a silk lily of the valley in the all-white waterfall bouquet. She hadn't seen Sean since she had been discharged, and hadn't expected to. But thinking about him made her realize how much she missed her father. Made her selfishly yearn to have him there if only for an hour or so. If only to walk her down the aisle.

Blinking back unexpected tears, she refocused on the bouquet. Merely looking at the fake flowers made her feel like a fake herself. She turned away, not sure she wanted to see the woman reflected in the smooth glass. Three months ago...

"Three months ago you were a fool in love with your career. And an even bigger fool in lust with Marc McCoy," she said softly.

She tossed the bouquet to the velvet chair and reached back to undo her dress, but she could barely move her arms. Joanie had trussed her in. It looked as if Joanie would have to let her out.

She sighed. "Just peachy."

Joanie poked her head around the corner. "Whatcha need?"

Melanie sighed with relief then tried to pinch the tiniest bit of fabric away from her waist. "You were right. It needs letting out."

"I was afraid of that." Joanie came to stand behind her, assessing the damage. "I really hate to tell you I told you so, but—"

"You told me so." Melanie watched her sister slide into her role as seamstress. While she may have spent the past eight years bucking tradition, Joanie had always been content with her life. More than that, she seemed to cherish the role she'd created for herself as everyone's best friend.

It struck Melanie as odd that she should be the one getting married when her sister was still inexplicably single.

Joanie sighed wistfully. "I really do love this dress." She smoothed the puckered seam. "I think it's the one I would pick, you know, if I was in your place." A shadow briefly moved over her pretty, freckled face. "You're lucky, you know? I don't think there's a time in my life when I can't remember Craig being around. And he's always had such a crush on you." She brushed a strand of red hair from her cheek. "You couldn't ask for a better man...."

Her soft words drifted off. Melanie watched her sister, wondering if she was going to mention that the most she and Craig had ever been were friends. The best of friends, but just friends. But her sister appeared to be thinking of something else entirely.

"Joanie?"

Her sister blinked then stared at Melanie in the mirror. "Sorry, must have drifted off there. I haven't had more than a couple hours sleep in the past two days."

Melanie looked at her a little more closely. "Are you sure that's all it is?"

"Sure? Of course I'm sure." She tried to pinch the back of the dress. "Wow, exactly how much weight have you put on since last month?"

She gently batted Joanie away from where she poked at her stomach. "Not all that much."

"Is it that time of the month?"

"No." Melanie wished it were that simple. If only she could tell Joanie why, exactly, she had grown out of her dress. But doing so would undermine Craig's generosity and would open up a whole different can of worms.

Two more days. Two more days and she could tell her sister and her mother.

Joanie pulled back. "No doubt about it. The seams need to be let out at least a half inch."

Melanie swallowed hard. The formal rehearsal dinner her mother had insisted on was only... She glanced at her watch. "Oh, God, I've only got a half hour to get to Bedford Inn."

Just then, an electronic bell rang, followed by a too-innocent, "Yoo-hoo!"

Joanie caught Melanie's gaze in the mirror.

"Mother," they said in unison.

"I'll take care of her," Melanie said, a heartbeat later. "You go finish up whatever you have to, so you can help me out at this dinner."

"Hmm. I don't know. A choice between dinner with Mother and your soon-to-be in-laws or playing voodoo doll with the bride next door? Tough call."

Melanie latched onto Joanie's arm. "Please don't make me go through this alone."

Her sister's green eyes widened in mild surprise. "Melanie, you're not facing a firing squad. Even if you were, you would be the one person I know who could handle it." She covered Melanie's hand with her own. "Okay, I'll be there." She laughed quietly. "But I have to say, you're on your own for the honeymoon."

Honeymoon. Melanie's stomach tightened to the point of pain.

She gathered fistfuls of her full skirt in her hands and led the way from the room. She'd like to say she was surprised by her mother's impromptu visit, but really couldn't. Her mother had always been good at reading her. She didn't doubt Wilhemenia Weber had picked up on the emotional turmoil she'd been going through for the past few months. And if she knew her mother, Wilhemenia wouldn't stop until she found out what was going on.

IN HIS JEEP outside the bridal shop, Marc McCoy absently rubbed the back of his neck, then flicked the air-conditioning on. He didn't know if it was the heat or his anxiety about what he was planning to do that made the temperature in the all-terrain vehicle intolerable, but if Mel took much longer, he was going to stalk in there after her. He grimaced. Who was he kidding? He wasn't going anywhere. He'd sit here and wait just as he had for the past forty-five minutes. All because he'd been too wrapped up in his thoughts when she'd gone in to see his plan through. Eight solid hours of planning, and he'd been knocked out of commission just at the thought of coming face-to-face with her for the first time in three months.

He directed the cool air vent toward his face, then let his gaze drift to the two glossy magazines on the passenger seat. He resisted the urge to grab the first one to find out exactly "what a woman looks for in a man." It wasn't long ago he wouldn't have been caught dead reading this stuff. But Mel's absence in his life had left him with a gaping hole and long, endless nights that he tried to fill with reason.

He grabbed the magazines and shoved them under his seat.

He looked at his watch, then returned his attention to the shop.

He didn't know why, exactly, he had hesitated when he first spotted Melanie leaving her mother's house. For Pete's sake, he didn't even know why he hadn't marched right into the house the moment he got into town.

Frustrated with his hesitation, he shut off the car engine, then reached for the door handle. His hand froze on the sun-warmed metal. Melanie's mother was walking down the street looking like a woman on a mission.

"Uh-oh."

Instantly, he was reminded why he hadn't gone into the small house on Cherry Blossom Road. Because of Mel's mother.

What was she doing here? In order to do what he had to, Mel had to be alone. She'd gone into the shop alone, and he'd expected her to come out the same way. What he hadn't banked on was Wilhemenia Weber, who looked as though she'd come fresh from sucking on a dozen lemons, deciding to pay a visit.

She could be here to see Joanie, Marc thought. *I hope she's here to visit Joanie.*

Five minutes later, the late afternoon sun reflected off the bridal shop door, and he sat up straighter.

"Show time." Mel stepped onto the brick sidewalk. At least it looked like Mel. Grimacing, he slid down his sunglasses and squinted at the woman leaving. Yep, it was her all right. Minus the jeans, T-shirt and blue blazer she'd been wearing when she went in. Now she was decked out in one very short dress. But it was definitely her. *It's about time.* What did she do? Decide to wear her purchase home? He reached for the door handle again. If he lived to be two hundred, he'd never understand what it was with women and clothes. He still had at least eight pairs of Mel's shoes cluttering the closet in his town house. Keeping his gaze focused on Mel, he began to climb out...then froze.

There weren't very many things Marc McCoy, Secret Service Agent, third of five proudly macho male siblings, was afraid of. But he was man enough to admit that Wilhemenia Weber was one of them. And when she followed Mel out of the shop, she threw a wrench the size of a semi truck into his plans.

"Damn."

Marc fought the urge to sink down in his seat. Not only to keep Mel from spotting him, but to prevent her mother from focusing her fault-finding gaze on him. Oh, yeah, he'd met her once. And that one time was enough to know the woman would never like him. He grimaced, finding it difficult to believe it was just over three months ago, before that stupid discussion about love and before Mel's injury, that she'd talked him into going home for Sunday dinner.

Mrs. Weber's disapproving stare had started when he sat on the couch, causing the thick plastic furniture cover to crackle in a way that had made him flinch even as Mel laughed. The Stare had followed him throughout dinner, where Wilhemenia had jerked his soup bowl out from under his nose—apparently because he wasn't convincing enough while trying to choke back the thick, cold green stuff—and ending when she'd practically slammed the door on him when he'd only been halfway out.

The only saving grace was that Mel had taken a perverse sort of pleasure in the whole ordeal. But he absolutely drew the line at returning to that woman's home. Unless she took that stupid plastic off her furniture and ordered in for pizza and beer.

He sobered, realizing that would never happen. Not until Mel invited him back into her life.

His gaze followed mother and daughter down the sidewalk of the quaint little town of Bedford. What was more than a little unsettling was that he still wished Mrs. Weber had liked him...at least a little.

The risk of being spotted gone, Marc scanned the street before he slowly switched his attention to Mel. And found it suddenly difficult to breathe.

He couldn't quite put his finger on it, but she looked different somehow. Her blond hair was slightly longer, brushing the top of her shoulders in a curly way that caught the rays of the early evening sun. But that wasn't it. Then it dawned on him. It was the dress. Well, not the dress, exactly, but the fact that she was wearing it. In muted pink with shiny flowery things stamped on the fabric, it was exactly the type of thing Mel wouldn't have been caught dead in before. He appreciated the sway of her bottom, thinking he'd have been okay with her wearing feminine attire if she'd asked him. But she hadn't. In fact, aside from the brief meeting when they'd first been assigned to work together, he'd never seen her in a dress. And then she'd been wearing a knee-length black skirt.

This thing...this thing barely brushed the middle of her thighs.

Then there were those heels.

Growing more than a little hot and bothered, Marc tugged at the neck of his T-shirt. The shoes added a good three inches to her five feet seven inches. That would bring the top of her head to his nose rather than his chin when they came face-to-face.

Mrs. Weber turned her head in his direction. Marc slumped in his seat, jamming his knees against the dashboard in the process. He cursed. But the words barely exited his mouth when Mel nearly toppled right off those high, sexy heels. He grinned, forgetting the pain shooting up his knees for a second. Now *that* was more like the Mel he knew and—

He bit back the word, an audible gulp filling the interior of the Jeep. What did he know about love? Hadn't Mel told him during their first and only argument that he didn't know diddly about love?

No, he didn't, couldn't love her. He just liked Mel's sexy backside enough to think it worth protecting from the guy who'd already shot her once.

"Oh, yeah? Then tell me something, McCoy. Why is that damn engagement ring you've been carrying around for three months burning a hole in your pocket?"

ADVENTURE, FREEDOM *and hot sex are overrated.* Melanie squeezed her eyes shut and repeated the sentence slowly.

"Melanie, dear, there are guests present."

She cracked her eyelids open to take in a generous view of Wilhemenia, who sat across from her in the dining area of the Bedford Inn. She wasn't sure why, but lately everything her mother said, no matter how innocuous, got under her skin. She offered a patient smile. "Of course there are guests present. It's my rehearsal dinner. I invited them, remember?"

She took in the gilded antique chairs, the crisp white damask tablecloths and the pretty flowered wallpaper, wondering exactly why the traditional event was called a rehearsal. It wasn't as though she or Craig needed pointers on how to walk down the aisle. That was a no-brainer. She smiled at Craig's father, who sat adjacent to her, and suppressed the urge to fidget, sure the unladylike move would elicit another public reprimand from her mother. Then realization settled in. The rehearsal part of it didn't have so much to do with her and Craig. Rather it was a preview of what holidays would look like from here on out.

The tickle of panic that had been with her all day grew to a pang.

Melanie tried to shake the images that crowded her mind. But like an unwelcome visit from the ghost of Christmas future, she envisioned her mother perched on the edge of a couch making comments that always somehow seemed like criticisms about the Christmas tree and covertly trying to get at the nonexistent dust bunnies under the coffee table with her ever-present embroidered handkerchief.

And Craig's parents? Melanie watched them as she chewed a bite of cold roast beef. Okay, so his father was a bit... overbearing. Suspicious almost. Which was only fair given the suddenness of the upcoming nuptials. Melanie's cheeks heated. Craig's mother, on the other hand, was almost effusively nice. Likely a result of spending the past forty years trying to compensate for her husband's bad manners. And her desire for grandchildren from her only child. The roast beef stuck in Melanie's throat. Doris was going to get one of those sooner than she expected.

Guilt ballooned to challenge the panic.

Craig's mother smiled at her brightly. Melanie smiled back, the tongs of her fork screeching against china.

She purposely avoided looking at Wilhemenia.

"Scary, isn't it?"

"Hmm?" She glanced at Craig, who sat next to her.

He leaned a little closer and lowered his voice so only she could hear. "The thought of these guys being in the same room for more than five minutes at a stretch." He cleared his throat. "Just getting my own parents to spend that much time together is asking for trouble."

His familiar grin eased her discomfort as he unwittingly fit his own welcome image in with the others stamped in her mind. It didn't surprise her that he'd been thinking the same thing she had. Throughout their nearly lifelong friendship, Craig and she had always understood each other.

She watched as the grin vanished from his face. He tugged at his tie. She thought he must be feeling as awkward as she was. He leaned in her direction again. "When this infernal thing is over, we need to talk."

"Sure, we can do that." Melanie was almost relieved to focus on someone else. She had been so wrapped up in her own thoughts, she hadn't considered that Craig might be as nervous about all this as she was. But the fact that his request was so very serious scared her. Was he having second thoughts?

She glanced up to find the table had gone suspiciously silent. "How about this heat wave?" she said, not comfortable with the way her mother was watching her.

Doris made some comparison between the heat and a tin roof that Melanie missed, but Craig's burst of laughter made her sigh.

Why can't you be more like Marc?

She jerked involuntarily at the unwelcome thought, sending her fork sailing through the air. She watched in horror as it spiraled above the table, prongs over stem, prongs over stem.... Finally it landed neatly in the middle of her mother's plate, spearing her roasted potatoes.

"Melanie!"

Her cheeks felt on fire. Of all the places for the sucker to land. She tightly clasped her hands in her lap where they were unlikely to do more damage.

"Pardon me."

"Are you all right?" Craig asked.

Melanie made a show of watching her mother pluck the foreign piece of silver from her food.

Look at him, she ordered herself. She did.

It wasn't that Craig Gaffney wasn't attractive. He was appealing in an all-American way that included surfer good looks, wide grin and a sharp mind for drugs. Pharmaceuticals, she amended. She thanked the waiter when he brought her another set of linen-wrapped silverware. Her mother cleared her throat. Melanie carefully freed the silver from the white linen and picked up the clean fork, though she didn't think she could swallow another bite of food.

Craig had a great sense of humor. Did it really matter that he sometimes didn't grasp a punch line? Or that his capacity for humor had somewhat dwindled since they announced their engagement?

She picked up her wineglass and took a hefty sip only to realize she shouldn't be drinking. She forced herself to swallow, then coughed. Craig's father narrowed his eyes, watching her far too closely.

"Wrong pipe," she said quietly.

Her fiancé was also very comfortable to be around, she continued, reviewing her Pro-Marriage to Craig column. A quality that had instantly cemented their friendship nearly twenty-five years ago when they were in kindergarten. He didn't judge her the way most people did then...and now. She glanced in her mother's direction. Wilhemenia was frowning...again. No, Craig had always accepted her for who she was. Which made accepting his proposal all too easy when she'd spilled her troubles to him.

Craig leaned toward her, giving her a hefty whiff of his cologne. *I can change that.* He lowered his voice. "You don't feel like you, well, you know, have to—"

"Throw up?" she said a little too loudly.

He didn't laugh. Instantly, she realized why. No one else at the table knew she was pregnant.

She searched for a way to cover her mistake. "I think I'm suffering from a case of pre-wedding nerves. Otherwise, I'm fine. Really." Which was true enough. She hadn't suffered through a moment of morning sickness, and she was two weeks into her second trimester.

Pregnancy. Baby. Marriage.

Suddenly, Melanie did feel sick.

Sick with fear.

What did she know about being a mother?

"I never thought Melanie would be the first of my girls to marry," Wilhemenia was saying to Doris. The comment caused Craig's father's gaze to sharpen. "Joanie was always the better bet."

More wife material, Melanie silently added, wondering exactly where her sister was and why she wasn't here defending her. And why was her mother discussing her as though she weren't even at the table?

Craig's mother tittered. "But you have to agree, she'll make a handsome bride."

Archie drained half his glass of beer. "Tell me again why you two are in such a rapid-fire hurry to have Pastor Pitts marry you?"

Melanie started. Craig squeezed her hand and said, "I think a twenty-five-year courtship is long enough, don't you, Pumpkin?"

Pumpkin? Okay, so soon she'd look as though she'd swallowed a pumpkin, but still... "You did ask me to marry you on the playground, didn't you, Pookems?"

He blinked at her.

Melanie was aghast at her behavior. She resisted propping her elbows on the table and covering her face as she considered exactly what was going to hit her and Craig once everyone found out she was pregnant. And learned just how far along she was. It wouldn't take a Ph.D. to figure out the math. Craig had been not only out of town at the time of conception—he'd been out of the country. In New Guinea. Doing whatever pharmacists did in third-world countries. That wasn't fair, because she knew exactly what he had been doing. While she...

Melanie finally gave in and rested her forehead against her hand, ignoring her mother's stare.

God, she *was* going to be sick.

She pushed away from the table. Everyone grabbed their glasses and silverware to keep them from becoming deadly projectiles. Tears burned her eyes. Could she possibly make this dinner any worse?

"Excuse me. I'm going to..." *What? Lock myself in a bathroom stall until the world makes sense?* "Powder my nose."

Her mother neatly placed her napkin next to her plate. "I'll come with you."

"No!"

The occupants of the head table stared at her in stunned silence, as did the half of the population of Bedford that had been invited to the dinner. Melanie tried to control her voice. "I mean, thank you, Mother, but I can see to this myself." Her mother appeared ready to argue. "I'm fine. *Really.*"

Melanie shakily stood her ground. Surprisingly, it worked. Her mother sat down. "Very well, dear."

Melanie looked for the tiny bag she'd brought with her, then saw it lying on the floor. She stopped herself from crawling under the table for it, smiled at everyone, then stepped as casually as she could toward the hallway.

She felt awful. Her stomach was upset, she felt bloated and her swollen feet ached. But it was more than that. She felt out of her element. Usually in command of every situation, she now felt inexplicably vulnerable. As soon as she was in the hall, she collapsed against the wall, blinking back hot tears. What was the matter with her? Hormones? Or did some part of her realize she was making the biggest mistake of her life?

Out of eyeshot of everyone in the dining room, she slowly slid her hands down her stomach, resting them over the exact spot where even now her child was growing within her.

Marc's child.

She briefly closed her eyes, wondering again if not telling Marc about her condition was such a good idea.

She wiped the dampness from her cheeks. Too late now, wasn't it?

Besides, Marc had made it clear he wasn't interested in anything permanent. She reached down and slid her aching feet from the torturous contraptions Joanie called shoes and tried to work the heel off one. She couldn't very well wear them if they were broken, could she? It wouldn't budge. She started in the direction of the rest rooms before someone caught her trying to snap the heel off from the other one.

Inside the pink-and-gold rest room, she locked herself into a stall and sank down on the seat. She needed a few moments to herself. Bolstering minutes to take a deep breath and pull herself together. She had to. Not for her sake. For her baby's. And, a guilty part reminded her, for Craig. He deserved better than a cranky bride who abandoned him to his mother-in-law.

Melanie swallowed hard, appreciating if not particularly overjoyed with the humor of the situation. After using up the better part of her life trying not to upset the delicate balance of her relationship with her mother, she'd spent the past eight years going through an odd, ambitious sort of rebellion. Not a planned one, by any means. But during her first year at college, all the emotion—all the hunger for adventure she had secretly craved—had just kind of gushed out, overwhelming her with its intensity. She'd been as unable to deny the change in herself as she would have been able to keep the sun from warming her skin.

Then, three months ago, she had paid for that "coming out" of sorts. But tucking away the thrill-seeking Melanie Weber was not an easy task.

The outer door opened. "Yoo-hoo."

Melanie closed her eyes and clutched her shoes, half wishing she could climb on top of the toilet so her mother couldn't see her stocking feet from under the door. Not that it mattered. She peeked through her eyelids to find her mother angling her head to peer through the thin crack between the hinges.

"I'm in here, Mother."

"Oh!"

She had to give her mother credit. At least she attempted to act as though she hadn't just been gaping into a closed stall.

She heard the door next to hers close. There was no rustling of clothes, meaning her mother wasn't doing anything in her stall, either.

"Mother?"

"Yes, Melanie?"

"Why are you so afraid I won't go through with...well, you know, with marrying Craig?"

There was silence, then the distinct sound of the toilet paper roll going around in circles. Melanie gave in to a sudden smile. At least her mother was attempting to make the situation look somehow normal.

"Well...I have to admit, I am a little concerned about your

unusual behavior these past couple days." Wilhemenia paused. "I don't know, your behavior reminds me so much of that time you came home from university for the summer and neglected to tell me you'd changed your major from business to pre-law." She made a quiet sound. "I won't say a word about how your choice of careers after graduation disappointed me."

You don't have to say anything because you already have. Every time you want me to do something I'm against.

Melanie propped her shoes on a metal shelf then toyed with her own toilet paper. "And do you really think hovering over me like a—" *jailer?* "—like a mother hen is going to prevent that from happening?"

Another brief silence. "It's not like that at all. I...I just want to be here if you need anyone to talk to."

Melanie caught herself ripping the paper to shreds, the pieces floating to land around her feet.

"Melanie?"

God, she was crying again. If she kept up the waterworks, she'd end up floating down the aisle on a wave of her own tears.

Her mother spoke again. "*Is* there anything you want to talk about?"

Melanie opened her mouth, but nothing came out. She swiped at her damp cheeks.

Her mother cleared her throat. "If this is about that Marc character, you should just put him out of your mind right now."

Melanie released a long, silent sigh, the words a vivid reminder of exactly why she couldn't talk to her mother.

"He's not the marrying kind, you know. More little boy than man. You'd only be miserable."

Melanie nodded, hating her mother's words but agreeing with them nonetheless. She was beginning to suspect that the only thing worse than being *without* Marc McCoy was being *with* him.

"Mom?" The shortening of the word mother should have sounded foreign, but oddly enough it didn't. "Did you love Dad?"

For the life of her, she couldn't figure out why she had asked that. Her father had died when she was three, right after Joanie was born. What did ancient history—especially her mother's ancient history—have to do with what was happening now?

"Never mind. Forget I just asked that question." Melanie got up and collected her shoes.

"Melanie?"

She stopped midway toward the door. "Yes?"

"I..." Wilhemenia's voice trailed off. "I just wanted to tell you that all I've ever wanted is for you to be happy."

Some of Melanie's tension melted away. "Marrying Craig will make me happy, Mom. Thanks." She gestured vaguely, though her mother couldn't see her. "Thanks for putting everything back into perspective."

Clutching her shoes in one hand, she opened the outer door. She skidded to a dead stop, finding herself nose-to-chin with a whole different barrier.

Marc McCoy.

Melanie's breath gusted from her.

That can't be right. This was her rehearsal dinner. Marc shouldn't be anywhere near the inn or the rest rooms, much less her, right now. Yet there he was, big as life and twice as tantalizing. She stumbled backward.

"Wrong way. You want to come out." Marc folded his fingers around her wrist and tugged her the rest of the way into the hall. Melanie's knees felt about as substantial as baby food. She had no choice but to lean into him, causing a wave of longing to flow through her body. Suddenly, three months seemed like a very short period of time, indeed.

"What's going—"

"Shh." Marc laid a finger against her mouth. The simple action was maddeningly sensual. Her gaze was glued to his lips. But rather than kissing her, he set her purposefully away from him, confounding her even more. She moved her hand to the side of her throat, feeling her pulse thrumming wildly, her skin searingly hot.

"Interesting conversation you and your mother were having in there," he said.

Melanie avoided his gaze. "You heard?"

She didn't realize what he was doing until he slid a mop handle through the door handle, securely barring her mother inside the ladies' room.

A hysterical laugh tickled Melanie's throat. She couldn't count the times she would have loved to lock her mother in a room. But wishful thinking was one thing; willful doing was quite another. She battled the irresponsible emotion.

"Let's go," Marc said, taking her hand.

Let's go? Had he actually just said, "Let's go"?

Melanie dug in her heels as best she could, considering she wore no shoes. Her stocking feet slid across the tile as Marc hauled her toward the parking lot. She swatted at him with the lethal shoes in her free hand.

"Hold on a minute, McCoy. Just where do you think you're taking me?"

He stopped. "Why, out of here, of course."

Melanie stared at the man who had the power to overturn every one of her well-laid plans. Her stomach pitched as she realized he intended to do just that.

Then he had the nerve to grin. Grin! Okay, he was rubbing the spot where her spike heel had nicely connected, but otherwise there was no evidence she had done anything more than blow a strand of his rich brown hair out of place.

"Hello, Mel. Miss me?"

Miss him? About as much as a bad sunburn. But her heart started to murmur something else. Melanie ignored it.

"What are you doing here? You weren't on the guest list. I know because I drew it up."

"I penciled myself in." Marc's reflective sunglasses prevented her from seeing his brown eyes, but his smile told her more than she wanted to know. His head tilted forward as he took a languid look over the tight-fitting silk of her dress, then up to where the sleek material hugged her waist and breasts. "Put on some weight, haven't you, Mel?"

Scorching heat spilled over her cheeks again as she fought the desire to cover her stomach. *He doesn't know*, she reminded herself.

"Looks good on you."

While her physical dimensions had altered a bit since she last saw Marc, he hadn't changed a bit. At six foot two, he was two hundred pounds of raw, muscled male. His military background was evident only in his tall posture. The easygoing grin and lazy casualness were pure Marc, as were his black T-shirt, jeans and the suede vest she knew concealed the 9mm revolver he always carried.

The mop handle rattled against the door. "Melanie?"

Oh, God. Mother. "You know, it's not very nice to go around locking people in bathrooms." Melanie tugged her hand, but he only tightened his hold. "Marc!"

"What?"

"Let me go." She considered whacking him with her shoe again. He finally released her.

"Aw, now is that any way to treat an old boyfriend?"

A handsome grimace creased Marc's face. A face she had tried to forget. A face chock-full of remarkable features she sometimes found herself wishing her child would inherit. *Their child.* Melanie swallowed hard.

"Ex-partner, then," he said quietly. "Surely you have a few minutes for your ex-partner."

Partners. Yes, they had been at least that. Although not in any permanent sense of the word, despite her present condition. Their partnership had been more professional than personal, and she had been dumb to forget that even for a second. As special agents for the Treasury Department's Secret Service Division, they had worked together for two years. Up until Melanie decided it was time to get out.

Wrong choice of words. She hadn't decided anything. The decision had been made for her. By a fellow agent who had turned his gun on her...and by a doctor's innocent words.

"Ex-partners do not lie in wait when all they want to do is catch up," she said softly. "What do you want?"

Marc had always been good at his job. When he wanted, he could be formidable. His physical appearance alone was enough to scare off any number of fanatics hoping for a shot at stardom by targeting a political candidate. But in his downtime, Melanie knew him to be an irresistibly handsome, rambunctious little boy who usually took nothing and no one seriously. Which gave her a definite advantage over him.

Melanie bit her lip. She didn't want to think like an agent anymore. In fact, she hadn't thought about her previous career for at least—well, half a day. Hooker had called her from jail that morning, after a two-month silence, despite court orders for him not to do so. Hearing his voice before she broke the connection had rattled her as much as his previous calls, not to mention the countless letters he'd sent her, which she had returned unopened. Out of the need to feel safe, she'd strapped her firearm on. An irrational act, considering Hooker was in custody.

"Yoo-hoo. Melanie, there's something blocking the door.

Could you open it, please?" There were rattling sounds as her mother tried to open it herself. "Melanie?"

Melanie swallowed hard, feeling Marc's gaze hone in on her despite the sunglasses. She suppressed a shiver.

"You're going to have to call off the wedding, Mel."

She blinked. "What?" she whispered.

"You heard me. Tell the poor guy you agreed to marry you're sorry, but there's been a change in plans."

Hysterical laughter again threatened to erupt from Melanie's throat. She thought of all the plans that had been made, the guests who had been invited, and realized she'd drop everything in a heartbeat if she thought for a minute that Marc loved her. But he'd already made it clear he didn't and never would.

No, Marc's appearance was just one more unfair occurrence in a day chock-full of them.

"Not on your life." She surveyed him. She noticed the way he stood, all too handsome and deceptively relaxed, then watched the casual way he shifted his weight toward the bathroom door. Melanie's gaze slid to the barrier, and her heart gave a triple beat.

"Melanie? Who's out there with you? Is it Craig? Maybe he can help—"

Melanie dove for the mop handle. Before she could pull it free, Marc's arms snaked around her waist. She gasped and thrust her elbow into his stomach with all the force she could muster, given her restricting apparel. She met with what felt like reinforced steel. While she'd gone a little soft around the middle, he'd gotten more than a bit harder.

"Come on, Mel, don't make me go to Plan B," he murmured.

Plan B? What was he talking about? And why did dread and anticipation spread through her at the humor in his voice? She stilled. "You can let go of me now," she said with forced calm.

"Why? So you can try to let your mother out again? No way. I've been trying to get you alone all afternoon. Now that I've got you, I intend to do what I came for." His breath stirred the hair over her right ear. She was powerless to stop an obvious shiver. "You *are* happy to see me."

She tried to loosen his grasp, but again he tightened it.

"Come on, Marc, where am I going to go?" She wriggled against him, hating that he could read her reaction so well.

"Mmm."

Melanie's knees threatened to give out at the sound of his soft hum. His palms had flattened against her hips and now nudged up toward the underside of her breasts. She gasped, every traitorous part of her body craving that all too familiar touch.

Marc buried his face in her hair and breathed deeply. "God, I forgot what it was like to touch you."

Need grew within her again, stronger this time. "Please let me go." She hated the helpless quality of her voice and tried to insert some metal. "Or else I'll do something you won't find very pleasant."

His chuckle stirred more than her hair. "You always were one for idle threats, weren't you?"

Somehow she found the energy to do what she had to. Curling her fingers around one of the shoes, she swung it backward, heel first, hitting her intended target. Air rushed from Marc's body. He stumbled back, releasing his hold on her and reaching for his crotch.

"How idle was that?" Melanie whispered. Clutching her shoes in one hand, she reached for the mop handle with her other.

"Oh, no, you don't," Marc said.

Melanie's stomach gave a small flip as she struggled to

open the bathroom door. She nearly had the mop free when Marc drove it home.

"Why did I think this would be easy?" he murmured.

The world tilted beneath Melanie. By the time everything stopped spinning, she found herself draped over one of Marc's wide shoulders, her shoes bouncing off the tiled floor. Her eyes were parallel with his jeans-clad rear end. And oh, what a rear end it was, too. Too bad she wasn't in the mood to enjoy it at the moment.

What was she thinking? She didn't want to enjoy anything about Marc. Not now. Not ever again. In two days she was getting married. And not to Marc. Because Marc had a bad habit of disappearing when she needed him most.

"I can't believe you just did that!"

"Yeah, well, believe it," he murmured. "I don't care what they say, sometimes drastic measures are necessary."

They? Who were they? God, she wished some of this mad situation would start making sense.

Marc suddenly stilled. "Everything's fine, sir. You just go on about your business."

Melanie peeked around his hips to see her uncle Fred worrying his tie in his hands. Bedford's most prominent banker scurried toward the men's room across the hall, not even attempting to help. Melanie suddenly wanted to cry.

A tentative knocking sounded on the ladies' room door. "Melanie? Are you all right?"

Drawing in a fortifying breath, she said, "I'm fine, Mother." Aside from feeling like a sack of flour. "Feel better now?" she asked him quietly.

"Much, thank you," Marc said lightly. "Now, tell me how I go about making you see reason."

"Reason? I'm not the one who just threw someone over her shoulder."

She felt a hot hand on her ankle. She fidgeted and tried to see what he was doing.

"Hold still, or you'll find a hand right where I'm sure you least want it," he said. "Tell me, Mel, do you still take that neat little nickel-plated .25 everywhere you go?"

Melanie's eyes widened as he cupped her right heel, then slowly slid his fingers up her calf, tickling the back of her knee. "Marc! Get your hands off me, you overgrown—"

His probing ceased just short of her panties. He stood silently for long moments. Melanie didn't dare breathe. Awareness tingled everywhere his hand had touched, and even now neglected parts of herself pleaded for the pleasure they knew Marc could bring.

"Satisfied?" she croaked.

"Not nearly," Marc said quietly. He moved his hand across her backside, eliciting a gasp, then slowly began down her other leg. "There she blows," he said, pulling her .25 free from her thigh holster.

Melanie groaned and pushed against him in exasperation.

"Tell me, Mel, does your fiancé know what you hide under your skirt?" he asked, not removing his hand. Instead, he caressed the spot around her empty holster with feathery, fiery flicks of his callused thumb. She wriggled against him, threatening to topple herself to the floor. The way she figured it, anything was better than subjecting herself to Marc's all-knowing touch.

"Put me down."

His hand abruptly disappeared from her leg.

Rather than relief, Melanie felt nothing but disappointment. She held on for dear life as he bent to pick up her shoes.

"I will," he said, the lazy teasing back in his voice. "Eventually."

2

MARC TOOK IN everything and everyone in the parking lot in one glance. He hadn't expected to spot Tom Hooker lurking in the shadows—the shooter who could even now have his gunsights set on Mel—but he hadn't expected Hooker to escape custody the day before, either. No matter how overloaded his senses were with Mel's nearness, he couldn't forget that all evidence indicated Hooker was not only on a direct route to Mel, he was armed to the teeth, as well.

He picked up his pace.

Well, *that* hadn't exactly gone as planned, had it? He shifted Mel's weight more evenly over his shoulder, ignoring her attempts to get him to let her down. Ignoring, too, the warmth of having her body against his again, even given present circumstances. He strode toward his Jeep, parked in the far corner of the lot. The smell of new fabric mingled with Mel's soft, subtle perfume. Linden flowers. That's what he had always likened the scent to. She had always insisted it was jasmine. One of these days he'd take her to his family home in Manchester, Virginia, to show her the linden tree in the back yard. The tree's brief but fragrant blossoms were the closest he'd ever gotten to any type of flower in the all-male household in which he'd been raised. Of course, while Mel shared his small town background, the only flowers likely to be found in her yard were of the rose variety.

"Where are you taking me?" Mel asked, wiggling to free herself from his hold.

"Cut it out, Mel. You're just making this harder." He tried not to focus on the way her breasts jiggled against his back and gave her bottom another squeeze. He grinned at her gasp.

"Is that what this is all about?" Her voice was raspy. Her movements stopped. "Are you doing this to cop one last feel?"

"Feel?" He opened the back door of the Jeep, thinking that touching her again would indeed be reason enough for him to kidnap her. "No, Mel." He laid her across the back seat, causing the tight, short skirt to shimmy up her thighs, baring her legs and other more secret areas for his scrutiny. He tossed her shoes into the back, his gaze glued to the tiny scrap of material that masqueraded as underwear. It didn't come close to disguising the soft, down-covered swell of sweet flesh it covered.

He concentrated on the tightening of his throat instead of the swelling in another area of his anatomy. Oh, how he longed to claim that mouth of hers with his, to skim his hands down her lush body, to trail a finger along the border of those panties, slowly, teasingly, watching as the silky material dampened with her reaction....

He reined in his thoughts. Speaking of groins, he'd be better off protecting his whenever he was on this side of her feet. The thought hit him just as she thrust her foot toward him.

He caught her ankle. Despite her actions, in her face he read the same longing he felt. He hadn't realized how much he missed small moments like these. When everything but Mel vanished into the background. When just knowing how quickly he could make her come apart sent his blood pounding through his veins and opened a peculiar sort of weightlessness in his stomach.

He shifted his hand up her calf, the languid move hiding the way he shook inside.

"Marrying Craig will make me happy."

Melanie's words to her mother just moments earlier echoed through his mind. His hand froze as he slowly tore his gaze from her face. The feel of her warm, satiny skin beneath his palm made him fear it would take a crowbar to lift his hand.

A glance around the parking area reminded him where he was and what he was doing. Gradually, the sound of his heartbeat lessened, and the drone of cars passing on the nearby street increased. He finally moved his hand and swallowed...hard.

"Nice view," he said, keeping his voice carefully neutral.

When he dared look at her again, her cheeks were flushed with color and she was avoiding his gaze. But it was the rough sound of her voice that betrayed her most of all. "Yeah, well, you might want to get a good look while you can." Mel battled with the skirt, pulling on the hem until it somewhat covered her.

I don't need to look. Everything about you is already burned into my memory.

Marc forced himself to reach for the handcuffs he'd left on the floor. He leaned toward her, careful not to let things spiral out of control again. Afraid it wouldn't take much.

"I'm really sorry about doing this, Mel." He grasped her wrist. He expected a struggle, but surprisingly he encountered little. He grimaced as he tugged her arm over her head. The metal teeth of the cuffs caught as he attached one side to her wrist, threaded the other through the handgrip above the window, then dragged her other arm up. He tried not to notice the way her chest heaved with every breath as he caught her legs under his weight. He took his sunglasses off and tossed them to the front seat. He was about to pull away when his gaze snagged on hers again.

God, it had been a long time. Too long.

Marc stretched his neck, thinking an ordinary man would

be a goner with one look into Mel's face right now. She looked altogether too kissable, too damned sexy. Luckily he'd never considered himself an ordinary man. He came from four generations of McCoys who had served in the military or law enforcement or both. He had once been a Marine. Nope, none of the five current McCoy brothers, if asked, would ever admit to knowing the meaning of the word *ordinary.*

Only problem was, the pep talk wasn't doing diddly to douse his need to taste her lips....

Before he knew it, he was leaning closer to her, his breath mingling with her wine-scented breath. He eyed her mouth, groaning at the way she moistened her lips with a quick dart of her pink tongue.

"Marc, you better, um, not do what I think you're about to."

"Do what?" *Get it under control, McCoy.* "Kiss you?"

She made a sound that was somewhere between a whimper and a warning. It took Herculean strength to leave her mouth untouched, her lips slightly parted, no matter how much he wanted to claim both. *Because* of how much he wanted to. Instead he brushed his lips against the sensitive shell of her ear. "Remember when we used the handcuffs for reasons that were...not professionally correct?"

"That...that was a long time ago." She fairly croaked.

"Not so long ago that you can't remember." Not so long ago that he couldn't remember, either. Even now he hardened painfully at the images that slipped through his mind. Sex with Mel had always been intense. But, somehow, looking at her now, he found it hard to believe this prissily dressed example of upper-middle-class bliss could still be an inventive spitfire between the sheets.

He heard the click of her swallow as she moved restlessly beneath him.

Oh, she remembered, all right. He could tell by the way she

arched against him even as she sought to put more distance between them. Impossible, given their current position.

"I don't think it's a good idea for either of us to remember," she said quietly, turning her head away when he would have pressed his mouth against her jawline.

He forced himself to pull back. "I think it's the best idea I've heard in a long time."

She turned her head toward him. "Just one of the many examples of how differently we think, isn't it?"

He recognized the shadow of pain in her eyes. He'd seen it once before. The night before she was shot. The night they'd had their first and, as luck would have it, last argument. The night she had asked if he loved her.

Remembering the moment, Marc found swallowing almost impossible. But upon closer examination, he discovered there was something else in the depths of her eyes that was somehow unlike the pain she had so clearly felt then.

Before he could pinpoint exactly what, she moved one of her legs up, catching him off guard, though her stockings guaranteed her attempts were ineffective. He grimaced, thinking it was a good thing he'd tossed her shoes into the back or he'd have been in trouble.

"You're getting rusty, Mel." He patted her legs then reluctantly drew back. "I guess a dress and a couple months under Mother Wilhemenia's roof will do that to a person."

He watched the color return to her cheeks, though she still refused to meet his gaze. "And you're still as reckless as you always were, aren't you, Marc?"

"You used to tell me my...how did you put it? My adventurous nature was what you loved about me." He cringed at the loose use of the L-word.

"What?" The cuffs clanked as she shifted to look at him. "I never said I loved that about you. That trait is exactly what made me—what made us so different."

Marc eased himself out of the car and closed the door. He drew in a deep breath and worked his shoulders to loosen the muscles there. Yes, Mel had always appealed to him in a way he'd never wanted to examine too closely, but this... He thrust his hand through his hair, frustrated by his inability to define what he was feeling. One thing he did know was that he'd have to control it if he was going to protect Mel in the way she needed to be protected. And if he was going to get her back into his life.

He glanced toward the inn. Why didn't it surprise him to find Mrs. Weber marching through the door? He grimaced, watching as she motioned to a man about his own age. Marc clutched the driver's door handle. Mel's groom, he guessed.

No, this wasn't going as planned at all.

Then again, nothing with Mel had ever really gone as planned. If it had, she would still be with him and the division and she wouldn't be getting ready to marry some other fool on Saturday morning, putting herself at more risk than she knew. And making him feel lonelier than he'd ever thought possible.

He climbed in and slammed the door so hard the Jeep rocked. He started the engine.

"Where are you taking me?" Mel asked again. The persistent clank of the cuffs told him she was examining them. He didn't have to look. She knew as well as he did there was no way she could free herself. Not unless she carried a key in her bra. Something he doubted, but he had prepared for the possibility anyway by making sure she couldn't reach it if she did have one.

"Just sit back and enjoy the ride, Mel. You're not exactly in a position to do much else."

She pushed at the back of his seat with her feet. Marc leaned forward. She might have gotten a little rusty, but she still packed a hell of a punch. And he wouldn't put it past her to have enough strength in those long legs to send him flying through the windshield.

He should have brought some shackles.

Stick to the plan.

Just because the plan was off course didn't mean he couldn't proceed with the rest of it.

He thought back to a magazine article he'd recently read. When having problems, focus on the good things.

"Mel?" he said quietly.

A long silence, then a tentative, "What?" drifted from the back seat. He looked to find her still examining the cuffs. Marc faced the road again.

"Remember the time we were on the vice-presidential detail in Seattle?"

Silence.

"You remember. He was in Washington for the preprimary debate, and we were placed on extra alert—"

"I remember," Mel interrupted, apparently giving up her study of the cuffs.

He glanced to find her staring at him. "Then you remember what you did when you saw that perp in the hotel kitchen? You wrestled the guy to the floor before he had a chance to identify himself." She turned her face away. "Good thing the vice president's ticker was strong, or you would have given him a heart attack."

No response. Marc tightened his hands on the steering wheel. Maybe that hadn't been the best memory to use.

"Of course you couldn't have known he liked to walk the streets incognito, picking up a paper or two. Hell, none of us knew."

Silence.

Marc cleared his throat. The art of conversation was obviously not an inherited skill. His father was a pro at it—at least with others—as was his brother Mitch. Given Mel's response, he guessed he was still an amateur. "Not in the mood for reminiscing, Mel?"

"Don't call me Mel," she said finally. He exhaled in surprised relief. An angry Mel was much easier to deal with than a silent one. "My name's Melanie. And no, I don't feel like revisiting the past, Marc. I'd just as soon forget it."

He turned onto the on-ramp for I-270 South. "It wasn't that long ago."

"Ninety-two days. Two-thousand, two hundred and eight hours. One hundred, thirty-two thousand—"

"All right, I get the picture already," he grumbled.

"—four hundred and eighty minutes," she finished, her voice little more than a whisper. "That's a lot of time. Enough time for a person to completely reinvent herself." She paused. "I'm not rusty, Marc. I'm not the person you knew."

Maybe she had a point there. Marc rubbed his fingers across his chin. Then again, his reaction to her hadn't changed. While Mel still carried her .25—strapped to her milky thigh, no less—she didn't call herself his partner anymore, in either sense of the word, no matter how much he wanted to lose himself in her. Now more than ever. Three months without Melanie had done that to him.

He resisted the urge to rearrange a certain painfully erect body part into a more comfortable position. He reminded himself that his plan had as much to do with physical urges as it did with the threat that loomed over Mel's head. And the changes in her merely amplified her need for protection.

What would she do when he told her Hooker had escaped from custody en route to his hearing? That it was strongly suspected he was coming after her to finish the job?

He looked at her in the rearview mirror, flinching when the rock she wore on her left ring finger reflected the sunlight. He thought about the velvet pouch in his pocket. His ring was nothing compared to the one she had on. Little more than costume jewelry. Why had he decided an emerald was prettier than a diamond?

He grimaced, wondering why he carried the stupid thing around, anyway.

Marc mulled the situation over for the half-hour ride into the city, finding no easy answers to his questions or the ones Mel kept asking. Honesty to a degree. That's what a piece in last month's issue of *It's a Woman's World* had said. But what was that degree? He absently thrust his fingers through his hair. Sure, he knew enough not to tell a woman her hips looked big in a certain pair of jeans or that a shade of lipstick looked awful when it did...well, most of the time anyway. But how much did he tell Mel about what was going on? Was it best to keep the truth from her altogether? Was it better to let her believe he'd kidnapped her to keep her from marrying someone else? Which wasn't exactly a lie...

He slid the velvet pouch to the side of his pocket. Who in the hell had colored in so many shades of the truth, anyway? He really couldn't guess how Mel would react. All he knew was that her injury must have scared her but good, or she would have never quit the division.

"God, you're not taking me to your town house, are you?" Mel's voice broke into his thoughts.

He cleared his throat. "So you still recognize the way. Given the number of times you've visited lately, I'm surprised."

She whispered something he couldn't hear. He turned to look at her. He'd noticed before that she'd let her hair grow. He watched the setting sun bounce rays off the golden strands, making it appear as if she wore a halo. Only he knew how much of the devil resided within her, even if she chose to forget.

"What was that?" he asked.

Metal clanked against metal, but she said nothing.

"Let's see, what could it have been? Hmm. Could you have been commenting on how many times I visited you in that colonial mansion wannabe on Cherry Blossom Road in Bedford you now call home?"

Her continued silence told him what he wanted to know.

He grew more agitated. "I was afraid your mother wouldn't tell you how many times she turned me away—"

"She did not." Another nudge to the back of his seat nearly threw him against the steering wheel. But it was the loud tearing of material that caught his attention.

Marc pulled into the garage of the two-family town house he had lived in for the past ten months. With a flick of the remote, the garage door started to close, clipping off the sunlight. He turned to see Mel's frown as she took stock of the rip in her dress.

"Tsk, tsk," he said softly.

"Go to hell, McCoy."

He climbed out of the Jeep. "Oh, me and hell are coming to know each other very well lately," he said to himself, then opened the back door. "Are you going to cooperate? Or should I leave you out here until you cool down?"

He watched her school her features into a mask of calm. Only the bright spots of red on her cheeks gave away her true feelings. "I'll cooperate."

He grinned, not buying her act for a second. "Good."

He took the key to the cuffs out of his front jeans pocket and released her. She rubbed at the red rings around her wrists, then stared at the tear in her dress.

"I can't believe you did this," she said as she scooted to the door. Marc stepped out of the way. "Where's the phone?"

She glanced around the garage to where a telephone extension had once hung next to the door to the kitchen.

"Phone?" he asked.

Her gaze warily shifted to him. "Yes, you know, that little

banana-shaped instrument you use to contact others. Where is it?"

He glanced at her, taking in her shoeless feet. "Let's go inside, why don't we?"

He placed his hand at the small of her back, silently groaning at the way the silk of her dress complimented the warm hollow. She didn't budge. "I'm not going anywhere with you."

He cocked an eyebrow. "Oh? You're here, aren't you?"

"Not by choice." She moved away from his touch, and he saw the ten-inch tear in the side seam of her dress.

He dropped his voice an octave, doubt briefly tainting his intentions. "What makes you think you have a choice now?"

Wrong thing to say. He knew without any magazine telling him that. No one liked to be boxed in. Especially a woman like Mel.

He watched as her eyes widened slightly. For the first time in the years he'd known her, he spotted fear lurking in her face, in her stiff posture. Never had Melanie Weber been afraid of him. And he didn't like the thought that she was now, even if it was for her own good. He molded his fingers gently around her upper arm and urged her toward the door.

"Come on. If you're still hungry, you can raid the fridge while I see to some things."

She tried to tug her arm from his grip. "I don't want to raid your fridge, Marc. I'm supposed to be in the middle of a perfectly wonderful dinner with—"

"I know. Your groom-to-be, his parents, your mother and all of Bedford. I hate to tell you this, Mel, but I think your guests have figured out you won't be back."

Her gaze fastened on his face, but she kept walking. He steered her through the door, then closed it and turned the key in the dead bolt. He pocketed the key, then let her go, oddly disappointed he no longer had a reason to touch her.

She ran her hand absently over the marble-tiled countertop that had been the deciding factor in his taking the town house, though he had yet to understand her fascination with the piece of rock. She turned toward him, her eyes soft and watchful.

Marc barely heard the loud, curious meow and the clicking of nails against the kitchen floor until Brando wound himself around Mel's ankles.

"Oh, God, you still have him." She bent to lift the cat into her arms and cuddled him close. For a moment, a crazy moment, Marc allowed himself to believe Mel was here on her own steam.

"Of course, I kept him," Marc said quietly, turning away. He tensed, half expecting her to mention all the times he swore he'd toss the scruffy scrap of gray fur from the place after she'd dumped the stray in his lap. But after Mel disappeared from his life... Well, the arguments on how the new town house and the cat wouldn't get along meant little. And having something of Mel meant a hell of a lot more.

He felt her probing gaze on him. Well, that bothersome habit hadn't changed, had it? She still looked at him as if she could see to the core of his soul. And, stupidly, he still felt the need to hide it from her. Especially now.

He opened the refrigerator, using the door to block her gaze. "Why don't you go wait in the living room. This shouldn't take long." Peripherally, he saw her finger the empty phone perch on the far kitchen wall. Then the pat of her shoeless feet against the tile told him she had left the room.

MELANIE MADE HER WAY through the all too familiar town house, trying not to notice the changes. Or, more importantly, trying not to register all that hadn't changed.

She didn't want to see the paperback she had readily abandoned on the side table when Marc had tackled her on the leather sofa.

She didn't want to remember how they had a wallpaper glue fight while decorating.

She rested her hand on the dining room table, trying to erase from her mind what had happened the one and only time they had attempted to have a civil meal, only to end up with her right elbow resting in a plate full of mashed potatoes. It had taken three washes to get all the gravy out of her hair.

She closed her eyes. No phones. Not a single one of the three extensions was in sight. She swallowed the panic that had been accumulating in the back of her throat all day. During the drive, she had come to the conclusion that she couldn't return to the dinner and pretend nothing had happened; that much was obvious. But at least she could tell someone she was okay and that they shouldn't worry.

"Who would you like to explain this to, Melanie?" she whispered, absently stroking the purring cat in her arms. "I've got it. You'd call Craig. He'd be upset, but surely he'd understand. No, no, you'd call Mother and make her worry even more that you're going to run out on your groom."

She leaned against the living room wall and closed her eyes, not wanting to be reminded of the past. But everything in this place brought the memories rushing back. Marc hadn't changed a single thing since their breakup. She came awfully close to indulging in a smile, thinking she could check back in fifty years and everything would probably be the same, only a lot older. His battered leather recliner was still a mile away from the television set, though he'd argued with her for weeks after she had convinced him to move it there. Her short-lived plan had been to arrange his things so that when she moved in, he wouldn't have to move anything to accommodate her stuff.

It was a stupid plan.

She swallowed, trying to forget all about that time in her life. Staring at spilt milk wasn't going to get it cleaned up, as her mother was fond of saying.

She thought about Craig and all he offered, comparing him to Marc and the thrilling impermanence of a life spent on the edge. Craig was practical, thoughtful and predictable. Marc was exhilaratingly irresponsible, selfish and boyishly irresistible.

But, ultimately, the absence of a father in her life made Melanie desperately long for her child to know one. And Craig would give her child everything he needed. Her baby deserved that.

Marc... Well, Marc wasn't interested in being a father.

No matter what happened, she knew she had to marry Craig.

Still, the sadness that filled her was overwhelming in its intensity.

As her gaze slowly focused, it settled on the coffee table. A pile of well-thumbed magazines littered the top. Melanie bent down and let Brando go. The cat scampered toward the kitchen, as she moved toward the table.

Cosmopolitan? Redbook? Working Woman? She slowly leafed through the magazines strewn across the surface between empty beer bottles and a doughnut box

"Mel, I was thinking—" Marc's words abruptly stopped.

Before she had a chance to blink, he was across the room, gathering the books. "Never mind those. They, um, were delivered here by mistake."

Melanie turned over the one she held and found his name on the label. She blinked at him, a curious warmth spreading through her chest.

He jerked the magazine from her grasp.

She decided he had gone mad. He might look like the same

hunk who had swept her off her feet two years ago with his charm and devil-may-care take on life. But his actions now... She was afraid they marked him a few croutons short of a full salad. So what if he looked even more in control than he ever had? He had kidnapped her, for God's sake. Swiped her from her wedding rehearsal dinner not ten yards away from a roomful of guests. Threw her over his shoulder and hand-cuffed her in the back of his Jeep. And he was reading women's magazines. That more than anything proved he wasn't in full charge of his faculties.

Yet the fact that he was reading women's magazines some-how touched her.

"I should have left you handcuffed," Marc grumbled.

"Let me guess, you like the pictures," she said, forcing her gaze to the French doors leading to the back yard. He was so outrageously embarrassed, reminding her of a young boy who'd just got caught with a *Playboy* under his bed. "Actually, I'm surprised you didn't. Leave me handcuffed, that is."

He stuffed the magazines into a garbage can. "I didn't think it was necessary. The way I figure it, you run, I'm on you before you can get ten feet." He tugged at the collar of his T-shirt. "So you might as well sit down until I'm finished." Tin cans clunked together as he tossed a handful into a large brown bag.

She watched him, not sure what to make of his behavior. He was still so much a little boy wrapped up in a gorgeous man's body. On the job he was a confident professional, but when it came to matters of the heart, she was afraid Marc could qualify for the role of Dumbest in the sequel to *Dumb and Dumber*. She swallowed hard. She pushed aside her at-traction to those endearing qualities and reminded herself that she needed a responsible adult.

She absently sat in his recliner, but the action wasn't as easy as she had hoped. The hem of her dress hiked up to her panties. She tugged at her sister's idea of a dress, wishing she had gone with something a little more conservative.

"Do you want a coffee? It's your favorite," Marc said.

She shifted to look into his face. He held out a hefty mug to her. The aroma of French vanilla made her mouth water. She accepted the mug, longing for a sip, though she couldn't drink it. Caffeine and all that. Still, she decided it best not to argue with him right now. She'd pretend to drink the coffee. Then she would talk him into letting her go. It was as simple as that.

Marc continued doing whatever it was he was doing, passing through the room several times carrying bags. One bag in particular caught her attention because it wasn't plain brown paper like the others, but rather a glossy pink with purple handles. She squinted to read the words printed across the outside: Old Towne Bed and Bath Shoppe.

She sat upright and made an attempt at pulling the ripped seam of her dress together even as she tugged at the hem. "Okay, let me phrase my question in a way even you can understand, Marc. What, exactly, is your objective?"

"My objective?" He stood and stuffed something into the pink bag.

She fidgeted. "You didn't go through all this just so you could serve me a coffee." She glanced at the untouched coffee in the cup she'd put on the table, then eyed him. "Did you?"

He rocked on his heels, then folded his arms across his chest. "No, you're right, I didn't."

Hope shot through her. He was beginning to sound reasonable. Good. That meant she would soon be out of this place and back to her new safe, predictable life in Bedford in no time. "So?"

"Ah, yes, my objective." He reached to scoop up Brando, who sat on the floor. The casual move made Melanie remember when she'd brought the scrappy cat home from the shelter after having him neutered and declawed. Marc had picked up the tiny, shivering kitten, drew him close to his chest and said, "I coulda been a contender," earning the cat his name.

Marc cleared his throat. "Let's just say it's important for you to spend some time with me, that's all."

"Time?" Melanie focused on the conversation, not liking his vague answer. "How much time are we talking about here? An hour? Two hours?"

He lifted his head to meet her gaze. Melanie's throat closed at the determination she saw in his eyes. "As much time as it takes."

"What?" Melanie rose from the chair. "As much time as it takes for what?" Certainly he wasn't trying to... "I am going to marry Craig, Marc."

He stepped closer to her, then appeared to change his mind and stepped back. Despite the distance that separated them, Melanie felt as if he'd touched her.

"All this, your getting married...it's about that night, isn't it?" he asked.

She knew he had to be talking about the disastrous discussion they'd had about love just before she was shot. Melanie swallowed her surprise. She had seen Marc McCoy in various hair-raising situations. But never had he been so eager to understand.

"It's about more than that night." She fought to hold his gaze, though she wanted to look elsewhere, fearing what she might give away. "Marc, I know my getting married must have come as a shock to you." She tried to feel her way. She didn't know what to say. Especially when he dragged a hand through his dark hair, tousling it in that way she loved. "For Pete's sake, we don't even know each other."

She stopped and looked him in the eye. "I mean, we *know* each other. But not very well." She was faltering and she knew it. There were some areas where they knew each other only too well. "I've never even met your family. You've met my mother, but just the once." She cleared her throat. "I'm not even sure what your favorite color—"

"Green."

She gave a shaky smile. "And mine?"

He stared at her, seemingly at a loss. She wished he would say purple, as if that in itself would prove he cared about her.

But he remained painfully silent.

Finally, he said gruffly, "I'm going to finish up. Why don't we have this little talk later, okay?"

"Talk," Melanie repeated numbly, her point more than hitting home. "Yes, yes, we do need to have a talk."

She watched him set Brando down and leave the room, incapable of all but the simplest of movements. Like blinking.

She desperately needed to convince him that they weren't meant for each other—before his mere presence swayed her the other way. She needed to remind him that he didn't love her, no matter how much it hurt to face that inescapable fact.

Brando brushed against her foot. She absently scooped the tom up and stroked him, then glanced at her watch. She caught herself bouncing the cat as if he were an infant and forced herself to stop. She didn't understand why she had to explain anything. Hadn't it been Marc who said he never wanted children? Hadn't it been Marc who was nowhere to be seen when she was lying in a hospital bed after surgery to remove the bullet she'd taken? When she'd learned she was pregnant?

She realized she was close to tears. She couldn't deal with this right now. She really couldn't.

Her legs were no longer able to support her. She sank into the beige leather couch, listening to the sound of running water from the kitchen. Marc's peculiar behavior wasn't the only cause for concern. There were her curious feelings for the man, reignited the moment she saw him standing outside the inn's ladies' room. She blamed his absence from her life, the shock of seeing him again after so long, for most of her reaction. But she knew she couldn't easily dismiss the other feelings that had stirred to life. Her blood ran thick; her lips were forever dry, as though waiting for him to moisten them with his kiss; her body trembled in a way she had somehow forgotten it could but all too readily remembered.

But it was more than that. She had missed him. Missed his boyish smile, his adolescent sense of humor—

"Are you sure you don't want something to eat before we leave?"

Marc's question pulled her from her thoughts. At the mention of food, the cat leaped from her lap and meowed. Melanie swallowed the lump in her throat. Marc acted as if this situation were nothing more than two old flames catching up, but the fact that he'd carried her there, not to mention removing all the telephones, told her she was little more than a prisoner.

Prisoner.

"Uh, yes, I am a little hungry," she said, trying for a smile. His grin told her he wasn't buying her change in behavior. Still, Melanie tilted her head and desperately kept smiling. Finally he said something under his breath, then returned to the kitchen.

Her heart racing, Melanie got up from the couch so quickly she was sure she heard another rip of fabric somewhere in the back of her dress. She tugged at the hem and hurried toward the French doors—the obvious choice for escape. Too obvious.

"Think, Mel, think." She started at her use of her old nickname. Everyone at the division had called her Mel. Initially, she had encouraged the habit. The male name did away with a lot of the pre-meeting sexual discrimination so inherent on the job, especially since out of two thousand secret service agents, only one hundred twenty-five were women. Of course, it hadn't meant a thing after she met someone face-to-face, but with her knowledge of tactical techniques and natural skill with firearms, she had more than held her own in the male-dominated field.

The bedroom.

She bit her lip. Marc would probably expect the bedroom to be the last place she'd go. Given his ego where his libido was concerned, he would think her too weak to confront the memories of their lovemaking.

She tried the door to the bedroom, then caught sight of the bathroom. She hurried across the hall and turned on both faucets, then pushed the auto lock in and closed the door before stepping into the bedroom.

Twilight filtered through the miniblinds on the windows, slanting intimate shadows across the unmade king-size bed. Melanie swallowed. If Marc had judged her too weak to come in here, she had a sinking feeling he might have been right. They hadn't spent a great deal of time in the town house, but what little time they had was spent primarily in this room.

She edged along the wall and the closed closet doors, irrationally afraid that if she got too close to the familiarly rumpled bed, she might be tempted to climb in. Her pulse racing, she made her way to the closest window. The other one would require her to step around *that* bed. Her palms grew damp, and she hoped she wouldn't have to do that.

"Mel?"

Every molecule of air froze in her lungs as Marc's voice filtered through the closed door. There was a quick knock against the bathroom door across the hall. She hurried to the window. Hoisting the miniblinds, she stared outside, then tried to unlatch the window. It wouldn't budge. She glanced over her shoulder to make sure the door was still closed and blindly tried to open the window. *Nothing.* She stared at the previously easy-to-turn latch and found that a tiny lock had been secured to it. She considered using the brass clock on the night table to break the glass. Then her gaze caught on something else.

Slowly, she lifted the turned-down picture frame next to the clock. Her breath caught when she looked at a picture of herself.

Where? How? Neither of them had ever owned a camera. Heat swept across her cheeks. At least not while they were together. Now she owned a top-of-the-line camera with all the extras in preparation for the birth of her—their—baby.

But this picture...

She scanned the background of the photo and realized she hadn't posed for the shot. It had been taken on the job. Marc must have had a copy made and had her image cropped and enlarged. Her heart gave a tender squeeze.

"Nice try."

Melanie jumped, nearly dropping the picture as she turned toward the door. There was a time not so long ago when no one could have entered a room without her knowing it. Obviously that was no longer the case. She turned to find Marc filling every inch of the doorway, his hands on his lean hips, his sexy grin peeling back the layers of her resistance.

"I..." She what? Melanie swallowed and put the picture frame on the nightstand. She had tried to escape. It was as simple as that. "You can't keep me here, you know. By now a lot of people will be looking for me." She stared at him. "You're well versed on the legalities, so I won't bother with those." She squared her shoulders. "But I don't know if you understand how morally incorrect this is. If you have one ounce of feeling left for me, Marc, you'll let me walk out the front door. Please."

"I have more than an ounce of feeling left for you, Mel.

That's why I can't let you go." His expression shifted briefly. "Take it off."

"What?" Melanie's gaze slid to his face. She must have misheard him. Certainly, he wasn't suggesting—

"Take off the dress, Mel."

Her heart started beating double time. Her gaze slid to the rumpled sheets on the bed next to her. Her hands absently stroked her slightly rounded stomach. "Did you hear one word of what I just said?" she asked.

"There's nothing wrong with my hearing."

She fought not to fidget. "No, there probably isn't. Now, your thought processes are a different matter." Melanie pushed away from the window and strode toward the hall, pretending a bravado she didn't feel. She stopped when she reached the door—and him—but refused to meet his gaze. She focused on his chest instead, then decided that wasn't much safer. "Excuse me, but I think I'd, um, feel better if we moved to the other room."

His eyebrows rose. "You're the one who led me in here."

"Led you?" She looked into his eyes, something she swore she wouldn't do but did anyway. This close, the black of his pupils seemed ready to take over the brown of his eyes. She'd always loved his eyes. "I didn't lead you anywhere." Her thrumming body disagreed. "I was trying to escape. Big difference."

"I can't let you do that."

Melanie wasn't sure what she wanted to do more as hot tears blurred her vision—slug him or cry.

He looked as though she had gone ahead and slugged him, apparently as shocked by her tears as she was.

"I didn't...I mean, that's not.... Oh, hell." Finally, he moved. Just enough to let her into the hall. Except that would mean brushing against him. Not a good idea. Especially since she couldn't seem to control the faucet to her waterworks. *It has to be the hormones.*

Melanie rapidly blinked back the dampness. She had not walked away from Marc McCoy because she had stopped wanting him. She doubted the chemistry that existed between them would ever be completely gone. Neither would their history, considering the child that was even now growing inside her.

She cleared her throat then swept past him, her breasts and hips brushing against him for the briefest moment. Tingles ignited at the points where they touched, then swept throughout her limbs, making her momentarily dizzy. Her ability to go on with her life had depended a great deal on Marc's absence. Now that he had reentered the picture—despite the Neanderthal way in which he had—she had a problem on her hands. Especially if he intended to see through this plan of his to hold her hostage. Melanie held her head straight as she led the way into the living room. Brando was in the middle of the couch, giving himself a thorough bath. Melanie sat fidgeting next to him, rationalizing that if Marc decided to sit next to her, he would have to—

He moved the cat.

Melanie got up from the couch quicker than she thought possible. "I can't believe you're doing this. I don't know what you're trying to prove."

"Take off the dress, Mel," he said in the same exasperated tone he'd used in the bedroom.

"Why?"

He sank to the couch and rested his arms on his knees. "For one, if you keep pulling on that hem you won't have anything left to take off."

Melanie caught herself trying to elongate the length of the dress by sheer will alone. She switched to pulling the tear in the side together. "I always said you were about as romantic as a rock."

"Yeah, well, even a rock knows that dress and the other you plan on wearing on Saturday make you an easy target."

Melanie's throat tightened. Target? Her gaze honed in on his face.

He said something under his breath. "As long as you're wearing that thing, there's a chance you'll try to escape again."

"What did you mean by an easy target?" she asked tightly. "Target for what?"

"You're trying to change the subject, Mel."

She hesitated. Something about the way he said that further unnerved her, and he wasn't meeting her eyes. Whenever he refused to look at her, it meant he was lying. "Marc—"

"Take it off, Mel," he said.

Anger won out over paranoia. "I see. You figure if I'm nearly naked I won't make a run for it."

"Uh-huh."

She swallowed, hating that he looked relieved.

He shrugged, his half-boy, half-rogue grin melting her insides. "If you'd like you can also consider this a form of punishment for trying to escape."

She attacked her hem with renewed vigor. "So now it's a punishment."

He pushed to his feet and rounded the coffee table. "Can you just be quiet for a minute, Mel, and take off the damn dress?"

3

So MUCH for all the advice he'd picked up. So far he was batting zero for two. Revisit the past, they said. He mentioned Seattle, and she clammed up. Let her know with small gestures how you feel. Mel looked about ready to jump out of her skin.

Marc eased Mel around, the feel of silk and her firm, warm flesh confounding him. In all the thought that had gone into this plan, nowhere had he left room for the riot of emotion that charged him every time he came within smelling distance of Melanie Weber. And now that he was touching her— well, it was better he didn't think about that.

He eyed the back of the dress. "Where's the zipper?"

Mel was so tense he swore her hair trembled. "There is no zipper," she whispered.

She tried to pull away, but he held her. "Yeah, well, if there's a way into this thing, there has to be a way out, right?" He spotted the buttons that stretched from the neck all the way down to her softly rounded rear end. He cleared his throat, his patience dwindling fast.

"I suppose this is a woman's idea of romance," he murmured. He'd read his fill on how to fix a soothing bubble bath and knew what type and color every piece of lingerie meant. Pushing a tiny pink button through a silky loop, he winced at the sight of his callused thumb against the delicate material. He didn't think the editor had him in mind when writing about stuff like this.

The herbal smell of her hair reached his nose, and he battled a groan. Ravishing Mel was no way to protect her. Or to convince her not to marry the other guy. Yes, he'd missed touching her. But more than that, he'd missed her and everything that was her. Her laugh. Her quiet strength. Her sharp mind and even sharper wit. His thoughts shifted to Tom Hooker and the bullet that had taken all that away from him. The man who even now posed a threat to Mel's life. He chose to ignore that things had gone awry before then.

Suppressing the desire to rip off the ruined dress, Marc tried to make quick work of the buttons, but the closer he got to the small of her back, the quicker his pulse pounded. It usually took a whole lot more than undoing somebody's buttons to arouse him. Then again, Mel had always been able to turn him on with little or no effort. His painfully aroused condition proved that hadn't changed.

That's not why we're here, he reminded himself. Yes, he wanted to take Mel right here and now. On the carpet, on the couch, against the wall. Just like old times. Lose himself in her and forget the past three months. Forget that damn hospital and the battle he'd fought and lost to go in there to see her. Forget that even now, out there somewhere, Hooker was looking for revenge against Mel because she was the one responsible not only for foiling his assassination attempt, but for his arrest.

He suspected, from the trembling of Mel's fingers where she stubbornly held the rip in her dress together, that she wouldn't put up much of a struggle if he pulled her into his arms. He had guessed that the instant he'd met her eyes at that stupid rehearsal dinner. But sex had never been their problem. It wasn't the reason she had left him. And it wasn't the way to bring her back.

Neither is kidnapping her, his conscience taunted.

As each button gave, the material of the dress gaped open,

baring her creamy flesh. Marc's jeans tightened uncomfortably. The closer he moved to the arch of her back, the louder the blood roaring in his ears got. Finally all the buttons were undone. He touched her back with his rough fingertips, then drew them down until they rested at the top of her panties.

He absorbed her shiver.

"Please don't," she whispered, breathless.

While she said one thing with her mouth, her body was speaking a whole different language. A language even he could understand. She leaned into his touch and tilted her head to the side, baring her neck to his gaze. One thing he was coming to learn was that no meant ño, and that included *don't*. But when her lush rear end pressed against his erection, everything he'd read in the past three months vanished, and he knew nothing more than an urgency to touch Mel in a way he hadn't for a long, long time.

He lowered his mouth to her neck, laving the silky skin there. He circled her rib cage and filled his palms with her breasts. The need that surged through him was almost frightening in its intensity. She whimpered and pressed her bottom against him more insistently. He nearly lost it right then and there.

"Please don't," she whispered again, her face flushed. But this time she moved away, her hands tugging her hem down and uselessly trying to hold the dress together at the back.

Marc's gaze dropped to her mouth. Her lips were slightly parted, her elegant throat trying to swallow. Funny, he had never noticed how long and graceful her neck was. He'd always thought of her as mouthwateringly attractive, but he had never stopped to define by degrees how each part equaled the delicious whole. Outside the bedroom, he'd always thought of her as his equal. Part of that might stem from the fact that they had been partners before lovers, but Marc suspected most of the reason was his own witlessness.

"What are you afraid of, Mel?" he asked, trying to crush the desire threatening to burn right through his veins. "Do you think I can't even unbutton your dress without wanting to jump your bones?"

A shadow of a smile flitted around her eyes, making him want to coax it out. She realized as well as he did how close he'd come to doing just that. "Three months ago you wouldn't have gotten past the third button."

"Three months ago I was a different man," he said, using her words against her. She backed up toward the couch, uncertainty on her face.

He cleared his throat. "Aren't you forgetting something?"

She stared at him blankly, color still high on her cheeks.

"The dress."

"You're serious, aren't you?"

"Uh-huh."

Something flashed in her eyes, reminding him of the Mel he had always admired. The one who never passed up a challenge, a person who could play the I-dare-you game just as well, and often better, than the guys. Her gaze never leaving his, she tugged at the material, pulling first one, then the other, sleeve free. Then with an expression that seemed to ask him, "What do you think of that?" she released her grip, and the dress glided to the floor in a shallow puddle of pink silk.

She stood in front of him, arms stiffly at her sides, nothing but a strapless strip of material covering her breasts and a tiny scrap of triangular silk barely concealing the hair between her legs. Marc's throat closed as his gaze followed the toned line of her inner thigh down to her sexy feet. It took everything he had not to drag her into his arms. All she needed was that pair of stiletto heels he'd tossed in the back of the Jeep, and she would be every man's idea of a dream come true. Problem was, she already was his dream. Even with the scar he couldn't bring himself to look at somewhere above her bra line.

"Impressive," he said, vaguely registering that his voice still worked. "Tell me, Mel, will The Fool appreciate your effort to make sure the wedding night is something to remember? Or has he already tasted the sweets in the candy store?"

The redness in her cheeks told him he'd said the wrong thing...again. Marc bit back a curse, watching as she quickly bent to pull the dress on.

"Trust you to make everything sound dirty. And his name is not The Fool. It's Craig."

He roughly caught her hands. "Has he, Mel?"

He'd told himself countless times it didn't matter if Mel had slept with another man. In fact, he had already accepted that she probably had. But seeing her nearly naked, the slightly rounded muscles of her stomach drawn taut, her womanhood so proudly accentuated by the naughty panties, shot his efforts all to hell. He was back to square one, back to when he had wallowed in a jealous funk at the thought of another man touching her.

She glanced away. "What does it matter?"

He forced her to look at him, aware he was being rougher than necessary but unable to help himself. "Answer me, Mel. Have you slept with him?"

She met his gaze, the moisture in her eyes despite the courageous way she held her head nearly knocking him over. She said nothing for a long moment, merely stared at him in that unblinking way that always drove him crazy. Then she lowered her lashes and looked at the dress pooled around her feet. "Not that it's any of your business, but...no. I haven't slept with him."

She said the words so quietly, Marc wasn't certain he had heard her. But the relief that eased through his tense muscles told him all he needed to know. What he had suspected. What he had hoped.

She hadn't been able to be with anyone else, either. Good.

Of course it did little to solve that other little problem. The fact that she was still getting married.

He couldn't help grinning. "Do you remember the first time we went to that hot dog place down on Mission? The one with those old-fashioned mustard bottles?"

She tugged herself free of his grasp. "This is stupid."

She reached for the dress again. He established his hold. "Oh, no, you don't." She fought him, this time with the strength that had made her one of the best in the business. "I told you the dress comes off, and it stays off until we leave."

"What kind of game are you playing, Marc?" she asked hoarsely, the ragged emotion in her voice like a punch to the gut.

He nearly let her go.

"It's no game, Mel. It's punishment, remember?" His gaze flicked over her flushed skin. "You tried to escape, and now you're facing the consequences."

"So you just expect me to sit around here for how ever long you decide...." She hesitated. "Butt naked?"

Marc's grin widened. "Not butt naked, Mel. At least not if you behave yourself."

She moved her head in a way that flipped her hair over her shoulder. And oh, what a shoulder it was, too. At least the part he allowed himself to view. The other side and the scar that loomed in his peripheral vision remained untouched by his direct gaze. "So what do I have to do to get my...clothes back?"

A dozen, impossible, improbable ideas sprang to mind. "Oh, I don't know. I suppose we could work out some sort of merit system." He thought for a moment. "Tell you what.

You cooperate with what I have in mind, and I'll award you points."

"Points?" The wariness was back in her eyes. "What kind of points?"

He sighed. "Not the type you're thinking. And here we thought I was the one with the dirty mind." He released her wrists, then reached for the dress. She quickly stepped out of it, and he tossed it to a dining room chair behind him. "I may have sunk to kidnapping, but I'm no rapist."

"That's a relief."

Though she tried for sarcasm, her tone fell just shy of the mark. "Is it, Mel? Could it be true that you haven't thought about us at all?"

She was silent. Marc found it incredible that he was standing in front of a half-naked Mel and had no urge to look past her face for the answers he might find there.

"Is this one of the questions that will earn me points?"

"No," he said, his frustration building. "This is one of the questions that will help me figure out where I went wrong."

Mel stilled, staring at him in a way he couldn't interpret.

The mechanical din of "One Hundred Bottles of Beer on the Wall"—the tune that served as his doorbell—echoed through the town house. They both stood completely still until it rang again.

"Seems we have a visitor," she said quietly.

Marc glanced toward the door, then crossed his arms. "I have a visitor. You're marrying someone else in two days, remember?"

Which, now that he could think about it with objectivity, didn't make any sense at all. He grimaced. He hadn't been the only one not interested in marriage. Going into any relationship, he was usually the one worried about the woman's intentions after intimacy. But Mel had made it clear the first night they nearly tore each other's clothes off that she wasn't interested in picket fences.

Why, then, was she getting married?

Oh, hell. While she still had a lot of fight in her, Marc watched a lone tear slide down her cheek. She sighed and rolled her eyes toward the ceiling, apparently not liking the display of emotion any more than he did. "Oh, I remember, all right. I think you're the one having trouble with your memory."

Marc shifted uneasily, tempted to give up the whole thing right there and then.

But he couldn't. Not yet. He'd never failed in an assignment, and he wasn't going to start now.

Marc moved toward the front windows and pushed the curtain aside. He grimaced when he spotted the familiar red sports car parked at the curb. *Roger.*

"I'll be back in a minute," he said under his breath. "Don't go anywhere."

Her stare told him she didn't appreciate his attempt at humor.

Marc walked to the door and opened it, frowning at the partner assigned to him a week after Mel left the division...and him.

"What's up, Rog?"

"Oh, not much with me. I'm wondering why you didn't show for work detail this morning, though."

Roger Westfield tried to look around Marc into the town house. Marc made it difficult. Easy to do, considering Roger was at a disadvantage on the doorstep. His thirty-something face was annoyingly handsome, but it was his sharp blue eyes that betrayed exactly how capable he was. Like Marc, he'd never been married, never came close, and he'd been a good partner so far. Marc hadn't taken any points off because Roger had been partners with Hooker when Mel had stumbled on to her would-be assassin's moonlighting endeavors. Too bad Roger was screwing up Marc's good impression of him.

Roger's gaze settled on something inside the town house, then he looked directly at Marc. "You went and did it, didn't you?"

Marc glanced at Mel, where she stood in the middle of the living room, stubbornly making no attempt to cover herself. He pushed Roger outside, then stepped out, leaving the door slightly open so he could keep an ear out for Mel's movements. He wouldn't put it past her to whack him in the back of his head with a lamp and leave him for dead.

And he wouldn't put it past Roger to let her walk right out of the town house and into the line of fire.

Marc thrust his hand through his already disheveled hair. "I knew I never should have said anything to you." Actually, he'd had little choice in the matter. The night before last, after the bulletin went out on Hooker's escape, Roger and he had gone out for a beer. After one too many, Roger had shared the nasty details of his close calls with women...and Marc had spilled his guts about what had happened between him and Mel, including his half-baked plan to take her into what he saw as protective custody.

This morning a report went out on Hooker's surfacing in the area, and the whole department had been put on alert. And Marc had decided to put his plan into action.

Roger said, "You're right. You shouldn't have told me. But since you did, and I know you used your training to take that woman in there against her will—" He stopped abruptly. "Have you lost your mind, McCoy? Do you know what will happen if she presses charges? I won't say anything about your job, but the legal—"

"She won't press charges."

Roger frowned. "Excuse me for saying so, buddy, but it

doesn't look like Melanie Weber is a very happy camper right now."

Like he needed to be told *that*. "What's up, Roger? I know you didn't come here to offer emotional support."

"Emotional support? You've been reading those damned magazines again, haven't you?"

Marc stiffened, not about to respond to the question. When Mel had taken that bullet, then disappeared from his life, he'd tried everything to figure out exactly how to make things right with her. And that included reading those damned magazines, as Roger had an irritating habit of referring to them. He jammed his fingers through his hair. In all honesty, he thought a few of the articles directly addressed exactly where he'd gone wrong with Mel.

Then he'd bought that stupid ring that even now was a leaden weight in his pocket.

"Look, you're right." Roger nodded. "I didn't come by to badger you about your personal business. It's your life, feel free to screw it up."

"Gee, thanks."

"Don't mention it." Roger tried to look through the crack in the door. "Just thought you might like to know a certain somebody's mother contacted our boss demanding an address for you." Marc stared at him. "She was calling from a sheriff's office somewhere in Maryland."

Adrenaline rushed through Marc's body, thick and all-consuming. "Damn, I've got to get her out of here—"

"Whoa, hold on to your shorts there, cowboy. I know your heart is in the right place, but don't you think it would be a good idea to just let her go and let the division protect her?"

What Roger left out was that the division wouldn't give her the protection she needed until after Hooker squeezed off another potshot.

Marc thrust his hand through his hair again. "You'll have to cover for me."

Roger shook his head. "No can do. When the shit hits the fan, that little lady in there is going to tell everyone and his brother I was here. You can put your own ass on the line, but keep your hands off mine."

"I can't let her go," Marc muttered. "Hooker is out there right now, possibly casing Mel's every move. I can't allow him to target her again. I won't."

Why couldn't his plan have gone off without a hitch? Why'd he have to lock her mother in the ladies' john and spill his guts to Roger?

Roger broke into his thoughts. "Come on, McCoy. You don't know that Hooker has her on his shortlist. His emergence in the area could mean he wants to take another shot at the senator."

"Come on, Roger, you know as well as I do that Hooker's cell mate let spill that Hooker planned to seek Mel out. Then there are those letters he sent and all those calls Mel reported to the U.S. attorney's office."

Marc stared at his new partner, feeling ill at ease but unable to describe exactly why. "Just sit on what you know for as long as you can, okay? Long enough for me to get her out of Dodge."

Roger shook his head. "I think you're making a big mistake here. She left you and is about to marry someone else. She's not your responsibility. What's it going to take to get that through your thick head?"

Marc resisted the urge to grab Roger by his neatly starched collar. "Excuse me if I don't take advice from a man who calls a one-nighter a relationship."

"Ouch. This from a guy who thinks *love* is a dirty word." Roger turned and started walking toward his car. "Good luck, buddy. You're going to need it."

Marc stepped inside the town house and slammed the door, causing it to shake on its hinges. What in the hell had Roger meant about *love* being a dirty word?

It was then he realized Mel's dress was no longer draped over the dining room chair...and Mel wasn't there, either.

MELANIE'S SKIN felt hot, and the yearning just a couple of Marc's innocuous touches had awakened threaded through her in an endless ribbon of need. That he had kidnapped her at all should have been motivation enough for her to want to escape. Strangely enough, it wasn't. It was the earnest reaction of her traitorous, hormone-ridden body moments before, as he had slowly, awkwardly unbuttoned her dress, the feel of his slick mouth pressed against her skin that had rocketed her moderate desire to get home to an urgent need to get as far away from Marc McCoy as quickly as possibly.

Even now, she wanted to press her fingers against her un-kissed lips, to satisfy the tickle of wanting there that had gone unsatisfied. Instead, she held the doubled-up towel against the bedroom window and carefully tapped it with the brass clock.

Melanie cringed. The sound of breaking glass was louder than she expected as the pieces fell onto the tiled patio outside. Ignoring her thudding heartbeat and the urge to take a moment to see if Marc had heard her, she quickly pulled out the remaining shards, then folded the towel over the sill.

It wasn't a long drop. Maybe only five feet or so. If she lowered herself carefully, there wouldn't be any drop at all. No risk of hurting the baby. Still, that didn't ease the knot of fear that had remained with her since the night...

She drew in a deep breath and tried to swing her leg up, but her dress forbade the movement. Hiking the skirt up to her hips, she ignored the irony and swung her leg over the sill. Had she been thinking straight, she would have grabbed a T-shirt and a pair of sweats from Marc's drawers.

But she didn't have time now. She had no idea how long Marc planned to talk to his visitor—God, was Roger Westfield really his new partner?—but she didn't gather it would be long. Her leg slipped, and she grabbed onto the wood window molding for dear life. Taking long, measured breaths, she leveraged her other leg through the window, her edginess having more to do with her still raging hormones than concern about getting caught.

Okay. Now all she had to do was turn around and with the strength of her hands and arms, lower herself down.

Easier said than done.

Inside the town house she heard the slamming of a door. Her heart threatened to leap from her chest. Right this minute Marc was probably rushing toward the bedroom. She quickly maneuvered her body around and through the window, her gaze cemented to the closed bedroom door. It remained closed. In one arm-testing move she lowered her feet to the ground, cringing when glass bit at her stocking feet. But she didn't care. What were a few scrapes and ruined panty hose compared to having her heart broken all over again?

She turned and ran straight into Marc's chest for the second time that day.

4

DESPITE HER THWARTED escape attempt, Melanie was thrillingly aware of every inch of Marc that brushed against her. Her heart beat an uneven cadence in her chest that had little to do with the exertion of climbing from the window and more to do with the irrational hunger she felt for him. The type of craving that did crazy things to her head and made her body hum. The kind of need that had made her press her backside against him minutes before. The sort of irrational yearning for him to be the man she needed right now.

"God, Mel, you're killing me here," he said hoarsely, his fingers clutching her hips not quite against his, but not pushing her away, either.

She swallowed hard, wondering just who was doing the killing when she could feel every glorious inch of him crowded against her stomach.

He groaned and set her firmly away from him. "I take it you're ready to go."

The overdose of hormones combined with sexual frustration made her want to sock him in the nose. She settled for whacking his arm with her open hand.

"Oh, I'm ready to go all right. Home. My home. Now." *Before I do something stupid like make love with you.*

Marc's fingers curled around her chafed wrists, eliciting a shiver. "Sorry, Mel, but that's not an option."

The somber, almost regretful way he said the words made her uneasy. "It is if you let it be."

He said nothing, but the bemused expression left his face. Melanie fought to keep her gaze locked on him, though she wanted to look away.

"Where are we going, then?"

"Somewhere safe."

All at once, the details of the past hour clicked off in her head. Marc saying they wouldn't be staying at the town house long. His haphazard packing. The visit from his new partner, Roger Westfield. She felt the pounding of her pulse where Marc still held her wrist, remembering the ominous words she caught of Marc's conversation with Roger before she slipped into the bedroom and out the window.

Hooker had escaped.

She felt suddenly faint. That meant Hooker hadn't called her from jail that morning, as she'd assumed... He'd already been out.

"Okay."

One of Marc's eyebrows rose. "Okay?"

Melanie's throat seemed unbearably tight, but she managed a smile. "Yes. Okay."

He instantly released his grip. "After you."

Walking with as much dignity as she could muster, given her torn dress and thwarted escape attempt, Melanie led the way to the French doors and waited patiently as he unlocked and opened them.

SHE KNOWS. Marc admitted he might be a little dense when it came to relationships, but he knew Mel. He took the cat carrier from her and put it into the back of the Jeep. Her new awareness didn't manifest itself in the obvious way. No. She was far from demanding an explanation, but her acquiescence was more unsettling. There was a worried tension around her mouth, and her movements were stiff and awkward. Her only demand was that they take Brando with them when he had been about to pour a hefty amount of food out for the old, fat tom.

Damn. She must have overheard his conversation with Roger. Sure, he knew he'd have to spill the beans sooner or later and let her in on the reason he had swiped her outside the john at her own wedding rehearsal dinner. But he'd planned to play his cards close to his chest at least until he could figure out a way to break the news to her gently.

He eyed the way she nervously pulled at the tear in her dress and tried to reassure Brando, who was meowing up a storm in the carrier. Her skirt-pulling wasn't nervous in the way it had been earlier, when he suspected her intention was a vain wish to keep him from sneaking a peek. No. Mel looked ready to jump right out of her skin. And that bothered him.

Before he could stop himself, he brushed his knuckles against her cheek. "You all right?"

The worry vanished from her green eyes an instant too late. "Sure, I'm fine. Considering I've been kidnapped by a madman."

He grinned at her feeble attempt at humor. *This* Mel he could deal with, even if she wasn't running at full speed. He reached for the cuffs in his pocket.

Mel eyed him. "Don't tell me you're going to shackle me up again."

Marc fingered the cool, heavy metal. "Given your new habit of creating an exit where one wasn't meant to exit, I think it's a pretty good idea, don't you?"

"Trust me, I'm not about to go jumping out of a moving vehicle."

"No?"

"No."

"I'd really like to take your word for it, Mel, but considering we both had the same training, and I figure you're at least as good as I am at rolling out of a moving car..." Marc placed one of the cuffs around her left wrist. She yanked on it angrily.

"Pig."

"Mule."

He hustled her toward the driver's door. Only when her back was turned did he attach the other cuff to his right wrist. Mel tugged.

"Watch it, will you," he grumbled. "I'm attached to that arm."

She swung around, glaring when she saw what he'd done.

"Get in the Jeep, Mel."

She yanked on the cuffs again and smiled at his scowl. "Doesn't feel so hot when the cuff's on the other hand, does it?"

"Bite me, Mel. Now get in."

When she continued to hesitate, he maneuvered her around and boosted her up, his palms blessedly full of her sweet behind. She squeaked, and he gave her delectable cheeks a good squeeze, liking that he still knew some of her buttons to push. She immediately scrambled inside and over to the passenger seat, nearly taking his hand off in the process.

"I don't know what you hope to accomplish by acting like a cad," she said, giving the cuffs a tug for emphasis after he was in the Jeep.

I hope to keep you at arm's length, Marc thought, tugging her hand so he could turn the ignition. He needed to keep his wits about him now that they were going into the open. More patrols looking for him meant fewer on Hooker's trail. "Hey, can't blame a guy for taking advantage of an especially advantageous situation, can you?"

Mel turned toward the window and whispered something under her breath.

"I'm over here, Mel."

"I'm very clear on where you are, Marc. At least physically."

He grimaced, wishing the tightness of his jeans away. She didn't have any idea about his physical position.

"So, tell me," she said, her voice dropping an octave, "how long have you and Westfield been partners?"

He shrugged, but didn't feel any of the nonchalance the action indicated. Not when she'd been lying in a hospital bed recovering from a bullet wound that had nearly taken her life. "A week after Hooker was arrested."

"Oh." She turned away again, but this time she spoke loud enough for him to hear her. "How are you two getting along?"

Not as good as you and I did. "Fine. He can grind on a guy's nerves after a while, but otherwise he's on the ball."

Her smile caught him off guard.

"What?"

She shook her head. "Nothing."

He hated when she did that.

She sighed. "I was just wondering if there's anyone out there who's capable of *not* grinding on your nerves."

He looked at her squarely. "You were okay."

"Oh, no, I wasn't. At least not in your book."

He frowned. Mel was the best damned partner he'd ever worked detail with. Didn't she know that? She pulled at her short dress again, jerking his hand in her direction. He guessed she didn't have a clue how he really felt. "I thought we were pretty good together."

"At least up until the point where I nearly got myself killed."

Marc shifted his fingers the fraction of an inch needed to cup her knee. He was frustrated by the stockings that separated her skin from his. "What happened to you could have happened to anyone, Mel. You were doing your job." *And if I had been doing mine, I would have taken that damned bullet for you.*

Her gaze was unwavering. "Where in the job description does it say I have to take down one of our own?"

"Hooker stopped being one of our own the minute he shot at the senator."

Marc's fingers stilled on her knee, and the silence stretched. She turned her engagement ring around and around on her finger.

"Did I ever tell you Hooker and I trained together at VMI?" He shook his head, recalling how green he'd been back then. A regular know-it-all and do-it-all who took crap from no one.

He sensed rather than saw Mel's gaze on him.

"One night after really tying one on with some of the guys, it was Hooker who saved my ass." He remembered how he'd tried to take the other, smaller man on after Hooker had told him and the others to cool it. It might have been because of his compromised condition, but quicker than he'd been able to blink, Hooker had pinned him to the ground and told him there was going to be a surprise midnight inspection and he was too damn good a candidate to screw things up now.

Marc realized he'd never thanked Hooker for straightening him up. Two of the guys he'd been with had been booted out that night, no questions asked.

He grimaced, thinking it really didn't matter now. "I never would have thought him capable of something like this. I guess a lot can change about a person in eleven years, huh?"

"A lot can change about a person in three months," Mel said softly.

"You can say that again," he answered just as quietly.

Her .25 was in the glove compartment, where he'd put it. He decided not to worry about it since she didn't seem too intent on escaping anymore.

"Look, Mel, I put off telling you about Hooker because I didn't want to scare you. But I do think it's a good idea if we talk straight now." She nodded, but averted her gaze. "I don't know how much you heard back there, but Hooker told his cell mate he was coming after you."

He watched her swallow.

"So far we have reports of clothes stolen from a clothesline at one place, firearms taken from another, both houses just outside D.C., not too far from here."

She looked at him, her eyes round.

"There, I said it."

A charged silence fell between them as they racked up the miles.

"Thanks," she said softly. "You know, for telling me everything."

He gripped the steering wheel more tightly. "No problem."

He felt her gaze on him again, probing, seeking out chinks in his armor. He rubbed his chin against his shoulder, wondering how the conversation had gotten so serious so fast. And how, exactly, he could steer it back to safer territory.

"Where are we going?" she asked.

Marc studied the highway with exaggerated interest. He thought they'd passed a milestone, but he couldn't be sure. "You'll find out soon enough," he said, preoccupied.

He moved to rub his palm against his jeans, accidentally dragging her hand along for the ride. She gasped when she found her fingers within inches of his zipper. A car horn pierced the air, and Marc realized he'd veered into the next lane. The Jeep nearly went on two wheels as he quickly made the needed correction.

If he didn't watch it, he wouldn't have to worry about Hooker's intentions because both he and Mel would be out of the picture.

"I see your driving hasn't improved much."

The chuckle that vibrated in his chest released some of the tension. "Yeah, well, if I recall, you're not much better behind the wheel."

"Guess that's why neither of us had been given driving detail, huh?"

He briefly locked gazes with Mel, grateful for her tactful ability to drain the stress out of any situation. He supposed it was a gift of sorts, the way she wrapped things up neatly and put them aside. If only that same gift hadn't allowed her to neatly box him up and put him in the closet of her past so easily.

Marc moved to rub his neck, but the clanking of the cuffs told him he'd better not. Instead, he laid his clenched hand on the seat between them, inexplicably irritated by the careful lengths to which Mel went to avoid touching him.

He thoroughly searched the road in front of and behind the Jeep, keeping an eye out for local and state police. The last thing he needed was another monkey wrench thrown into his plans.

THE HANDCUFF around Melanie's wrist felt strangely heavy. Not so much physically, although the metal was hard and unyielding. The peculiar sensation that made her acutely aware of her shallow breathing stemmed more from the symbolism of being attached to Marc than anything else. A physical depiction of what she'd felt mentally for the past three months.

She brushed errant tendrils of hair from her face with her free hand, admitting she'd been wrong to think the baby was the cause of any unfinished business between her and Marc. The truth was that without closure, she may as well be chained to Marc when she walked down the aisle in two days. There was still so much between them. Unresolved emotions. Sizzling tension that arced between them like a visible electrical current. She was aware of his every movement, every tap of his index finger against the steering wheel. Every flex of his thigh muscles as he accelerated or slowed to match highway traffic. Erotically aware of the snug fit of his black jeans across his groin.

Catching her bottom lip between her teeth, she turned to the window, watching the city quickly give way to the lush greenery of the country. But it was the low heat in her lower regions, and not the roadside, that got the bulk of her attention.

Aside from brotherly goodnight kisses, she'd never shared physical closeness with Craig. She'd told herself it didn't matter. Her failed relationship with Marc was an example of why relationships based solely on physical attraction were doomed for failure. But though nothing but a short chain connected her and Marc, she felt his presence more strongly than a physical touch. She was aware of the dampness between her thighs and the involuntary, sporadic tightening of her thigh muscles that caused shivers to shimmy up her stomach and her breasts to swell.

She closed her eyes and dragged in a deep breath. It wasn't fair. How could she still want Marc so much with her body, yet know with her mind that he wasn't the man with whom she could share forever? With whom she could raise her child in a stable, loving environment that included two parents?

She slowly opened her eyes. She'd be better off focusing on where Marc was taking her rather than trying to rehash all the details that led to their breakup.

Breakup. Now there was a word. Had she and Marc really broken up? Not in the traditional sense. They'd had that heated discussion about love that had broken her heart, but there had been no vocal parting. Rather their relationship had suddenly ceased. She'd gotten shot, found out she was pregnant. Her mother had taken over, and Marc had disappeared from her life.

"Hang in there, Mel, it isn't much farther."

She slid her gaze toward Marc, blinking at the familiar words. He'd said exactly the same thing when she was in the ambulance, with him bending over her and smoothing her hair from her face.

"What?" she whispered.

He eyed her closely. "You look like you just saw a ghost."

Maybe it was because she had.

Until that moment she'd completely forgotten the snatches of consciousness between the time when she'd first spotted Hooker to when she'd been hit in the chest. She'd felt her knees give out, one by one, then she'd slumped to the ground. She couldn't remember anything in one uninterrupted piece after that, only in snatches. And in every snatch there was Marc's boyishly handsome face creased in anger and concern just inches above hers.

Melanie tugged at the hem of her skirt, then stopped when she found Marc's hand resting on her knee. She looked at his well-shaped fingers and the way they curved just so against her skin. Then, afraid of reawakening the deep well of feelings for him, she removed those same fingers from her too hot flesh and laid his hand firmly on the seat between them.

"Not my fault," he said, giving her a full-wattage Marc-the-irresistible-playboy grin.

She trained her gaze out the window. "Nothing ever is, is it, Marc?" she whispered, unsure if he heard her, if it really mattered.

5

MARC CURSED the absence of the moon as he blindly tried to insert the key into the lock. Mel stood beside him, but she was apparently trying to make out where the waters of the Potomac lapped against the shore. Dusk had settled completely, and aside from what little light the multitude of stars provided, they were enclosed in darkness.

"Do some investing?" Mel asked.

The key finally hit home. With a quiet whoosh, he pushed the door open, then eased her inside. "My brother Connor loaned me the place." Which was as much as she needed to know. He closed the door, then searched for a light switch. When a naked bulb in the cracked ceiling fixture illuminated dingy walls, a threadbare plaid couch, a scarred coffee table and little else, he grimaced.

"Charming," Mel whispered.

This certainly wasn't going to earn him any points. "I didn't exactly have time to scope out the place, Mel," he said, inexplicably irritated. In fact, he was lucky to have found the remote cabin on the shores of the Potomac. All he'd been going on was a brief conversation he'd had with Connor, who'd stashed a federal witness there before trial about six months ago. Marc had lifted the keys from his brother's pocket that morning after verifying the cabin was empty.

Mel yanked on the cuff, nearly pulling him over. She smiled at him innocently.

"Is that your not so subtle way of telling me you want loose?"

He fished the key from his jeans pocket and released his side. He pocketed the key.

"Oh, come on, Marc. You're not going to leave these things on me, are you?"

"I haven't decided yet." He spotted a radiator on the far side of the room.

"No, you don't." Mel began backing away from him. "Don't even think—"

The catching of the metal teeth sounded unusually loud in the quiet room as Marc fastened the free cuff to the radiator pipe.

"Just for a minute, I swear." He wanted to go out and check the place to make sure it was as effective at keeping someone in as it was at keeping unwanted people out. He stepped toward the door, not about to fool himself into thinking that darkness and unfamiliarity with the area would keep Mel inside.

"WHEN I GET OUT OF THIS MESS, I'm going to..."

Melanie's words broke off. What would she do? Have her baby's father thrown in jail? She shivered, briefly giving in to the urge to smooth her palm down her stomach. She closed her eyes, amazed that such a small move always managed to calm her, remind her that no matter what was happening, there was something more important she should be thinking about.

No, she wouldn't, couldn't have Marc arrested, the big dummy. His heart was in the right place—he only wanted to protect her. Besides, despite everything that had happened in the past few hours, she was quietly coming to admit that with Hooker on the loose, there was no physically safer place on earth than right here with Marc McCoy.

The safety of her heart, though, was another matter entirely.

She stared at her engagement ring. It flashed, reminding her of a completely different flash of light. A flash that had momentarily blinded her. The night that had changed everything raced through her mind. Her throat tightened, her lungs ached, and a deep sense of loneliness saturated her.

She couldn't remember exactly what had alerted her to the seriousness of the situation when she pulled up to Senator Turow's house. It could have been the all-encompassing silence. Or the fact that no one was where they should have been. Or both, with a generous pinch of gut instinct that told her something was wrong. One minute she and Marc were running a simple errand to see if Hooker or Westfield had found the watch she'd lost earlier in the day, the only thing she had left of her father. The next, chaos erupted.

Melanie forced a swallow through her dry throat. Funny thing was, there had been nothing especially urgent about the detail. Your run-of-the-mill watch of a senator who had declared his candidacy for president. And he wasn't a particularly controversial candidate. No hate groups out there with his name at the top of their political hit list. No ex-wives with a bitter ax to grind. Just a normal, everyday guy who happened to make his career in politics and had made himself an unwitting target. But not a target for a right-wing fanatic. Rather he'd been targeted by one of his own.

Well, one of his own secret service personnel anyway. It was never determined who, if anyone, had been pulling the strings behind the scenes.

The cuffs clanged against the pipe. Melanie looked down to find her fingers absently tracing the scar that lay below the patterned material of her dress. She dropped her hand to her side and gave a ragged sigh. Would there come a time when she wouldn't remember that night with such vivid clarity?

When she wouldn't awaken in a cold sweat, her heart beating loudly in her ears, Marc's name on her lips?

"All clear."

The relief that swept through her was frightening merely because it existed at all. "Think of the devil," she whispered as he closed and bolted the door.

"What was that?"

She tried for a smile. "I said, 'You're back.' Now are you going to take these things off or not?"

He appeared to consider the question, but was watching her a little too closely for comfort.

She gave up on the smile and shifted from foot to foot. "Knock it off, Marc. I'm not going anywhere, and you know it."

"How would I know that?" He took the key from his pocket and opened the cuff.

Melanie wiped her damp palms against her dress and rubbed her wrist. "Because we both know there's no safe place for me until Hooker is caught."

His complete and utter stillness riveted her gaze to his face. Never had she known Marc to be completely still outside work. During the long hours spent on detail, he could stand as still as stone, but even then the energy about him fairly pulsed. Now, his stillness transcended the physical, going deeper than she had ever witnessed. His eyes held a calm watchfulness, an understanding, a respect that made her swallow with some difficulty.

An electronic chirp cracked the tension. Melanie blinked as Marc slid a cell phone from inside his vest. *He's had a phone all along.*

"Hello?" He turned away from her, holding the slender receiver to his ear. "Hi, Roger. No word, huh?... No, we're in a safe place.... I don't think it's a good idea to tell you where."

He paced a short way and lowered his voice. "Call me the instant you hear anything. And I mean anything."

He closed the phone and slid it into his vest pocket. He turned to her. She wasn't sure what he saw but was surprised when he lifted his hand, skimming the back of his knuckles over her cheek.

"I'm going to get you through this in one piece, Mel."

She resisted the incredible urge to lean into his touch, to give herself over to the turbulent emotions swirling through her bloodstream. The desire that made her want to lose herself in the consuming sensations that came only when loving Marc. "As long as Hooker is out there, no one I know is safe if I'm around them. You know that, don't you?"

"Including me?"

"Especially you."

His halfhearted smile tugged at her heartstrings.

"Seems to me I've already made my decision in that regard."

"Yes, I guess you have." She searched his face. "The question is why? Why after all that's happened are you putting your life on the line for me?"

Now there's a question. Marc had expected many questions, many approaches from Mel, but this hadn't been one of them. What had happened to the spitfire he left cuffed to the cold radiator? The woman out for blood—namely his?

He grimaced, wondering if this was a new approach. A new tactic meant to catch him off guard and create a gaping opportunity for escape. But he'd never known Mel to be very good at deception. When she was mad, she showed it. Boy, did she ever show it.

No, this question had nothing to do with manipulation. She genuinely wanted to know the answer.

If only he had one to give to her.

He withdrew his hand and stalked toward the window.

"Guess I don't have to ask if there's an air conditioner in this place." He hoisted open the paint-encrusted window and gave the bars outside a shake to insure they were indeed solid. While the safe house didn't have much in the way of creature comforts, it *was* safe.

"Marc?"

He stepped to a rusted old fan in the corner, checked to make sure it was plugged in, then turned it on. It wheezed to life, oscillating ineffectively.

"What?" he said finally.

"Why?"

He turned toward her, not feeling much better now that ten feet of dusty wood floor separated them. "Isn't it enough that we used to be partners?"

Her sexy smile was spiced with a bit of challenge. "Somehow I can't see you kidnapping Roger in order to protect him."

"Yeah, well, I didn't used to sleep with Roger, either." Marc saw her wince. *You have a great way with words, McCoy.*

He plucked the decrepit fan from the floor and moved it to the coffee table, yanking out the cord in the process. Cursing, he moved the table closer to the electrical outlet. Still, the infernal contraption blew in every direction but where he wanted it to. "I thought we both agreed that you're now here by choice."

"Well, not quite by choice. But at least I understand the situation a little better." She crossed her arms. Marc's gaze followed the movement, appreciating the way the material of her destroyed dress pulled tight over her breasts. At least she wasn't yanking at the hem anymore.

He strode toward the door.

She quickly followed him, then stopped. "Where are you going?"

He eyed her. She looked altogether too nervous, too vulnerable. "Out to the Jeep to get Brando and the other stuff."

"Oh." Everything about her seemed to relax. What had she thought? That he was going to leave her here by herself? He narrowed his gaze on her face. She hadn't looked exactly right since he'd come into the house. What had happened when he was outside? Had something spooked her?

He rubbed the back of his neck, not knowing quite what to make of the situation. Nothing ever spooked Mel.

You only left the woman handcuffed to a radiator, alone, with no chance for escape while a madman is somewhere out there, after her, his conscience taunted. That would be enough to spook anyone.

He cleared his throat. "But there's no hurry. I could sure use a cup of coffee first."

MELANIE WAS only too happy to see to the coffee and insisted Marc at least go get Brando. She brought in two cups from the kitchen, one filled to the rim with instant coffee, the other with milk. Marc was sitting on the couch, reading some papers. She sat next to him, careful not to sit too close but acutely aware that all the distance in the world wouldn't be enough to keep her from wanting him.

"So what's the plan?" she asked, handing him the coffee.

"The plan?"

She reached for the papers he held. "Yes, the plan. You've been referring to this 'plan' of yours since you swung me over your shoulder." She looked at the top sheet and felt the blood drain from her face. It was the bulletin on Hooker's escape. Melanie had to scan it three times before she got the full scope of what the report said. Two days ago arrangements had been made to transport Hooker from the county jail to a holding cell at the courthouse. A guard had been escorting him from the cell to the courtroom when Hooker grabbed the guard's gun and made his escape.

But what caught her attention was a notation at the bottom of the page: Suspect believed to be seeking revenge against agent Melanie Weber.

Her hands shaking, she put her mug on the table then handed the papers to Marc, unable to read the report. She cleared her throat and looked to find him pointedly avoiding her gaze.

"Marc? You do have a plan, don't you?"

"You mean beyond keeping you safe?" He put his coffee cup on the table then sat back and stretched, but the coiled strength of his arm muscles revealed his true tension. "Nope."

Melanie stared at him. "You've got to be kidding?"

"Nope."

She glanced around the room, wincing at the bare bulb hanging from the ceiling fixture. "Let me get this straight. Hooker escapes from custody. You kidnap me. Take me first to your house, then haul me all the way out here to the coast of the Chesapeake—"

"Potomac."

She glared at him. "Okay, the Potomac. And now we're going to—"

"Wait."

"Wait for what? For Christmas?"

"If that's how long it takes for Hooker to be apprehended."

The weight of his words sank in. As did all the plans for her neatly mapped life. She moved her ring around her finger. "I can't just sit here for God knows how long waiting for Hooker to be picked up." Her voice dropped to a whisper. "I have things to do, Marc. Places to go..."

She realized what she'd said and looked at him. "I'm getting *married* the day after tomorrow."

"No, you're not."

She blinked very slowly. "What?"

He pushed up from his seemingly relaxed position and planted his well-toned forearms on his knees. "What I mean is that if Hooker is not caught between now and Saturday, you're not going anywhere near that church."

Why did she get the impression that's not what he meant at all? Could it be there was more behind the kidnapping than he was letting on? Was he merely taking advantage of the circumstances to stop her from marrying Craig?

But that didn't make a lick of sense. He'd had ample opportunity to seek her out before now. While she was in the hospital would have been a good time. After she found out she was pregnant would have been even better. But she hadn't received so much as a phone call from him. All this madness couldn't be about stopping her from marrying Craig.

Suddenly restless, she got up and started slowly pacing. "Tell me, Marc, why we're not going to do anything to help catch Hooker."

He immediately dropped his gaze, making his motives all the more suspect.

"You don't think I'm up for it, do you?" She moved to stand before him.

"Don't be ridiculous. You were my partner. You're just as capable as I am."

"Liar."

"I'm speaking the God-given truth." He reached for his coffee.

"Then why can't you meet my eyes when you say it?"

He looked at her, and she saw all she needed. She curled her fingers into her palms.

"You think that because I was shot, I'm some sort of invalid. Incapable of doing much more than sitting by idly while Hooker is caught."

His chuckle nearly knocked her off her feet. He took a sip out of the mug. He almost choked. "I don't think you're an invalid. Not exactly. Come on, Mel, I've been around others who have suffered injury in the line of duty, and it always takes a bit of time for them to get back up to snuff." He stared at the cup in his hands. "Milk?"

Melanie's face went hot as she realized he'd covered his cup with the report and had taken hers by mistake. She took her cup from him and put it on the table. "What makes you think I'm not? Up to snuff, I mean?"

"Seriously?"

She nodded patiently.

"Because if you were working at full tilt, you wouldn't be here right now. You would have laid me out the instant you saw me outside that damned rest room."

Melanie opened her mouth, but no sound came out. She clamped it shut. Slowly, her anger drained from her tired muscles, leaving her feeling suddenly vulnerable. He was right. At least partially. Of course, he had no way of knowing that her unresolved feelings for him had played a large role in her reluctance to fight him to her full capacity. And that just seeing him again had dealt a huge blow to her equilibrium.

Still, one well-placed blow to his solar plexus or his windpipe would have stopped him as effectively as any bullet. And she had done neither. Why? Up until now she had tried to convince herself she wasn't here of her own free will. What a crock that was. She'd been trained to stop professional assassins. Yet she had barely put up a token fight when Marc had thrown her over his shoulder and marched her out to his Jeep.

He cleared his throat. "Because if you were okay, you wouldn't have quit the division."

Melanie turned and paced, rubbing her forehead. She didn't know which was worse—having Marc think her incapacitated or having him know the real reason she had quit.

Still, spending the next unnumbered hours, days even, alone with Marc, doing nothing, was not an option.

"Maybe you're right," she said quietly. "But we could put some sort of plan together. You know, entrap Hooker."

His expression was dubious.

"Maybe this is just what I need. Something—a case—to sink my teeth into, you know, to oil my rusty skills."

He shook his head. "Nope. We stay here."

Renewed anger surged through her tense muscles. "And tell me, Marc, who died and made you all-knowing protector?" *No, no, no.* She wasn't going to get anywhere by arguing with him. *Think, Mel, think.* She continued pacing, carefully measuring her steps so as not to appear hysterical. "Okay. I admit I understand your initial motivation for kidnapping me. But we both agree that those aren't the circumstances now, right?"

"Uh-huh."

"Well, then, shouldn't we both have a say in what we should or shouldn't do?"

He turned his hands palms up, shrugged and sat back. "As long as it doesn't have anything to do with Hooker, sure."

Melanie bit her bottom lip to keep herself from swearing. "But isn't it in our best interest to make sure Hooker is apprehended as soon as possible?"

Marc laced his fingers behind his head, his expression growing decidedly playful. Mel fought not to watch the way his stomach muscles lengthened under the soft cotton of his shirt. "This is about that damned wedding again, isn't it?"

Melanie stared at him, wide-eyed. "This doesn't—I mean it isn't—"

"Admit it, Mel, everything was fine and dandy until I charged back into your life and messed things up."

It was suddenly impossible for her to swallow. "Don't you mean when Hooker escaped and restarted a nightmare I thought had ended?"

He rose from the couch in one long, languid move. "Nope. I mean when I charged back into your life."

"But you aren't back in my life, per se," she whispered. "We're no longer partners...." She trailed off, watching as he moved ever closer. She fought to hold on to her words. "We're not partners anymore. Not in any sense of the word."

"And you want me to believe that in three months, you found someone who could replace what took us two years to build?" He was within breathing distance, and Melanie did just that. She took in a long, slow breath, filling her senses with the utterly masculine smell of him.

Never one for expensive colognes, despite the many brands she bought for him for Valentine's Day, birthdays and Christmas, he preferred using a citrusy aftershave that enhanced rather than covered his unique smell. Obviously that hadn't changed. She fought the desire to hum, likening the smell to warm soap, lapping ocean waves and the pungent scent of a freshly peeled orange.

"I've known Craig for much longer than I've known you. A lifetime, in fact."

Marc reached out and caught a stray tendril of hair that had curled over her cheek. Suddenly incapable of drawing any breath at all, Mel merely watched him, shivering when he gently tucked the strand behind her ear. "Ah, yes, I remember you telling me about Craig. He was the one who lost his breakfast when you and he were assigned to dissect a frog in science class. Let's see if I can remember correctly. In the third grade, right?"

"Fifth," she said, her voice hoarse.

He met her gaze, the depths of his brown eyes dizzying. "Funny, Mel, I don't remember you telling me that you two had gone out."

"He was the first guy I ever kissed."

"On a dare."

This was not going well, at all. Yes, she knew she'd told him all this. She hadn't been aware he'd been listening. "There was always something between us...." Her gaze dropped to Marc's mouth, which was turned up in a teasingly suggestive smile. She licked her lips. "Between Craig and I, I mean." He didn't have to know it was friendship.

"Tell me something, Mel. Does he make you pant the way I did?"

The brush of his palm against her right nipple caused a massive shudder to travel the length of her body. She knew she should move away from him, protest the familiar, intimate touch, but she could do little more than stand transfixed, wanting him to touch her and...more.

"He makes me happy."

The smile finally vanished. "Outside of the bedroom. How's he going to make you feel inside?"

He cupped her breast, very obviously avoiding contact with the straining tip. She stifled a moan and tried to stop herself from leaning into his touch. "I'm sure he'll be very good."

"Oh? Has there been evidence of that?"

Another scrape of his thumb across her nipple, another shudder that seemed to begin and end in her heated core.

"I don't think this is a very good idea, Marc. We should, um—" she licked her lips again, her gaze fixed on his mouth "—we should be discussing how we're going to trap Hooker."

"Uh-uh." He slowly shook his head. "The only thing I'm interested in catching right now is you."

Despite all her arguments, she knew he already had her.

His mouth came down on hers. Mel gave up the fight and melted against him, surprised by how very much she had longed to feel Marc's arms around her. Only his arms weren't around her. His right hand still lay against her breast. His other arm was frustratingly at his side.

Melanie leaned closer, putting her arms around his neck and drawing him nearer, coaxing his tongue into her mouth, teasing him with little flicks of her own that she knew had once driven him crazy. Still he kept his free arm to himself.

Whimpering deep in her throat, she rubbed against him, pleased to feel his erection. Tilting her hips forward, she shimmied against him in a hungry way she knew not even he could deny.

And he didn't. Threading his fingers through the hair above her ears, he kissed her more thoroughly than he ever had, delving deeply into her mouth, his breath coming in rapid, telling gasps. Still, it wasn't enough for Melanie. She grabbed the back of his shirt, tugged it from the waist of his jeans, then plunged her hands under the soft material to touch the even softer length of his hot skin.

Before she was aware he had taken his hand from her hair, she felt his fingers graze the front of her damp panties. She nearly collapsed against him as a long shudder took hold of her, shimmering through her sex-starved body even as she moved her hips against his probing fingers. He groaned and slid his fingers inside the edging.

Oh, how long she had waited for this. Dreamed about this. Marc touching her...

"Yes, yes," she murmured against his mouth.

"No."

6

"No," Marc said again.

It took a long, bracing moment to realize the word had come from his mouth. Beneath his fingers, Mel's skin was hot. Against his body, hers was soft and pliable. Against his mouth, hers was wet and seeking.

No? *No?* Why on God's green earth would he ever say no? He stared into her sleepy eyes and nearly groaned. He'd wanted to bury himself deep in her ever since he saw her coming out of that damn bridal shop. Hell, his need for her went back further than that. Way further. Back when he'd stood outside that damned hospital, battling demons he hadn't known still existed, holding that stupid ring. Demons that wouldn't allow him to set foot inside that cold, antiseptic building where people were supposed to heal. The only memories he had of hospitals were of people dying.

"No."

This time there was no mistaking the word had come from him. He was harder than steel, his blood pumped through his veins like an overworked locomotive, and Mel was hotter than she'd ever been for him. Even now her hungry mouth slid to his ear despite his words.

He grasped her arms and pushed her away from him. Her face was flushed and provocative, but despite the groan that echoed through him, Marc knew he was doing the right thing. Mel would hate him if he took advantage of her like this.

Take advantage of Mel. He nearly laughed out loud. If only his tortured body wasn't battling him for control.

Mel's drugged eyes searched his face. "Isn't this what you wanted, Marc? To make me pant at your feet?" He watched her swallow.

His fingers dug into her soft flesh. "Not like this. Not this way."

"What way, then?" She tugged her gaze away from his face and whispered, "This may be your last chance. In two days I become somebody else's wife." Was it him or had her voice cracked on that last word? "You might want to take what you can, while you can."

If any words were capable of proving he'd made the right decision about pulling away, those were. He refused to have sex with her while she was still determined to marry that—that Craig.

Good comeback, McCoy.

He forced himself to turn away from her, the action one of the hardest things he'd ever done. It fell a solid second. The first thing on the list was visiting Mel in that infernal hospital.

"I'm...I'm going to get the rest of the things out of the Jeep."

MELANIE STOOD near the barred window and rubbed her arms despite the heat as Marc moved around behind her, unpacking. Her body still pulsed with need. Her head swam with confusion. She couldn't guess at the reason he had pushed her away. Her ability to understand anything he did or felt was notably faulty.

Before their breakup, she had convinced herself he loved her. She'd thought she felt it in his touch when their lovemaking had become somehow more...meaningful. Slower, more thoughtful and ultimately more thrilling. Had thought she saw it in the depths of his eyes when he looked at her. Then the night before her run-in with Hooker, while lying slick and breathless in his arms, she had made the mistake of saying she loved him.

She closed her eyes against the memory. But it was useless. The lines of his shocked face were forever etched into her mind. She hugged herself to keep from remembering the way he'd practically leaped away from her. She'd found him so damned cute despite her pain that she'd nearly cried.

Then she'd been shot, and he had left her lying alone in the hospital.

Melanie tried to ignore the dull ache in her heart as she slowly turned to watch Marc disappear into the bathroom. She reminded herself that it hadn't been the only time she'd misread his intentions. She absently examined her wrists. She'd thought he'd thrown her over his shoulder earlier tonight to keep her from marrying Craig.

Her cheeks burned with the knowledge of how wrong she'd been...again.

She'd known from the beginning that Marc wasn't the type to commit. She even admitted that his aversion to commitment had proved a magnet of sorts. What woman could resist seducing a man of Marc's caliber into their way of thinking?

The room was unbearably quiet. She tried to find some relief in the idea that she'd chosen someone like Marc. A man with honor, dedicated to his career. A man who knew wrong from right. But did it really matter if she'd chosen him or a Johnny-Be-Bad Biker, when all was said and done? Ultimately she'd fallen in love with a man she couldn't have.

A man who would have as much interest in being a father as he'd had in being a husband.

She tightly closed her eyes, trying to quell the little thrills of awareness that continued to slink through her body. Despite the hunger for excitement that had propelled her to become a secret service agent and had ushered her into Marc's arms, ultimately she had wanted what every other woman wanted: love.

"Mel?"

She looked up at the sound of his voice. His concerned expression made her put a hand to her face. She was crying... again.

Hating that her hormonally influenced emotions made her so weak, she scrubbed at her cheeks and whispered, "I must have some dust in my eyes."

He shifted, apparently uneasy. "Dust?"

She nodded, then lifted her chin. "Did you want something?"

He gestured toward the bathroom, where she could hear the water running. "Yeah, um, it's ready."

"Ready?" she repeated numbly, peering around him.

He seemed to hesitate, then moved aside. "Yeah, I thought, you know, maybe you would want to take a bath."

A bath? She blinked several times. Had he just said... No. He couldn't have. She hadn't taken a bath since...well, since forever. Both she and Marc were shower people. She looked into the bathroom and noticed the shower curtain had been tied back and that the showerhead was notably dry.

She also noticed that three dozen or so candles in varying colors and sizes had been lighted and placed around the small room.

Her gaze flew to Marc.

He was looking at the stupid fan. "I think I'll go fix us something to eat."

Eat? Melanie swallowed hard and watched as he hurried toward the kitchen, closing the door after himself.

For long moments, she stood firmly in place, staring first at the tendrils of steam rising off the filling tub, then the closed kitchen door. Finally, her brain began to work, however sluggishly, and she slowly entered the bathroom, closing the door behind her.

With the light from the flickering candles, the walls looked artfully worn rather than dingy. The illusion was helped along by the thick new towels folded neatly over the sink, the huge bath mat covering the floor and the nightgown hanging on the back of the door. She fingered the soft material, tears gathering in her eyes as she noted the high collar and the long length. Marc had always preferred her to wear lingerie that was a little more risqué, a little more transparent. That he had chosen this...

Her gaze trailed to the glossy pink bag she had spotted at the condo. It had been shoved into the wastebasket, one of the tags he must have cut dangling over the side. Everything before her indicated he *had* planned in advance. If only the overwhelming evidence didn't prove that this particular plan had nothing to do with protecting her from Tom Hooker.

She realized the water was about to overflow and moved to turn off the old-fashioned two-handled faucet. She trailed her fingers in the steaming water and breathed in the scent of— She picked up the bottle of bath oil. Her throat clogged. *Jasmine.*

She indulged in a watery smile. She didn't know what had gotten into Marc, but only he could do something so incredibly sweet at the most inappropriate time.

She stood up, not knowing quite what to do. Marc had not only carved out a safe haven for her by way of the cabin, he'd created an oasis of sorts, as well. She sat on the edge of the claw-footed tub and peeled off her panty hose, not sure what to make of his actions.

All she could think about was how heavenly the water smelled.

And how she should be careful not to read more into Marc's unusually thoughtful actions than was there.

MARC SET the last plate on the coffee table, then straightened, surveying his handiwork. The place didn't look so bad now that there were signs people inhabited it. He grimaced. At least he thought so. As for Mel...

His gaze trailed to the closed bathroom door. Left with nothing more to do until she came out, he stepped toward the door and listened. She'd been in there for a long time. If there had been a window in there, he would have guessed she'd be long gone by now. But there wasn't.

He hadn't known how Mel would take the bath bit. He'd half-expected her to label him crazy, and he'd come close to pulling the plug himself. He'd found the idea in an article, "Ten Ways to Win Back Your Lover for Good." He'd thought the notion was a bit twisted, but he admitted finding the bath tempting once he'd filled the tub.

There was a sound. Quickly stepping back from the door, he wondered if the nervousness that charged through him was noticeable.

So far every point of his plan had gone horribly, terribly wrong. Rather than convincing Mel to drop her wedding plans and take up where they'd left off, he was sure he had further alienated her, though he wasn't exactly sure why. Which just wouldn't do at all.

The door finally opened, making him jump. So much for keeping his cool.

And so much for that nightgown he'd bought to keep his libido under control.

Uh-oh. Marc's gaze was plastered to Mel's uncertain expression. He tried to ignore the jutting of one curvy hip and the inviting way her breasts pressed against the pale silk that nearly matched the shade of her hair. He failed miserably.

"Hungry?" he asked, clearing his throat and flinching at his word choice. *Keep it safe, McCoy. Keep it simple. And keep it far away from anything to do with sex...for now.*

"Um, yes, a little."

Mel responded to his question, but she didn't move an inch from where she stood. She gave him one of those sinful little smiles of hers, shifted her weight from one bare foot to the other, then slid her hand down the length of the silk. Marc swallowed hard, watching the pale material mold to her perfect body.

He let rip a vehement curse and tore his gaze away from her.

It took every shred of control he had to ignore her. He noticed the slight quake of his hands, and his blood pulsed so thickly through his veins he could hear the roar of it in his ears. But he couldn't let happen what he was afraid was going to happen until he could prove to Mel he had changed. Maybe not in all the ways she wanted him to—*love* was a word that had never been used in the McCoy household—but he did want her in his life, badly. Things had been good between them. So good. And they could be again.

And he was willing to do whatever it took to make sure that happened.

Mel finally moved, but the slinky way she did made him wish she had stayed where she was. With short, measured steps, she came to stand in front of him, the evidence of her arousal clearly evident by the two points smiling at him through the silk. His throat—along with another body part—tightened painfully.

"Shall I sit here?"

Before he could get a word out of his mouth, Mel turned to fluff the cushions on the couch. He'd always thought she'd had a great rear end, but the way the silk outlined the lush, rounded flesh...

It was then he realized there were no lines. *No lines.*

He'd forgotten to buy her panties.

I can handle this. I can handle this....

"Excuse me." His voice was barely a croak. "I'll be, um, right back."

He disappeared into the kitchen, switched on the broiler, then stood gripping the rim of the sink for dear life. He turned on the water and resisted the urge to plunge his head under the cold stream. Instead, he splashed his face several times.

He was afraid if he went back into the living room, he wouldn't be able to resist making love to her. And if he did that, he was sure he'd lose her forever. After Hooker was caught, she'd go away believing he'd only wanted her for sex. Which was what she'd accused him of before.

Nearly burning himself, he took the hefty helping of Cheddar fries and burgers from the broiler. Then he took a deep breath, praying for some major help to see him through this night.

He took the food into the living room and placed it on the table, along with the other things he'd set out. He'd made all her favorites. But as he watched her look it over, he thought she seemed about as hungry for food as he was.

He purposely knelt on the floor on the other side of the table, not about to test himself by sitting next to her.

"I...I bought some wine. Red. I know, um, how much you like red." At the time he'd thought it would help wash down the food if it hadn't turned out right. Now he realized how stupid the idea was.

His gaze was riveted on the outline of her soft, shapely breasts as he poured the ruby-colored liquid into two different-size tin cups. The wine spilled over his hand and splashed onto the coffee table.

"Mel..."

"I'll only have a sip or two." She avoided his gaze as she hesitantly took the smaller of the cups. "Yes?"

He watched her lips purse to sip, then her throat worked as

she swallowed. Just beyond his vision, he saw her breasts sway against the nightgown. He kept his gaze glued to her face as she picked at a piece of green lettuce on her burger, then nibbled on it. A dollop of mayonnaise clung to her upper lip. Her too pink, too wet tongue dipped out to slowly lick it off.

Marc felt a groan grow deep in his chest. She didn't have a clue what she was doing to him. As far as she was concerned, she was merely sharing a meal with him. Nothing more. Nothing less.

He should have bought one of those granny gowns, and to hell with the heat.

No longer able to help himself, he allowed his gaze to travel south.

Talk, McCoy, talk.

As much as he hated to broach it, there was one subject that would throw cold water onto his libido, but quick.

He folded his paper napkin. "Do you love Craig?"

Marc cursed himself up one side and down the other. He had meant to discuss her relationship with Craig, but not in that direct way. He vigorously rubbed both hands over his face. But that particular unasked question had been haunting him all night. It was just as good it was out.

He chanced a look at Mel to find she had finally lifted her gaze to his. Her green eyes were dark in the candlelit room.

"I..." she said, then quietly cleared her throat, apparently struggling for an answer. "Yes, Marc. I do love Craig."

But not the way I love you, Melanie thought.

Melanie was half-afraid she'd said the second part aloud. But as she searched Marc's face, taking in his sexily disheveled brown hair, she knew she hadn't. And she would likely never tell Marc she loved him ever again.

"I see," he said, looking entirely too crestfallen.

She'd never known a man as irresistible as Marc. Even

now, despite her hurtful confession. He'd taken off his T-shirt, apparently trying to beat the heat. The sight of his bare chest alone was enough to notch up her body temperature. She pulsed all over as her gaze followed the length of his hair-sprinkled chest—she longed to feel the crisp dark hair between her fingers—down to where his jeans hugged his well-toned waist.

She blinked and looked into his dark, shadowed eyes, longing for him to say something silly or make a wisecrack. Something, anything to break the growing tension, to slow the rapid beat of her heart. But he didn't.

She wasn't sure if it was the decadent feel of the silky nightgown against her clean skin or the sight of him looking so hurt and completely appealing, but she knew then exactly what she wanted. One more night with him. A few intimate hours to remember in the years to come. Quiet time before she told him she was pregnant. Before she married someone else.

She watched his gaze flick to her hands. She worried her engagement ring, then skimmed the clingy lines of the silk. But rather than avoid his gaze, as she had earlier, she sat up a little straighter, stretching her neck as a shiver started at the very tips of her toes and shimmied all the way up her spine. She felt, rather than saw, her nipples harden, and she opened her mouth to pull in more of the humid air. Marc might have failed Relationship 101, but she had plenty of proof that he had aced the course on body language.

Marc wasn't sure what had changed in Mel in the past few minutes, but he knew for a fact something had. He could tell by the way she sat up a little more provocatively, looking at him in that way that said so much. He'd never been able to refuse her. Never. It hadn't mattered where they were—in a restaurant, in the car—all she had to do was look at him that way, and he was all hers.

That hadn't changed.

Pure, primitive need filled him as he grabbed the edge of the table. He gave up trying to gain some leverage and instead tipped the table out of his way. The crash of tin, glass and plates was barely audible over his hammering heartbeat.

Threading his fingers through the hair above her ears, he suddenly stilled, holding her there, gazing deeply into her eyes. He needed to make sure this was what she truly wanted. If he saw a flicker of doubt...

Her hands encircled his wrists and slid up his arms, pulling him closer.

"Make love to me, Marc."

Her husky voice flowed over him like the silk that covered her lush body, chasing away any chance he had of pulling away from her. With a deep groan, he slanted his mouth across hers, tentatively at first, calling on every ounce of self-control at his disposal.

She tasted so sweet. Like a ripe pear begging to be eaten. Her tongue sought and found access to his mouth even as she slid closer to him, cradling him between her silk-clad thighs, pressing her breasts against his bare chest. He'd always thought that the closest he could come to heaven was through sex with Mel, but what he was feeling now, he couldn't begin to describe. It was like looking into the star-filled night sky, seeing all the answers to life's questions printed there and being unable to do anything more than admire them, bask in the peace they offered, but not being able to read them.

Tilting her head with one hand, he slid his other down the impossibly long column of her neck, feeling her pulse there. There was a sense of inevitability about this, their coming together now, tonight. As if he was no more in control of his actions than Mel was. His palm moved from the silk of her skin to the silk of her gown, finding very little difference except in the way the silk moved, gliding easily against her flesh as he cupped her breast.

She tugged her mouth away from his, gasping as she rested the side of her head against his. "You always knew just how to touch me," she rasped.

Her hands skimmed down his abdomen, causing him to catch his breath. She reached for and found the front of his jeans. Her knuckles grazed his skin as, one by one, she undid the metal buttons there, her mouth once again seeking his.

Marc drank deeply of her lips, groaning as she slid her hand inside his fly, freeing him and wrapping her silken fingers around his pulsing shaft. He nearly spilled his need into her palm right there and then. A part of his mind said it was because he'd gone so long without her. Another part told him what they were sharing was unlike anything they'd shared before.

Gliding the nightgown slowly up her long, long legs, he tried counting backward from a hundred, but lost track of the count when she flicked her tongue across his lips, then closed her mouth over his again.

Too soon. Too fast.

At the rate they were going, it was going to be over as soon as it had begun. He needed to gain some distance, and he needed to do it now.

Gently pressing her into the cushions, he ignored her needy protest, then grasped her hips and hauled her down so her rear end was even with the edge. Her lusty moan coaxing him on, he used his thumbs to part her and slowly bent to fasten his lips around the sensitive nub at her center.

Mel cried out and arched from the cushions, pressing herself against his mouth. He curved her legs around his neck, laving her with his tongue, reveling in her gasps and soul-deep moans.

She tunneled her hands through his hair, moving restlessly, both begging him to stop and pleading with him to give her the release she sought.

With his fingers, he spread her farther, running his mouth the length of her, licking, tasting her musky essence, then he slowly slid two of his fingers inside, readying her for him.

He knew her moment of crisis was near. Could tell by the way she almost desperately grasped the cushions, her hips going still. He fastened his mouth around her nub once more and gently sucked, holding on as she bucked from the couch in a series of uncontrollable spasms, contracting around the fingers he thrust into her slick wetness.

She looked at him through drugged eyes, her hair a tangled blond mass around her face, her lips parted provocatively.

He'd never wanted someone so much in his life.

Marc made quick work of taking off his jeans, his teeth gritted so he would keep from climaxing before he claimed her the way he'd been longing to for the past three months. She sought and found his erection and led him home. As she surrounded him, he threw his head back. Damn her for making him want her this way. Bless her for showing him what it felt like to be alive again.

No...not yet...

But he couldn't wait. It seemed like forever since he'd been able to lose himself in Mel. Three torturously long months filled with wet dreams and cold showers, haunted by memories of her needy cries and soft sighs.

She rocked against him, pulling him in deeper, and he lost all concept of time and place as he thrust into her.

The instant he heard her cry out his name, he let loose, every muscle going rigid even as he tried to keep up the rhythm of his thrusts. But it was a losing battle. His hamstrings locked and his hips drove forward one last time, spilling his need deep inside her.

For long moments they stayed like that, joined together,

connected in a way that somehow surpassed anything they'd shared before. Marc felt as if he was floating somewhere above his body, lighter than the heavy, humid air around them, curiously detached yet a part of every physical item in the room.

He reluctantly withdrew from her, then laid his head against her silk-covered stomach. He closed his eyes, unsure if it was his heartbeat he heard there, or hers.

MELANIE JOLTED AWAKE, her heart pounding in her ears, fear clogging her throat. Around her, the night was black and forbidding, the bed she lay in unfamiliar and hard. It took her a moment to realize where she was.

The safe house.

She'd dreamed. What? What had she dreamed? She desperately tried to hold on to the haunting images, to examine them, to understand why she had awakened and why she felt as if her heart was going to beat right through her chest.

Hooker.

In her mind's eye, she saw the shadowy figure somewhere twenty feet to her right near the first-floor window of the senator's house. The window was partially open, and the figure had been halfway in when she shouted. Then there'd been the flash of reflected light as Hooker had turned his weapon on her.

She closed her eyes and swallowed hard. The staff psychologist had told her the nightmares would lessen in frequency after a week or two. But here it was, three months later, and she still saw the vivid, haunting images almost nightly.

"Maybe the dreams are trying to tell you something," Judith Hamilton, the psychologist, had told her a couple of weeks ago.

"Yes, I think they are," Melanie had said. "They're telling me I did the right thing by quitting."

A low murmur brought Melanie's head around. Marc turned over and pulled her into his arms as naturally as if he'd been doing so forever.

For a long moment she stayed like that, trying to control her breathing, trying to enjoy the moment for all it was worth, all it signified—namely, the last time she and Marc would share a bed. But rather than wrapping herself in the warmth of his body, a bittersweet sadness gripped her from within. She burrowed against him, breathing in the smell of him, trying to ignore that he didn't have a clue what she had in mind.

After their frenzied lovemaking on the couch, they'd managed to salvage some of the food he'd prepared. She fed him the Cheddar fries, and he gave her bites of the salad with slow deliberation and languid care. The circumstances that had brought them together were taboo, and everything but the sound of the crickets had been off-limits. Melanie looked on their silence with the twenty-twenty vision of hindsight. She supposed that since Marc couldn't say the things she had so longed to hear, there had been nothing to say.

But their bodies still had plenty to communicate.

Melanie swallowed past the emotion clogging her throat. She'd never felt so thoroughly made love to.

At least in her eyes they had made love. But she knew better than to make that mistake twice. In Marc's eyes...well, he'd likely see it as the best sex he'd ever had.

Dear, thickheaded, love-impaired Marc.

She dragged his hand to her mouth and kissed his fingers, loving the warm feel of his skin against hers. When he stirred, she gently moved his arm around her waist and held it there, wishing the baby within her could know the touch of his father. She tightly closed her eyes, clutching the memories from the night before, holing them away the way a squirrel gathered the biggest nuts to see him through the winter. Only the memories Melanie had gathered would have to last her a lifetime.

WHAT IN THE HELL *was that infernal pounding?*

Marc dragged the pillow over his head and groaned, groggily trying to remember how much he'd had to drink last night. There had been many times over the past weeks that he'd awakened, convinced someone was using a jackhammer just outside his window, only to find the curtains flapping against the frame.

Then he remembered he'd had very little to drink and bolted upright in bed.

Mel.

A quick, sweeping glance told him he was the only one in the room. The pounding was someone knocking at the front door.

The significance of that hit him in the gut like a sucker punch. He leaped from the bed, pulled on his jeans and rushed the door.

"Mel?" he called, nearly tripping over a confused Brando. "Sorry, buddy."

They were out in the middle of nowhere. It didn't bode well that Mel was nowhere to be seen and that someone was at the door. He picked up his empty gun holster, noticed his cell phone was missing and cursed. Quickly, he checked his jeans pocket. Relief washed through him. Good. The ring was still there.

Improvising, he grabbed the leg that had broken off the coffee table the night before. He yanked open the door, then brought the leg down.

"Whoa!" Connor ducked, lifting his arms to ward off the impending blow.

Cursing, Marc tossed the leg into the overgrown grass, then stared at his eldest brother. "Jesus, Connor, I could have maimed you for life." He dragged in a breath. "What in the hell are you doing here?"

A scowl marred his brother's face. "I think the better question would be what the hell are *you* doing here?" He tried to push through the door, but Marc stopped him. "Imagine my surprise when Pops wakes me up in the middle of the night to tell me the Maryland state authorities have been by asking around for you. Then this morning I'm putting my keys in my pocket when I notice a certain one missing. Damn it, Marc, do you have any idea what kind of trouble you could get us both into by breaking and entering into federal property?"

Marc scratched his head and looked past his brother. He was relieved to see his car was still there. That meant Mel had to be around somewhere. "I'm just borrowing the place for a couple days, that's all. I really wish I had the time to explain—"

"That's all? Have you lost your friggin' mind, Marc?"

Time or not, it was obvious Connor wanted an explanation and he wanted it now. But with Mel only God knew where, and with Hooker...

He took a long look at his brother. No one had known where he was until now. Even one more person having that information doubled the risk of discovery.

Oh, God.

He grabbed Connor by his shirtfront. "Were you followed?"

"Let go of me right now, little brother, or else—"

"I asked if you were followed!" Marc said.

He abruptly released Connor then started to close the door.

Connor caught the barrier. How many times when they were kids had Marc pulled a fast one on his brothers only to have Connor following on his heels? And how many doors had Connor caught, preventing his escape?

"I'm not going anywhere until you explain this to me.

Now. And why don't you start with what in the hell was going through that deranged mind of yours when you kidnapped Melanie Weber right under her mother's nose."

Marc ground his teeth together. "Later, Connor."

"Damn it, Ma—"

Needing to find Mel and not knowing how to get rid of his brother, Marc tried to push Connor out of the way just as Connor was taking a step forward. Connor stumbled, all his attention on grabbing the rickety iron railing. Marc quickly reached out to control his fall, then reached into Connor's suit jacket to slide his gun from his shoulder holster. He said, "Sorry about this, Con. I'll get the gun back to you later." He went inside and slammed the door. Connor dropped to the ground.

7

THE COOL SAND sucked at Melanie's high heels, making each step an impossible struggle. She hadn't realized that three months of inactivity would leave her so out of shape. At this rate, she'd only get twenty yards before Marc realized she was missing. He'd probably find her on her knees, gasping and wheezing and offering her soul up for a measly cup of coffee. Just one. It didn't matter that she hadn't had even a sip of the heavenly brew for nearly three months. She needed the caffeine jolt right now.

Marc had never been a morning person. That's one of the reasons it had been so easy to sneak out. Another was that after waking from that nightmare, she hadn't slept another wink. It had been all too easy to slip from the bed long before dawn to map out her escape.

Her heart gave a tender squeeze. Leaving Marc lying there alone had to be one of the more difficult things she'd ever done. He'd looked so boyishly handsome—almost vulnerable—and downright sexy. It was almost too easy to let herself believe everything would be okay. She'd tell him the truth about the baby and he'd...

She tripped over a piece of driftwood. He'd have a coronary—after he gave her the devil for keeping the information from him for so long.

Her thoughts focused on the exact reason she needed to get away from Marc, and fast. Yes, Hooker may be lurking out there somewhere, but the physical danger he presented paled in comparison to the romantic fantasies she was starting to entertain after a night of loving Marc.

Exasperated with the tears that threatened to flood her eyes, Melanie set the heavy revolver in the sand and, still clutching the cell phone, took off the shoes Marc had brought in from the Jeep the night before. She looked between her torn dress and the revolver, then tossed the shoes into a nearby bush. She really hated to litter, but the shoes were the least important thing she had. And considering her impractical attire, there was no place for her to stick any of the items for safekeeping.

She picked up the firearm, making faster progress as she sprinted across the beach, barely aware of the sun rising to the east or the sounds of nearby gulls. When her gaze wasn't trained in front of her, it was darting behind her to the cabin that grew smaller and smaller as she ran.

Still no sign of movement. Relief and disappointment filled her. She was going to get away this time.

Stopping to catch her breath, she gauged the distance between her and an easily recognizable road. Not far. If she called her mother...

It occurred to her that Craig's name hadn't even emerged as a possibility. She tightly closed her eyes. Why was it that since yesterday, she seemed to look for ways to compare Craig to Marc? It wasn't as if she hadn't thought long and hard before accepting Craig's awkward proposal. She'd taken two weeks. Fourteen torturous days and sleepless nights alternating between crying and determining to put the pieces of her life back together.

Irritated with herself and her situation, she juggled the revolver and punched out her mother's phone number with her thumb.

Her mother picked up on the first ring. "Hello?"

"Mom?"

"Oh, good Lord, Melanie! Where are you? Are you all right? Is that—"

"Mom—"

"—madman still holding you hostage? I've been up all night worrying—"

"Mom!" Melanie's patience drained as she tried to edge a word in.

"—afraid he'd done something awful. You hear those stories in the news. Spurned lover kills his ex-girlfriend, chopping her into little pieces—"

Melanie tugged the phone away from her ear and stared at it. Chopping her into pieces? What was her mother watching?

"—they find her in some Dumpster in the back of a Chinese restaurant—"

"Mother! Listen! Are you listening to me? Look, if you don't be quiet for a minute... No, sorry, I really didn't mean to say be quiet—"

This conversation was worse than the sand that had nearly sucked off her shoes. Only with her mother, she'd be lucky to get out alive.

"And Craig! I nearly forgot about Craig. He's right here—"

"Mother—"

"Melanie? Melanie, is that you?"

Melanie instantly relaxed. "I'm fine, really I am, Craig. There's nothing to be concerned about." Craig would understand. Craig understood everything. She'd tell him where she was and he'd be here to pick her up.

"Melanie? This is your mother again."

Like she had to be told *that*. Her anxiety grew. At this rate Marc would find her in a heap on the sand bawling hysterically. She chanced a glance at the house. Her heart leaped into her throat. The back door was open.

She slapped her hand to her forehead, then lowered her voice. "Mother, look, I know you were worried about me...

Listen to me! No, of course I'm not whispering. I need you to pick me up—"

Suddenly her words were cut off as a shot split the relative calm of the dawn landscape, sending gulls squawking toward the sky. A millisecond later a column of sand spat at her like a geyser, spraying the front of her dress. Another shot followed, and the cell phone went flying from her fingers, her skin vibrating from the jarringly close call.

Oh, God.

Melanie hit the sand so hard it took her a full half minute to catch her breath. Those thirty seconds she used to scramble toward a nearby bush. Finally she was able to draw in air, and the raw, harsh sound stunned her.

Oh, God. Someone's shooting at me.

She looked toward the house. The door was still open, but Marc was nowhere in sight.

Then she spotted him. Crouched at the side of the cabin, he was barefoot and wearing nothing but that tight pair of jeans, a gun drawn as he scanned from his left to his right. Gun? She had his gun.

Another shot.

Melanie dove deeper into the brush.

She looked down to find her free hand covering her belly, an unconscious attempt to protect the life that grew there. Stinging tears flooded her eyes as the danger that had loomed around her like an intangible cloud for nearly twelve hours crystallized into stark, terrifying reality.

Wrapping her fingers around Marc's revolver, Melanie reached deep inside, seeking the stillness she had learned to count on to see her through on the job. Her heart thudded harder, and she choked back a tidal wave of panic. *Come on, come on.* Where once she had been able to count on herself, her talent for clear thinking, now it seemed every lick of knowledge had gone, leaving her feeling scared and vulnerable.

Think of the baby.

The harder she sought strength, the more panicked she grew. Then, suddenly, like a slow influx of cool air, stillness swept over her. It started in her chest and emanated outward, calming the tremor in her hands. She planted her feet firmly on the ground. She crouched, her breathing shallow but controlled, her sight swift and ears alert. *There.* The rising sun reflected off something dark and shiny near the road.

She quickly ducked and slipped the safety off the revolver. Hooker. It had to be him. Given the remoteness of the cabin, there was no way he could have accidentally found the place. He must have followed them from the inn or the town house. Not that it mattered. Right now, she was at a disadvantage. She knew approximately where he was, but he knew *exactly* where she was.

Forcing a swallow, she balanced the gun in both hands, the weight familiar and reassuring. She'd always been a crack shot. She prayed she hadn't lost her touch.

Another crack of gunfire. The bullet ripped through the bushes to her left. She sidestepped quickly, then revealed herself, aimed and squeezed off a round. The trigger had barely sprung back before she was under cover again and sprinting toward the house.

One yard, two yards...

Crack.

She dove into the sand headfirst, wincing at the mouthful of sand she took in. As soon as the round whizzed past, she was up, blindly shooting at her target, then running again.

"Mel, get down!"

She heard Marc's order, then fastened her gaze on him. He was nearer than she thought, and whatever sand remained in her mouth spewed out when he hit her head-on. He was shooting even as he fell on top of her.

The stillness she'd felt left her immediately upon coming in

contact with his body. She didn't know if it was the fear that
they might never be this close again, or if she was just awfully
glad to see him, but she felt on fire, despite everything going
on around them. The scent of gunpowder filled the air, and
the sound of a car's tires squealing against asphalt ripped at
her ears, but all she could think of was that she could feel the
rapid beat of Marc's heart against hers. Irrationally, she
thought, *That's just the way it should always be.*

She opened her eyes to find him looking at her. A quizzical
glint darkened his eyes as he scanned her features. She realized she was about to pass out.

"You okay?"

She nodded, struggling to regain her wits. "Fine. I'm fine.
Your cell phone's history, though."

His devilish grin made her smile. Her brain was on over-
load. One moment she was arguing with her mother on the
phone, the next she was eating sand while an escaped criminal used her for target practice. That would make anyone a
little loony, wouldn't it? But even as she tried to convince herself that's why she felt the way she did, her body told her
something else. And growing evidence of Marc's arousal
pressed into her thigh.

He rolled off her and leaped to his feet. "Get up, Mel." He
offered his hand.

She took it. Standing, she took inventory of the new tears in
the dress.

"Nice. Think we can market it?"

"Yeah, you can call it the hell-and-back look," she murmured.

Everything she'd been thinking, feeling, minutes before
was gone.

"Well, if that wasn't a sign that we've overstayed our welcome, I don't know what is." Marc sighed.

She looked at him. "Hooker."

His gaze was intense. "You saw him?"

"No. But who else could it be?"

"You're right." His expression grew pensive. He paced a couple steps, then hopped when he stepped on something in the sand with his bare feet. She shivered as he turned to face her. "Out for a morning jog, were you, Mel?"

Recalling exactly why she had tried to make her escape, she sobered. She futilely tried to brush the sand from her dress as she headed toward the house. "Something like that."

He grasped her arm, pulling her to face him. "Why?"

Her throat growing tight, she handed him his gun. "You know why."

His gaze held her still. "Are you telling me that last night..."

His words trailed off, leaving her speechless. She stared at the sand beneath her feet and squinted against the brightness of the rising sun.

"That last night was about lowering my guard so you could take off?"

Looking at her feet, she ignored the squeezing of her heart and whispered, "If the shoe fits." She winced at the words, hating how callous they sounded. The last thing she wanted to do was hurt Marc. But he was making it very difficult for her to do anything else.

She cleared her throat. "Don't you think we should be getting out of here?"

"Why? So you can just dump me at the first opportunity?"

She eyed him thoroughly. She didn't like what she'd said or the impact it had on him. But if it helped put her on equal footing, then that was what was important. Wasn't it?

One thing the last ten minutes had made painfully clear was that going home, returning to the neat little plans she'd made, wasn't an option. But she hoped where she went from here was.

"I promise not to ditch you if you agree to being partners on this," she said, pushing the words through her tight throat.

"Come on, Mel—"

Her heart beat an even, powerful rhythm, giving Melanie an important element of her life she'd lost months ago. *Control.* A sure sign was the echo of her mother's voice in the back of her mind telling her there were some things a woman wasn't meant to do. Couldn't do. Things the past few months had made Melanie believe she no longer should do. But right now, right this minute, her survival instinct kicked in pure and strong. She needed to protect not only herself, but her baby. And to do that, she needed to be in control of the situation. If not as leader, at least as partner.

"Marc, please listen to me. If what happened proves anything, it's that I am far from safe just sitting still waiting for the proper authorities to pick up Hooker. I'm going to have to track him as deliberately as he's tracking me." She cleared her throat, the reality of the words chilling her. "Either you're in or you're out. It's your call." She tried for a shrug as nonchalant as any he'd ever given her. "Makes no difference to me."

Suddenly, he grinned. Not a "You're killing me, Mel," grin, but a grin that said something more. She felt her face grow hot. Instead of turning away, she met his gaze.

"Now that's more like the Mel I remember." He handed her the gun. "So are you ready to go hunting, partner?"

MARC DIDN'T KNOW what to believe. He was acting more on instinct than wisdom. Why had Mel run? He watched her curvy little behind, clad once again in the pink dress, as she opened the door to a posh D.C. hotel room. He groaned. He didn't want to feel anything more than professional respect for her. Not any more. If she could leave him after last night...

Despite the partnership deal they'd struck, he was having

trouble indulging in conversation with the new, reanimated Mel. On their ride to the city, she'd broached nearly every subject. Correction—every subject that had anything to do with Hooker. Sharing with Marc the details of the first letters Hooker had written—she'd sent the rest back unopened—telling him the frequency of Hooker's phone calls where he professed his innocence. And of course she'd grilled Marc on everything he'd picked up over the past few weeks.

Throughout much of it, he'd remained silent, his hands attached to the steering wheel until he realized he was trying to pulverize it in his grip. All he could think of was he needed some space to think. Considering he'd had far too much space in the past three months, and that he'd been trying to get her to talk since he'd first put her into the back of his Jeep the day before, his reaction was not only unexpected, it was aggravating.

He rubbed the back of his neck. He felt used. Violated. Cheap.

He grimaced. He was reading too many of those damned magazines.

"We should be at some fleabag motel on the outskirts of town instead of in a four-star hotel," he said under his breath, holding open the door so she could maneuver herself and the shopping bags she carried inside.

"What makes a motel safer?"

He glanced around the long fifth-floor hall, scoping out the fire exit directly across from their room. "Escape routes."

She set the bags on a puffy, flowery ottoman and began rifling through them. "We've stood post at this hotel countless times. We both know exactly where the escape routes are, so what difference does it make?" She took a bra and a pair of panties from one bag, then a pair of jeans from another. "Besides, after where we stayed last night, I could do with a soft bed, cable and a bit of comfort."

Comfort? He felt as though he was soiling the room just being in it. And every negative comment she made about last night jabbed at him like a well-placed punch.

He put down the pet carrier and his bag.

He turned to find her emptying a small amount of kitty litter into a box. He pulled a can of cat food from his bag—the contents of which he purchased when Mel was buying clothes. He let Brando out, holding the can up when the overgrown tom wound around his ankles. "Well, you're none the worse for wear. You probably slept through the whole thing, didn't you, sport?"

He looked up to find Mel watching him in a way he couldn't immediately identify, a way he didn't particularly welcome. Her face had gone all soft while her eyes held a faraway look. "What?" he grumbled, shifting uneasily.

Her cheeks reddened, and she immediately dropped her gaze. "Um, I'm going to go take a quick shower, you know, before we get down to work." She glanced toward the bathroom door. "Why don't you order up some room service? Brando's not the only one who's hungry."

He opened the can, then put it on a bag on the floor. Brando swooped down on it like a ravenous fiend, making a rumbling sound between a growl and a purr as he knocked the smelly stuff back.

Despite the little they'd eaten in the past eighteen hours, food didn't appeal to Marc at all. But talking to room service personnel would give him something to do while he waited for Mel. And it would get his mind off trying to figure out exactly what he was feeling and why.

He hesitated when it came to ordering for Mel. Last night he'd fixed all her favorites, and she had eaten the salad and lettuce and tomato off both their burgers. When the room service lady got impatient with him, he made up his mind and ordered her a salad and a burger and fries for himself.

He slowly hung up the receiver and found himself right back to square one.

Sitting on the bed, he listened as Mel turned on the shower, and the restlessness within him grew larger than life. He realized that a lot of his agitation had to do with the fact that he'd been unable to protect her—again. She could have easily been hit, or worse, this morning. He shoved his fingers through his hair. Between when he figured out what was going on and when he tackled her to the sand, he'd known a fear unlike anything he'd ever experienced. It had paralyzed him. Made him focus on protecting Mel and Mel alone when he'd known the best way he could protect her was by incapacitating Hooker.

Instead, Hooker had gotten away and lived to shoot at her another day.

The new direction of his thoughts wasn't any more comforting than the last. Snatching up the receiver again, he put in a call to Connor at work. By now his brother should have recovered from the fall he'd taken, and his anger should have lowered to a slow simmer. At least that's what Marc was banking on because he had a few favors to ask.

"McCoy," his older brother answered.

"Connor, hey, it's Marc...."

After a good talking down and a promise for revenge, Marc found out Connor had been on the property when the sniper hit. He'd followed the plain black sedan with no plates but had lost the perp shortly thereafter. He'd returned to the cabin, but Marc and Mel had already gone. He also learned that no new word had been posted on Hooker's whereabouts. Connor promised to call if he found out anything, official or otherwise.

Marc hung up the phone, frustrated to still hear the sound of the shower. At this rate, the woman was going to wash herself down the drain.

He sprung from the bed and vigorously rubbed the back of his neck. Yes, he always experienced a certain charged tension after a close call, but this... His muscles were coiled so tight he expected them to pop at any second. His mind kept fastening on the image of Mel's wet, soapy body in that shower just a few feet and a wall away. *Damn.* Why had she run that morning?

He strode across the room and retrieved his bag from the top of the television. *The Feminine Mystique* was written across the glossy cover of the magazine he slid out. Glancing toward the bathroom where the shower was still running, he opened to the table of contents and found the page of the article. God, if Mel—much less any of his brothers—caught him reading this stuff...

He grudgingly admitted that he didn't believe Mel when she implied she used sex to distract him the night before. No woman could be that good at pretending. But why would she tell him that? It didn't make any sense. It could be, as the magazine suggested, she needed to keep a part of herself to herself. He wondered how much else Mel was keeping from him.

More than likely, her hurtful—God, where had he gotten *that* word?—remark was because she was afraid all her new, well-laid plans would get mussed up by their taking up where they left off.

He groaned. Only they hadn't taken up where they left off, had they? He stuffed the useless magazine under others on the phone table and started pacing. He was starting to relate on a personal level to the magazine pieces, which was not part of the plan at all. Why didn't men have a periodical that could help them understand what was going on with the opposite sex? Oh, yeah, he'd read that book that said men and women were from different planets, not once, but twice. Not that it mattered. He could read it a hundred times and still never really get what the guy was saying. Besides, he couldn't seem to budge the image of himself as an Invader From Mars alien every time he thought about it.

He picked up his pacing. Something about his feelings for Mel, his reaction to her, had changed since he'd carted her away the night before. He couldn't quite put his finger on what, but he knew they were more intense, vivid.

Then there was the sex.

God, he got rock hard just thinking about the way she had moved beneath him, over him, how it had felt to have her slick muscles surrounding him again. Things had always been great between them in bed, but last night...

This was getting him absolutely nowhere. He needed a safe distance between him and Mel. He needed to stay alert, keep his eye on the ball and catch Hooker before Hooker had another chance to squeeze off a round at Mel.

And he needed to keep away from all those damned magazines.

MELANIE LEANED against the wall, her breasts unbearably sensitive, her body pulsating with the rhythm of the water. Where was he?

She knew it was crazy, masochistic even, to want Marc again after the morning's events, but she was coming to accept that life didn't make much sense. How could she want a man so badly with her heart and body, and know with her head he was all wrong for her? How could she run away from him, knowing it was the right thing to do, then try to tempt him into making love with her again?

She knew finding Hooker should be top priority right now. But she also knew that when he was found, there would be no excuses left to be with Marc. And that understanding opened up a whole new ache in her heart and made her want to take as much as she could while she could.

Peeking through the half-open shower curtain, she saw no sign of Marc. How long was she going to have to stay in here waiting for him?

She swallowed hard. She had lobbed quite a blow at his ego on the beach when she'd suggested their lovemaking had been nothing but a way to freedom. She closed her eyes and leaned her forehead against the tiled wall. What had she been thinking? She *hadn't* been thinking. At least not all the way through to the end. All she'd known at that moment was that Marc had charged back into her life and turned everything upside down. And she was having a hard time accepting that.

And that was saying nothing of his new attitude toward her. He acted as if she hadn't gone through the exact training he had, covered the same assignments, protected the same subjects. Suddenly, to him, she was this helpless little thing who needed taking care of. Needed someone to take the load from her fragile little shoulders. A big, strong man to make all the bad things in the world go away.

She moved her face into the spray. Marc was going to have to get it through his thick head that she could take care of herself, thank you very much.

An image of the sniper flashed through her mind, and she groaned.

Okay, so maybe she had lost her touch since taking that shot three months ago. Maybe the wound and the resulting shake-up of her life had undermined her confidence, clouded her thinking. She slowly ran the bar of soap over her belly, reflecting on all the changes that had resulted from that one moment. Fear itself was healthy, necessary, as long as she had some control over it. It was when she lost that control that things became dangerous.

It had been fear that had paralyzed her and fear that had shown her the way to the stillness she had lost what seemed like a lifetime ago.

The spray continued to pound. She peeked through the open bathroom door. At this rate, she was going to turn into a prune before Marc figured out what she was up to. She clutched the melting soap and began lathering herself all over again from the neck down.

Come on, Marc.

Last night...

She swallowed hard. Their time apart may have played a small role in the heightening of emotions, but last night there had been something more, a sensual intensity, an acute liberation in their coming together.

She tried to remember what it was like at the beginning of their relationship. Before she heaped so many expectations on top of it. But even then, there had been a shadow of hesitation, a list of reasons why they shouldn't be doing what they were. She supposed it stemmed from the fact that they worked together. Even the first time was supposed to have been their last. An accident, Marc had said. Yes, an unfortunate turn of events, she agreed.

Then came the second and the third times, and the excuses lost their edge until they stopped making them at all.

Melanie sank her teeth into the flesh of her lower lip, thinking that would have been about the time she started falling in love with him.

And what about all her plans? She had believed herself independent, liberated, and now she was mapping out a traditional route as if her life were a road impervious to earthquakes, floods and all forms of natural disasters.

Then came Hurricane Marc.

She looked down to find her hands resting over her stomach as if protecting the growing life within.

An image of a little boy emerged in her mind. A little boy who had her light hair and Marc's large brown eyes. A child who would have all her practical traits, yet would face life with the same zeal his father did.

Following closely on the heels of that image was one of her mother. She was probably climbing the walls. But not the walls of her house. She'd likely be camped out at the local sheriff's office, directing activities. From the minute, making sure fresh coffee kept running, to the elaborate, ordering deputies to comb the countryside for her.

The thought might have made her grimace before, but Melanie found herself smiling. There were a lot of unresolved issues between her and her mother. But ever since she learned she was pregnant, her perception of her mom had shifted. Wilhemenia had spent more than half her life obsessing over her two daughters, fighting to keep their house, working to keep Melanie and Joanie in tennis shoes. She had sacrificed her life for the sake of her children after the death of her husband. No, she had never remarried. No, Melanie couldn't recall her mother ever going out on a date. Not even after she and Joanie had left the nest.

She understood her mother better now. She felt the same fierce need to do everything it took to protect and provide a loving environment for the baby growing within her. Even if it meant sacrificing her needs to do so.

"Mel?"

Startled, she instinctively reached for the shower curtain to cover herself. Which went against her decadent plans.

She opened the curtain. Marc stood in the bathroom doorway, looking at everything in the elegant little space besides her.

He cleared his throat. "You planning on using all the water in the hotel?"

She wanted to shake him. Instead she pushed the curtain open even farther.

"Jesus, Mel, you're getting the floor all wet."

License to Thrill

Without looking at her, he yanked the curtain almost all the way closed.

She grabbed his hand with her wet one. Finally his gaze moved to her face.

"You know, McCoy, sometimes you can be as thick as shag carpeting."

His eyes narrowed. "Thick, huh? No, I think thick would be me climbing into that shower with you." He craned his neck, obviously struggling not to look at anything but her face. "Look, you want to go, the door's right there. You don't have to sleep with me to escape."

Melanie opened the curtain and slipped her wet fingers along his jaw and into his dark hair. "I don't want to go anywhere, Marc. Not right now."

"Come on. You're getting me all wet."

Melanie smiled. "That's the whole point."

Finally, a reaction. A flick of a gaze to where the water sloshed over her breasts. Melanie swallowed hard. *Yes.*

"No." Marc grasped her wrists and tugged her hands from his face. "Room service will be here any minute."

Forget room service. Melanie fought to hold on to her smile.

His gaze dipped a little lower. A languid shudder ran through her. He hesitantly lifted his fingers, and she stopped her movements, realizing he was looking at her scar.

Last night it had been too dark for any visual exploration. And while the physical reminder of what she had gone through had been a constant presence for her, Marc had never seen it.

She swallowed hard as he gently ran the tip of his index finger across the pink, puckered skin. Then his eyes met hers.

Before she knew it, she was in his arms, her slick, soapy body against his clothed one.

8

MARC LANGUIDLY TRAILED a finger across Mel's belly, lightly touching the damp tangle of hair between her thighs. He grinned at her quick intake of breath.

"Again?" she rasped.

His chuckle shook the bed. "I don't think so." He gently tugged on her hair, earning him a laughing shriek. "I need at least a week to recover after today."

Her sudden stillness tipped him off to the change in her demeanor. He dragged his head from where it lay against her breasts and glanced at her face.

Sure enough, the light had drained from her green eyes, and when she sighed, it was as if she bore the weight of the world on her stomach instead of just him.

"What's the matter?" he asked, running a fingertip over the scar that represented so much in their relationship.

"Nothing."

Nothing? "Hey, that's my line."

She finally looked at him rather than through him. Then he realized what had precipitated the change in her mood. He'd mentioned time. *I need at least a week to recover....*

She reached for a towel that lay nearby, and Marc let her up so she could wrap it around herself. He wanted to protest the covering of her delectable flesh, but bit the impulse back. He might not know what was going on in her head, but he knew the meaning behind her physical movements. He wouldn't have a week to recover for another bout.

He rolled onto his back and draped his arm across his forehead. He couldn't imagine his life without Mel in it. While he was sure he and Mel had gotten physically closer, he also felt an emotional rift no amount of advice could help him bridge.

And it hurt like hell.

He rubbed his hands over his face. "I never thought I'd hear myself say this, but I almost hope you get pregnant."

She jumped off the bed so quickly, the movement of the mattress nearly catapulted him off the other side.

"What?" Her voice was a hoarse rasp.

Despite the tightness in his chest, he was amused by the way she clutched the towel—as if he already hadn't tasted everything that lay beneath it.

He shrugged. "Have you noticed we didn't use any protection?"

She remained mute, staring at him unblinkingly.

He cleared his throat, not entirely sure he liked her reaction. Was she so averse to the thought of having his child? "You know, we didn't use a raincoat, a rubber, a cond—"

"I know what protection means, Marc." He grimaced, watching her hands shake as she tucked in the towel.

He sat on the bed and reached for his briefs. "You don't have to act like I just suggested you become a live organ donor, for God's sake."

She started shaking her head in an odd way. "No, no, it's not that. I..." Her hand went to her throat as if trying to work the words out. "I want to know what you meant when you said you wished that I was pregnant."

It was his turn for the words to get caught. And boy, did they. To make matters worse, they seemed to have claws, and clutched at his throat for dear life. "I said I *almost* wish. Big difference."

Uh-oh. The homicidal look on her face explained why he'd had difficulty saying the words. Unconsciously he knew they would get him into a heap of trouble. And he knew Mel wasn't reaching for that pillow because she was tired. Although Lord knew she should—

She hurled it at him.

He caught it easily, and she made a sound of frustration. Dropping the pillow, he raced across the mattress and grabbed her, pulling her onto the sheets even as she clutched the bedside lamp in both hands.

"Give me that."

She struggled against him. "Let me go!"

He was glad her towel had come loose and circled her legs, pinning them—it kept her from causing any major damage.

"Give me the lamp, Mel." She sank her teeth into his shoulder. "Ow! Would you stop that!"

He pried the lamp from her fingers and dropped it to the floor. It shattered, despite the plush carpeting. He cringed, wondering how much that little knickknack was going to cost.

"What is it with you?" he asked, catching her chin, preventing her from taking a hunk of flesh from his shoulder. He searched her face. He'd never seen her this worked up. "Is it because I said I *almost* wished you were pregnant?"

Her answer came by way of a kick to the shin.

"Geez, Mel, would you tell me what in the hell is going on?"

The towel was coming loose.

"Come on, we talked about this a long time ago. Even before we started sleep—er, dating. I told you I didn't want kids."

She went suddenly still. He didn't dare move his hand, though. Not until he was sure this wasn't a diversionary tactic.

"Besides, aren't you the one who's marrying somebody else tomorrow?"

Aw, shit. Were those tears in her eyes?

He finally let her go and quickly moved to the other side of the bed. "What is it with you, anyway?" He ran his hands through his hair, his blood surging through his veins. He could handle almost anything from her. Silence. Her penchant for whacking him in the arm. Her sexy seductions. But her tears—he couldn't handle those.

The first time he'd seen them had cut him to the bone. The night Hooker shot her. She had gritted her teeth and paid close attention until she was sure Hooker was in custody, but the instant she looked down, her voice had cracked.

"So much blood."

Marc had stared at her, unsure who had said the words, her or him. It had been all over, the blood. So much, he wasn't sure exactly where she'd been shot or how many times. Then Mel had started crying. *Crying.* That more than anything had scared the hell out of him. Mel wasn't a crier. She was one of the guys. She was supposed to be telling crude jokes, keeping a stiff upper lip and all that.

He leaned his forehead against his hands. That night had driven home how very different they were.

"I don't get you, Mel." He pressed his thumbs against his eyelids to block the images. "Three months ago you just break things off. No explanation, no goodbye, no I hope it was good for you, too. Then the next thing I hear you're marrying somebody else."

She rounded the bed and stood in front of him. "Do you really want to get me, Marc? Do you want to know the real reason I quit the division?"

He narrowed his eyes, trying to ignore that she was still naked. Trying harder still to ignore his instant arousal. "Yes."

She picked up the pillow he'd dropped. She whacked him a good one. "I am pregnant."

Marc sat ramrod straight on the side of the bed, dumbfounded, the pain from her hit not stinging nearly as much as her words. "What?" His voice was a croak.

She lifted the pillow again, then dropped it and sank onto the mattress beside him. She whispered, "I said I am pregnant, you twit."

Since she was no longer directly in front of him, he stared at the window. A strange tingling began at the base of his skull, then inched over his head, chasing out every chaotic thought, every coherent word. "When? How?"

Out of the corner of his eye, he saw her press the pillow to her belly. "You *really* don't want me to answer that, do you?"

He imagined he could hear the creak of his neck as he turned to look at her. Her eyes were squeezed shut, and she clutched the pillow so tightly he expected it to split open and cover them both with feathers. "Either Craig is a very fast worker—"

She sprang from the bed, but before she could whack him upside the head with the pillow again, he grabbed her wrists, holding her still.

"Would you just hold on for a minute? You didn't let me finish." He strengthened his grip. Not because she still needed to be restrained, but because he needed the connection to ground himself. "What I was going to say is—and don't you dare hit me again or I swear to God I'll tie you to the bed—either Craig is a very fast worker, or I'm..." The thought of tying her to the bed was preferable to the words he couldn't seem to push from his throat. "Or I'm—"

"Going to be a father," Mel finished softly for him.

Marc felt as though he'd been caught on the wrong end of Mike Tyson's left hook. He worked his mouth around some kind of agreement, but no words came out. He could only stare at her. His gaze lingered on her face, dropped to her still bare, still wonderfully, deceptively flat stomach, then to her face again.

Then odd details combined to make a supportive whole
The urgency of her wedding plans. The fact that she drank
milk rather than coffee. Her quitting the division to become a
security consultant.

She nodded slowly.

"Well." He thought the word had come from his mouth,
but he wasn't entirely sure. It sounded too high-pitched, too
contrite to have possibly been his voice. But since he was
watching her mouth, and nothing had come out of there,
then—

"You're hurting me, Marc."

He winced and quickly released her wrists, watching as she
rubbed them.

"Sorry," he mumbled.

She stepped quickly away from him and put on one of the
hotel robes. She looked crazily small and delicate in all that
thick, white terry cloth. "For what, Marc?" She knotted the
belt and swiveled to face him. "Are you sorry about running
out on me three months ago?"

Running out on her? Who ran out on her?

"Are you sorry for kidnapping me yesterday?"

Kidnapping her? He thought they'd moved past that.

"Oh, no, wait, I know what you're sorry for. You're sorry
I'm pregnant." Her voice cracked. "Aren't you?"

He opened his mouth, then snapped it shut again.

Her gaze dropped to the floor. "Too late," she whispered.
"I'm well past the twelve-week mark, so abortion is out. Not
that I'd have one, mind you. I found out I was pregnant when
I was in the hospital. Alone. With no one but my mother and
sister around to prove that someone *did* care about me."

"I didn't mean—"

"Didn't mean what, Marc?" She seemed to shrink into the
depths of the robe. "Tell me."

Yes, Marc, spit it out, man. He silently cursed himself. "I meant I'm sorry for hurting you. Your wrists, I mean."

She looked at the ceiling and gave an exasperated groan that made him cringe. He'd said the wrong thing. Again.

Why was it he could never say the right thing to her? No matter what his response, it never failed to send her straight over the edge.

"What?" he asked, growing irritated. "What did you expect me to do when you sprung the news on me, Mel?" He grabbed his jeans, putting them on without his briefs and giving up on buttoning them after several failed attempts. He stalked toward her. "Or *were* you planning on telling me?"

A SHOCK OF PANIC shot through Melanie. She had expected anger from Marc. Had even planned for his dumbfounded expression when she blurted the news. What she hadn't predicted was the formidable, sober man facing her.

She turned and tugged on her panties under the privacy of her robe. Her cheeks burned, her heart thudded, and even she knew her dressing was a way to buy more time. She gave Marc credit when he didn't interrupt. He stood silently while she put on the jeans and the tank top she had bought.

"Of course I planned to tell you," she said softly, not daring to meet his gaze as she draped the robe over a chair back.

"When, Mel? When were you planning to tell me?" His voice was low.

She shivered, then bought a little more time by putting a sheer white blouse over the teal blue tank. She made a ceremony out of tying it at the waist. When? Good question. She really hadn't known when she was going to tell him. That had always loomed somewhere out on the horizon. The only thing she had been sure about was that she *would* tell him.

Then came yesterday, and the kidnapping, moving the time scale up so fast she got dizzy just thinking about it.

What a difference a day makes.

Marc took a step closer to her. Her gaze was riveted to his stony face. "When, Mel? After you got married?"

She didn't answer. She was too surprised by the myriad emotions plainly visible on his handsome, unshaven face.

While he was obviously hungry for an answer, she also noted pain lurking in the depths of his eyes. Before yesterday she had never seen him so serious, so direct. Suffice it to say she would never have used those two words to describe Marc McCoy at any point in their relationship.

He crossed his arms, emphasizing the clean lines of his forearms. "Well, seeing as your wedding is only a day away, I think it's safe to say you were planning to tell me *after* the nuptials." His eyes narrowed. "Although I'm not convinced you planned to tell me at all."

"Of course I was going to tell you. I told you now, didn't I?"

"Only under duress."

Duress? Yes, she would describe what she was feeling as duress.

You deserve every harsh lash he can dole out, her subconscious taunted.

God, how bad was it when her own subconscious berated her?

Very bad. Awful.

"Look, Marc, I..." Her heart contracted. "I did plan to tell you. You'll have to trust me on that." She anxiously brushed her hair from her face. "I do have to admit I don't really know *when* I would have done it."

He stood, a tall and silent sentinel, waiting for her to finish. Problem was, she was done. That's all she had to say. She had thought in vague terms. She envisioned Marc playing a role in their child's life. Long weekends, some holidays, things of that nature. Even though merely imagining him standing on her doorstep on a weekly basis and not being able to touch him turned her inside out. But that all had depended on her telling him he was going to have a child.

"Does...he know?" Marc shifted, appearing uncomfortable. "Craig?"

It was the first time he had said her fiancé's name in an uninsulting tone, which alerted Melanie to the seriousness of the question. And warned of the consequences should she tell him the truth. But if her current situation proved anything, it was that putting something off didn't avoid the hurt. It only made things worse.

She closed her eyes. "Yes," she breathed.

He didn't curse. Didn't yell at her. He didn't even blink. He nodded once, as if understanding something she couldn't quite decipher.

Melanie hurried about the room, burning off the nervous energy filling her. After she had collected discarded towels, placed all the dishes on the service cart, wheeled it into the hall and stuffed her ruined dress into the shopping bag, she turned to find Marc hadn't moved.

Her heart surged into her throat, choking off her air supply, filling her eyes with tears.

"Marc?"

He didn't respond, just stared at the spot where she'd been standing earlier.

"I'm sorry," she whispered.

She stood with her hands fisted at her sides, willing herself not to turn away. In all the scenarios she'd envisioned when she told him she was pregnant, she never thought she'd be the one apologizing. Until this very moment, she'd adamantly believed she was the one who deserved the apology.

Now she realized she'd punished him for crimes he hadn't committed.

I was alone and pregnant.

He didn't know she was pregnant.

He won't make a good father.

She'd never thought she'd make a very good mother until the choice was taken away from her.

He's going to run in the other direction when he hears this one.

He hadn't.

He finally moved. She jumped without knowing why. The suddenness, maybe. The fact that he had moved at all.

"Tell me, Mel, how does this, my knowing, impact your plans?"

Everything that had happened in the past three months slipped through her mind. The hospital. The doctor's shocking news. Marc's unexplained absence. Craig's proposal of marriage.

"I honestly don't know." And she didn't. After all that had passed between Marc and her, she couldn't see herself marrying anyone else. Not even Craig.

He blinked once, slowly. Then he moved again. He finished dressing and came to stand in front of her.

"I know what you're going to do. You're getting married tomorrow," he said, his gaze lazily traveling the length of her body and lingering on her stomach. "But it's going to be *me* you're marrying."

9

MELANIE STARED at the passing countryside with no concept of where they were or where they were going.

After Marc's staggering pronouncement, he'd hustled her out of the hotel via the back entrance and deposited her in the Jeep. She was aware of little more than taking the pet carrier he'd given her before leaving the room.

What had he meant by saying she was going to be getting married tomorrow to *him*? The mere thought was enough to start her heart racing. Swallowing, she vaguely registered that they were still in the city. Was he taking her to the town house? She looked in his direction to find him almost relaxed. As if their recent conversation hadn't taken place.

She watched a woman, stranded at the side of the highway, fixing a flat tire. It struck her that she once thought that would be one of the worst things to have happen, to be stuck out in the middle of nowhere. Now she knew better. But she also knew enough to know that no matter what the situation, things could always get worse. Her heart gave a triple beat. Or better.

She shifted in her seat to face Marc, her knee brushing his thigh. "What did you mean back there?"

"Back where?" he asked a little too innocently.

She kept her gaze steady.

He shrugged. "I meant exactly what I said."

She gestured nervously. "Which is?"

"Are you losing your hearing along with the good sense God gave you?" He grinned from ear to handsome ear.

Melanie barked with laughter, surprising herself.

She tried to school her expression into one more befitting the situation.

He'd told her once about his father's fatherisms. "With the good sense God gave you" was a popular one. That he'd used it to lighten the mood gave her hope. Hope that this was nowhere as serious as she'd feared.

She bit her bottom lip, unable to completely wipe the lingering smile from her mouth. "So let me get this straight. Tomorrow," she said, drawing the word out and indicating a point on her jeans with her finger, "I'm getting married."

"Uh-huh." He flicked on the blinker and exited the highway. Moving away from the city, she noticed distantly, as he continued west on a two-lane state route.

"But I won't be marrying Craig."

He nodded as if indulging a particularly slow child. "Uh-huh."

Her smile widened. "And the reason I'm not going to be marrying Craig is because I'm going to be marrying you."

"Right."

Melanie's smile vanished. "Wrong," she said hoarsely.

She turned to face the dashboard, her stomach tightening to the point of pain. She suppressed a groan.

"Oh, no, Mel, I'm right as rain." He reached over to take her hand and ran a callused thumb over her sensitive palm. "You see, I have every intention of becoming your husband tomorrow."

Husband. Marc.

She tugged her hand away. "Please...don't touch me."

He laughed, the robust sound making her stare at him as if he had gone insane. "No, that may be what you've been saying to Craig the last three months. Me? Admit it, Mel." He moved his hand to her leg and brushed it up the inside of her thigh. "Me, you can't get enough of."

Incredibly, she felt like opening herself to his touch.

Panic swelled sure and strong in her chest, chasing the air from her lungs. His repeating the words didn't make her understand his announcement any better. Marriage to Marc would be— A peculiar melting sensation flowed throughout her body. Marriage to Marc would be wonderfully exciting, unpredictable, impossible.

The emotional roller coaster she'd been on for the past two days provided all the proof she needed that marriage to Marc would be a disaster. He was by turns irresistibly handsome, foolishly inexplicable and ultimately irresponsible.

"Where are we going?" she whispered.

That made him move his hand away. "Someplace safe."

She tightly closed her eyes. "We're not going back to that, are we, Marc? We agreed we were partners in this." She forced herself to stop worrying her hands in her lap. She'd tried to get the ring off at the hotel, but it wouldn't budge past her first knuckle. Her fingers must have swollen more than she realized. "That means sharing information. That means I get just as much say in where we go as you do. Someplace safe just...well, it doesn't cut it right now."

"It's going to have to cut it because that's all I'm giving you."

She fervently battled hysteria. "We're partners—"

"That was before I found out you're carrying my child."

She stared at him, puzzled. "Your child?" she whispered. "A little over an hour ago, you didn't even know I was pregnant."

He gazed at her from under his eyebrows. "Okay, *our* child."

"Which brings us back to the partners thing."

He slowly shook his head again. "Oh, no, Mel. The way I

see it, our roles now are completely bipolar. You—" he gently jabbed a finger against her collarbone "—are officially in charge of eating right, exercising, taking your vitamins and creating a healthy internal environment for our child."

Her anger flared. "Who in the hell died and named you ob-gyn?"

"The way I see it, your being pregnant gives me license to do a lot you might not be happy with, Mel." He grinned. "Anyway, those are your duties. Now my duties..." He flexed his hands against the steering wheel. "My most important duty is to maintain a healthy external environment. Namely, keeping you safe." He glanced at her. "Nine months of hard labor is the way things look right now."

"Five months," she corrected absently. "And I'm the one who's facing labor."

Marc wants to take care of me. She rubbed her forehead with a shaking hand. The thought was appealing in a sort of medieval sense. Me man, you woman. Wasn't that the way things used to be? And while women had come a long way, baby, they still had a long way to go. Sure, small concessions had been made. In wedding ceremonies, it was no longer, "I now pronounce you man and wife," and men were known to wash the occasional dish or two. She flicked a glance at Marc, admitting that he not only washed dishes, he could whip up a pretty good meal with the help of the microwave, frozen vegetables and a broiler.

She squeezed her eyes shut. What was she doing? While her view of the future had been knocked askew, it was dangerous to make room for Marc in it. She felt as if she was wandering through a dangerous daydream where being handcuffed—literally and otherwise—to Marc didn't seem like such a bad proposition.

She shifted on the seat as they put the D.C. suburbs behind them.

"We can't even agree on anything, Marc. What makes you think we could make a family work?"

His expression never faltered. "We'll make it work."

Then it occurred to her that Marc wasn't doing all this because he loved her. He was doing it because it was the right thing to do. Marrying her was a duty. A job. And one he thought he was up for.

Her heart expanded painfully.

No, for the good of her baby, she couldn't marry either Craig or Marc.

While Marc's heart might be in the right place, the signal got scrambled somewhere between his chest and his head.

I'M GOING TO BE a father. Marc waited for panic, for anger, to set in, but all he felt was this strange kind of weightlessness. *I'm going to be a father.*

He glanced over to Mel, twisting that rock around her finger. He wanted to tell her to take it off, wished he could replace it with the one in his pocket. But now didn't seem like the right time.

Okay, he admitted he hadn't been overly enthusiastic when they'd initially discussed how they felt about children a year or so ago. He grimaced. Who was he kidding? He'd adamantly said he wouldn't even consider having kids. And he hadn't.

Boy, in light of the day's events, did that seem a lifetime ago.

His reasons had been solid enough. Raised in a family of four other males, with a male who barely got passing grades as a father and was far in the hole when it came to mothering, he wasn't the only one of the McCoy bunch to decide children weren't in the cards. His decision had come as a result of a long, middle-of-the-night conversation with Connor after his youngest brother, David, had run away. It had taken them some eight hours to find him.

Marc acknowledged that it hadn't been David's running away that had upset him so much. It had been where the four-year-old had run to.

His brothers and father had been about to report his disappearance to the local authorities when they got a call from their closest neighbor, three miles up the road. They would have called sooner, they said, but they hadn't known David's real name because he was calling himself Grover, after his favorite *Sesame Street* character, and said he didn't have a home.

Pops had driven Connor and him over to pick David up. Only when they tried to pry him away from the family, who were having dinner, their little brother had kicked and screamed, insisting that this was his home. No one could blame him. The neat little family, complete with mother and father and other children, would be anyone's ideal.

The entire humbling experience had made Marc realize he'd had a heart. More importantly, he'd learned that same heart could be broken.

"Mel, what I said...you know, before you told me you were pregnant..."

She looked at him in that way that made him squirm. It was worse than facing a crowd of protesters while guarding the president.

"Well, you have to know I had no idea...."

"I was pregnant?"

He nodded. "Right."

"No problem."

He glanced toward her, but she had turned to stare through the window.

He tried again. "I know I once said I never wanted to have children."

He watched as her chin quivered slightly.

"Well, I don't feel that way anymore."

She made a sniffing sound, then finally looked at him. "And how exactly *do* you feel, Marc?"

It wasn't the first time she'd asked the question. He couldn't count the times he'd been caught on the wrong side of what he called her "put your feelings into words" game. Still, he knew he had to try or risk a whole lot more than a whack in the arm.

"Happy?" he said cautiously.

Her short burst of laughter dismayed him.

"What?" he asked, frowning.

She appeared as caught off guard as he did, and she quickly looked away. "The way you said 'happy' in the form of a question." She cleared her throat. "So, are you happy or not?"

He hesitated. Not because he didn't know how he felt. He was afraid of falling into a carefully laid trap. "Yes. Yes, I am."

She didn't answer, and he couldn't see enough of her face to see her response.

He grew tense. "You always told me I was never any good at putting my feelings into words, Mel," he said gruffly. "But I want to try to explain this one to you, if you'll hear me out."

She nodded, but still didn't look at him.

He trained his gaze on the road disappearing under the wheels of the Jeep. "Two days ago I didn't think there was a chance in hell of ever seeing you again." It had been a difficult realization. But with Mel's wedding date fast approaching, and without a clue how to get to her, he'd given up hope of repairing things between them.

"Then Hooker escaped," she said.

He nodded, then said, "No, no. I mean, yes, of course he escaped, but that's not what I'm working at."

He finally earned her attention. He didn't know if that was

good or bad. What he did know was that he was quickly running out of road, and if there was anything to be said, he better say it now, because he might not get a chance later.

Spit it out, McCoy.

"I don't know what I'm trying to say," he grumbled, ticked off at himself. "But I do know that when you told me you were pregnant...well, I know you and—that a year ago when we talked about having kids...well, I thought I didn't want any."

He chanced a glance in her direction.

Get to the point already, man, you're losing her.

He clenched the steering wheel tightly. "And when I found out you were marrying somebody else...it shocked me, you know?" He bit back a curse. "My gut reaction was that something had to be going on, but I had no idea it was..."

She turned to the window.

"No, don't turn away," he said urgently, touching her arm. He couldn't define why, but it was important he say this to her, important she understand.

He withdrew his hand and exhaled loudly. "What I'm trying to say to you, Mel, is that when you told me you were having my...our baby, I knew it meant you weren't only going to be a part of my life...." He swallowed. "But that you were going to stay that way for a long time to come." He released the wheel and turned his hands palms up. "And I...I was happier than I've been in a long, long time." He rubbed the back of his neck so hard his skin hurt. "Maybe ever."

The silence in the Jeep was deafening. Marc kept his gaze fixed on the road, afraid he'd screwed up again.

But when seconds dragged into minutes without a reaction, he gave in and finally looked at her.

And found her crying. "Aw, hell, Mel, don't go turning on the waterworks again."

She made a sniffling sound that made him groan. "That's the sweetest thing you've ever said to me."

Despite the stiff way he sat, a funny feeling exploded in his chest. An odd mixture of pride and hope. "Yeah, well," he murmured, wondering if his face was red. "I wouldn't recommend looking for me to do it again. That was hard enough for me to say and I...I don't know if I can do it again."

MELANIE REACHED OUT and took his hand, ignoring his prickly posture as she cupped his palm against her cheek. For a long, glorious moment, she reveled in the rough feel of his skin against her. Tears plopped over his fingers, but she didn't really care.

He grew more tense, and she smiled, aware of how much the admission had cost him. He was right. She had constantly accused him of keeping his thoughts and feelings from her. But if this was any example of what lay dormant inside him, then she hadn't given him nearly enough credit.

"Come on," he said, opening the glove compartment. "Somebody will think I hit you or something." He handed her a tissue.

She wiped her cheeks and blew her nose, laughing at his horrified expression.

"Hell, Mel, if you don't stop, I'm never going to say stuff like that again."

She whacked him on the arm as a fresh bout of tears sprang to her eyes. "Must be the hormones," she said, wondering at her extreme emotional reaction to his gruff confession.

The Jeep fishtailed as Marc screeched to a stop on the two-lane road, earning him a honk from the truck behind them. "Good Lord. Do you have to be sick?"

Melanie glanced through the back window. "What are you doing? You could have gotten us killed."

The truck pulled around them, honking once more as it passed.

"So you're okay, then?"

Melanie laughed. She was more than okay—she was euphoric, delirious, thrilled. Despite the knowledge that his confession wouldn't, couldn't lead them anywhere. "I'm fine, Marc. Not every pregnant woman gets sick, you know."

His grimace was endearing. "No, I didn't know." He rubbed the back of his neck. Something she noticed he was doing often lately. "Why do I have the feeling there's a whole lot about this I'm not going to know?"

Melanie hid her smile and glanced through the window as he got under way, going noticeably slower. She appreciated the deep green of the tobacco fields, the patches of wild rhododendrons, the utter stillness of the land around them. Then it dawned on her where he must be taking her.

Sure enough, ten minutes later she spotted a buckshot-peppered sign announcing they were entering Manchester, Population 1,999. She craned her neck at a small diner, then stared at a bar and gawked at a cute general store with the requisite old man sitting on a rocking chair whittling.

Melanie's heart dipped into her stomach. He was taking her home.

ALONG WITH the initial jolt of excitement Marc had felt at the news of his impending fatherhood, fear twisted in his gut. What did he know about being a father? He'd never been around kids. Well, aside from his brothers.

Boy, am I ever going to catch hell for this one, he thought, envisioning those same four brothers.

Marc slowed to the speed limit, spotting Sheriff Percy Mathison sitting in his usual place on the outskirts of town waiting for speeders. He waved, and Percy waved back tersely, apparently upset he wasn't able to get another hefty contribution to the Manchester County coffers.

It was late afternoon, and everyone was either home or on their way. The general store had its share of customers, as did the diner, but it was the absence of Connor's car at the bar that made Marc wince. That meant Connor was either working late or he was already home. He sincerely hoped it was the former, because he really didn't need another run-in with his older brother right now.

"This is...nice," Mel said quietly.

Nice. Now there was a word. But it certainly couldn't be used to describe Manchester. Small, maybe. Perhaps even okay. But definitely not nice. He grew more uncomfortable the closer he got to the family house. He grimaced. Mel would take back her words the minute she got a gander at the McCoy place.

Set back from the road, the old, sprawling farmhouse looked ready for the wrecking ball. Then there was the barn. The instant he thought about it, it came hulking into view, little more than a haunted, weatherworn, gargantuan structure whose slats had shifted long ago. It was no safer to enter than it looked. Not that it mattered. They hadn't had any animals in a long, long time. Unless you counted Mitch's dog Goliath. Even when his quarry darted inside, Goliath stood outside and barked up a storm. The old slobber puss never went in.

Marc shifted, nearly knocking his knee against the dash. He wasn't sure why he'd never brought Mel here, but as they approached, a prickly knot pulled tight in his stomach. He glanced over to find her attention glued to the scenery. No matter how she might react to the McCoy place, it was too late to turn back. Besides, it was the safest place for Mel and the...baby. No one would dare mess with the McCoys. No one.

He groaned when he spotted the cars parked in the rutted

drive. It figured—every single McCoy male was home. While it meant more protection for Mel, it also meant a hell of a lot more trouble for him.

In all the years he'd lived here, not one of his brothers—or his father, for that matter—had ever brought a woman to visit. The youngest, David, had posted a sign on the front porch when he was six and had been burned by his first-grade girlfriend. It had said, No Girlz Allowed. Marc cringed when he saw the unvarnished piece of wood still hanging there, creaking ominously in the spring breeze.

Wait! Marc's black mood lightened as he brought the Jeep to a stop, blocking in everyone else. Mitch had brought a woman home once. Liz something or other. His hope deflated when he remembered that on the day of their wedding, Liz had run off, leaving Mitch standing high and dry at the altar.

"This is home?" Mel asked quietly, her eyes huge as she took in the overgrown grass, the drooping fence, the demolished front steps.

"Yep. This is it."

He climbed from the Jeep, sensing rather than seeing Mel step to his side. He cleared his throat. "The place isn't usually this..." He coughed, catching the lie before he finished it. Of course the place was usually this bad.

Marc spotted Connor looking out the side door. He was filled with a sudden urge to hustle Mel into the Jeep but managed to hold his ground.

He exhaled. "Guess we'd better get this over with. Come on."

He wasn't sure what Mel had expected, but when he realized she wasn't next to him, he looked to find her frowning at his back before reluctantly following.

"Aw, hell." He backtracked and held his arm for her to take.

She kept her hands stoically at her sides. "I'm okay."

"Take my arm, Mel."

Her eyes flashed. "I said I'm okay. Pregnant women can walk on their own."

He bit back a curse and grabbed her stiff, cold hand. "Why does everything have to be a fight with you?" He noticed he'd quickened his step and purposely slowed it. "Oh, and about the, um…"

"Baby?"

"Yeah, the pregnancy thing. Let's say we keep that information to ourselves for a while, okay?" He didn't want to send his father into cardiac arrest. "Anyway, I think it's a good idea if we tell them we're getting married first."

She tried to pull her hand away. He held fast.

"Marc McCoy, I'm not going to marry you."

"Sure, Mel, sure," he said, decidedly distracted.

JUST WHEN SHE THOUGHT Marc had passed some major milestone, he'd say or do something that completely destroyed it. Now was no exception.

"Marc, I—"

He grimaced at her. "We'll talk about this later, okay?"

"Okay."

"Good."

She looked at him long and hard. Was it her, or was Marc McCoy anxious? She noted the way his mouth was pulled into a nervous line, no trace of the happiness he'd proclaimed a short time ago. She followed his gaze. Someone stood at the side door. They were similar in size and hair coloring, but that's where the similarities ended. One of Marc's brothers? It seemed the obvious guess. As they drew closer, she saw the glum expression on the other man's face, and knew for sure that it had to be true. Only a blood relative of Marc could pull off that don't-screw-with-me look.

"Marc," he said.

"Connor."

Melanie waited for an introduction, but not for long. Marc pulled her inside the house with barely enough time for her to make eye contact with Connor.

For a ridiculous moment, she was afraid he intended to take her inside and stuff her in a closet away from his family, away from where she might get him or herself into any trouble. He pulled her into the kitchen. She stopped cold, her breath freezing somewhere en route between her lungs and her nose.

Oh, God.

Marc finally released her hand, leaving her standing in the doorway, barely aware when Connor gently budged her out of the way so he could pass and join the room full of other McCoy males.

The house had appeared enormous from the outside. But looking at it now, filled to the brim with prime male flesh, she didn't think there was a house large enough to hold the amount of testosterone in the room.

"Hi," she said hoarsely.

10

MELANIE WAS AFRAID she had spoken a foreign language. No one responded to her choked greeting. Her gaze slowly drifted over five devastatingly handsome faces. They stared back. Despite the size of the table, which could easily fit a family of ten, it looked puny with these guys sitting at it.

Suddenly, everyone spoke at once. But it was the oldest, maybe Marc's father, who rose.

Melanie blinked slowly. It couldn't be. It wasn't possible. "Sean?"

His grizzly warm grin told her it could be and was. Then it dawned on her. Sean hadn't been at the hospital to visit anyone else, as she had assumed. He had never corrected her. Sean was Marc's father.

A missing puzzle piece shifted into place, completing a picture she hadn't known was there. All at once, she recalled how he had defended Marc's actions, offered practical reasons Marc hadn't come to visit her. At the time, she hadn't thought it odd that he should try to defend someone he didn't know. She thought it was a man thing.

"Maybe he can't get away from work," Sean had suggested.

When that one hadn't worked during their third visit— when he'd smuggled in eggs, bacon and hash browns from a nearby family restaurant because she wasn't eating the hospital fare—he'd said quietly, "Maybe there's something about hospitals that bothers him."

When she had quietly disagreed, he had gone on.

"I don't think it's so far-fetched. This is the first time I've...well, that I've spent so much time in a hospital in a long, long time. You see, my wife died...."

Melanie's mind reeled with the images and words, her thoughts a jumble as she realized how much she knew about the family before her, though not through normal channels. During her long conversations with Sean while her mother had been busy ordering the hospital personnel around, while Craig had been working and Joanie had been snowed under at her shop, she and Marc's father had spent hours talking, seemingly about nothing. She had thought he was humoring her by telling her about himself. And even then she had wondered if what he was sharing was true, or was just a way to get her mind off her own problems.

She now knew every one of his stories had been true.

Her gaze drifted over the four other men in the room. She realized she could pick them out based on what Sean had told her.

The tall one who had been at the door had dark eyes that looked as though they had seen more than any one man should. He offered her a chair. She would have known without Marc's calling him by name that he was Connor. Sean had said Connor had been more of a father to the others than he had ever been. It appeared he was still playing the role. She sat down and murmured a thank-you.

Then it occurred to her that Sean knew an awful lot about her. She felt her cheeks go hot, remembering all she'd shared with him, thinking him a stranger she could confide in with no risk of her troubles becoming known to anybody else.

"Evening, Mellie. You'll have to excuse us," Sean said with a grin Melanie realized was reminiscent of Marc's. "We're not used to having women around here."

Shocker, Melanie thought, and returned his smile.

"Can I talk to you in the other room for a minute?" Connor said to Marc.

Panic swelled in Melanie's throat. *No.* Marc couldn't leave her here with...with *them.* She could barely manage him—if that's what you could call what she did with him—much less four other brothers exactly like him. Well, not exactly like him. One of the brothers had sandy blond hair. One of them looked as though he had missed his last two appointments at the barbershop. But given their gift for gab so far—

Sean put a hand on her shoulder, seeming to sense her uneasiness. She instantly relaxed. "Are you hungry? Here, why don't I fix you a plate."

She slowly shook her head, feeling a little better. "No, really, I'm not—"

"I already fixed her one, Pops." Marc plopped a plate full of meat loaf, mashed potatoes and corn in front of her. Her stomach growled. A quiet laugh next to her said she wasn't the only one who heard it. She looked to find the blond brother—a dead ringer for Brad Pitt—watching her. He would be David, she realized.

"Excuse us for a minute, will you?" Connor said, aiming a grin at her. He slapped a hand against Marc's back and moved it toward his neck. The way Marc bent slightly told Melanie he didn't have much choice in the matter.

She hid her smile and watched the one with long dark hair—he would be Mitch, ex-FBI, now PI—as he put a glass of milk in front of her.

"You must be Melanie," he said, sitting down.

She nodded and filled her fork with potatoes.

"Nice to meet you. I'm Mitch."

A chair screeched as the blond one scooted closer. "I'm David. And the quiet one over there is Jake. Don't let him scare you. He's probably wondering if you have your green card."

That's right. Marc had told her once that all his brothers

were in law enforcement. The information combined with
what Sean had shared gave her a jumping off point. "That
must make him the one with Immigration and Naturalization
Services."

"And do you?" Jake asked.

She choked. "Excuse me?"

"Have your green card."

She laughed. "Better. I have a copy of my birth certificate."

He didn't respond.

"Showing I was born here."

David chuckled. "Don't pay him any mind. He's just yanking your chain."

Popping a bite of meat loaf into her mouth, she considered
him. "Let's see, you're David, so that must make you with the
police department."

"Right."

She gestured toward the table. "Please, eat."

"She's right," Sean said, and sat down. "We're making her
uncomfortable."

"No, really, you're not," she lied. "Food just tastes better
with company."

She saw Mitch topping up her glass with more milk and
Sean putting more meat loaf on her plate. Then it hit her. The
reason everyone had responded so unusually to her when
she came in. Why Connor had quickly offered a chair, why
Mitch had poured her milk instead of soda or beer, why Sean,
David and Mitch were hovering over her like a trio of mother
hens. Devastatingly handsome, testosterone-laden mother
hens.

She fearfully sought out Sean.

His shy grin told her he knew exactly what she had just realized. "Sorry, Mellie. But I couldn't keep, well, you know,
the secret once we got word Marc had made off with you."

The mashed potatoes stuck to the roof of her mouth. Marc

didn't have to worry about telling his family anything about the baby. They already knew.

"You don't look pregnant," David said next to her.

Mitch swatted him on the arm. "Are there any vitamins or anything you should be taking? Would you like some water to wash them down with?"

"I'm fine—"

"You look tired," Jake said in the same accusatory tone he'd used when inquiring about her green card. "Maybe you should lie down after you eat."

"I'm fine, really, I am." Melanie was unsure how to react to the onslaught of male attention.

David pushed her plate closer to her. "Eat before it gets cold."

Melanie managed another forkful. "Um, Sean, I don't remember you telling me exactly what you do for a living."

Connor came into the room and patted his father's arm. "Pops here is still walking the beat for the D.C. Police Department." He reached across the table. Melanie quickly wiped her hand on her napkin and shook his hand. Was it her imagination, or had he cringed at the pressure of her shake? "Sorry I was rude. I'm Connor. That house Marc holed you up in last night is the property of the U.S. Marshal's office."

She nearly choked. David handed her the glass of milk. Jake moved his chair a little farther away. "You mean it was a government safe house?"

"Uh-huh."

Speaking of Marc, where was he? Melanie glanced nervously toward the door.

"He'll be back in a minute," Connor said. "He wanted to...clean up a bit."

Clean up? She wasn't aware he'd been dirty. Her mind provided a vivid image of their shower together mere hours ago.

She had finished half the plate of food when Marc finally

reappeared. He looked none too happy. And the red smudge under his right cheekbone told her why.

"Oh, God!" She jumped to her feet and hurried to him, ignoring his protests.

"He's got and given lots worse than that, Mel," Jake said.

She was growing angrier by the second. She swiveled toward the table full of men, including Marc in her disbelieving sights. "Is that the reason you two left the room? To get into a fistfight?"

Marc tugged on her shirtsleeve. "Uh, Mel—"

She shrugged him off and looked at Connor.

"Just a bit of payback for the shove I took this morning," he said.

"This morning? You mean you came to the safe house?"

He nodded and rubbed his knuckles. His wince made her cringe.

Marc cleared his throat. "Mel, I think we'd better—"

She ignored him and visually swept the rest of the table. "And all of you knew what was going on when they left the room?"

"Mel—"

She shushed him.

The way the McCoy males instantly avoided her gaze told her they'd known and hadn't done a thing to stop it from happening. She supposed she should be glad they spared her from seeing the exchange.

"I can't believe this. Is this the way you settle problems between each other? A shove here, a punch there?" She shook her head. "Haven't any of you heard of verbal communication?"

Jake caught her attention as he scratched his chin. "What better way to let each other know you're royally pissed then a punch in the jaw?"

She planted her hands on her hips and stared at each of

them in turn. "I sincerely hope none of you act this way on the job."

They all denied that at once. Melanie wanted to put her hands to her ears as she turned toward Marc. "Did you really hit Connor this morning?"

"I didn't hit him, I...well, I kind of pushed him and he, um, he fell down the stairs. Can we go in the other room now, please?"

"Apologize."

Marc blinked at her. "What?"

A quiet chuckle came from the table. Melanie turned toward the culprit. David looked away.

"I said apologize to Connor. Now."

"Hell, Mel, he already got in his lick—"

She grabbed his hand and tugged him across the room toward his older brother. "Shake."

Connor looked at Marc's hand, his arms crossed stoically. Melanie raised an eyebrow. He cleared his throat and reluctantly took his brother's hand.

Marc remained silent. Melanie elbowed him in the ribs. He mumbled contritely. "Sorry, Connor."

"For what?" she prompted.

"Aw, come on, Mel—" He sighed. "I'm sorry for shoving you and taking your gun when you came by this morning. It's just—"

Melanie slapped her hand over the mouth she had thoroughly kissed a short time ago, feeling the heat of his flesh against her palm. "There's no justifying when you apologize."

The two men dropped hands, both looking enormously uncomfortable.

"Now we can leave the room," she said.

Marc stared at her. "What about Connor? Doesn't he owe me an apology?"

Melanie nearly laughed at his boyishly offended expression. "I don't have any control over what Connor does or doesn't do, Marc."

She caught a glimpse of Sean, who sat on two chair legs, grinning. He winked at her, and she felt herself blush from head to foot.

Who'd have thought she had *that* in her? Certainly not her. More of her mother must have rubbed off on her than she realized. Or maybe her impending motherhood had set off some sort of gene she hadn't been aware she had. Either way, she felt oddly at peace with herself...and at ease.

I KNEW there was a reason I never brought her here, Marc thought. It had been more than the fear of what she'd think of the place. More than being afraid she'd take the move the wrong way. He'd somehow known she wouldn't understand him and his brothers.

He followed Mel as she led the way into the living room. His gaze was glued to her nicely rounded backside. It had been a long time since he'd seen her in a pair of jeans. And these ones did her bottom proud.

He turned on a light as she turned toward him, no doubt to give him what for. But while he still wasn't entirely clear on what had happened in there, he hadn't yet lost the ability to knock her off track.

"Now, before you go getting your panties in a twist, you should know Connor and I did more than go at each other in here." He held her gaze. "I had Connor scour the beach for one of the bullets this morning."

He watched the wind slowly disappear from her sails as she blinked.

"He handed it over to David, who had D.C. ballistics compare it with the one you, um, took three months ago." He cleared his throat. "Perfect match."

She stood still for a long moment, then sat on the edge of the sofa. "So trading shoves and punches isn't the only thing you and your brothers are capable of."

He grinned. "Honestly, that doesn't happen often." He ran his fingers through his hair. "I think the last time Connor and I came to blows was over a decade ago."

"Over what?"

He shrugged, then turned and sat in his father's recliner. "I wrapped his Goat around a tree that used to be in the front yard."

"You hurt an animal?"

"No, no. The Goat is a car. A GTO."

Her answering smile warmed him all over. "Yes, I'd say that would deserve a punch or two."

He crossed his arms, affecting nonchalance, when inside his every muscle tensed. "He broke my jaw in two places."

He watched her horrified expression. Her gaze dropped to his jawline. He figured sharing that was enough. She didn't have to know the rest. How his father and Connor had dragged him into the emergency room. How he'd fought the intern and ended up strapped to a gurney. His throat tightened unbearably. How a school bus had been involved in an accident at the same time and in all the excitement, he'd been forgotten, left by himself for four and half hours, untreated, next to a young boy they hadn't been able to revive.

Her soulful eyes lifted to his. "You sent Sean to the hospital, didn't you?"

He hadn't expected the question and didn't quite know how to respond. "Yes," he said quietly.

"Why didn't you come yourself?"

He hated the lump in his throat. "I...I couldn't, Mel. I just couldn't."

His gut twisted into knots. He hated his weakness when it came to hospitals. But this late in the game, he supposed there wasn't much either he or anybody else could do about it. If he couldn't bring himself to go in when Mel was shot...

"Does it have anything to do with your mother?"

He coughed. "Pops told you about that, huh?"

She nodded slowly, not helping him. He figured he deserved it. She was completely right in her argument that he didn't share enough of himself, his past, his thoughts, with her. It wasn't because he didn't want her to know. It was just that he didn't think the words worth saying. Who cared if he nearly hyperventilated—him, two hundred pounds of prime secret service agent—every time he spotted a hospital? What did it matter that his mother had died when he was young? Lots of children lost one or sometimes both of their parents and still managed okay. Mel had grown up without a father.

He realized she was still waiting for an answer. He gave her the only one he had. "I associate hospitals with death, Mel." His thick swallow sounded loud in the room. "I couldn't have stood it if I lost you in one, too."

He looked away, hating that his eyes burned, hating that she looked at him in that pitying way. "Sorry, that came out a little rougher than I meant it to. I'm not used to talking about, well, you know, feelings." He clamped his hands together. "I guess being raised in an all-female household has its advantages," he said carefully.

Mel's gaze was soft. "Trust me, Joanie and I had our fights, but they usually involved destruction of clothing."

He welcomed his unexpected laugh, but the smile had vanished from her face. Before he knew it, she had crossed to him, threading her fingers through his hair and forcing him to look up. Giving in to the need to feel her, he laid his head against her belly, finding it amazing that in there somewhere beat the heart of their child. A child they had created together.

Mel would make a wonderful mother, he realized. She

would be strong and witty as well as loving and nurturing. He could already see her singing the baby to sleep in the middle of the night. Imagine her coaxing the toddler to eat food he disliked. Hugging the child when he came home after having been teased at school. He saw all of this.

And he wanted to be a part of it so bad it hurt.

She slowly drew away. "So," she said quietly. "Now that we know Hooker is the one who shot at me this morning, where do we go from here?"

He cleared his throat. "We don't go anywhere, Mel."

She looked at him for a long time. "Don't you even—"

He held up his hand to stop her. "David's already passed on the information to those who need to know it."

She stood a little straighter. Marc's gaze was drawn to her stomach. He didn't know if it was fact or if he was imagining it because he knew she was pregnant, but he swore he could make out the new fullness of her belly.

"Was he able to get any other information on Hooker?" she asked. "Have the authorities checked out his house? His sister's place? Staked out all his usual hangouts in case he surfaces?"

He nodded. "They've done and are doing all that, Mel."

She turned and started pacing. He grimaced. The whole point of bringing her here was to make her feel safe. It wasn't going to help if she insisted on being a part of things.

She abruptly faced him. "You already have a plan, don't you?"

He didn't respond.

"And you're not going to let me in on it, are you?"

He wasn't sure if he liked where this was heading.

"God, this really stinks, you know, McCoy?"

He grinned. "Better watch out. You're in a house with six McCoys now."

She looked toward the kitchen, her palm going to her forehead as she considered what he said. When she looked at him, he could see she was still angry, but she was also undeniably concerned. "I'm putting my life...the life of our baby in your hands, Marc. Please take care of us."

For the first time in his life Marc knew what absolute fear felt like. "I will."

MELANIE LEANED against the kitchen counter, trying to sort out the details of her life. Despite the newfound closeness between her and Marc, she couldn't envision a future for them together. The whole marriage thing... She swallowed hard. Well, she would just have to straighten that out once the threat that loomed over her head was gone.

An odd warmth spread through her chest. She had to give the guy credit, though. Marc McCoy was a boyish adventurer ninety-nine percent of the time, but when it came down to the important things, he did the right thing. Both by her and the baby.

If only he could give her what she yearned for most—his love.

She idly watched as David rinsed then loaded plates in what had to be the biggest dishwasher they made. She glanced around the room. In fact, it was probably the only appliance that had been bought within the past ten years. An old commercial-size refrigerator hummed in the corner, and she was afraid that if she looked more closely at the six-burner stove, she'd find it had a compartment for wood.

She reached for a towel and absently folded it, hating that she didn't know what was going on in the other room, where the remainder of the McCoy males were discussing her future. But she knew giving in to Marc was a wise choice. For three months she'd based her decisions on what was best for her baby. Now that her existence was threatened, this was probably the most important thing she could ever do for her child. Especially since she couldn't marry his father.

At least she'd been given phone privileges. Marc had loomed over her, but he hadn't interfered while she let her family know she was all right.

Her gaze wandered to the door.

"Do they do this often?" she asked David.

"What? Call family meetings?" He gave her a half grin, reminding her again of how very much he looked like Brad Pitt. "No."

Melanie looked at him closely. He couldn't be more than a shade over thirty—her age—if that, but his blue eyes reflected the wisdom of a sixty-year-old. *Good, a McCoy who doesn't feel he has to wisecrack his way through everything.*

She turned to the counter and folded her hands on top of it, pretending an interest in the sunset she could see through the window overlooking the back yard. *Back yard?* It seemed as if half of Virginia stretched behind the McCoy house, crisscrossed with sagging fences.

"Do you mind if I ask you a question?" David said.

She glanced at him. "Shoot." She grimaced, thinking she'd seen enough shooting to last her a lifetime, thank you very much.

"I...I'm having a few women problems."

Women problems? Melanie battled against a smile and lost. "Sorry." She motioned with her hands and returned her attention to the sunset. Only *she* would find herself on the brink of a conversation regarding someone else's love life. "I don't think I'm exactly an expert on male-female relationships." *That was an understatement.* "But I'll do the best I can."

He didn't say anything, and she turned to him. He was scratching at something on the edge of a plate. His hands were long and lean, and he looked so deep in thought, Melanie felt the inexplicable urge to know what was on his mind.

She quietly cleared her throat. "This woman. Have you known her long?"

"Only a few weeks." He put the plate in the dishwasher and closed it. "She's my partner. That's why I thought talking to you about my predicament might help."

Melanie worried her bottom lip, wondering exactly how much he knew about her and Marc.

David piled the pans in the sink.

"Here," she said, pushing away from the counter. "Let me get those."

He grinned. "I could hold my ground with the dishes, but you could get yourself in trouble offering to do these." He glanced toward the door. "Only don't tell anyone I let you do anything more than sit at the table. They'd have my hide."

She laughed and pushed him gently out of the way. It might help if she had something to do while she waited for Marc. She didn't mind helping David with his problem. If he ever got around to sharing it.

Then it occurred to her that she had some bargaining power. David wanted advice on his love life. She wanted, needed to know more about Marc.

David reached into a cupboard, took out a mug, then poured a cup of coffee.

"Before you go on," she said, filling a couple of the messier pans with hot water and soap and putting them aside, "I'd like to make a deal with you."

"Deal?" He pushed a lock of golden hair from his forehead.

"Yeah. I answer your questions, then you can answer some of mine."

He eyed her over the rim of his cup. "Ah, Marc's a bit of a mystery man."

She smiled. "A bit."

"I don't know if I can help because we haven't been able to

figure him out yet either, but..." He gave her a crooked grin. "It's a deal."

"Good." She rinsed a pan and put it in the drainer. "You first."

He pondered for a minute while she poured half a can of cleanser into a stainless steel skillet.

"Tell me, Mel, what is it that women really want?"

Melanie dropped the cleanser in the sink, then scrambled to pick it up. Why did she have the feeling answering David's question wasn't going to be as easy as she thought?

11

MARC TURNED OVER yet again, tempted to punch the floor to make it softer. If only it had a chance in hell of working, he would have. He threw his head against the pillow and winced, knowing being away from Melanie was as much to blame for his agitated state as his sleeping arrangements on the floor of Mitch's bedroom.

"Can I ask you a question, Mitch?"

The bedsprings squeaked. Marc looked at his brother, as comfortable as you please in the double bed. "Hmm?"

"Why are you such an awful host?"

Mitch's chuckle grated on his nerves. "You were the one who went and made an ass of yourself by tossing and turning and got kicked out of the bed, not me."

Marc sighed and draped his arm across his head. "Good thing that's not my question, then, isn't it?"

The springs squeaked again, and Mitch squinted at him through the darkness. "Will you just ask your question already so I can get some sleep?"

Marc grimaced. "Yeah, life must be pretty tough as a client-less PI."

"I have clients. I'm just taking a bit of a leave, that's all," Mitch corrected. "Anyway, I meant we both need our sleep if we're to keep up with this rigid schedule we came up with to keep a constant watch on the house."

"Yeah, you're right." Marc lay back, reviewing what he, his father and brothers had worked out earlier in the evening.

First had come the objectives. Keeping Mel safe was definitely at the top of the list. He really didn't want to think about how they knew she was pregnant, but they all did. The best he could figure, Mel must have told his old man a lot more in that hospital than Pops had let on.

Second was to catch Hooker so he could never prove a threat to her again. In conjunction with the first objective, all five brothers had agreed to take two-hour watches until Hooker was caught, with Pops staying in the house as the final barrier between Hooker and Mel.

To see through the second objective, Marc had put the word out on his and Mel's whereabouts. If Hooker wanted her, Hooker would have to go through the McCoys to get her.

He frowned. His only concern now was his inability to get through to his partner, Roger Westfield. He wasn't on the schedule for post duty and he hadn't answered his phone, leaving Marc to believe he was out with one of his many dates.

The only obvious drawback to the plan was that it would soon eliminate the reason Mel was with him. As much as he'd like to believe in his ability to convince her to marry him, he knew it was far from a done deal. And if she went back to Bedford and started working at her new, cushy position, his job would be very tough, if not downright impossible.

Marc stretched his neck and swallowed hard. He'd never really talked about relationship stuff with any of his brothers. Well, not anything that went beyond comparing been-there, done-that lists, anyway. And just because he needed some information didn't necessarily mean he'd find anything out. Especially since given the subject of his question, Mitch was more liable to slug him than answer him.

He cleared his throat. "Mitch, do you remember, oh, I don't know." He hedged, thinking about chucking the whole question. "Seven years ago."

Mitch was unusually quiet. There was no squeak of the bedsprings, no noticeable sign of his breathing.

Marc pressed on. "What I want to know is, do you, you know, ever regret not going after her?"

When the silence dragged on, Marc lifted himself on one elbow, wondering if he should have said her name. He lay down. No. Out of all of them, Mitch had been the only one tempted to try the marriage route. He'd gotten as far as the altar before Liz Braden stood him up. There was no way a guy forgot something like that.

"Yes."

The word filled the room but sounded oddly far away. Marc rubbed the back of his neck, wondering where his brother was right now. Here? Or somewhere out there with Liz?

"No."

Marc frowned and sat up, staring over the side of the mattress at the empty bed. Where did he go? Then he realized Mitch must have climbed out the window and onto the roof over the front porch. He'd done it often when they were younger, earning him his share of ribbing for being what they all saw as a dreamer.

Marc sat on the bed and looked out the window. He wasn't about to go out there after him. He'd done it once as a teen and nearly got tossed over the side for his efforts. "That roof is going to collapse on you one of these days, you know."

Mitch stretched his jeans-clad legs in front of him, his back against the house. "Let it."

Marc grimaced and looked out at stars. There were so many of them. "So you didn't tell me which was your answer, yes or no."

Mitch crossed his arms over his bare chest. "Both, I guess." The night was dark, the only sound the crickets. "I would have liked an explanation why, I guess." His deep swallow was audible. "But at the same time, my damn pride wouldn't let me go after it, you know?"

"Yeah, I know."

"Anyway, that's muddy water under a bridge that washed out a long time ago." Mitch shifted to look at him. "Why do you ask?"

Marc shrugged. "I don't know. Just curious, I guess."

"Curious, my ass. What's going on in that head of yours, Marc?"

Marc moved to his makeshift bed on the floor, pondering what Mitch had said and ignoring his question.

"You know," Mitch said, his voice muffled, "I'm surprised you haven't tried to sneak into the room down the hall yet."

Marc grew agitated and punched his pillow. "The old man hasn't started snoring yet."

Mitch's laugh threatened to wake the whole household. Marc picked up his pillow and tossed it out the window.

MELANIE HAD BEEN afraid they'd never leave her alone. Jake had brought her a thicker blanket—though the room was so hot she could barely stand the sheet. David had brought her a nubby blue terry robe. Mitch had asked if she wanted to talk about anything, to which she had smiled and said no. Sean had brought her some milk and cookies, then knocked on the door every five minutes until a half hour ago, asking her if she was okay.

Finally, blessedly alone, Melanie snuggled into the single bed and filled her nose with the smell of Marc all around her. Marc's bed. Marc's pillow. Marc's sports trophies reflecting the moonlight from a shelf on the wall. She smiled and rolled over, more content than she suspected was safe. But since no one was looking, there was no harm in indulging in the connection to the father of her child.

She'd enjoyed it when Sean had made it clear she and Marc

were not to share a room. Marc had argued, but to no avail. Especially when his four brothers had joined in and agreed that there should be no sinful shenanigans under the McCoy roof. Even though her pregnancy was proof that they'd indulged in plenty outside the McCoy house.

Sinful shenanigans.

She gave a little shiver of anticipation, for the first time really seeing what life was going to be like with a baby in it.

She glanced at the clock, knowing there was no way Marc wasn't going to violate his father's dictate. In fact, she'd expected him to sneak into the room long before now. Where was he? She rolled over and sighed, wondering if maybe he'd fallen to sleep in Mitch's room.

The way she understood it, the only McCoys who still lived in the house were Sean and now Mitch. He'd moved back shortly before David had moved out. Marc, Connor, Jake and David all lived in D.C. or the suburbs, for convenience. But all of them called this old house home, and returned as often as they could, usually Wednesday nights and weekends, sharing meals, probably shooting the breeze and likely holding on to all that bonded them together.

Melanie sobered. Given what Marc had grudgingly shared with her while they were alone in the living room, what David had haltingly told her in the kitchen and what she had learned from Sean, she knew the glue that bonded them together was of the super adhesive type.

She didn't know all the details, but from what she understood, Marc's mother had died during childbirth some twenty-eight years earlier, when David was two. She worried her bottom lip, calculating that Marc would have been five. David said he couldn't remember anything about her but her scent. The rest of the brothers recalled bits and pieces, and Connor was good about sharing memories with them all since he was the oldest.

Connor had taken on the role of father when Sean had been helpless to stop himself from sinking into a depression so black he'd sometimes disappear for days, leaving the five young boys to fend for themselves.

She stilled her hand where it lay flat against her belly, swearing she felt movement just beneath the surface. Her doctor had told her she should start becoming aware of the baby's movements some time during her fourth month. After long, quiet moments with no further sensation, she thought she must have imagined it.

She shifted restlessly, hurting for Sean but most of all hurting for Marc because he remembered his mother and more than likely had memories of her being pregnant. In her mind's eye, she saw this precocious five-year-old touching his mother's belly, excited and challenged by the life growing inside her. A life extinguished along with his mother's.

Melanie swallowed tears, her hands touching her belly, remembering how protective Marc was of her. She guessed a lot of his behavior stemmed from his childlike pride and his admitted fear of never seeing her again. But she now understood a hefty measure came from losing not only his mother, but also his baby sister, when he was so young.

The floorboards outside her door squeaked. She sat instantly upright, her heart thundering in her chest as she reached for the revolver on the nightstand. Cocking it, she pointed it at the wooden barrier.

Slowly, the doorknob turned. She waited, holding her breath, her finger surprisingly calm where it rested against the trigger.

Marc.

Exhaling, she dropped the .22 to her lap and rolled her eyes heavenward. "You scared the daylights out of me," she said.

"Shh." Marc peered down the hall, then quietly closed the door. "I thought the old man would never go to sleep."

The fear that Hooker had somehow gained access to the house diminishing, Melanie put her gun, which Marc had given back to her, on the nightstand. She remembered Sean's stern warning before they'd retired to their rooms—all except Jake, who'd stayed on in the kitchen—and fought a smile. She felt as if she was in high school and her boyfriend had just thrown a stone at the window. Only Marc probably would have broken the window, she thought, smiling.

"Move over," he said, lifting the sheet.

"I thought you'd never ask." Scooting over as far as she could on the single bed, Melanie sighed contentedly when he climbed in behind her, spooning her against his warm length. "Nice," she murmured.

How long had it been since Marc had held her? Just held her? Never, she realized. There was really never a time when they had snuggled for the pure pleasure of snuggling.

And you shouldn't get used to it now, either, a voice inside her warned.

Pushing aside all the questions that demanded answers she wasn't yet prepared to give, she reached behind her.

"Mm, even nicer."

Marc trapped her hand in his, his voice low. "Stop it, you tease."

She raised her eyebrows in the dark. "Stop it?" That's the second time Marc had put off her seduction attempts. She must be losing her touch.

She shifted, causing the bedsprings to squeak.

"Quiet, or you'll wake the ogre who lives down the hall."

She laughed. "I wouldn't call him an ogre."

She made out his grimace in the moonlight that drifted in from the window above the headboard.

"You didn't have to grow up with him."

She ran her fingers along his smooth jaw, remembering it

had once been broken. "I'd trade you my mother for your father any day."

His chuckle shook the mattress. "No, thanks."

She listlessly moved her hand to his chest. She was used to him wearing nothing to bed, but out of consideration for their surroundings, he wore a pair of boxer shorts. She let her fingers dip lower across the velvety skin of his stomach, reveling in his low hiss.

He caught her hand in his again. "I said stop it, Mel."

She leaned over and kissed him, slowly, thoroughly, loving the taste of toothpaste on his tongue. She closed her eyes and pressed her nose against his. "Your reluctance wouldn't have anything to do with my...condition, would it?"

She felt rather than saw his grin. "Condition?"

She took his hand. "Ever since finding out I'm pregnant, you've been treating me with kid gloves." She kissed him again, a moan building in her throat as he willingly let his fingers be led to her wetness. "There isn't any need to. I'm perfectly capable of having a normal sex life until I'm well into the third trimester."

This time he kissed her, and she could sense the urgency lurking behind a thin barrier of caution. "Are you sure?"

She nodded.

No longer in need of her talents as a guide, he flicked the tip of his finger over her pressure point, causing her to shudder in pleasure. She tightly grasped his biceps and laughed. "Hmm, I'd say you adjust quickly."

She moved to push him on the mattress and nearly succeeded in toppling him from the bed. She laughed, and he pressed a finger against her lips as he righted himself beneath her.

"Keep up the chatter, Mel, and you'll end up spending the rest of the night alone."

She tugged her T-shirt off and let it drop to the floor,

pleased when he cupped her breasts. "Now that would be a real shame, wouldn't it?"

She arched into his touch, loving the feel of his palms against her breasts and the way he feathered his thumbs over her nipples, causing them to ache.

There was something decidedly sinful about making love to Marc in his family's house, with his brothers and father just down the hall. She cradled Marc's erection between her thighs, causing him to groan. She quickly covered his mouth with her hand. He nipped at her skin with his teeth, and she pulled back, laughing quietly.

She'd long accused Marc of being a breast man, and he obviously intended to prove her point now. She shivered, not about to stop the thorough attention, reveling in the texture of his tongue, the flick of his thumb, the squeeze of his fingers, knowing that the complete passion behind his actions was more responsible for the flames licking inside her than his touch.

His movements slowed, and he lay back. She could feel him watching her. When he spoke, his voice was quiet. "David told me that you and he had a long talk earlier."

Melanie stilled the rocking of her hips. She tried to make out his features and covered his hands where he was still touching her. "Yes. Yes, we did."

"He said you weren't going to marry me."

She touched his cheek, running her fingers along the fine line of his jaw.

There was so much Melanie wanted to explain to him, so much she wanted to say, but now wasn't the time. She couldn't help fearing that there wouldn't be a time, that the opportunity for them to discuss such intimate matters had already passed. And that scared her even more than the man hunting her.

"Let's not talk about that now, okay?"

Slowly, she bent toward him, pressing her mouth against his, communicating her feelings and urging him to share his. When he buried his fingers in her hair and languidly returned her kiss, she knew this time she wouldn't be denied.

MELANIE SLOWLY AWOKE to a cardinal calling outside the window. She stretched, aware of the thoroughly sated condition of her body. She reached out, only to realize she was the only one in the small bed.

Propping herself up, she pushed back one of the curtains to peer outside. The purple smears across the eastern sky told her it was very near dawn. Somewhere around five, Marc had left her, murmuring something about his turn at taking watch. She scanned the grounds but saw no sign of him.

She eased down on the bed, her contentment slowly seeping away no matter how hard she tried to hold on to it.

Over the past three days it had been all too easy to let her plans for the future fade to the background. When faced with the urgency of her present situation, it was no wonder. Out there somewhere, Hooker was waiting in the shadows.

But if everything Marc said was true, and if the trap he was setting for Hooker panned out, then the urgency would end and she would be smack-dab in the middle of the mess she'd made out of things.

She lay on her back, staring at the ceiling. Well, she hadn't exactly created a mess. Despite all that had happened, her blazing attraction for Marc and their very sinful shenanigans, not much had changed. She was still pregnant. And even though she knew she could never marry Craig, as far as everyone else was concerned, judging from her conversation with her mother the night before, she was still set to marry him in... She glanced at the clock. Six hours.

That sent her into a coughing fit.

Six hours?

She stared at the window. Marc had closed it—for safety reasons, he'd said. She knelt on the bed and pushed it open, needing some fresh air.

As she lay down, she mechanically counted off all the reasons she had once thought Craig would make a better husband and father than Marc. He was dependable. Stable. She knew him and he knew her better than anyone else. Outside work, they held much in common. He was thoughtful and loving and completely unselfish.

But all those were reasons he made a great friend.

His job doesn't require he put his life on the line.

She kicked off the covers. That point wasn't entirely fair. She had put her own life on the line, and was still doing it, if present circumstances counted. But that was before she found out she was pregnant.

That had changed everything. The moment the doctor had come into her hospital room, beaming with the news, her entire life had crowded around her as if a plastic snow dome had been clamped around it. And she hadn't particularly liked what she saw. Through the eyes of an expectant mother, she viewed herself as a girl, tugging off her hair bow and all the ruffles on her dress and tossing them into the trash the first day of school. As a teenager, making every school team—including football—just to get a rise out of her mother. As an adult, seeking every thrill and adventure she could.

Her mother's face had loomed, superimposed, yes, pinched with disapproval, but also etched with worry. In that moment she realized she had another life to consider now. She also understood that she would always worry her mother. The condition went hand-in-hand with motherhood.

But she couldn't help thinking that if her father had been alive, if he had played a role in their lives, the load would have been easier for all of them.

Melanie rolled over and pressed her face into the pillow.

The insight had not come easily. After she had been released from the hospital and was at home, sitting in a daze in the back yard, and Craig had proposed—she had accepted.

A proposal it was important for her now to reject. For both their sakes. And she owed it to him to discuss it face-to-face before telling anyone else.

She sat and let her gaze wander around the room. There was something comforting about being in Marc's room. She got up and ran a hand over a poster of a race car. The tape had come off the bottom right corner. Looking closer, she rolled it up a bit. No, it couldn't be....

It wasn't difficult to loosen the yellow tape on the left corner. She rolled up the poster to confirm her suspicions. Grimacing, she stared at the definitive pinup poster. Farrah Fawcett. Well, that explained some things. Like why Marc was so obsessed with her breasts. Gad, this poster had to be...

She looked at the flip hairstyle even she had emulated, not wanting to think about the time or the fact that she could remember it.

She sighed and tried to smooth the race car poster. It immediately rolled halfway up. Didn't these people ever paint?

She smiled, counting all the things she had learned about Marc in the past twenty-four hours. His reluctant capacity for deep emotion. She pulled on her jeans, leaving on the faded Redskins T-shirt Marc had given her to wear. His close bond with his brothers. She slipped into her new athletic shoes. The tragedy in his past that had taken the only female influences from his life.

Biting solidly on her bottom lip, she tried to ignore the things that came together in her mind. The poster that told her Marc held on tightly to the past. His cautious admission that he was afraid he'd never see her again.

The only problem was the realization came about three months too late.

She quickly made up the bed, then left the room and all its puzzles behind, descended the stairs and moved toward the side door. She hadn't seen Marc, but she guessed he was probably outside watching the place. Which was just as well. Right now she really needed to talk to Sean.

She was glad to find him in the kitchen, nursing a cup of coffee.

"Morning. Sleep well?"

Melanie's face heated, remembering she hadn't done much sleeping. "Great. I slept great." She cleared her throat. "That coffee fresh?"

"It's drinkable."

She absently mimicked David's movements from the night before, taking a mug from the cupboard and pouring herself a half cup of the hot java. A couple of sips couldn't hurt.

Sean took the cup from her hands and dumped the contents down the drain before she could open her mouth. "Jake dug out some decaffeinated something or other for you. Here it is." He picked up a red-and-white box. "Tea."

Melanie grimaced. "I'd much rather have the coffee."

Sean filled the teapot, his actions his only response.

Resigned, she sat at the table and pulled the crossword he'd been working on her way.

"Hungry? Mitch read over the nutritional information on all of the cereal boxes and said this had the most vitamins." Sean nudged a box in her direction.

She laughed. "That's the first time I've heard someone call sugar-coated cereal nutritious."

David stumbled into the room, his jeans slung low on his hips, shirtless, his hair sticking up at all angles. "I thought I heard you." He reached into a cupboard and produced a banana. "Here. I saved this for you."

Melanie shook her head in disbelief. She'd thought Marc was a handful. Five more of him was too much.

Still, it was much easier to accept the banana, pour the cereal into the bowl he handed her and allow Sean to pour some milk than it was to argue.

Sean frowned at his youngest son. "David, don't you think it would be a good idea to put some clothes on, what with a guest in the house and all?"

David glanced at himself, seemingly unaffected by his half-dressed appearance. She guessed she was lucky he hadn't wandered in in his boxer shorts. She shook her head again, the origins of Marc's behavior becoming less and less a mystery. *It must be genetic.*

David shrugged, then stumbled out of the room, leaving her and Sean alone.

Melanie crunched on the cereal. "Sean," she said tentatively between bites. "Do you remember what you said to me in the hospital?"

She watched him stiffen. He faced the stove, apparently watching the kettle. "Depends on what you're referring to."

Melanie shifted, uneasy. "About my deciding to keep the baby?"

He slowly turned in her direction, his blue eyes serious beneath his bushy salt-and-pepper eyebrows. "What, that I thought it was a good idea if you got married?"

She nodded, remembering she hadn't thought the advice outdated coming from him. He had seemed genuinely concerned about her raising a child on her own. Which was funny, because she would have suspected a conspiracy had her mother broached the subject. "You meant that I should marry Marc, didn't you?"

He was quiet for a moment before he said, "At first I did. I'd never seen my boy as worked up as he was while you were lying in that hospital. He hounded me night and day until I agreed to go in there, you know, on the sly."

His expression grew serious. "But the more I got to know you, and, well, after I met that Craig fellow..."

Melanie stared into her cereal bowl, remembering when Craig had come to visit while she was talking to Sean.

"And he appeared like a decent enough sort. Well, I thought that you were the better one to make the decision about who you should spend the rest of your life with." He coughed. "You know, who should play the role as father of your baby."

She squinted at him. "But you're the baby's grandfather."

Sean turned as the kettle began to whistle. "My first. I know." He took the kettle from the burner but didn't make a move to fill the mug sitting on the counter. "Hell, Mellie, I didn't do a very good job bringing my own boys up. I didn't have any right telling you what you should do with your own child." Silence reigned as he finally poured the water to let the tea steep. "I will say I'm awfully glad Marc knows about the child and that I'll now get that chance to play grand-daddy." He smiled at her sadly. "That is, if you'll let me."

"Of course I'll let you," Melanie whispered, her throat clogged with tears.

She took her bowl to the sink, rinsed it and put it in the dishwasher. She joined Sean at the table. They sat across from each other.

"Sean?"

He lifted his gaze to hers.

"Thanks." She gestured absently with her hands. "Not just for now. But for...well, for being there when I was in the hospital."

She saw a depth of emotion in his eyes that made her chest tighten. A curiously familiar expression she swore she'd seen in Marc's eyes. "Anytime, Mellie. Anytime."

12

MARC SPOTTED MEL the instant she opened the door. His heart did a funny little thing in his chest just seeing her coming from the house he'd grown up in. She even caught the door before it could slam, as though she'd been doing it for years.

He kicked the back of his boot against the large rock he sat on, wanting to call out to her but not sure if he should. While she slept last night, nestled safe and warm in his arms, he'd been wide-awake, mulling over everything.

He watched her run a hand over her belly, appearing completely oblivious that she did it. He experienced a mixed burst of pride and fear and forced himself to swallow a huge dose of reality.

She doesn't want you, sport.

He looked around. The grass was overgrown, trampled beneath his and his brothers' footsteps. He rubbed the back of his neck. The trouble was, he really couldn't blame Mel for not wanting to marry him. The minute he'd learned about the baby, nearly the first words out of his mouth were, "You're marrying me." No romantic proposal, no declarations of love.

Love.

There was that word again.

He grimaced. What in the hell did he know about love? Sure, he supposed he loved his family. But Mel? She walked to the front of the house, away from him. He did know that the first few days she'd been in that hospital he'd hurt like hell. And that when he'd thought he'd lost her... Well, the ring was still burning a hole in his pocket.

He knew why he'd bought that engagement ring, but he didn't really know *why*. He'd told himself it was because it was what Mel had wanted. But not even that excuse held water anymore. Not when he remembered how nervous he'd been when he'd decided on the ring because it matched the color of her eyes. Not when he'd felt both proud and scared to death when he'd stood outside the hospital, then later, outside her mother's house, all decked out in a suit, ready to propose to her, only to discover she was marrying someone else.

But did he *love* her?

He bit off a curse. Mel at least deserved someone who knew what love was and knew how to show it.

And his son? Or daughter, he quickly reminded himself. What did he or she deserve?

"Someone who knows how to be a parent," he said quietly.

Truth be told, along with the excitement he felt about becoming a father, he was also more scared than he'd ever been in his life.

Mel turned in his direction, apparently having heard him. He rubbed his face and looked at his watch. David should be taking over soon. He needed the break. While it was part of his job to go for long stretches on watch, the way his mind had been working overtime...well, he could use a good, long shower and a couple cups of coffee.

"Here."

He looked up to find Mel standing directly in front of him, holding out a cup of what he'd just been dreaming about. He mumbled his thanks and took a long sip. He tried to hand it back.

"I can't have it, remember?" she said with a small smile. "Anyway, you look like you need it more than I do."

"Gee, thanks."

She sat down on the rock next to him. "You're welcome."

He scanned her profile, thinking she appeared as sober as he felt. Obviously she'd been doing some thinking of her own.

"Well," he murmured.

She gave him a weak smile.

A few minutes had passed in silence before she said, "I saw the poster of your old girlfriend on your wall."

He squinted against the rising sun. "Huh?"

She looked at him for the first time since sitting down. "Farrah?"

He continued to frown until he registered what she was saying. "Oh." He cleared his throat. "Unfortunately I had to share her with the entire male population." *Just like I'm going to have to share you with one male in particular.*

The thought came out of nowhere.

"I wanted to tell you that I...understand about your past," she said.

He scanned her face. What did a picture of a woman in a swimsuit have to do with his past? He grimaced and shook his head. He didn't get it.

And that was just the point. He would never understand how her mind worked. No matter how many women's magazines and relationship books he read, none of it would help him when it came to Mel. "Connect to your feminine side," one of the books had encouraged. He bit back a curse, finally admitting he might not have one of those. The stupid thing was, he wasn't sure if he was upset about that—or relieved.

He and Mel existed on two separate planes, their differences outnumbering their similarities. That had bothered him since the beginning. It might very well be what made him hang back when she had sought a closer connection.

He rubbed his palm against the rough denim of his jeans. "You'd better go inside. I don't want you to catch a chill."

"I can take care of myself."

He sighed. "Let me rephrase that. My watch is over, all right? I'm going inside. Would you like to come, or do you want to stay out here?"

She lifted her chin. "I think I'll sit out here awhile longer."

Marc shrugged, pretending he didn't care. "Have it your way."

He began to get up, then sat down. "By the way, I think you're right. You shouldn't marry me. In fact, I think it's a pretty good idea if you go ahead and marry Craig."

MELANIE SAT in stunned silence, watching Marc squirm next to her.

"I'm sorry, I didn't mean for it to come out quite that way," he said, looking torn. He cleared his throat and met her gaze head-on. "You said you loved Craig. And I'm sure he loves you. And the baby... Well, I can still play a role in his life, can't I?"

Melanie's mind refused to register what he was saying.

"Look, Marc—"

He shook his head. "It's okay. You don't have to do any more explaining. Your reasons for not marrying me have finally settled in. I won't be bothering you anymore." He rose from the rock and started walking toward the house.

Melanie finally convinced herself she wasn't hearing things and leaped up.

"What?" she asked, hurrying after him. "What did you just say?"

She reached him and nearly ran right into him. "You can't just say something like that, then walk away! I want an explanation."

She would have thought he looked altogether too cute, too tortured. If only she wasn't feeling as if he'd ripped her heart out.

"What's there left to explain, Mel? You love Craig. I'm assuming he loves you. I don't want to stand in the way of your happiness. It was wrong of me to do so to begin with."

She didn't know whether she wanted to hit him or burst out crying.

The sound of a car engine broke the early morning silence. It took a second for her to recognize it. By the time she did, Marc had pulled the gun from the waist of her jeans and was hustling her toward the house.

"Get inside."

"I'm not—"

"Come on, Mel, now is not the time for an argument."

Her gaze flicked toward the approaching car. It looked familiar, but she couldn't be sure from this distance. The door opened, and Sean pulled her inside just as David and a half-dressed Mitch came thundering into the kitchen.

Melanie's heart beat double time. She looked down, realizing Marc had taken her gun. Her hands rested solidly against her belly, as though protecting the child there.

She caught Sean's expression. Emotions Melanie could recognize swept through the older man's eyes. Joy, sorrow, undiluted fear for her and his grandchild. Had he heard the exchange between her and Marc? Did he know Marc had told her to marry another man?

The moment was broken when Jake ran by, buttoning a shirt over his unfastened slacks. Melanie stared, dumbfounded by how quickly they got going. Sure, they were all in law enforcement, but these McCoys... As witless as they appeared on a personal level, they were like a well-tuned military unit used to dealing with situations like this. She shuddered, wondering if that could be the case.

No...

"Oh, no, you don't, Mellie." Sean blocked her way when

she was ready to bolt out the door. "You're going to stay inside and keep yourself and my grandchild safe."

For the second time that morning, Melanie felt her face go hot. If the command had come from Marc, she would have fought him. But his father she couldn't refuse.

"Do you really think it's Hooker?" she asked.

He frowned. "I don't know, but I suspect the boys will find out soon enough."

She nodded and stayed in the living room. For the sake of her baby.

She sank into the recliner and rested her head in her hands. She pondered exactly how she had gotten into this mess and whether or not anything would ever be the same again.

She started to get up to look through the front window when an arm snaked around her from behind, pinning her to the chair.

"Don't move," a male voice warned.

Oh, God.

Cold fear ran straight through Melanie, paralyzing her as much as the command. It had to be Hooker.

Her mind raced crazily. How did he get in? She flashed to that morning, when she'd found the house stuffy and had rebelliously opened a window Marc had locked. She smelled the fresh Virginia air on Hooker's clothes. He had likely just gained access, which meant he'd likely come in while she had been talking to Marc.

She closed her eyes. If anything proved her decision to resign her position with the secret service had been right, her actions that morning did. She'd allowed emotion and just plain insolence to interfere with the protection against a serious threat, undermining the actions of those who had sworn to help her. Every one of the McCoy brothers was even now swooping down on what might be an innocent visitor, while she had not only let Hooker into the house...she was utterly alone with him.

Her throat tightening, Melanie reached for a gun that was no longer there.

"Stay quiet." Her assailant released his grasp and rounded the chair. Melanie's stomach hurt so much she thought she might experience her first bout of morning sickness.

"Hooker," she whispered.

"This isn't exactly the way I planned things, Mel. You have to understand that." He appeared nervous. Melanie knew from training and experience that a panicky man was the most dangerous one. He was more apt to act out of fear than to think things through. Her gaze was glued to the gun in his shaking hands.

"I tried calling you. Why didn't you take my calls? Why wouldn't you listen to me, Mel?"

She looked him full in the face. "All the talking's been done, Hooker."

"No!" He pointed the gun at her. "You've got to listen to me!"

Melanie tried to make herself one with the chair upholstery, hardly daring to breathe. *Keep your eyes raised. The hardest thing to do is to shoot someone while looking into their eyes.* The snippet from her training did nothing to make her feel better.

"I mean, no," he said a little more calmly. "Not nearly enough's been said. You need to know the truth. I'm here to tell you what really went down that night." He swiped at the sweat on his forehead with the cuff of his denim shirt, a shirt Melanie knew he'd stolen from a clothesline. "I asked... demanded to talk to you after everything went down, but you...you'd been shot. They wouldn't let me explain things." His eyes held a desperate, crazy pleading. "You're the only one who can help me, Mel."

Melanie felt the ridiculous urge to cry. For the second time in as many days, she appreciated the irony of her predicament and hated it. She couldn't be more than fifty yards away from five prime, well-trained males, and she'd entered the only unsafe place on the property.

Hooker's hands shook so violently, she was afraid he would accidentally trip the trigger.

Keep it together, Mel. Keep it together.

"You don't understand. I didn't do it. It wasn't me, Mel. It wasn't me."

She attempted to push a response from her throat. "Then why have you been trying to kill me?"

"Kill you?" He stumbled back a couple of steps. "I haven't been trying to kill you. I've been trying to talk to you. Why...why would I want to kill you? I've been trying to save my ass." There was the sound of slamming car doors. Hooker jerked his head to listen, his anxiety quotient nudging up even further. "You're confusing me. I need to get this out, don't you see?"

There it was. The stillness she needed settled over her as a rare opportunity gaped wide-open.

Hooker continued. "That night... It's kind of like a blur to me, you know? One minute I'm checking out a suspicious noise, the next I'm waking up on the cold ground with your boyfriend's knee in my chest." His voice rose in pitch as he continued. "Don't you see? It wasn't me, Mel. It was—"

Vaulting from the chair, Melanie acted on pure instinct. With her right hand, she forced the barrel of the gun away while she slipped her left leg behind his right knee and pushed against his shoulder. As he fell, she tugged the gun out of his grip, then planted her foot solidly against his solar plexus, pinning him to the floor.

She locked the safety on the gun, then allowed herself a moment to enjoy the afterglow. Oh, yes, she still had it.

Hooker started to struggle. Afraid he might get loose, she

started to pull her hand back, the weight of the gun she held promising more strength to the impending blow.

"Damn it, it wasn't me!" Tom Hooker flinched. "It was Roger!"

Her hand connected with the side of his head just as his words slipped through the protective adrenaline haze clouding her thoughts.

MELANIE'S MIND reeled as she stared at the unconscious man she had slowly, methodically bound with curtain ties. Hooker's last words echoed as if he were saying them over and over.

It was Roger.... It was Roger.... It was Roger....

After three months of replaying the memories from that night, of reliving the horrifying moments in her sleep, feeling as if there was something she was missing, something that didn't ring true, she knew the reason. That shadowy figure she had caught trying to slip through the senator's window, the faceless man who had shot her hadn't been Hooker. It had been his partner, Roger Westfield.

A man now Marc's partner.

Facts that supported Hooker's claim accumulated in her mind. Hooker's repeated attempts to contact her. His unwavering proclamation of innocence. The staff psychologist saying the recurring nightmares were trying to tell her something. Marc telling her during the drive to the safe house that he would never have thought Hooker capable of doing what they all thought he had done.

"Yoo-hoo, Melanie. Are you in here, dear?" A pause, then, "Let go, you wicked creature!"

Melanie's heart dropped somewhere down around her ankles as she heard her mother's voice from the kitchen. Caught somewhere between shock that she could have been so wrong and alarm that the man responsible for almost taking her life was still out there somewhere, she absently checked the tie around Hooker's feet, then haltingly stepped toward the other room. Just short of the door, she stopped, gathering her wits. Despite everything that had just happened, she realized a new fear. The fear that her mother would instantly know what had happened between her and Marc the past two days. As sure as if Melanie had a scorecard taped to the front of her T-shirt.

"Melanie Marie, where— Oh, there you are, dear."

Melanie stepped into the kitchen to find the cramped quarters solidly divided into two camps. The McCoys stood beside her or behind her—large, hulking men who made her feel slightly intimidated but also as though she had the power of God on her side.

On the other side of the kitchen was her mother along with two state police patrolmen and...Craig.

Melanie's heart skipped a beat, and her skin burned with guilt. But there was no anger in Craig's eyes. Instead she watched worry turn into obvious relief, then curiosity as he eyed her disheveled appearance, then looked at Marc. When he gave her a small smile, relief washed through Melanie's tense muscles. She knew without asking that she hadn't lost her best friend.

Her gaze shifted to a movement closer to the floor.

Oh, God.

Goliath.

Her mother had taken a time-out when Melanie had entered, but now returned to the losing end of a game of tug-of-war with Mitch's Saint Bernard, Goliath. Melanie rushed forward, realizing it was her bridal bouquet that was locked in Goliath's jaws. White lily petals sprang from the arrangement like mammoth snowflakes, covering the tile and her mother's pink shoes.

Craig tried to distract the dog as Wilhemenia yelped for

someone to help. Then she lost her grip. Before Melanie could do anything, the hulking hound of a dog galloped from the room, triumphant.

There were several undisguised snickers from behind Melanie as her mother finally turned toward her, her face red, her hair sticking out from her usual smooth chignon. "Melanie, I want you to explain to me this minute what's going on."

"I—"

"For three days I've been worrying myself to death over your well-being—"

"Mom—"

"Ever since this twit—" she waved impatiently in Marc's direction but seemed to have a problem isolating exactly which one he was "—kidnapped you from the powder room."

"He's not—"

"Then yesterday morning you call, trying to tell me something—" Melanie rolled her eyes, remembering she hadn't been able to get a word in edgewise "—and I nearly go deaf from this horrible sound, and the line goes dead."

"That's because—"

"Poor Craig has been as worried as I have. He's not left my side, or Joanie's, once throughout this entire ordeal. Except to go do what nature intended, of course, but that's excusable considering all the coffee he's—"

Craig gave Melanie an understanding look then touched her mother's arm in an obvious effort to stop her. "I think she gets the picture, Mrs. Weber."

"Then we pull up here and that overgrown creature—"

"Mother!"

Wilhemenia gave Melanie a reprimanding look. "You're right to raise your voice to me. Here I am chattering away when we should be seeing to unfinished business. Officers, arrest that man." She gestured toward where she thought

Marc stood, but instead pointed to Jake. She started to tuck her hair into place. "And I think you should be able to work up something by way of accessories with the—" she faltered as she looked over the McCoy bunch "—rest of them."

"Over my dead body will you touch any of my boys," Sean said, his voice booming commandingly through the room.

Wilhemenia fell silent. *Silent.* Melanie stared at her. She'd never seen anyone capable of quelling her mother's incessant tongue. Lord knew *she* was incapable of it.

She looked between Sean and her mother, both powerful personalities. She recalled that every time Sean had come into her hospital room, her mother had made herself instantly scarce.

Craig seemed to notice the odd reaction and raised an eyebrow at Melanie.

Wilhemenia finally regained her voice, though it was noticeably softer, more self-conscious. "Your wedding is in three hours, Melanie. I think—"

"Until Hooker is caught, Melanie isn't going anywhere," Marc said, stepping next to Melanie and crossing his arms.

She wanted to scream as she watched Marc size up Craig. That's all she needed. For Marc to coldcock her best friend because, like her mother, he didn't understand that there wouldn't be a wedding. She wasn't going to marry Craig. Craig knew that without her having to say a word. The only reason he had proposed to begin with was that she'd been convinced Marc wasn't going to play a role in her baby's life. One look had told Craig that all that had changed.

She stared at Marc, exasperated. Why couldn't he be more observant? Or was he acting on emotion, as she had that morning when she opened the window?

She raised her voice. "Will everyone just shut up a minute and let me speak?"

The room went suddenly, blessedly quiet.

Melanie tried to figure out where to start. She looked at her mother first.

"Mom, I'm sorry you had to worry about me, but there isn't going to be any arresting here. Not of Marc or any of his brothers." Wilhemenia opened her mouth to speak, but Mel hurried on. "While I didn't agree at the time, Marc took me because the man who shot me three months ago had escaped from prison. So he did what he did to protect me. It was the right thing, the only thing to do."

She glanced at Marc, remembering his cryptic words earlier when he told her she should marry Craig. She looked at him, wishing they could have finished that conversation. She knew there wasn't going to be a wedding. But after what he'd said, should she tell him that?

"As for Hooker," she said quietly, "while all of you were outside protecting me from my mother and my...fiancé—" she had to push the last word out "—Hooker was already in the house." She took some pleasure in their dumbfounded expressions. "He's tied up in the living room."

"What?" Marc asked as his brothers bolted into the next room.

She nodded. Normally, she might have enjoyed a moment like this, proving she could still hold her own under fire, but she couldn't. Not knowing what she did. Not knowing that Hooker hadn't been the one who shot her. And especially since she'd knocked Hooker out for all his efforts.

"So," she said, wanting to deal with Marc and the sticky situation she found herself in the middle of before telling him his new partner was the real shooter.

"I still think—"

"Keep out of this, Mother," Melanie said.

Shocked by the firm order, her mother opened and closed her mouth several times, reminding Melanie of a hooked bass.

"Did you mean what you said this morning?" she quietly asked Marc. "You know, about my marrying..."

Her heart contracted in her chest. She waited for his response, some sign, a flicker in his expression, but there was none. And he was taking far too long to respond.

If ever she needed Marc to speak his mind, it was now.

Her mother touched her arm. "Melanie, dear, I really hate to interrupt—"

"I thought it was your life's occupation." Her mother looked as if she'd been slapped. Melanie cringed. "Sorry, that was uncalled for."

"I meant every word," Marc said, his expression stony. "I wish you and Craig every happiness."

Melanie would have whacked him if only her heart weren't cracking in half. "That makes two of us. Only there isn't going to be a wedding. Craig and I are not getting married."

Marc and Wilhemenia stared at her as if she'd lost the last of her marbles while Craig slipped his arm around her shoulders, supporting her every step of the way. A move she was thankful for, because she was going to need his friendship to see her through this.

She cleared the tears from her throat. "But that's not all. The man tied up in the room next door is not the one we should be looking for. The man who shot me is Roger Westfield."

13

SHELL-SHOCKED. That's the best way Melanie could describe how she felt. After all that had happened, it felt really weird sitting in the church antechamber pretending to get ready for her wedding. It seemed a shameful waste, really, seeing as she had planned everything out. Well, Joanie had planned everything out, and she had agreed, right down to the little nosegays the bridesmaids were going to wear, and the rosebuds being passed out instead of rice to toss at her, and...her groom.

Problem was, she didn't have a groom. And she probably never would.

Craig.

At least she still had her best friend. He really didn't know what to make of what was going on between her and Marc. *She* didn't know what to make of it, for that matter. One minute they were having the most incredibly touching sex of her life; the next he was telling her, no, *ordering* her to marry Craig. It didn't make any sense. None at all.

But Craig didn't need it to make sense. Yes, he'd told her during the long drive home, he was a little disappointed.

"I wouldn't be human if I didn't admit that my pride has taken a hell of a blow," he said, getting a hug for his admission, although not the type of hug Mel shared with Marc. The affection she traded with Craig was of a brotherly nature, and could never have been anything more, she realized. "I'd also be lying if I didn't say I'm relieved." He'd smiled at her. "I love you, Melanie, but…"

"Not in *that* way," she had finished for him. "I love you the same way, Pookems."

She only wished her feelings for Marc were as easy to sort through and settle.

She was coming to expect that from her relationship with Marc McCoy. Her heart gave a painful squeeze. From here on out, he'd play a role in her life, but only that of her child's father, not her lover or anything more.

There was a brief knock at the door. Quickly sitting up, she rubbed her cheeks to put some color into them.

"Yoo-hoo," her mother called out as she opened the door.

Melanie made an effort not to slouch.

Wilhemenia quietly closed the door.

"How is everything?" she asked, coming to stand behind her daughter.

Terrible. Awful. I want to crawl into bed and cry for a month. "Fine."

Wilhemenia fluffed the back of her hair, then rested her hand on Melanie's shoulder. "You look beautiful."

Melanie blinked at her in the mirror. Had she heard right? Had her mother just given her a compliment? No, it wasn't possible. Especially not when all of Wilhemenia's carefully approved plans had been ruined. Besides, there was always something wrong, some different way she could have done her hair, an alternate color of lipstick or at least a reprimand about her poor posture. "Excuse me?" she heard herself say.

Wilhemenia smiled. "I said you're beautiful." Her gaze faltered, and she began toying with the sleeves of Melanie's dress. "I know I probably haven't told you that nearly enough, but I've always thought it." She paused. "I just wished your life could have turned out different from mine."

Melanie's dress rustled as she turned to face her.

Certainly her mother wasn't telling her what she thought she was? It couldn't be possible. Had Wilhemenia been pregnant when she married? Her face went hot. She reminded herself that her mother didn't know of her condition. She peered at her a little more closely. Or did she?

"Are you trying to tell me something, Mother?"

Wilhemenia pulled a chair from the corner. She *pulled* it. She didn't pick it up and carefully move it. She hung her purse on the chair, then sank into it. But she still didn't say anything.

"Mom?"

"Do you remember what you asked me?"

Melanie watched her take papers from the cavernous depths of her purse.

"You know, in the bathroom, during the rehearsal dinner?" She avoided Melanie's gaze as she put the papers in her hands. "It's difficult to believe that was just three days ago. It seems like a lifetime."

You can say that again. Melanie smiled to hide her thoughts. "Sorry, I don't. Remember what I asked you, that is."

Wilhemenia cleared her throat, an odd sound considering how elegant she usually was. "You, um, asked if I had loved your father."

Melanie stared. Her mother stroked her hand. "I remember now."

"The truth is, yes, I did love your father. More than life itself."

Melanie looked at her. In the years since her father died, her mother had if not quietly cursed her father, at least blamed him for leaving her with two girls to raise. Melanie realized she had never tried to look into her mother's heart for the truth. She'd merely accepted it, and yes, even judged her on it.

Her mother stared at the ceiling. "Yes, I know you're pregnant, Melanie." Her gaze shifted. "I overheard the day you told...well, when you told Sean about it." Color touched her cheeks. Melanie guessed it was because of embarrassment. "I was coming back from the nurse's station and saw him sitting with you, as he often did. I didn't want to interrupt, but..." She trailed off and gave a guilty little smile. "But that's not what this is about."

"You were pregnant, too, weren't you? When you and Dad married?"

Her mother nodded. "Not that anyone knew. I was very careful about keeping it a secret. In those days when a young woman was single and pregnant in a small town, it was more than scandalous, it was..." She laughed weakly. "Talk about taking the long way around the bush. I'm just going on, aren't I?"

Melanie peered at her closely. She had always thought her mother rambled on because she wanted, required command of the conversation. She'd never thought for a minute that she chattered because she was nervous.

"Anyway," Wilhemenia said, "I think you ought to know I always considered you my miracle disguised as an accident."

Melanie's throat thickened. So much was shifting into focus.

"And I did love your father. I did. But I was miserable. I let that love get in the way of a happy marriage. Nothing was ever enough. He didn't do things the right way. He must not have loved me as much as I loved him. The list was endless. And when he died, I was so angry at him because I thought he had failed me in the ultimate way. He hadn't loved me enough to fight to stay with me."

Melanie shifted, unsure what to do, what to say. She'd never shared confidences with her mother.

Wilhemenia gave a quiet, humorless laugh. "There I go again." She cleared her throat and gazed directly into Melanie's eyes. "What I'm trying to say here is that I saw you heading down that same path with Marc. And I had to...I had to intervene."

Melanie let the words sink in. "Are you telling me what I think you are? That you..." *What? Chased big Marc McCoy away? Sent him packing?* "You orchestrated our breakup?"

Wilhemenia patted her hand. "I didn't have to orchestrate anything, Melanie. It was happening all by itself. I merely stepped up the beat a little."

Melanie got up from the chair. "I can't believe you did that." She paced across the room. The references Marc had made about her mother not passing on messages, turning him away when she was recovering... She hadn't believed him. She'd thought her mother had no reason to want them apart. True, Wilhemenia had never liked Marc, but she had never meddled in Melanie's life to that extent before. Now she saw her mother had the most potent reason there was—she'd wanted to protect her daughter from suffering the same heartache she had suffered.

The reason, combined with Wilhemenia's tenacity, explained a lot but changed little. Not now. The sad truth was that what her mother said made a lot of sense. She stopped pacing and stared at the papers in her hands. *They were all notes from Marc.*

But she had been willing to settle for a loveless marriage with Craig. Well, not completely loveless. They had the bond created from lifelong friendship.

But marriage to Marc would be torture. Her love for him—without his love in return—would be the destructive, passionate, demanding type. That was the threat and always had been.

"I think I'd better go join everyone in the back of the chapel before Marc comes and pulls me out," her mother said quietly. "I'm sorry, Melanie. I...I just wanted to let you know that."

Melanie nodded, worrying her bottom lip between her teeth.

She sank into the chair in front of the mirror, not really seeing her reflection, her thoughts jumbled. She stared at the papers in her hands, then shoved them into her purse. It didn't matter anymore, did it? It didn't matter that her mother had played a role in securing her and Marc's breakup. That there were reasons behind Marc's absence at the hospital. None of it mattered because she and Marc just weren't meant to be.

There was another knock at the door. Melanie blinked back stinging tears. When Craig walked in, she blurted, "I love him, Craig."

MARC SAT in the back of the nondescript van, oblivious to the heat as he stared at the chapel across the street. Bedford. The small town was neat and manicured and seemed to demand, "Do not enter unless you, too, are equally orderly." Not for the first time, he found it odd that a product of a place like this—much less a woman—had run off and joined the secret service. He grimaced and absently rubbed the back of his neck. Then again, Mel didn't live to satisfy anyone's expectations.

Just when he thought he had it all figured out, she changed all the rules. She wasn't marrying Craig. A part of him was relieved. A greater part ached because she wasn't marrying him, either.

He recognized a late-arriving guest as the uncle he'd encountered outside the men's room at the rehearsal dinner. He spoke into the two-way radio and asked the plainclothes officer just inside the chapel door to escort him to where all the other guests were, to the pastor's quarters in the back. Considering the time element and the need for everything to look normal, he and Mel had decided the ceremony should appear to go ahead as planned. Even the guests didn't know why they had to wait in the back rather than take a seat in one of the pews. It hadn't been easy, but he and his brothers had called in favors from every law enforcement official they knew to fill those same pews with fake guests. Every guest in that chapel was armed to the teeth and ready to take out the shooter within the blink of an eye.

"You're nuts, you know?"

Marc was so engrossed in trying to catch a glimpse of Mel, he had forgotten Mitch was in the van with him, along with two surveillance experts. "To keep you out of trouble," Mitch had said after he and Mel had questioned a barely conscious Tom Hooker, then put together what looked like the last of their plans.

Hooker had been hauled off by the state police. A hearing was already scheduled for first thing Monday morning. Mel had taken off with Craig and her mother, and Marc had sat at the kitchen table making phone calls, his four brothers and his father staring at him and shaking their heads while Brando meowed piteously at his feet.

"What?" he'd said after the stare fest had gone on a minute too long.

"You picked a hell of a time to lose the good sense God gave you, Marc," his father had said. "That girl is family."

"What would you have me do? Trade places with her last groom?"

Their silence told him all he needed to know. And he'd answered them with a series of choice curse words that raised even his father's eyebrows.

Marc grumbled, earning a chuckle from Mitch. "You know, there's something bothering me about this whole thing," Marc said under his breath.

Mitch took a long swig of coffee and glanced at his watch.

"Yeah, I'd say having your woman the target of an assassin is cause for bother."

Marc glowered at him. "Not that. Well, yeah, that, too, but there's something else."

Mitch stretched over one of the bucket seats and turned the ignition key. The van roared to life. He turned the air conditioner on full blast. One of the other men thanked him. "What is it?"

"I don't know. I keep thinking I should have known." He remembered going into the other room to find Hooker as good as hog-tied. Pride had filled him to know Mel had done that. Sorrow had also pierced him. She could take care of herself. Pregnant, single or any other way.

Marc caught sight of a girl of around six in a pink frilly dress hurrying up the chapel steps, her skirt blowing around thin legs. His throat grew tight as he watched her and her father being ushered inside by the undercover officer. In so many years he might find himself with a little girl like that. Or a boy. What would it be like to be a father? Not just a part-time dad, but a real, honest-to-goodness dad? Despite the cool air circulating through the van, he broke out in a sweat.

"You know, all along Hooker maintained his innocence."

"You can't blame yourself, Marc. You know what Pops always says."

"All guilty men plead innocent because they have nothing to lose." Marc rubbed his chin. "That's all well and good, but Pops was never in the academy with the one in question." He shook his head.

"And Bundy might be a senator by now, if not president, if he hadn't been caught. Come on, Marc, we both know appearances have nothing to do with it."

"Still, I should have known." Marc went silent. He thought about the tests that had been run on Hooker's service revolver. They had come up negative. He had dismissed it by saying Hooker had another gun and had disposed of it before he was caught. Only it wasn't Hooker's gun they should have been looking at, but Roger Westfield's.

If he had been wrong about Hooker, what else had he been wrong about?

"Damn." Marc jerked open the van door, causing the men inside to scramble for cover.

Mitch caught his sleeve. "Where are you going?"

"He's already in there."

14

MELANIE NODDED to the plainclothes officer keeping watch over the balcony entrance, then hurried up the stairs to watch the impostor bride walk down the aisle in a thick, gauzy veil. Clutching her revolver, she crouched a little lower behind the balcony railing in the back of the chapel, the sound of the organ at her elbow nearly deafening her. Her heart thudded dully in her chest as she methodically scanned the full pews below.

She didn't know how Marc had pulled all this off. Not able to pull in recognizable secret service agents, he'd relied instead on the vast network of law enforcement personnel available through his brothers and Sean. All the real guests—it had been too late to cancel the wedding, and besides, if they had, the setup might not have worked—had been safely and discreetly escorted to the pastor's private quarters at the back of the church, where, she was sure, they were all trying to figure out what was going on.

The bride finished the walk and stood next to a guy who looked an awful lot like Craig, but wasn't. Despite everything, Melanie fought back a smile. As far as brides went, this one—well, this one really took the cake.

The organist finally stopped playing and left the balcony, as instructed. Melanie backed up, hiding behind the large instrument, wishing she had had time to change out of the uncomfortable wedding dress she wore. But Joanie had been too intent on getting the stand-in's dress on, and her mother had been busily helping explain things to the real guests. In the chaos, Melanie couldn't even find her jeans.

It was probably for the best, because Marc hadn't wanted to let her out of his sight, and she wasn't about to tempt herself unnecessarily by undressing in front of him. No one knew as well as she did that nudity, specifically her own, and Marc were a lethal combination. She had a lot to work out, and she didn't need sex messing things up.

The fact remained that Marc had offered to marry her only for their child's sake, nothing more. Besides, he'd rescinded the offer that morning when he'd told her she should marry Craig.

She considered peering through the fan-shaped windows to look at the dark brown surveillance van parked on the street, but doing so would give her presence away. After a heated debate, it was decided that Marc shouldn't be seen anywhere near the chapel, in case Roger Westfield spotted him and figured out he was being set up. Melanie briefly closed her eyes. She only hoped they could get Westfield before he got them.

A rustling sounded behind her. Frowning, Melanie peered around the organ. Instead of the silver head of the organist, she saw a familiar dark one.

Roger.

Moving so he wouldn't spot her, Melanie slowly slid into the shadows, her palms growing instantly damp. *Not good.*

MARC RUSHED into the chapel, his breath coming in ragged gasps as he stuck to the shadows. He scanned the backs of the phony guests, making sure Roger hadn't somehow sneaked by, then turned to the door. The stand-in pastor's voice droned on, pretending to marry the couple down the aisle. Marc clutched his revolver close to his chest and wiped his forehead against his shoulder.

His instincts told him Roger was already here. So far nothing had been said about Hooker's recapture, so the scumbag would think it was safe to continue his campaign to eliminate Mel and any possibility that she might remember what really happened three months ago. The idiot didn't know Mel had no idea Roger was the true shooter until two hours ago. Hell, neither had he, for that matter.

The best he could figure the situation after talking to Tom Hooker, the night of the assassination attempt it had been Roger, not Hooker, who had moved against the senator. Marc silently cursed, remembering his new partner's top-of-the-line sports cars and his many expensive outings.

He moved to the other side of the chapel.

Roger must have knocked Hooker out, and when Mel showed up, he shot her. Hooker had been already out of commission, coming to when gunshots were fired.

Marc wondered what it must have been like for Hooker to be fine one minute, then wake up on the ground the next with two agents on him—one of them his own partner—accused of attempting to assassinate the senator.

Running true to form in most assailant cases, when Hooker had tried to contact Mel to persuade her to listen to his pleas of innocence, she had refused to talk to him.

Then Roger's luck had run out. Four days ago Hooker had used his training to escape en route to his pretrial hearing and had managed to elude recapture. Marc grimaced. The guy had been good enough to get past him and his brothers, which was saying a whole hell of a lot. Only problem was, everyone knew he was heading for Mel. Which made Roger's plan pitifully simple: do away with Mel, and Hooker would take the fall for the crime forever.

Marc's chest tightened painfully. He only hoped Roger wasn't as good as Hooker.

His attention was pulled to the altar. From this distance,

not even he could tell that the groom wasn't Craig and the bride wasn't Mel.

The stand-in pastor—who was a desk jockey ex-priest from his father's D.C. precinct—looked up and addressed the audience. "Speak now, or forever hold your peace."

Marc watched the groom hesitantly lift the bride's veil.

"Kiss me and you're dead meat," Jake said to the Craig look-alike.

His brother's threatening words made Marc wince. Not yet, you yo-yo. Westfield had to believe Jake in drag was Mel if they were to have a chance in hell of making this work.

He anxiously stepped forward, searching the guests again. He froze when he spotted Roger crouched behind the balcony railing, his rifle aimed straight at Jake.

Dear Lord, where's Mel?

"Yoo-hoo!" a familiar voice called a second before Mel's mother came in from the back. "I just thought you should know the natives are getting—"

"Hit the deck!" Marc shouted.

Jake tackled Mrs. Weber, covering her in wedding dress white, his cowboy boots peeking out from underneath as Marc aimed. The guests scrambled for cover, pulling out firearms, so the chapel was filled with the echoes of chambers loading, all of them looking for the unseen threat. Before Roger could squeeze off a shot, Mel appeared to his left. She whacked him in the arm with her revolver as he fired. The bullet harmlessly penetrated a plaster column.

Blood roaring in his ears, Marc thought about everything that had happened in the past three months. Mel being shot...finding out about her pregnancy...the recent attempts on her life. The revolver in his hands felt remarkably light, his focus on his target notably clear. He pulled off a shot, only at the last second lowering his aim.

Everything seemed to happen in slow motion. The bullet

slammed against Roger's right shoulder. He dropped his rifle. It fell from the balcony to the marble tile near Marc's feet.
Roger swayed, leaning precariously against the railing. Mel
clutched him to prevent his fall, and Roger grabbed for her.

The railing creaked.

Marc's heart hiccuped in his chest.

Mel, no!

Then, suddenly, Roger was no longer against the railing,
and Mel was carefully leaning over.

"Got him."

THERE WAS a certain surreal quality to the day, Marc thought,
standing next to Mel on the chapel steps. For some odd reason, colors seemed brighter, the birds louder, and the air definitely smelled sweeter. And the decision he'd come to the instant he saw Mel was all right seemed all the more clear.

He moved out of the way as a paramedic hurried out and a
federal criminalist headed in. Roger Westfield had been
carted off on a stretcher, two marshals under the command of
Connor and a pair of handcuffs guaranteeing he didn't have
a chance to pass Go or collect $200.

When they'd wheeled him past, Roger had asked how he'd
known he was the real shooter. Marc told him he'd be better
off asking Tom Hooker that.

"Nice ceremony," Marc said to Mel as they waited, with
the real and stand-in guests, for everything to be sorted out.
Mel's relatives and neighbors buzzed with excitement, some
of them still not completely grasping that there wasn't going
to be a wedding, after all.

"I'd say it was memorable," Mel said quietly, giving him a
broad smile.

Marc felt as if he'd been socked in the gut. "It'll be the talk
of the town for, oh, I'd say well into the next generation."

Her expression told him she hadn't missed his reference to

their baby. Their eyes met. No matter how hard he tried, Marc couldn't rip his gaze away from her. Lord help him, but he wanted to throw her over his shoulder and kidnap her all over again. And this time he'd do it right. Not because there was some madman out there who wanted to take her life. Not because she would be the mother of his child—children, he amended, suddenly deciding he wanted a horde of them. No, he wanted to handcuff her to him in more ways than one because he loved her more than anything else in this godforsaken world.

He loved her.

The realization surprised him in that it *didn't* surprise him.

His grin widened, and his heart skipped a few beats. Mel had always told him he was the last to catch on when it came to matters of the heart.

Jake walked by, Mrs. Weber lecturing him about a tear in the dress. Marc chuckled, then cleared his throat. "Do you think your guests are disappointed you and Craig aren't getting hitched?"

Mel eyed him closely. Her sexy green eyes shimmered in the midday sunlight. "Not too much, I don't think." She glanced at Craig, who stood with Joanie and his parents. "If there are a few, they'll forget all about it after the free food and drinks." She flashed him a smile. "Anyway, they got some great gossip."

Marc scanned her from forehead to chin. "So where does that leave you?"

She gazed toward the chapel doors and shrugged, looking particularly delectable in the dress she'd changed into at some point between Westfield's arrest and subsequent transport to the ambulance. Sure, maybe the hem was a little long and the shoes too flat, but the rich material hugged her in all the right places.

"I guess it makes me a single parent in the making," she answered.

"Yeah, me, too," he murmured. "Shame, seeing as we're so good together."

"I'm not marrying you, Marc."

He winced. "Ouch." He clasped his hands behind his back. "Why not?"

"You know why not."

"Because you think I only want to marry you because of the baby."

She looked at a nearby woman, who was craning to hear their conversation. She whispered, "Something like that."

"So live with me in sin, then."

To his surprise, she bellowed with laughter.

He shrugged. "Hey, I'll take it any way I can get it."

Mel started to walk away. Marc caught her arm. "Have I ever told you how much I love your smile?"

She hesitated. "No, I have to say that's a first." A wary shadow eclipsed her eyes. "I've never heard you utter the word love in relationship to anything."

He glanced down. "Anyway..."

She peered at him a little more closely.

"I guess the excitement's over, so I'll just be on my way."

He didn't miss the puzzled wrinkling of her forehead. Obviously she had expected more. "Okay." She started to turn away, then hesitated. "I'll keep you posted on how everything goes. You know, with the baby."

He gave her one of his biggest grins. "Oh, don't worry, Mel. I'll be in touch."

15

DESPITE HIS WORDS, Marc hadn't tried to contact her over the next two weeks.

Melanie sat on the front porch swing trying to catch a stray breeze while Joanie and her mother discussed catering menus inside. Brushing a strand of hair from her cheek, she thought it was funny how things could happen right under your nose without your being aware of it.

For the past twenty-five years Melanie, Joanie and Craig had been the terrific trio. And in all that time, she had never noticed that her sister and her best friend had secretly been in love with each other. She shook her head. If anything good had come out of the whole fiasco, it was the acknowledgment of that truth. While Marc had held her under lock and key, among other things—her cheeks burned with the memory— the mere act of being so close together for a prolonged period of time had created a veritable hothouse of romance for Craig and Joanie, as her mother told the story. Melanie smiled.

Hothouse of romance, indeed.

She rocked the swing and ran her hand over her belly. Overnight, it seemed, her stomach had gone from being flat to swelling into a noticeable mound. Joanie and Craig's impending wedding plans weren't the only good thing to come out of recent events, she amended. While in the days immediately following the "non-wedding of the century," as the townsfolk were referring to it, she had leaped on the phone every time it rang and had absently searched passing cars for signs of Marc, she had since found a certain, quiet peace. A peace that closely resembled the stillness she once felt as an agent. She'd come to terms with her impending single parenthood and knew that her baby would have all the love he would ever need right here with her, her mother, sister, and yes, even with Craig, in his role as uncle rather than father.

She'd started her new position as a security consultant at Beane and Sons and had begun mapping out plans for branching out on her own.

All in all, life was pretty good. Despite the bone-deep longing she often felt in the middle of the night.

If Marc wanted to play a role in their child's life—

Beneath her hand, she felt a nudge. Her breath catching, Melanie sat very still. That was very definitely a nudge.

She'd felt her baby move.

"Mellie?"

She glanced up to find Sean walking up the steps. She was so excited, she didn't stop to think it odd that he was there. She motioned him over.

"Come...sit down. I just felt the baby move for the first time."

Sean took the space next to her and hesitantly held his hand above her stomach. She smiled and pressed his fingers against the side of her belly.

They sat like that for a long moment. Melanie started to get discouraged. Maybe it hadn't been the baby, after all. Her doctor had said she should start to feel movement any day now, but—

"There!" she whispered in awe. "Did you feel it?"

Sean chuckled. A deep, proud sound that vibrated right through her. "I think you've got another McCoy male on your hands there, Mellie."

She glanced into his eyes. "Is something wrong? Is Marc all right?"

Sean smiled and hesitantly removed his hand from her stomach. "Marc's fine. As nervous as all get-out, but fine."

Melanie frowned. "Nervous? Why would he be nervous?"

"Hi, Mel."

She would recognize that sweet voice anywhere. A fascinating feeling not all that different from what she'd experienced when the baby moved spread through her as she turned her head.

There he was. Marc. In all his six-foot-two glory, grasping the porch column as if afraid to come up the steps.

Melanie didn't know if it was due to the pure delight she'd just experienced, but she didn't think he'd ever looked so boyishly handsome, so completely lovable.

She cleared her throat and quickly got up from the swing. Sean moved to help her, and she smiled at him. "I'm not at that point yet."

Sean scratched his head. "I hope you don't mind I came along for the visit, Melanie."

"No, no, of course not." She slid a quick glance in Marc's direction. He was standing in the same spot. All at once the peace she had found scattered, leaving her feeling confused and out of sorts. "Why don't you come in? I'll get you something to drink."

The screen door spring squeaked as she led the way in. She motioned for them to sit in the living room, then she hurried to the kitchen. She needed a few moments by herself to adjust to Marc's sudden appearance. She heard the crinkle of the plastic furniture covers as she started to step into the kitchen. She nearly hit her mother with the door.

There was Wilhemenia, a pitcher of lemonade and a couple

of glasses already on a tray, along with a heaping plate of
cookies.

Her mother smiled. "I've got it."

Melanie's heart skipped a beat as she realized her excuse
for escape had been stolen from her. She briefly closed her
eyes, then followed her mother into the living room.

"Melanie, dear, help me take this plastic off, won't you,
honey?" Sean and Marc awkwardly got up and stood to the
side as Wilhemenia started fussing with the cushions. "You
know we take this off when we're entertaining."

Melanie's gaze locked onto Marc's, and they shared a small
smile. Wilhemenia *never* took the plastic off her furniture, unless it was to change it.

"Of course," Melanie said. "I don't know what I was thinking."

After all the plastic was off and Melanie had taken it into
the other room, she hesitantly settled into a chair, trying to
figure out what Marc wanted. And why he hadn't come on
his own.

One possibility struck her, and her gaze flew to his face. He
didn't think she'd renege on her agreement to allow him to
visit their baby, did he? Is that why he'd brought Sean along?
To work out a more binding visitation agreement?

Wilhemenia kept up pleasant chatter, telling Sean all about
the aftermath of Roger's capture and how she might have
been shot herself if his son Jake hadn't saved her life. And
didn't he have just a handsome bunch of boys, anyway.

Marc grinned at Mel, and she automatically smiled, feeling
suddenly, oddly shy.

He motioned toward the front porch. "Can I talk to you
alone for a minute?"

She stared at him blankly. "Um, sure." She got up. "But
why don't we go out back instead?" She gave him a weak

smile. "I think we've already given the town enough to talk about."

Wilhemenia and Sean didn't seem to notice their going as Sean started telling Melanie's mother about Mitch being left at the altar some years before. Melanie looked at Marc. He didn't appear to be tuned in to the conversation. In fact, he looked so nervous, he made her even more nervous.

She led the way to the back steps, then into the yard, moving toward the gazebo. Only when Melanie started to enter did she realize how romantic the setting was. She stopped just outside the ivy-covered structure and looked at Marc expectantly, struggling to hold his gaze when just looking at him made her hurt all over.

He didn't say anything for a long moment as he shoved his hands into his jeans pockets. It was then Melanie realized he wore a yellow oxford shirt rather than his trademark black T-shirt, and nowhere to be seen was the ever-present vest he wore to hide his firearm.

Her gaze flicked to his face. "Marc, listen, I, um, just want you to know that I'll let you play as big or as little a role in our child's life as you want."

A half-smile turned up the corners of his lips. "That's what you think my being here is about?"

She looked toward the neighbor's. Mrs. Jennings was peering over the hedge she was trimming. "I didn't know, what with Sean being with you and all."

He chuckled quietly. "I brought Pops along because he wanted to come." He paused, and she returned her gaze to his face. "If I'd have known he could handle your mother that way, I would have brought him with me three months ago."

She frowned. *Three months ago?* What did he mean? She swallowed, realizing he must have meant when he tried to visit her, only to have her mother turn him away.

His gaze trailed to where her hands covered her stomach. He looked altogether awkward and irresistibly at odds with himself. "Is it true? Did you and Pops feel him move?"

Her answering smile was wide. "Or her," she reminded him. "Yes."

"Is he...or she still moving?"

Melanie's throat clogged with emotion. She wasn't sure if it was such a good idea to encourage Marc to touch her. "Would you like to feel it?"

Unlike Sean, Marc barely hesitated as he laid his hand against her belly. She closed her eyes and guided his fingers to where she had felt the movement earlier. *Come on, baby, move for Daddy.*

As they stood there, birds rustling in the trees, the air carrying the keen scent of freshly mown grass, Melanie had never felt so right, so complete.

"Holy cow!" Marc exclaimed, tugging his hand away.

Melanie laughed at his childlike reaction, taking as much pleasure in his response as she had in her own. "Weird, isn't it?"

He gently put his hand back again. But this time, the tender emotion erupting inside Melanie was almost too much to bear.

If only things had been different....

"What's it like?" Marc quietly broke into her thoughts. "I want to know everything you're feeling."

Melanie told him.

Marc felt as if someone had completely pulled the earth out from under his feet as he watched myriad emotions cross Mel's face.

She finally broke eye contact. "I think he's tired himself out."

He took that as his cue to remove his hand, and he did, however reluctantly.

For a moment there, one sweet, miraculous moment, he'd felt connected to Mel in a way he never had before. Gone were the reasons they shouldn't be together. Gone were any doubts he or she might have had in the past. It had just been the two of them—and their baby.

He didn't want it to end.

She started to turn away. He gently caught her arm.

"I have something to show you, Melanie."

Her eyes widened slightly, most likely at his use of her full name.

Despite all the times he'd visualized this moment during the long drive from Manchester, he still fumbled with the damn velvet pouch as he slid it out of his back pocket. It fell to the ground between them.

Both of them stood staring at it, unmoving.

Then Marc knelt, staying there on the soft grass as he revealed the emerald ring blanketed in a pool of white silk.

He cleared his throat, forcing himself to look at her even though it appeared she didn't know quite what to do. "I love you, Mel. There's no way you can't know that. Baby or no baby, I want to marry you." Her hands covered her stomach. "But of course I'm glad there is a baby," he said quickly.

Her skin glowed a warm rose in the early afternoon sunshine as she whispered, "Tell me why I should believe you, Marc."

He swallowed hard. How did he go about doing that? "Would it help if I told you I bought the ring the day after you got shot? That I got this harebrained idea, after you asked me if I loved you, that what you really wanted was to get married?" He grimaced. "Only the idea turned out to be not so dumb, because the day I came over here to propose to you was the same day I found out you were engaged to Craig."

He cleared his throat and looked at the ring that had paled in comparison to the one she had been wearing two weeks earlier.

"It may have taken me a long time to realize it, but you were right back then, you know, when you asked if I loved you. I did love you. I do. Only I didn't know for sure until the day I nearly lost you in the chapel."

Mel stared at him long and hard, a suspicious dampness in her eyes. He wanted to groan but kept it in check. He supposed this was one of those times when women were allowed to cry. Even Mel. Especially Mel.

Then she turned away from him and moved toward the house.

"Mel!" He scrambled to his feet. "I'm serious. Look—" He searched his pockets as he hurried after her. "I've even got the receipt to prove it."

As quickly as she turned away, she turned back, catapulting herself into his arms and nearly knocking him over. He stood stupidly, holding the ring in one hand, the receipt in the other, as she pressed her body against his, their baby very noticeably between them. He couldn't see her face, and she was squeezing him so hard he couldn't breathe.

"Mel, you're killing me here."

She threw her head back and laughed, then kissed him full on the mouth. "Why couldn't you have said all that three months ago, you big dope?"

He frowned. "What? You're killing me?"

Her smile softened. "Yeah. That, too."

He opened his mouth to respond, then refrained. "Does this mean what I think it means?"

Her eyes sparkled more brightly than the gem in his hand.
"Yes, it may scare me to death, but it means exactly that."

Everything that had swirled around like pieces from different puzzles three months ago suddenly settled into place as
he looked into her face. Never had he been so sure that he was
doing the right thing.

He swept her into his arms and started marching toward
the house, ignoring her laughing demands to be let down.

He grinned at her. "Uh-uh. Not until we're standing in
front of a real pastor...."

I THEE WED

Anne McAllister

Chapter One

Cambridge, Massachusetts, February, 1988

"No, Ma. *No*. Ma, I just can't…I have things to do, that's why."

Diane watched, amused, as her roommate rolled her eyes and strangled the phone receiver with her hands.

"Besides, the North End's miles from here," Annie went on. "Miles."

The Arctic Circle at least, Diane thought, silently applauding her roommate's theatrical ability. Annie had theatrical ability in spades, but she was never in better form than when she was arguing with her mother. Diane watched as expressions of first agony and then weariness crossed Annie's face.

She gave up for the moment on the obscurities of Hegel, lay the book beside her on the bed, stretched her full five feet six inches, wiggled her toes and grinned. Her own life was so deadly predictable, so completely boring. It was one of the reasons she enjoyed living with Annie. There was so much opportunity for vicarious angst.

"Yes, I know you called on daytime rates, but I don't want to meet him. No! Ma…Ma… Really…"

Poor Annie. Diane stuffed the pillow back under her head

and propped Hegel up again on her stomach. But her mind drifted from the conflict between theses and antitheses to Lucia D'Angelo's conflict with her daughter.

Diane knew she should be ashamed of her unabashed eavesdropping. It wasn't the thing, her very proper grandmother would have told her in no uncertain terms. And even her less assertive mother would have doubtless made an effort to pretend that Hegel fascinated her.

But she could hardly help it, really. A 15-foot x 30-foot studio apartment didn't offer much opportunity for privacy.

Lucia and Annie's running battle over the men that Lucia wanted her daughter to meet and marry and that Annie had no intention of meeting, much less marrying, had been a constant in Diane's life since she had met Annie as a freshman at Harvard four years before.

"Besides how gorgeous he is," she heard Annie say. "Besides how smart he is. Besides whose nephew he is. I don't care whose nephew he is! Remember Guido Farantino? Remember him? He was your cousin Maria's nephew and he was a dork!"

Another furious volley from Lucia.

"Ma, I don't care if he goes to Harvard Business School. Just because a guy goes to Harvard Business School does not mean he is not a dork! On the contrary…"

Diane grinned and picked up her book.

"What do you mean I have to?" Ominous silence.

A storm gathering, Diane could tell.

"What did she promise him?" There was a deadly note in Annie's tone now.

Diane's brows lifted. She raised her head and peered over the top of Hegel to watch.

Annie was standing ramrod straight now, glaring out the window across their two-inch-wide view of the Charles as if it were Lucia D'Angelo and not a fleet of sailboats she had in her sights. "Mother…"

Diane waited, watching. When Ma became Mother it was only a matter of time. There was another long silence. Then Annie expelled a long, pent-up breath. Her shoulders slumped. She bent her head.

"What time?" A pause. "All right."

And before Lucia could say another word, Annie dropped the receiver back onto the phone with a thud.

"Let me guess." Diane said into the silence. "His name is Luigi Capoletti. His family are wine growers from Piedmont, and he's been sent to Harvard Business School to learn how to best earn the family more and more millions."

"His name," Annie said, turning around and fixing Diane with a hopeless look, "is Dominic Granatelli. His family is in the restaurant business in St. Louis. And he's at Harvard Business School because he is fulfilling the American dream." She tore at her long, dark hair with both hands. "God, where on earth does she find them?"

"I thought he was somebody's nephew."

"He is. Her godmother's best friend's sister's…or some damned thing. How should I know?" Annie made a face and sank down onto her bed.

"And is he gorgeous?"

Annie gave her a baleful look. "Are any of them gorgeous?"

Point taken.

"Why do I let her talk me into these things? I need to go rehearse tonight. I have a paper due in Greeley's class tomorrow. If Wallace calls, I'm supposed to go in to work." She slapped her hands down on the bed in exasperation.

Diane gave her a sympathetic smile. "Who knows?" she said lightly. "Someday she might actually find the right man for you."

Annie glowered at her. "I thought you knew better than that. There is no right man for me. I don't have time for a man, right or otherwise. I have ambitions of my own, and a man would only get in the way."

Annie was going to be the next Sarah Bernhardt or Dame Edith Evans. She was consumed with a passion and a fire for her actor's vocation that at times made Diane's head swim. It always left her out of breath. She couldn't have matched it if she lived to be a hundred.

She never wanted to. She was content for life to come to her. She wasn't going to go out and wrestle life. "So are you going to go or not?"

Annie grimaced. "What do you think? But only briefly. *Very* briefly. And only because Ma promised her godmother I'd be there and *she* already told Granatelli. He's 'expecting' me. And if I don't go now, he'll probably end up here, worried that I'm lost or have been abducted or something. And if he comes here, God knows how I'll get rid of him."

"He might be nice," Diane felt obliged to point out.

Annie shrugged. "They're all nice, but that doesn't mean I want to marry them. You want to marry them? You come with me." She brightened at once. "Yeah! You come with me. It's not an exclusive party, just Patty Lombardi's engagement."

Diane shook her head quickly. "I can't. I have Hegel."

"You have a week to finish Hegel."

"I also have my Paul Valéry paper to work on. Plus a test tomorrow in Italian."

Annie laughed and grabbed her hand. "Gotcha. You can practice your Italian on him."

"I don't want—"

"Of course you do. You're always blathering on about people needing to expose themselves to other cultures. 'We must open our minds and hearts to those different than ourselves,'" she quoted one of Diane's international relations papers with a pomposity belied only by the twinkle in her eye. "Isn't that the garbage you're always spouting?"

"It's not garbage," Diane denied.

Annie spread her hands. "Well, what could be more different for a blue blood like you than an Italian engagement party in the North End?"

"It's not—"

"It is. So if you believe all your blather, come with me. Open your mind and heart to an Italian from St. Louis. Cripes, you're from St. Louis, too. It probably won't be different at all. You probably have more in common with him than I do."

"Annie, I—"

Annie pulled Diane to her feet. "Please. Come. Come on, Di." She was imploring now, putting every bit of the vast D'Angelo theatrical potential to work. "Please. For moral support. You know I don't want to do this. You know I hate it."

Diane looked at Annie pouting, pleading. She looked at Hegel, gray and dog-eared. There was no contest.

"All right," she said. "But only for an hour or so, mind you."

Annie threw her arms around her. "I knew you'd be a sport."

"But," Diane added with a sternness born of experience, "I'm not going to meet him instead of you. You're not going to try any of those tricks this time. You promised to meet him. You're going to meet him."

"Of course," Annie said equably.

But Diane had heard that tone of voice before. She didn't trust it. Not a bit.

"WOULD YOU BE TELLING ME again why I'm doing this?" Jared Flynn's soft Irish accent broke into the Feinemann

Plastics case study that Nick was analyzing in his head as they walked.

"You're my friend," Nick said frankly, "and I bullied you into it."

Jared gave him a slow grin. "That I know. But why? An engagement party doesn't sound so very threatening, un-less—" the grin broadened "—you're the one getting engaged."

"No fear." Nick shook his head adamantly. "I need a little protection, that's all. I promised Aunt Lucy I'd do this. Her cousin set it up." He grimaced. "And apparently she owes her cousin. So I have to meet the girl."

"And I?"

"Have to sweep her off her feet."

Jared rolled his eyes. "There's optimism. She won't be looking twice at me with a handsome devil like yourself standing alongside."

Nick laughed. "You haven't noticed the girls dropping like ten pins when they see you behind the counter at Fiorello's?"

He was scarcely exaggerating. The girls who came in to eat at the funky Mass Ave restaurant used to stare at him as he dashed in and out of the kitchen bearing plates of spaghetti and linguine. But since out-of-work actor Jared Flynn had come to work there, Nick scarcely got a glance. His thick, blond-streaked brown hair and reasonably good looks had paled in comparison to Jared's tousled dark hair and craggy handsomeness.

He was hoping that, whoever Anna D'Angelo was, she would prove equally susceptible. He wanted nothing to do with her himself.

It wasn't that he wasn't interested in women.

At other times, in other places, he was very interested indeed.

But he was far too busy to be bothered this year. The first year at Harvard Business School didn't leave a man time to breathe much less to look at women. He couldn't remember the last time he'd had a date.

Yes. Yes, he could. It was at Christmas, when he'd gone home to St. Louis and his sister Sophia had invited him to a party at her house and had told him to bring Virginia Perpetti.

Ginny Perpetti was maybe twenty-three. A year or so older than his sister Frankie. She was pretty, soft and smiling. As dark as he was fair. Sicilian where he was Lombard. A couple of generations back that would have mattered. Now the fact that she was Italian was enough.

He suspected Sophia's motives, but he didn't demur. He'd called for Ginny, took her to the party, and afterward, on the way home, they'd walked around the neighborhood.

Ginny had pointed out the classroom at St. Ambrose's where she taught second grade. Then she had shown Nick the new house her brother Eddie and his wife had bought right behind it.

It had started to snow by then and the flakes caught on her lashes. They sparkled, tempting him, and before he knew it, he had bent his head to kiss them away.

Ginny had laughed, embarrassed, and batted at him, ducking her head shyly when he'd tried again.

Ginny.

"That Ginny Perpetti, she'll make a good wife," his mother had said the next morning.

It was no secret where his family's thoughts lay.

Right now she seemed light years away.

She might as well be. Sophia had mentioned in the letter

he'd got yesterday that Ginny was busy cutting out cherry trees for Washington's birthday.

Cutting out cherry trees with a bunch of second graders at St. Ambrose's was a million mental miles from Harvard Business School. Maybe more.

But, he thought—and sighed as he thought it—her counterpart, Anna D'Angelo, was right here.

Another shy Italian girl on the lookout for a husband. The daughter of somebody who was related to somebody who was related to him.

He understood how it worked.

He didn't think it was necessarily the best way to meet someone—and certainly not tonight.

But someday—who knew?

In a couple of years he'd be in the market himself. And if Ginny Perpetti weren't available, he might need to know someone who knew someone who had a daughter.

In the meantime, he would, as always, play his part.

Never let it be said that Nick Granatelli didn't pay his dues.

So, in half an hour or less, he was going to have to smile at her, make small talk with her and, hopefully, throw Jared at her and make his escape.

He glanced at his watch. It was seven. He still had another fifty pages of the Feinemann Plastics case to read and take notes on. His study group would be meeting by eight. He was going to be late; that was a given. But he didn't want to be very late.

"Come on," he said to Jared, beginning to sprint. "Let's get this over with."

IT WAS, in fact, a cultural experience. Diane Bauer had, in the course of her twenty-two years, participated in her share of sweet-sixteen parties and debutante balls back home in

St. Louis. During her junior year at Harvard, which she'd spent abroad, she'd partied at university get-togethers at bierstuben in Munich and heurigen in Vienna. And wherever she'd been, as long as she could remember, she'd danced and dined her way through plenty of black-tie affairs.

But she'd never seen a celebration that equaled the engagement party of Patty Lombardi and Greg Delvecchio.

For one thing, it was a crush. She'd read about such things in regency novels. She had no idea they still existed in Boston's North End.

But there was no other word to describe the pulsing throng of humanity that had crowded into the small private club.

The smoke, the laughter, the jovial press of people surging this way and that as they congratulated the happy couple and moved on in to talk to each other and get something to eat overpowered her.

She stuck close to Annie, trailing in her wake.

Annie, for her part, was muttering under her breath, craning her neck, peering first one way and then the other, obviously trying to ferret out Dominic Granatelli.

"How are you going to know which one he is?"

"I told my mother to tell him to stick a carnation in his ear."

"You didn't."

Annie rolled her eyes. "No, I didn't. He's supposed to be wearing a blue T-shirt that says something Italian on it. Campanella's or some such. The name of a restaurant. That ought to narrow things down."

Diane, who'd been scanning the crowd for the short dark type of guy Annie's mother seemed generally to come up with, found her eye caught suddenly by a tall, muscular man in a blue shirt with *Fiorello's* scrawled across it. She stared. "Him?"

Annie followed her nod and did a double take.

Diane understood why immediately. If ever any man was destined to make a woman forget her resolve to remain celibate in pursuit of a higher ideal—be it acting or the Church—this man was it.

He was, perhaps, a shade over six feet, with sun-streaked brown hair and lively blue eyes. His shoulders were broad, his arms muscular.

For the first time in her life Diane began to think there might be some redeeming social value to be found in wet T-shirt contests, providing this man was wearing one.

He wore a pair of faded jeans and ratty-looking tennis shoes and, on the whole, looked about as unlikely a member of Harvard Business School's class of '88 as she could imagine. There was undoubtedly some mistake.

But Annie apparently didn't think so. She threaded her way through the throng and strode right up to him and stuck out her hand.

Diane followed, pushing past several already tipsy revelers, in time to see the man nod and to hear him say, "Nick. Everybody calls me Nick."

Heavens above! *This was actually the man Annie didn't want to meet?*

Diane took a close look at her now, trying to see how being confronted with such a hunk of masculinity was affecting her resolve.

But Annie was saying quite bluntly, "Sorry you got roped into this. It wasn't my idea."

Nick laughed. Diane felt her heart kick over at the sight of his grin. She wondered why her mother never thought to send her men like this. Cynthia Bauer had a disgustingly hands-off policy where her daughter's love life was concerned.

What love life? a tiny voice inside her chided.

And that was true, of course. But Diane refused to do more than acknowledge it at the moment. She was far too interested in Annie's new man.

He had turned and was hauling another man forward now. A man not quite as tall as he was, but with dark, tousled hair and reasonably good looks.

"I'd like you to meet my friend. This is Jared Flynn. Annie D'Angelo."

Annie spared the friend a brief glance, said, "How do you do?" then reached behind her with the ease of long practice and latched on to Diane, tugging her forward. "And this is my friend Diane Bauer."

All sound, all movement stopped.

It was, Diane thought later, as if the heavens had opened and a voice had said, "Well, kiddo, here he is."

It was, Diane thought later, the moment she'd been waiting for since the age of four when she'd decided to be like Mommy and have a husband, too.

At the time she didn't know where she'd get him. Like everything else in her life, he would, she'd always expected, simply show up when the time came.

But she hadn't expected the time to come now!

She was amazed, startled, distracted.

And what a man, too, she thought.

Annie's.

Annie's man. The man Lucia D'Angelo had sent to meet her daughter. *Remember that,* Diane told herself and abruptly tore her eyes away from the dark blue ones fixed on her own.

She took a deep breath. "I'm pleased to meet you," she said with all the facility of years of polite upbringing. "And you," she added almost as an afterthought to his friend.

"Likewise," Jared said.

His gaze, unlike Nick Granatelli's, flickered from Annie

to her, then back to Annie. Nick's never wavered. He never spoke, either. Just looked. At her.

For the first time in her social life, Diane felt flustered.

"Can't stay long," Annie bellowed at Nick over the pounding of the music. "I'm rehearsing."

He blinked, then focused for a second on Annie, before his eyes turned once again to Diane. "You're searching?" he said to Annie, not looking at her.

"Re-hears-ing," Annie said, breaking it into syllables. But she spoke with more forbearance than Diane imagined possible. "I'm an actress."

"Right," Nick mumbled. He licked his lips, swallowed, then seemed almost physically to pull himself together.

"Does he speak English?" Annie asked Jared.

Jared shot his friend a sidelong glance, then grinned. "After a fashion."

Annie looked doubtful. "I wondered," she said darkly.

"Sorry," Nick said. There was a hint of red beneath his tan. He raked his fingers through his hair. "I—I have a study group tonight. And I haven't finished my case study. I—" The music suddenly evolved into something recognizable as a slow dance tune. He held out his hand to Annie. "Want to dance?"

"I suppose," she said with bad grace.

Diane looked to see how Nick was taking this stunning lack of enthusiasm.

The smile she got in return was in danger of melting her right where she stood.

She stood, bereft, and watched Nick take Annie into his arms and dance away.

"Shall we?" Jared Flynn asked her, and she turned back to see him hold out a hand to her.

Diane pasted on her best smile. "Thank you. I'd like that."

She did her very best to listen when Jared talked, to make sane and sensible responses to his questions, to be the perfect partner she'd been taught to be.

Annie told her later that Jared was an actor, that he was Irish, that he was waiting tables at Fiorello's and working on a construction crew while he auditioned for acting parts.

For all Diane knew he could have been a Syrian taxi driver from the Bronx.

She smiled and nodded and made all the small talk she could think of. Her eyes and her mind were following Nick Granatelli around the room.

"How will I know him?" she'd asked her mother when she was five.

And Cynthia had got a faraway look in her eyes for just a moment. Then she'd pulled herself together and patted her daughter's hand. "Don't worry, lovely. It will happen. And when it does, you'll know."

"Did you know?"

For a long time Cynthia hadn't answered. She'd sat staring into the mirror at her dressing table. But then her gaze caught that of her daughter's reflected behind it, and she'd smiled. "Yes, darling. I knew."

Later, when it became clearer to Diane that her mother had been married twice, that Matthew whom she'd always known and loved as her father, actually wasn't, that there had been another man who'd once, briefly, been Cynthia's husband, she'd wondered. Which of the two had Cynthia known at once was the man for her?

She'd never asked. She almost never talked to her mother about the man named Russell Shaw. There were topics too painful even for a mother and daughter as close as Cynthia and Diane to share.

When the music ended, Diane found herself standing next to the punch bowl. Jared got her a cup of punch. Nonalcoholic. She didn't need any other mind-muddlers tonight. Nick Granatelli was quite enough.

He and Annie had finished dancing on the far side of the room, and she wondered if it might be possible to sort of wander over that way, if there was any nonchalant way of threading her way through fifty or sixty people and looking available the next time the music began to play.

But she had barely formulated the thought when the music started up again.

And at the first strains of the clarinet solo of "Stranger on the Shore," Nick materialized in front of her, holding out his hand.

Diane had a punch cup in hers. Wordlessly he took it, handed it to Jared, drew her into his arms and danced her away.

Afterward she could remember every second. Every sensation seemed imprinted on her memory forever—the firm strength of the arms that held her, the soft cotton of his T-shirt, the rough calluses on his hands. They weren't Business School hands, Nick Granatelli's. But they were capable hands, strong, yet gentle hands.

She would have trusted her life to them, and she'd known him all of fifteen minutes.

She remembered what they talked about, too.

"Annie said you're from St. Louis," he began.

She nodded. "Frontenac."

Nick grinned. "A little ways from The Hill."

"Is that where you're from?"

The Hill, Diane knew, was a largely Italian neighborhood first substantially settled in the last years of the nineteenth century. Italians first from northern Italy, then later from Sicily, settled there to work in the clay mines and the foundry. A strong, insular, largely working-class neighborhood, it was not the St. Louis she knew well.

Nick seemed to think the same. "Yes, it is," he said and there was a flash of defiance in his blue eyes.

Diane met it, looked right at him and asked, softly, "Does that make a difference?"

For a moment he looked taken aback. Then he shook his head quickly and firmly. "No. Of course not. No."

She found that she'd been holding her breath. And at his reassurance, she let it out, and her breasts brushed the front of his shirt. The contact seemed to startle him as much as it did her. He drew an unsteady breath, bit down on his lower lip and pulled her more closely against him.

It was like coming home.

She couldn't help it; she nestled in, laying her cheek against his shoulder, letting her hand slip a little farther around his waist. She felt his cheek brush against her hair. She sighed and felt Nick smile.

Together they moved as if they were one, and the music wrapped them in a world all their own.

IT WAS PITCH-DARK and three o'clock in the morning. Diane's eyelids wouldn't close. She lay in her bed, all her nerve endings, all her muscles, all her emotions at attention—exactly the way they'd been since she'd come home an hour ago.

She'd tried tiptoeing and discovered promptly where she'd left Hegel, abandoned on the floor. Her muffled curse had prompted an equally muffled "mmph," from Annie's bed.

Diane hadn't seen her since she'd left for rehearsal at eight, taking Nick's friend with her.

Over her shoulder Annie had tossed a casual "Nice to have met you. Have a good time" at Nick. But that didn't necessarily mean she condoned Diane's stealing the man meant for her.

"You awake?" Diane whispered. Quietly. Guiltily.

"Mmmph."

"Annie!"

"Mmmph!"

Diane sighed. They'd have to talk about it in the morning, she supposed. She wouldn't feel right about it, until they did.

She'd stripped off her clothes and tossed them onto the desk, then padded into the bathroom and brushed her teeth and washed her face in the dark. Then she crawled into bed and willed herself to fall asleep.

No such luck.

An hour later she had tossed and turned so much that she had a nest of tangled bedclothes, but she was still no closer to dreamland. Her mind, her heart, her very being seemed entirely consumed by Nick.

She flipped over again and banged her elbow on the bookcase. Her grandmother would have been shocked at her response.

It apparently jolted Annie, too. She sat up straight. "Wha'?"

"Sorry. Nothing. I just banged my elbow."

"Oh." Annie still sat there, so quietly and for so long that Diane thought she'd gone to sleep sitting up. Then she turned her head slowly so that she was facing Diane. "Wha' time'd you get back?"

Diane hesitated a moment, then opted for the truth. "Two."

"In the morning?" Annie sounded aghast. She squinted at the clock, then lay back down. "I wanted you to distract him. You didn't have to stay out all night with him."

"I didn't," Diane said indignantly. Then spoiled it by adding, "But I'd like to."

Annie jerked upright again. "What!"

Diane glared defensively. "I would," she said firmly. "I'd marry him, if I could."

"Marry?" Annie choked. "It must've been a hell of an evening."

"It was," Diane said simply.

Annie stared, then shook her head. "Better you than me."

"You...don't mind?"

"Me?"

"Well, he was yours."

Annie rolled over onto her side, obviously fully awake now. She propped her head up on an elbow. "Are you drunk?"

"No!"

There was a moment's silence. Then, "He must've done something."

"He's a nice guy," Diane said firmly. "Very nice."

"Better than the usual from my mother," Annie admitted, then added, "But that doesn't mean you have to marry him."

"I know that."

"Then why'd you say...?" Annie couldn't even bring herself to repeat it.

"Because I meant it," Diane said with all the earnestness she was capable of. "There's something about him. We're on the same wavelength or something. We connected. We—"

"You didn't!"

"Didn't what?"

"Connect," Annie said. She reached over and flipped on her study lamp, bathing the room in a garish green glow while she fixed Diane with a basilisk stare. "You didn't sleep with him?" She sounded horrified.

"Of course not!"

Annie heaved a sigh of relief. "Thank God. That's all

right, then. I mean, I would've felt terrible. I know you take your duties as a friend seriously. And I know I told you I had to get to rehearsal. But, believe me, I would never want you to go to that length just to distract him. Really, I—"

"Annie." Diane was laughing. "Don't worry. I won't sleep with anyone just to keep them from disturbing your rehearsal schedule. I honestly like Nick Granatelli."

Annie looked doubtful. "Enough to marry him?"

Diane gave her roommate a stunning smile. "On the basis of gut instinct, yes."

Chapter Two

If some classes at Harvard Business School, Nick told Jared the following morning, could be likened to aerial dog-fights, his 8:30 course in management techniques the day following his meeting with Diane Bauer was the one during which he went down in flames.

He sat in the kitchen at Fiorello's, watching Jared get ready for the noontime rush, nursing a cup of black coffee, and tried to forget the mess he'd made of the Feinemann Plastics case study that morning.

It wasn't as hard as he'd expected; his mind was full of Diane Bauer. Still.

His verbal fumblings and mumblings and the well-aimed chip shots that had reduced him to incoherence all seemed to fade in comparison to his memories of Diane.

He couldn't ever remember being so taken with a girl. There was something about her smile, about her warm brown eyes, about the welcoming way she'd looked at him, that—the moment he saw her—made him forget everything else.

He'd certainly forgotten his study group. He'd taken one look at Diane Bauer and Feinemann Plastics had gone right out of his mind.

He'd done exactly as he'd intended, foisting Annie

D'Angelo off onto Jared. But instead of heading back to campus to a night of work, he'd found himself spiriting Diane off to a little coffee house in the North End and, later, to an all night café on Mass Ave, not far from her apartment, where they'd sat and talked for another two hours.

It was crazy and he knew it. Aberrant. Foolish. He had no business getting mixed up with anyone now—especially someone like Diane Bauer. It was the wrong time, the wrong place, and she was, without question, the wrong girl.

She was beautiful, charming and, he could well imagine, loving, given the right circumstances. But the circumstances were far from right.

And even if they had been right, there was too much difference in their backgrounds. Ginny Perpetti might make a terrific wife for the man who ran Granatelli's Restaurant on The Hill. But, even if eventually he also ran a whole series of Granatelli's restaurants across the country, Diane Bauer was out of his league.

Forget it, he told himself. *Forget her.*

So when Jared stopped long enough to ask, "Will you be seeing her again?" Nick shook his head. "No."

Jared's eyes widened. "And why not?"

"No future in it."

Jared's mouth quirked. "There's got to be a future?"

But there would be a future with a girl like Diane Bauer. There was always a future with girls like her. Nick sighed again. "Yep."

Jared still looked skeptical, but finally he shrugged. "Whatever you say."

Nick pushed back his chair. "I say I've gotta go," he said, getting to his feet and stretching. "I need to see if I can salvage something out of the day."

Jared grinned. "And the best o' Irish luck."

Nick flashed him a brief smile. "I'll need it."

"I HAD THE STRANGEST DREAM last night." Annie stood brushing out her long dark hair, but her gaze was on the Diane she could see in the mirror.

"Mmm?" Diane, sitting cross-legged on her bed, had all her Valéry notes spread out around her and was wishing whoever the patron saint of term papers was, he would bring it all together; she certainly didn't seem able to.

She hadn't got a thing done all day. She'd slept through her linguistics course, and while she'd managed to make it to Recent European History, what went on at Gallipoli was likely to remain shrouded in mystery forever, unless she read it in a book. She'd skipped lunch, knowing Valéry was waiting.

And Valéry was still waiting and it was almost three o'clock.

She didn't need Annie's contribution to her scattered state of mind. But Annie was her friend, and regardless of how pressed Diane was, she never ignored her friends.

"Dream?" she mumbled, her gaze flickering up to meet Annie's.

"Mmm-hmm. I don't remember what I was doing, but all of a sudden you were with me, and you told me you were going to marry Nick Granatelli."

"I did."

Annie blinked. She stopped brushing her hair. "You said you're going to marry Nick Granatelli? I didn't dream it?"

"You didn't dream it. But whether I'm going to or not—" she shrugged and gave her friend a little smile "—that remains to be seen."

In the clear light of day her pronouncement should have seemed outrageous, but somehow, oddly, it didn't. She still felt that certainty, that sense of inevitability, that she'd felt the night before.

"Good grief," Annie said, eyes wide. "What did you two *do* last night?"

"Talked."

"About getting married?" Annie was aghast.

"No." But about nearly everything else. Life. Death. Eternity. Childhood memories. Family squabbles. Favorite poets. Beloved tunes. You name it, Diane thought, she and Nick had probably touched on it.

"We talked in Italian," Diane said with a grin. "He says I do pretty well."

"He speaks it?" Annie didn't. Or not much anyway. But then, she was three generations removed from Rienzo, whereas Nick's parents had only emigrated right before his birth.

"He speaks it," Diane affirmed. "He learned it at home, of course. But he also spent two years in Italy after he graduated from college. He worked for his uncle at a restaurant in Milan. That's why he's going to Harvard."

"So he can run his uncle's restaurant in Milan?" Annie's eyes bugged.

Diane made a face at her. "No, so he can expand the business. He's definitely got the American dream. The whole family does. His dad runs a restaurant in St. Louis. When he mentioned it, I remembered where I'd heard his name before. It's quite well known, but Nick wants it better known. He wants a Granatelli's in every city of over one hundred thousand people."

"More power to him," Annie said.

Diane nodded. That was one of the things she'd picked up on right away with Nick—the sense of destiny, the determination. Very much like Annie, actually.

Not in the least like herself. Diane knew she was a background person. She always had been. But, she told herself, the world didn't need only leaders. It needed people who came along and mopped up as well. She didn't think she'd mind as long as she could mop up after Nick.

"And you're going to marry him?"

Even though the baldness of the statement when someone else said it made Diane give a nervous little giggle, she still didn't deny it. "I know it sounds crazy, but I really felt some very strong vibes the minute I saw him."

"It's called sexual chemistry," Annie said dryly. "Or lust, if you prefer."

"There is that," Diane admitted. "But it's more than that, too. I don't quite know how to explain it. It's like we communicate on some deeper level."

"Oh, brother." Annie rolled her eyes.

Diane threw a paperback copy of Valéry's poems at her friend. "Cynic. Wait till you meet someone."

"I'm never—"

"What about that friend of Nick's? Jeremy somebody?"

"Jared." Annie shrugged. "He's okay. He went to rehearsal with me. He's an actor looking for a break." She sighed. "Aren't we all?" She began brushing her hair again. "Anyway, he's waiting tables and working construction right now, haunting the casting calls and waiting for a chance to do what he really wants. Another dreamer—straight off the boat from County Cork."

"Is he any good?"

Annie shrugged. "Who knows? He was interested, though. Hung around until the end and walked me home."

"Maybe it wasn't the play he was interested in," Diane teased.

Annie shook her head. "It was the play. Otherwise he wouldn't have spent the entire walk explaining how, when he played Hamlet, the Ophelia in the cast had taken an entirely different approach than mine."

"He played Hamlet?"

"So he says."

"He must be good, then."

Annie shrugged.

"I'll ask Nick."

"When are you seeing him again?"

"I don't know." They hadn't set a date. But he knew where she lived. She had given him her phone number. He would call. She didn't know when, but she knew he would.

HE DIDN'T.

Days went by, then weeks. February in Boston was unrelievedly soggy and gray. Not unusual, Diane knew after having lived there four years. But this February seemed soggier and grayer than any she'd yet experienced.

It was, she admitted at last, because she never heard from Nick.

"He knows where you live?" Annie asked as they tossed a Frisbee back and forth in front of Widener Library. Today for the first time this winter, the sun was shining and the temperature seemed almost balmy. It looked like spring was coming—everywhere except in Diane Bauer's life.

She nodded. He did indeed know where she lived. He'd walked with her all the way to the front door before heading toward his own place.

"He has your number?" Annie persisted.

"Uh-huh."

"And it was really as wonderful as you thought?"

Was it? Diane was beginning to wonder.

As a teenager she'd read magazine articles about what to do when "he didn't call." They had been interesting, she supposed, but only academically. It had never happened to her.

For her the phone had rung off the hook. Tom Switzer, Cal Grable, Andrew Daly, Stephen Peterson, Mike Cambridge, Jeff Steinmetz, Hank Forrester. The list went on and on.

There was another list of names equally long of the men who had called her since she'd come east to college four years before.

No one said, "I'll be in touch," and left her flat. No one but Nick.

She wasn't so much angry as she was puzzled. She was usually a good judge of character. She sized people up easily in a matter of moments. She didn't think she'd been wrong about Nick Granatelli's interest in her.

So why hadn't he called?

"Call him," Annie said and flung the Frisbee so high that, leaping for it, Diane practically impaled herself on a tree branch.

"I couldn't!"

"Why not?"

"Women don't call men. It isn't done."

Annie shrugged. "I do it all the time. Just yesterday I called Jeff Grissom and told him he'd damned well better return my tennis racket if he wanted to live to graduate."

"Not the same thing," Diane said gently, tossing the Frisbee back.

Another shrug as Annie caught it. "Same principle. You want to talk to him, call him up."

Diane shook her head. She couldn't. She wouldn't.

Annie sighed. "You and your antiquated scruples. Run into him, then."

That bore some consideration. "How?"

"Like Freddy in *My Fair Lady*. On the street where he lives."

"I never go over there."

"So go."

"I..."

"Listen, do you want to marry this guy or not?"

Now, almost a month after their first meeting with no further contact, her expectations sounded idiotic. Marry a man who never even called her back. Come on, Diane, get real, she chided herself and knew her blush told Annie exactly what she was feeling. But, oddly, Annie didn't tease.

"Maybe he's shy," she said. "Bowled over by his feelings and fearing you don't reciprocate."

Diane doubted it. Annie was flinging the Frisbee with great abandon now, and Diane felt like an Irish setter fetching for its mistress as she bounded after it.

"Maybe," she panted. "Or maybe I was wrong about him in the first place."

Annie stopped and looked at her. "Do you really think so?"

Diane held the Frisbee against her chest, thinking back on the night, on the man, on the wonder of them both. "No," she said slowly. "I don't."

"Then you have to see him again. I'll go with you. Don't know why I didn't think of it before. I'll stop over and tell Jared about the casting at Hayward. They're doing *Elephant Man.* Come on."

"Now?" Diane felt her stomach knot.

"Why not? No time like the present. Unless you want to sit around fretting about it all day. Do you?"

Diane gave a rueful grimace. That was the trouble with Annie—she knew her roommate far too well. She knew that, given a choice, Diane would much prefer to have things over with, finished, settled. Sitting around worrying drove her crazy. And she would definitely sit around worrying about what she would say if, when they went, she did happen to run into Nick.

Happen to? she mocked herself. Did she really think for

one minute that Annie would leave anything to chance? She girded herself mentally, emotionally.

"All right," she sighed, resigned. "Let's go."

Harvard Business School, on the other side of the Charles River from the main campus, was a world unto itself. Used to the occasionally seedy, sometimes pompous air of Harvard itself, Diane thought the neo-Georgian red brick buildings of the Business School simply exuded purpose. They were made for the men and women who were destined to lead, not for thinkers but for doers, and certainly not for contented followers like herself.

Nick and Jared, she knew, shared an attic apartment not far from the campus. Diane wasn't too familiar with the area. She'd have been quite lost, but Annie knew exactly where she was going.

"I've been here before," Annie said when Diane expressed amazement as she practically trotted after her friend who marched purposefully down the street.

"You have?"

"Mmm-hmm." Steps quickened.

"To see…Jared?"

"Mmm-hmm." Annie rounded a corner at breakneck speed.

Diane's mind was working furiously. "Are you…you and Jared…?"

Annie stopped dead, and Diane barely avoided crashing into her. "No, we are not!"

"I didn't mean—"

"Yes, you did. You always do. But just forget it, will you? I am not interested in Jared Flynn! He is a friend. A fellow actor. And I have no desire to marry him!"

"I know you don't."

Nothing made Annie angrier than the suggestion that she

might find something—or someone—who might interfere with her accomplishing her professional goals.

"All right, then." Annie began once more to walk. "So long as you don't get any stupid ideas."

"No, of course not." Diane caught up with her friend. "Have you—I mean, did you—I mean, was Nick—" She stopped, floundering.

Annie grinned. "If you're going to marry him, you have a right to ask."

Diane felt her cheeks burn. "Forget I ever said that. It was insanity speaking."

Annie shrugged. "Whatever. Anyway, I haven't been keeping anything from you. Jared and I were reading some plays together, working out scenes. He is good," she admitted. "But Nick was never around. He lives in the library, I think."

"Oh." It was on the tip of Diane's tongue to say that maybe they should lurk around the library then. But once Annie had made a decision, there was little chance of changing it.

Besides, Diane didn't really want to lurk around the library. It would be all too obvious what she was lurking about for. Accompanying Annie wasn't nearly as obvious. She hoped.

The three-story red brick building in which Nick and Jared lived was even seedier than the one she and Annie shared. Diane liked it as much as she liked her own.

She remembered how it had horrified her grandmother, but her mother had said she thought it was fine. Diane wasn't sure even her mother would accept Nick and Jared's building. She stopped, swallowing hard, reconsidering.

"I don't know, Annie. Don't you think…" she began, but Annie went straight up the steps and rang the bell.

Moments later she heard a window rattle open above and Jared's dark head poked out.

He grinned when he saw Annie. "Oh, it's you. Come on up, then."

Diane still hesitated, but Annie took her arm and hauled her through the door.

The stairway was narrow and dark, winding its way upward, ever upward. When they reached the top Jared had already opened the door and stood waiting, a welcoming grin on his handsome face.

Nervously, Diane found herself trying to see behind him, to catch a glimpse of whoever else might be in the room.

"Got to leave in a hour," Jared said, ushering them in. "I traded lunch for dinner today. I heard there was a casting."

"At the Hayward." Annie flopped on the lumpy sofa, making herself at home. Diane lingered just inside the door.

"Ah." Jared nodded. "You going?"

Annie shook her head. "Not me. I've got enough work on campus. But I thought I'd tell you."

"Yesterday in the restaurant I heard talk of it, but I didn't want to ask. It's less than thrilled Fiorello gets if you do more than wipe tables and set out the plates. So I thought I'd check a few of the theaters this afternoon. Now I don't have to. Thanks."

His gaze shifted from Annie and for the first time he seemed to notice Diane still standing just inside the door. There was a knowing look in his eyes that made her want to slip right out beneath the door. She half expected him to say, "Come for Nick, have you?"

But he didn't. He smiled and pointed to the sofa where Annie was sitting. "It isn't comfortable, but it's all we have. Want a beer? A soda? Tea?"

"Tea," Annie said, surprising Diane. Her friend noticed

her lifted brows and shrugged. "He makes a good cup of tea."

Taking a seat next to Annie, Diane smiled. "Then I'll have one, too."

She perched on the edge of the sofa—or rather, tried to. But the sofa had long ago given up the last of its springs, and the stuffing seemed intent on swallowing her. Finally the effort of remaining on the edge was too much for her and she settled back, finding that as she watched Jared puttering around in the end of the room that served as a kitchen, she was actually able to relax a little.

Perhaps it was the fact Jared didn't question her presence, or the fact that Nick was nowhere to be seen. Or maybe it was the very everydayness of Jared's movements and the casual conversation between him and Annie that she let simply flow over her. But by the time Jared handed her a cup—with milk, no sugar, just the way she liked it—she felt much, much better.

She sat and sipped, feeling more relaxed by the minute, chipping in now and then when the conversation veered away from plays and toward a subject she knew something about. Outside Jared's neighbors tromped up and down the stairs, laughing and chatting, banging against the walls as they went.

Diane stopped fretting about meeting up with Nick who was, Jared mentioned in passing, studying somewhere and not expected back for hours.

Annie looked as if she were going to take this as an excuse for leaving, but Diane cut in quickly, "We're not really in a hurry, are we? What part of Ireland are you from, Jared?"

His answer, followed by another question, effectively settled Annie in again.

Ireland was a subject Diane knew little about. But years

of exercising her social graces had taught her how to make conversation with the best of them. It was no strain to talk to Jared Flynn.

They were discussing Irish poets, in particular Yeats, when there came more thundering up the stairs. The door flew open and Nick appeared.

He stopped dead at the sight of her.

On the way over, the worst scenario she had imagined was that he wouldn't remember who she was. The reality, she discovered, was far worse.

He remembered her well. And the memory—whatever it was—was clearly not what she had hoped.

He turned white, then red, then swallowed hard and dredged up a caricature of a smile from somewhere south of his toes. He looked as if he wished he were anywhere else but here.

Diane wished a rabbit hole might appear down which she could bolt. Not surprisingly, none did.

She managed a nod. Anything else would have to wait until she unstuck her tongue from the roof of her mouth.

"You're back early," Jared said brightly into the silence. "Have a cup of tea, why don't you?"

Nick looked at him, stunned. Diane was sure Jared was normally nowhere near that solicitous of his roommate.

"Come on, join us," Jared went on with the aplomb of the perfect host. "We're having a go at Yeats."

Nick shook his head quickly. "Can't stay. I forgot my Porter and Cain."

He strode into the room, stepping across Annie's and Diane's feet. Annie left hers outstretched, Diane retracted like a turtle into a shell. There was a brief shuffling of piles of paper, then Nick snatched a book off the desk, gave a small triumphant wave of it and headed back for the door.

Doorknob in hand he turned, his eyes scanning the room

before lighting on Diane. Aeons passed. Or maybe it was only seconds. His eyes spoke volumes, but Diane couldn't read a word they said. She could only look back at him, baffled and oddly hurt.

He pressed his lips together for a moment, then opened his mouth as if he were going to speak. He didn't. Finally he gave a tiny shrug and a faint apprehensive smile flickered across his face.

"I gotta go," he said. Diane thought his voice sounded rusty.

SHE HADN'T FORGOTTEN HIM.

You thought maybe she had? Nick berated himself. He leaned back against the glass phone booth and stared unseeing out across the rush of traffic going past. No, he hadn't ever thought that. He'd simply *hoped* she had.

It would have made life so much simpler.

But when had life ever been simple? he asked himself.

It certainly wasn't now. Harvard Business School was not designed to make your life simple. It was, he thought, designed to streamline your priorities.

School was number one on that list. Also numbers two through nine. A distant, fast-vanishing ten, was Fiorello's. As it was, he barely had time to breathe. A woman like Diane Bauer was the last thing he needed.

He'd thought it would take a few short days to forget the effect she'd had on him.

He was wrong.

She'd been there, lurking, in the back of his mind throughout his days. And nights.

Sometimes half a day would go by without him having time to think of her. But then, all at once, he would hear a laugh that sounded like the soft feminine chuckle he had managed to elicit during that one evening they'd shared. Or another time he would overhear a comment that brought to mind one that she had made, one that had made him smile, or think, or nod his head in agreement.

It was odd how strong an effect she'd had on him in the space of those few hours.

It was, he'd told himself at the time, because he had been otherwise deprived of female companionship. She was the first and last woman he'd gone out with this year—if you didn't count Annie D'Angelo, of course.

He didn't. He found Annie perfectly nice—albeit a bit intense—and a far cry better than the usual women his family or friends dredged up for him. But she held nowhere near the attraction to him that Diane did.

Seeing her again, however, would have been crazy.

What point was there? he asked himself. It would only make things more complicated than they already were.

Besides, chances were, the feelings were all on his side. A girl like Diane Bauer probably had her pick of men. Pretty, smiling, wealthy blondes usually did.

If he were to call, she wouldn't even remember him, he'd told himself. So he turned back to his work and tried to put her out of his mind.

Sometimes, lately, he thought he was getting better at it. Whole afternoons would go by in which he managed to get lots of work done. Like yesterday afternoon.

He was steaming away on his case study, remembered something in the Porter and Cain that he wanted to look up, hurried back to the apartment for it, and—there she was.

Smiling, wide-eyed. Tempting. Vulnerable. And hurt.

He could see it in her eyes. The bewilderment. The sense of rejection. The wondering. She hadn't forgotten.

And for the rest of the day, neither had he. So much for his powers of concentration. So much for all the work he'd been planning to get done.

Instead he'd spent the rest of the afternoon staring into space. He couldn't even remember what he'd wanted to look up in Porter and Cain when he held it in his hand.

Finally at six, when he was sure she'd be gone, he went back to the apartment, irritated, ready to snap at Jared for having invited her there. Jared wasn't there.

When he did come in, Jared had stared at him like he'd lost his mind.

"Annie came to tell me about a casting, and Diane was with her. What's the matter?" He gave Nick a conspiratorial wink. "Guilty conscience?"

That was part of it, yes. But it wasn't only guilt. It was also desire. She touched some chord deep within him that he didn't ever remember having been touched before.

He was an idiot, and he knew it, but the desire to feel that resonance again hadn't left him in the month he'd tried to forget her.

So, what was he going to do now?

Call her.

Two words. Surely not difficult. You simply picked up the phone and punched out the number.

He still had her number; he'd been carrying it in his wallet for weeks. He didn't want to think about the number of times he'd slid his fingers into the pocket of his billfold and pulled out that much-folded piece of paper. He didn't want to remember all the times he'd been almost to the phone when he'd thought better of it and pulled back.

No longer.

He couldn't get her bewildered expression out of his mind. He couldn't rest until he'd explained why he'd done what he'd done. He certainly hadn't meant to hurt her.

He dropped coins in the phone box, took a breath and dialed.

It was Annie who answered.

"I—" He cleared his throat. "Is…Diane there?"

There was a pause. "Who is this?"

He hesitated. "Nick," he said. "Granatelli."

Another pause. A slight scuffling sound in the background. The receiver being handed over. Then another voice, softer, also hesitant. "Hello?"

"Hi. It's Nick."

"Oh."

It was amazing how many emotions he heard in that one word. They sounded as tangled as his own. "I'm…sorry I had to cut out the other day when you were at the apartment."

"I wasn't expecting—"

"I would've liked to have stayed. I had a report to finish."

"I never—"

"But I got it done this afternoon, and I was wondering…was wondering if…if you'd like to…come out for a cup of coffee?"

She didn't speak for an eternity. So he'd botched it, had he? He was cursing his ineptitude, when he suddenly heard her ask, "Now?"

"If…if you don't have a class or something. If you do, I understand. It was just a thought. I realize you weren't expecting—"

"I'll come." Her reply cut right across his objections. "Shall…shall I meet you somewhere?"

"How about Fredo's? Do you know it?" It was a relatively new place, about halfway between his place and hers.

"Yes. All right. When?"

"Half an hour?"

She hesitated. "I have to be back to do some tutoring at five."

"No problem." In fact, he thought, all the better. It meant

they would only have at most an hour together. Surely that would be enough time to make explanations, to see her, to tell if the whole thing was a fluke, the case of an overworked male with temporarily undersatisfied hormones.

And if it was, he'd know. He could drink a cup of coffee with her and then get on with his life.

And if it wasn't?

He wasn't going to think about that.

Chapter Three

Fredo's was supposed to be noteworthy for its fifties' ambience, its chrome-and-Formica counter, its neon advertising behind the bar, and its horrible coffee. As Nick drew her into the diner, Diane didn't notice anything except the warm pressure of his fingers wrapped around hers.

Witlessly she followed him to one of the booths at the back, sitting down and watching as he sat down opposite her.

He hadn't had a haircut in the month since she'd met him. His sun-streaked hair was rumpled and brushed the collar of his shirt. He wore a navy chamois cloth shirt and jeans and looked to Diane as if he should be outdoors chopping wood, not cooped up in graduate school.

The waitress appeared, smiled and batted her eyes at Nick. "What'll you have?"

Nick looked at Diane, his smile all for her. "Coffee," she said recklessly.

"Two coffees," Nick said without shifting his gaze.

The waitress looked disappointed, shrugged and left. Diane felt once more as if she and Nick were the only two people in the world.

Don't, she tried to tell herself. *Don't hope.*

But she couldn't help it.

"I should have called you." Nick raked a hand through his hair, rumpling it further. His smile was rueful now. "I...wanted to."

Diane, not knowing what to say to that, didn't say anything, just looked at him and savored the moment.

He shrugged awkwardly. "I've had so much to do. I thought I'd better concentrate on it. On school."

"I understand," she said, giving him a smile she hoped was reassuring.

He looked minutely reassured. His smile became a grimace, then he sighed. "Yeah, well, I'm sorry. When I saw you yesterday, I knew I'd made a mistake." He traced on the Formica with his fingertip, finally venturing a glance at her from beneath his lashes. "I had a great time that night."

Diane breathed again. She smiled. "I did, too."

"I'd...like to do it again. If I haven't blown it too bad."

Diane shook her head. "You haven't blown anything."

It wasn't the way one played the game; she knew that. Girls were supposed to be coy, distant, lead men on. And, in the past, to be truthful, she'd done her share of it.

But she couldn't seem to do it with Nick. With Nick she always felt as if she weren't wearing her heart so much on her sleeve as plastered across the front of her shirt.

Nick must have got a good look at it for he said, "Good," and smiled at her.

The waitress slapped the coffee in front of them.

"Thanks," Nick said absently, his gaze remaining on Diane.

He had trouble thinking when she looked at him like that. He'd been having trouble thinking since she'd come around the corner of the diner, her cheeks rosy from the cold, her fair hair flying free behind her, her bright blue scarf knotted casually around her neck. Whatever he felt for her, and whatever it might have to do with underworked hormones, he knew it was also more than that.

She made the day brighter, made the dreary New England spring seem to bask in a golden glow. And the fact that her smile seemed all for him made him stand straighter, breathe deeper, become more the man he wanted to become.

Now he tried to think of something clever to say, something worthy of her note, and could only come up with, "Were you really talking Yeats with Jared?"

She nodded.

"I know from nothing about Yeats." He grimaced again. "About poetry in general. It's all been business with me."

"Well, I don't know much about Yeats, either," Diane admitted. "But I've had plenty of poetry being a French major, so I tried."

"Jared was impressed."

Her brows lifted. "Oh, yes?"

Nick nodded grimly. "He said if I wasn't going to take you out, he was."

Her eyes widened now. She sipped her coffee, her gaze never leaving Nick's face.

"I'd rather not give him the chance."

Diane smiled slightly and cocked her head.

He shrugged and bit down on his lip. "So, I was wondering, what about having dinner with me Friday night? Would you like to?"

Diane nodded. "Yes."

He grinned. "Good."

The hour passed faster than it had any right to. It seemed to Nick like less than five minutes had passed when Diane glanced at her watch, grimaced, and began pulling on her coat.

"I've got to go," she said ruefully. "I have a couple of students to tutor in French this afternoon."

That surprised him. "You tutor?"

She shrugged. "It's a job."

"You need a job?" His skepticism was obvious.

"I like tutoring," she said defensively.

Immediately he regretted his question. "Yeah. Better than slinging hash at least."

"The kids are nice. They're Dr. Edmonds's children. Do you know him?"

"Luther Edmonds?" Nick knew him all right. Luther Edmonds sat somewhere just to the right of the god of the business management pantheon.

"They're going to France this summer," Diane told him as she stood up. "And he wants the kids prepared."

He wanted everyone prepared, all the time, Nick thought. It was in Edmonds's class that the Feinemann Plastics fiasco had occurred. He winced at the memory, then got hastily to his feet.

He should be heading over to the library right now and settling in for a long, hard slough through the pile of material Edmonds had heaped on them just this morning. Above all, he should bear in mind that furthering his acquaintance with Diane Bauer was a pointless exercise, one destined simply to distract him from the task at hand.

Instead he took her arm. "Come on," he said and tossed a couple of bills on the table. "I'll walk you back to your place."

AND, AS SIMPLY as that, it began.

Nick needed a social life. At least that was what he told himself.

A man couldn't live by business courses and care packages of Granatelli's own prosciutto and *biscotti* alone. He needed the occasional walk along the river in congenial company, the rare dinner date with a member of the opposite sex.

After all, he thought, a third of the members of his class were married. *They* had a social life. Why shouldn't he?

So he met Diane for a quick lunch at the Snack Bar in Gallatin on Wednesday. He took her out for another cup of coffee Thursday. And, as he had suggested, they went out for dinner on Friday night.

It was another marathon date. They left her apartment at five-thirty. He didn't bring her home until after two. They talked about life, about hopes and fears, joys and sorrows. She told him about her mother and stepfather, Cynthia and Matthew Bauer. It was a different view of the society swells than Nick had got growing up on The Hill.

He thought he would like her mother. She sounded as generous and loving as his own mother, though in quite a different way. And while Matthew Bauer sounded every bit the staid, responsible businessman he was reputed to be, he didn't sound like a bad father to have. He said so.

Diane tossed her mane of golden hair and smiled. "They are lovely parents," she admitted. "They love me a lot. They want what's best for me. So does my grandmother," she added. "But she isn't as easy to be around."

Privately Nick thought Diane's maternal grandmother Gertrude Hoffmann—the woman who insisted on an hour of piano practice and an hour of flute every day, who thought the Palmer Method couldn't hold a candle to Copperplate and required that Diane learn to write that way as well, who criticized her living quarters, who had always decreed which schools her granddaughter should attend— sounded like a virago.

He hoped devoutly that he never had the displeasure of meeting her. He didn't say that.

"She's a dear, really," Diane said philosophically. "You just have to know how to deal with her."

Nick didn't imagine he would ever know that.

"What were your grandparents like?" Diane asked him.

"Not like yours." He traced a pattern on his plate with the tines of his fork. "I only knew two of them really well. My father's parents stayed in Italy. My mother's lived down the street. And after my grandmother died, my mother's father came and lived with us. He was a fantastic man. The best. He died when I was seventeen."

"You must miss him dreadfully," Diane said, her eyes warm with sympathy.

Nick nodded. Even now, just thinking about his mother's father, Nick felt his throat get tight, his eyes burn. He swallowed hard. "He used to let me watch him work."

"What did he do?"

"When he was young he apprenticed to an instrument maker in Cremona. Violins and cellos and stuff. He loved music, but he loved working with wood more. So he packed up and went off to Cremona to try to combine the two. But he missed home and family, and he went back to get married."

The waiter removed their plates and refilled their coffee cups. Diane didn't speak, just waited for him to continue.

"His wife didn't want to leave, so he stayed there and made furniture instead. He made beautiful furniture," Nick said softly. "The care he lavished on it. The detail." He shook his head. "It was a labor of love. As I got older he taught me how to do it." The memory made him smile.

Diane smiled, too. "He sounds marvelous."

"He was. He saved my life."

Her eyes got big and round. "How?"

"Figuratively, I mean. He gave me breathing space. I was supposed to be in the restaurant working every evening after school. And most evenings I was. But sometimes I needed a break and *Nonno*—my grandfather—provided it.''

''I envy you,'' Diane said, and he could see she meant it from the look in her eyes.

''I envy me, too,'' he said, reaching across the table to take her hand in his. ''And never more than right now.''

THAT WAS THE WAY it went.

Lots of conversation, sharing. Plenty of smiles. Some touching. The occasional mind-shattering kiss. But on the whole they behaved themselves. He might have wanted to go to bed with her—no, there was no *might have* involved; he *did* want to—but he didn't even try.

It was a miracle.

No, he thought. It wasn't. A guy just naturally behaved himself around Diane Bauer. She brought out a protective instinct not a predatory instinct in him.

Not, he realized, because she was defenseless. She had, she'd informed him with a completely ingenuous smile, taken two years' worth of lessons in tae kwon do.

No, it wasn't defenselessness that prompted him to watch over her, but rather her fundamental openness and generosity of spirit that he didn't want to see compromised or lost.

''It's like she's my little sister,'' he explained to Jared the next Saturday afternoon when he was preparing to meet Diane to go rowing on the Charles.

Jared, who had only met one of Nick's sisters, stared. ''Little sister? Don't be daft, man. Diane has as much in common with Frankie as a goldfish does with a piranha.''

Nick grinned. ''Not that little sister. Paula, I meant.''

Jared still looked doubtful. Nick didn't blame him. Diane wasn't really like the less fiery, more ethereal Paula, either.

Nor, if he were honest, did he feel about her the way he felt about Paula.

But even though he liked her, even though he wanted to go to bed with her, he wasn't serious about her. Not really.

It would be asinine for Nick Granatelli to get serious about Diane Bauer.

Even though she was the nicest girl he'd ever met, even though his heart beat faster when she smiled and his whole body trembled when she kissed him, he knew better than to think this relationship was going anywhere.

They might be a couple here and now. But here and now was not forever. Forever, for the two of them, would never work. There was far too much distance between them.

He tried to make sure she remembered that, too.

He tried to tell her he was too busy, that he couldn't see her. And she'd nod and say, okay. And then he'd relent and call. But even when he saw her, he brought it up whenever he could.

He said it again the Saturday they went rowing on the Charles. He should have been in the library and wasn't. He should be feeling guilty and, unfortunately, he did.

But he wanted to spend time with her, and even though he half considered phoning her at the last minute and begging off with too much work to do, he couldn't do it. For one thing, she'd understand. She'd say, "Do your work. It's important."

And it was. But it didn't feel, at the moment, as important as Diane.

Unlike any other girl Nick had ever dated, Diane could row and wanted to. It amazed him, and he commented on it.

"No big deal," Diane said, moving the oars efficiently as they skimmed down the river. "I'll row you downstream. You can row back." She gave him an impish grin.

Nick shook his head, grinning, too. "How'd you learn?" he asked her. It didn't seem like the sort of accomplishment a debutante would have.

"Fourteen years at summer camp," Diane informed him. "After that many years, who wouldn't know?"

Nick nodded in agreement. But somehow the camp notion nettled. Visions of little pigtailed blondes in snappy uniforms came to mind. Privileged little pigtailed blondes. Wealthy little pigtailed blondes. "Where was that?"

Diane continued to slice the oars rhythmically through the murky green water. "In the mountains of North Carolina. Pine forests. Lakes. Real log cabins. It was beautiful." She smiled at the memory.

Nick, though still nettled, couldn't help smiling at her. His only experience with camp had been a week-long baseball day camp in a local park when he was ten years old.

All the boys in the neighborhood had come, wearing their holey jeans and too-small T-shirts. But they thought it was the greatest thing on earth, learning the finer points of baseball from their elder brothers, cousins and uncles, some of whom were on a first-name basis with homegrown stars like Joe Garagiola and Yogi Berra.

Still, in comparison to Diane's experience, it seemed a joke. He told her about it, stressing the makeshift quality of the operation. "Not exactly the same quality as yours."

"Sounds like fun to me. I always wanted to play baseball. At camp I did. But the minute I got home, I had to quit. My grandmother didn't think it was proper."

There was very little, Nick thought, that Gertrude Hoffmann seemed to think was proper. He could imagine what she would say if she knew her granddaughter was rowing on the Charles with a guy like him.

"What about you? Where did you learn to row?" Diane asked. The April sun was warm and turned her winter-dulled

locks a burnished gold. He fought back an impulse to reach
out and touch it. She lifted her face to the sun and closed
her eyes for a moment, then opened them again and focused
on Nick, waiting for his reply.

He cleared his throat, shifted carefully on the seat trying
to ease the tightness in his jeans. "On the Mississippi."

"You had a boat?"

"Hardly. We used to skip school and go down along the
riverfront and 'borrow' any boat we could find."

"Sounds a bit daring," she said.

Nick shrugged. "The owners just used 'em on weekends.
They never even knew. We were always careful to put 'em
back where we found 'em."

"Clever." But she didn't sound censorious.

"Illegal."

"Yes, I can see what a hardened criminal you've turned
out to be." Her eyes were laughing at him.

He scowled, irritated that she didn't take his transgres-
sions seriously. She wouldn't have had to joyride in someone else's boat. "It isn't funny."

"No." But she still didn't sound put off.

"I bet you've never done an illegal thing in your life."

Diane stopped rowing, her face growing pensive, her gaze
shifting to the middle distance. She pondered, then brightened visibly.

"I have, you know. I am a chronic jaywalker."

"That's not what I meant."

"Well, it's as silly as you're being," Diane countered,
beginning to row again. "What am I supposed to say, you
were a terrible child? All right, you were a terrible child.
Now, are you satisfied?"

He wasn't. He wanted her to back away from him, dislike
him, disparage him. He wanted her to see how unsuitable
their growing relationship was.

He wanted her to tell him to get lost because he couldn't tell himself. The longer he was around Diane Bauer, the more he wanted to stay around her for the rest of his life.

HE WAS REALLY, Diane thought as she rested the oars in the oarlocks, behaving ridiculously.

Not exactly unusual of late, she had to admit. Every time they were together Nick seemed absolutely intent on pointing out to her how little they had in common.

He was quite wrong.

Diane had met a lot of men in her twenty-two years, and she'd never met a man she had more in common with than Nick Granatelli.

Of course he hadn't had the same monetary advantages she'd had. He hadn't had her vast experience of attending debutante balls and country club soirees. But Diane couldn't see that that had been a particularly enlightening part of her education nor a particularly enviable one. She'd done it because it was expected of her. It meant no more to her than that.

But other things did matter. And it was those things she discovered that she shared with Nick. He loved his family; so did she. He was a Catholic; so was she. He was a Cards fan; she'd been one since birth.

When he went home at Christmas, he, like Diane, went out to root for the St. Louis Blues.

Their schoolday memories were not that different, either. She might've gone to the best of the private Catholic girls' schools in the area, whereas he had divided his time between Shaw Elementary and St. Ambrose Grade School, but they both had plenty of nun stories to tell. And he understood immediately when she talked about literally sweating through thirteen years in St. Louis schools.

"You mean you didn't have air conditioning?" He'd looked at her horrified.

"Never," Diane had assured him. "We were hothouse plants in the very truest sense of the word."

She tried to point out to him all these areas of compatibility. But he just argued with her.

The beauty of it, though, as she told Annie, was that he never left mad, and he always seemed willing to come back and argue some more.

"I don't have time to come around," he'd told her just yesterday. "You better find another guy to go out with."

But Diane had said, "It doesn't matter. I'll wait for you."

He'd tried arguing with her about that, too. But she meant it.

"I'll be here. If you get finished, fine. Come by. If you don't, don't worry about it."

She didn't know whether he'd worried or not, but at least he came.

She wouldn't have blamed him if he hadn't for she did understand the pressures he was under. On the phone just last week she had mentioned to her parents that she was dating a man who went to Harvard Business School.

Cynthia had wanted to know if he was a nice guy. Matthew had asked her how he had the time.

So she was well aware that Nick was pressed. She was grateful for the time they got.

Annie, she was sure, thought she was a sap to wait for the few hours here and there that Nick could give her. Every time it happened Diane expected her roommate to call her a spineless idiot without a will of her own.

But for once Annie kept her opinions to herself. And if she looked at Diane with worry in her deep brown eyes, Diane didn't want to know.

She even allowed herself to go back to daydreaming about someday marrying Nick.

It wasn't outrageous. No one but her grandmother Hoffmann would think it was. And she was confident that, when the time came, she could talk her grandmother around. When it mattered, she always could.

The biggest problem, so far as she could see, was convincing Nick.

Sometimes she thought he believed their relationship was going nowhere, that they were friends and nothing more. At others she thought his feelings were as deep as hers.

She didn't know. She wasn't sure. But she didn't despair. They had time, she thought. The rest of the school year. The summer.

He was going home to work at the family restaurant for the summer, he told her. And Diane, who had been planning to tour Europe before she started at the Sorbonne in the fall, suddenly changed her mind.

"I'll be in St. Louis, too," she told him one late April afternoon when they were lying on the grass in the Public Garden.

They rarely came into Boston. Their lives seemed contained at their respective schools. But this afternoon Nick had had to observe the workings of a small, but growing corporation and do a critique of it.

He'd asked her if she wanted to meet him afterward and grab a bite to eat. It had been almost two weeks since they'd been rowing. They'd shared coffee on the run three times. They'd sat across from each other in the library one night. And on Tuesday, he had met her at her apartment and they'd walked together to the Laundromat, where Nick had spent two hours reading a case study about something to do with the takeover of a mustard factory while Diane read Maupassant in between loads of his and her laundry.

"You washed his clothes?" Annie stared at her, as if she had just confessed to the most heinous of crimes.

Diane had shrugged. "I did mine, too."

She didn't mind. She didn't even care that Annie rolled her eyes and said, "I suppose you think it's romantic to fold his shirts."

In fact, it was. Being with Nick, in whatever manner, was enough for her. But the opportunity to go on something even remotely resembling a real date was not to be sneezed at, either.

So when he called and suggested she meet him in Boston, she just asked, "Where?"

Then she rearranged her tutoring, prayed that her modern French poetry instructor would come down with a communicable disease so tomorrow's paper wouldn't be due till Monday, and set off to meet Nick by the swan boats at five o'clock.

It was still warm when she got there. Spring had arrived full flower. Blossoms danced on the forsythia. New leaves budded on the trees. New downy ducklings trailed their mothers across the pond. And when Nick suggested they take a ride, Diane was thrilled.

It felt childish and frivolous and wonderful just to be able to lean back against the bench of the giant swan with Nick's arm snug around her, her head on his shoulder while the warm spring breeze teased her hair.

Sometimes she wished they could do more things like this—simple things, gentle things. Things just slightly more sensually rewarding than doing laundry and studying together.

But she knew that as long as Nick was in grad school it couldn't happen. She understood that.

But it would happen. Someday it would. She knew that, too. Just as she knew when she looked into his eyes that he was the most important person in her life and always would be.

And after the ride was over, they walked across the lawn and sat down on the grass. Nick told her about the corporation he'd just visited, about a summer job offer they'd made him and about having to decline. That was when he said he was going back to St. Louis.

And that was when Diane had said she was, too.

"I thought you were going to France?" Nick was sprawled on the grass, looking up at her with heavy-lidded eyes. Diane wanted to reach out and touch him, run her hand along his arm, slide her fingers inside the buttons of his shirt and touch the firm muscles of his chest.

She knotted her fingers together and shook her head. "I'm going home, too," she said, paused, then smiled hopefully at him.

Nick didn't say anything for a moment, but the eagerness she'd hoped for wasn't there. Finally he pressed his lips together in a firm line. "Your St. Louis isn't mine."

She stared at him, disbelieving.

His jaw tightened. He scowled. "It isn't."

"That's the dumbest thing I've ever heard," Diane exploded.

But he just looked at her. "Is it?"

And she heard a real question in his voice.

It struck her forcibly for the first time that he really did worry about the differences in their backgrounds, that he really might fear there was no future for them. She thrust out her chin. It was a replica of her grandmother's, though most people didn't notice.

"Yes," she said firmly, meeting his gaze. "It most certainly is."

Nick didn't say anything. He lay there, propped on one elbow, looking at her, then letting his gaze shift toward the

swan boats cruising in the pond. The look on his face reminded Diane of the look he got sometimes when he was
wrestling with a case study, weighing the alternatives, trying
to see the future.

She had seen the future—and it was theirs, if he would
only let it be.

But she didn't speak, only held her breath and waited.

Finally his gaze came back to rest on her face. A slight
smile lifted the corners of his mouth. "Yeah," he said.

Yeah.

"ONE FOR YOU, and one for me. And another for me. And
another for me." Jared tossed Nick his one letter, then
dropped a sheaf of thin blue air mail missives onto his own
bed.

Nick looked up from where he lay and scowled. "The
Jared Flynn Fan Club at it again?"

"It's jealous you are." Jared grinned and slit open a letter, then sank down onto the edge of his bed to read it.

"Not me," Nick denied, picking up his own letter and
studying it for a moment. "Got my own fan," he said with
deliberate smugness, waving the perfumed letter in Jared's
face.

Jared looked up. "Oh? Who's that?"

Nick ran his finger along the edge of the envelope, ripping
it open. "Ginny Perpetti. She teaches school back home."
He scanned the letter, barely digesting it, knowing he was
only using it to hassle Jared a bit, not because it—or
Ginny—really mattered.

Jared, unhassled, laughed. "You're not interested in her."

"What makes you so sure?" Nick countered.

"Diane. Every waking moment you're not buried under
the bloody case studies you're with her."

"We're…friends."

"Pull the other one while you're at it."

"We are," Nick protested.

"And that's all, then?"

Nick started to say it was and stopped. He thought about Diane, about all the times they'd spent together, about the way she looked at him, the things she said to him, about the way he was growing to feel about her.

"I don't know," he admitted.

"Looks serious," Jared said simply.

Nick sighed, then lay back on his bed, staring up at the ceiling. It felt serious, too.

Ever since their conversation in the Public Garden last week, Nick found that he no longer automatically rejected the notion of a future with Diane Bauer.

For the first time it seemed remotely possible that while he was making the Granatelli name in St. Louis, he might make Granatelli Diane's name as well.

Chapter Four

"So you're not going to Europe?" Annie sounded equal parts aghast and amazed.

Diane shook her head, which was a mistake. She should have known better than to move while she was trying to put on mascara, but she so rarely wore it these days, she tended to forget. She wouldn't be wearing it tonight if it weren't for the play Jared was in.

She and Nick were going. It was going to be a date.

A real one, he promised her; as if that mattered.

Diane had considered all their cups of coffee on the run, all their Saturday afternoons in the Laundromat or Sundays in the little rowboat on the Charles to be dates. As long as they were together, she didn't care in the least.

"So have you told Mama, then? Or, more to the point, Grandmama?"

"I haven't told anyone," Diane said. "But you. And Nick."

"And is Nick pleased?" Annie finished knotting her long dark hair on top of her head and poked the last pin in place.

"Yes." He wasn't jumping for joy. But then, Diane realized, Nick was not the jumping-for-joy type.

Still her commitment to spending the summer in St. Louis

seemed to have made him happy. At first he'd looked doubt-ful, but the last few days he'd seemed less irritable, calmer, more likely to smile.

"He ought to be pleased," Annie said darkly. "I wouldn't give up a summer in Provence with Auntie Flo for anyone. Haven't you told her yet, either?"

Diane started to shake her head again, remembered the mascara, held very still and concentrated on her eye. "I'll write her. She won't care. Aunt Flo never cares what I do."

"How very unBauerlich."

Diane grinned. "Very. It's what makes her such a dear." Her stepfather's older sister, Florence, was the closest thing the Bauers had to a black sheep.

At twenty she'd married a German baron three times her age and moved to New York. Widowed at twenty-two, she remained in the east and never came back to St. Louis unless absolutely unavoidable family obligations required it. The last time she'd been there was in 1966 for her mother's funeral.

The baroness Florence Von Dettmeyer was a dream aunt. She ran an art gallery on Madison Avenue, traveled exten-sively, sent her only niece outrageous presents and provided her with plenty of opportunities to broaden her midwestern horizons.

Grandmother Hoffmann thought Flo barely to the right of unrespectable and didn't hesitate to say so. She had saved herself from damnation only by having married well. Grand-mother Hoffmann forgave many sins of those who had the sense to marry men of whom she approved.

Once, when she'd had a tad too much vodka, Flo had told Diane she thought Grandmother Hoffmann, had she been asked, might have married Baron Von Dettmeyer herself.

Diane, who'd heard tales of the hard-nosed Teuton who'd

been her aunt's husband, thought privately that he and
Grandmother Hoffmann would have been well matched.

"So what are you going to do instead? Wait tables at
Granatelli's?" Annie persisted.

"I doubt it. Not that I wouldn't. But I don't think Nick
would approve."

She could imagine the reaction she'd get if she even suggested it. She could hardly believe he was ashamed of her,
but on several occasions when he'd talked with his father
on the phone in her presence, he hadn't mentioned she was
there.

She didn't want to sound pushy, but afterward she
couldn't help asking, "Does he know about me?"

She'd been disappointed but not surprised when Nick had
said no.

"He has enough on his mind," he said, giving her a hug
and a smile. "He's trying out some new wholesalers. Every
time you think you've got things settled, they're screwed up
again. Supply dries up, the prices skyrocket, the source goes
belly-up." He shook his head.

"Sounds difficult," Diane sympathized.

"It is. Besides, Aldo, my brother-in-law, is setting up a
new accounting system. And the maître d' just quit. It's all
he'd need," Nick grinned, "hearing I'm being distracted by
a beautiful woman when I'm supposed to be working my
butt off here so I can go home and increase the family fortunes a hundredfold."

Diane knew that that was the plan. Other people used
Harvard Business School as a glorified employment agency,
getting their degree and expecting, as a reward, a clear entry
into a Fortune 500 company. Nick was there to learn all he
could and go home to make Granatelli's Restaurant a force
to be reckoned with in St. Louis.

"Are you distracted?" Diane asked doubtfully.

He'd pulled her into his arms and given her a resounding kiss. "What do you think?"

Diane didn't know what to think. She could only wait. And hope.

NICK WAS LEARNING to hope, too. Diane was right about one thing—he never would have let her wait tables at Granatelli's. He was having a hard enough time convincing himself that he could make her the owner's son's wife. But he was, for the first time, actually considering it.

He was also considering how he might best introduce her to the family—and the family to her. He would broach the subject carefully once he was home this summer. He'd call Diane sometime and invite her out, drive her through The Hill area, maybe take her past the restaurant.

Then, another time, they'd stop, and he'd take her in, introduce her to his dad. She'd like his father. At least he hoped she would.

As if by some odd chance she didn't, Diane would never let it show. She was far too well-bred to show her feelings.

His father wasn't. Dominic Granatelli never hesitated to show you what he thought about anything.

Nick knew he'd have to do a bit of preparation there.

Even if he did, he still didn't know if his father would like her. Not that there was anything to dislike about Diane Bauer. Nick had never in his life met a woman who was sweeter, kinder, more genuine.

But Dominic Granatelli had his own agenda, made up his own mind.

Nick doubted that the Bauer Brewery and Hoffmann Hardware heiress was exactly what his father'd had in mind as daughter-in-law material. She didn't come with a built-in familial connection to basil growers and olive orchard owners the way Ginny Perpetti did.

Still, Nick felt hopeful. If all went well after she'd met his father, he could ask her to come for a meal. She could meet his mother and Frankie and—

No, not Frankie. His sister's strong personality and unhesitating outspokenness would overpower a gentle girl like Diane.

She could meet Paula, though. Paula, in her last year of high school, was young and sweet. She could meet Carlo, too. His brother was in the seminary in St. Louis. Carlo could be counted on to be polite.

He'd save Frankie and Sophia—surely Ginny's biggest supporter—and his youngest brother Vinnie, who had long hair, an earring and a penchant for drumming on things, for another time.

But he was getting ahead of himself.

"One day at a time, fella," he counseled himself as he bounded up the stairs to Diane's apartment. "One day at a time."

She was ready when he got there, waiting just inside the door, wearing a lightweight spring coat over a demure rose-colored dress, her long honey-colored hair swept up into a barrette at her crown from which it fell in silky, shining splendor over her shoulders. The smile she gave him made him melt, and the last thing he wanted to do tonight was go watch Jared's play.

"All set," she said brightly, holding out her hand to him.

He drew her close, slipping his arm around her shoulders and kissing her. It was not a brief kiss. It simply fed the hunger that grew inside him, making him forget his purpose, his good sense, his intentions.

Someone behind Diane cleared her throat.

Nick jerked back. "Er, hi. *Annie?*" Of course it was Annie. Who else would it be?

But he had never seen her like this—all dressed up, wearing a dramatic black cape over a dress of ivory linen. Nothing demure about her.

"You're coming to the play," Nick said, unable to hide his consternation.

"Not with you," Annie said pointedly. "You don't have to be a French major to know what *de trop* means."

"Really, you're very welcome to come with us," Nick lied.

Annie rolled her eyes. "Get out of here," she said. "I don't like all that mushy stuff. When I go to a play I go to concentrate." She glowered at them both.

"She's right," Nick said. "If we don't hurry, we're going to be late."

He hadn't the slightest interest in *Look Back in Anger* himself. He had agreed to go because it was a good excuse to take Diane out on a real date and because his friend was in it.

If you had asked him he would have assured you that he was always certain Jared had talent, but he'd never seen him act until tonight.

He found out at once how right he was.

It didn't even seem to be Jared up there onstage. The man who left the cap off the toothpaste, who left dirty socks on the coffee table, warbled off-key in the shower and burned toast in the kitchen was nowhere to be found.

The lean, intense, dark-haired man who played Jimmy, Osborn's protagonist, didn't even seem to resemble Jared, except perhaps superficially.

The Irish brogue had vanished. In its place Nick heard an increasingly strident Midlands accent. The droll smile had fled, replaced by sneers and bitterness, then genuine anguish.

Nick had thought the play would give him a chance to

do a little bit of petting with Diane. He found that it captured his attention entirely.

So trapped was he in the web of emotions developing onstage, that he forgot Diane. And when it was over, and the curtain came down, he was as exhausted and drained as a man who'd run a marathon.

One look at Diane told him she felt the same way.

It was a shock to see Jared, sweating and grinning as he took his bows, looking once again just like the man who couldn't make a piece of toast.

"He was amazing," Diane said. "I never would've believed it."

"*You* wouldn't have?" Nick laughed, but he still felt shaken.

His roommate had so much potential in him, such incredible talent that he'd never suspected. It had simply taken the right circumstances to bring it out. He helped Diane with her coat, but all the time his mind swirled and he shook his head, still awed.

"He asked us to meet him backstage after," Nick said, steering her up the aisle. "He said we'd go out and grab a bite." He shook his head again. "I wonder he can eat."

"I know." Diane turned and smiled at him. "But I bet he can. Annie's the same way."

"Speaking of whom," Nick said, "where is she?"

They found her already backstage, on the edge of a group of theatergoers surrounding Jared. Everyone else was babbling and chattering, tugging at his arms or poking their faces in his.

Annie simply stood and stared.

She didn't speak, she didn't move. And when Diane and Nick came up to her, she didn't even acknowledge their presence. She just looked at Jared.

Gradually, slowly, his congratulators drifted away, and

Jared breathed deeply, stripped off his sweaty shirt and mopped his brow.

"Cripes," he muttered, giving them a grin. "Bit of a mob scene, this is."

"You were wonderful." Diane put her arms around him and gave him a hug. "I couldn't believe it was you."

"Me, either." Nick clapped him on the back.

"Thank you very much." Jared grinned. Then his gaze found Annie and he frowned. "What's wrong?"

She blinked, then shook her head. "Nothing." Her voice was flat, colorless. It made Nick frown, too, and Diane leaned forward, looking concerned.

"It's something," Jared said. His brows came together. "It was that bad, then?"

Annie blinked again, then looked at him, astonished. "Bad? It was marvelous. *You* were marvelous. I just...I just..." She shook her head, dazedly. "I never thought..." she said, her voice trailing off into a whisper.

"Marvelous?" Jared brightened. "You think so?" Again a moment's doubt flickered on his face.

"You were incredible," Annie said with authority, and bestowed on him a smile such as Nick had never seen.

At that Jared smiled, too, and took her arm. "Come and tell me, then," he commanded, hauling her with him toward the dressing room. He glanced over his shoulder. "Be right back," he said to Nick and Diane. "Give me a few minutes to get cleaned up."

Nick grinned. "And have your ego stroked a little."

Jared laughed. "That, too."

"He deserves it," Diane said, watching them go.

Nick nodded, bent his head and kissed her ear. "He does."

IT WAS A NIGHT to remember for all of them.

For Jared, obviously, because it was his first triumph on

the American stage. It would not, Diane was certain, be his last.

For Annie, Diane found out later, it was equally memorable because she had finally found someone whose talent she could respect.

"I thought perhaps he was a kindred spirit," she told Diane later that night. "But I didn't know until I saw him onstage. Now I do."

And for Diane and Nick it was a time to be together, to share the present, to hope for the future.

As if the play itself weren't wonderful enough, there was the after-theater supper at Gregoire's, a small cozy French bistro with a string trio playing danceable oldies not far from the theater where they started out as a foursome.

Halfway through the onion soup, Jared and Annie were so far into an analysis of the third scene that Nick had pulled Diane up into his arms and said, "Let's dance."

No one else was, but for once the etiquette of the situation was beyond her. Diane put her arms around his neck and let herself go.

They danced between courses. They kissed, they nibbled, they smiled. Jared and Annie moved on to the fourth scene, their discussion becoming as heated as Diane's blood.

After dinner Jared and Annie left them, still discussing, to go back to the apartment. She and Nick remained behind alone.

The other diners danced now, but they no longer did. Instead they sat close together at the table, talking with their eyes as much as with their mouths, saying things they couldn't yet bring themselves to put into words.

It was on the tip of Diane's tongue to say, "I love you."

She did love him. She knew that beyond a shadow of a

doubt. She, like the Biblical Ruth, would drop everything and follow him. He had but to say where.

She didn't speak because it wasn't her place. She had done most of the running; she knew it and was willing to acknowledge it. If she hadn't reappeared in Nick's apartment with Annie that afternoon last March, chances were he'd have never called her again.

But she had. And he had. And things had gone along from there.

Now, set in motion, they would continue, just as she'd always known they would. She and Nick were destined for each other. There was no hurry.

"All things come to she who waits," her grandmother Hoffmann used to say with asperity whenever Diane, a bouncy child, was impatient for something to happen.

So Diane waited. She smiled. She touched her lips to his. Nick cleared his throat. "I have something to ask you."

Diane smiled, hoping.

He looked uncomfortable all of a sudden. There was a tension in his face that hadn't been there before.

"What is it?" She deliberately made her voice soft, unhurried.

He eased his collar away from his neck, then tugged at the knot of his tie. "I shouldn't even ask you, I guess. It's an imposition, what with it being the end of the school year and all, but…"

Diane still waited. Surely he couldn't want to elope now?

He hesitated, tugged at his collar again, then went on, "You know Bennett Hamilton in my study group?"

Diane nodded. She'd met him once in passing. He looked and dressed every bit the third-generation blue blood that Nick did not.

"Yeah, well, his family's putting on an—" he raked his fingers through his hair "—hell, I don't know what you'd

call it…affair, I guess, to celebrate his brother's passing the
New York bar exam. Black tie.'' He grimaced. ''Next Friday down at their place in Newport. The 'cottage' Ben calls
it.'' Another grimace.

''On Bellevue Avenue, no doubt.''

''Is that money?''

''Mmm-hmm.''

''Then that must be where it is.'' He tugged at his tie
again. ''Anyway, he invited me. And a guest. 'Come for
the party and stay over,' he said.''

Nick made it sound as if he'd been invited to be the
recipient of a round at a firing squad.

''So, will you come? Be my 'guest'? Show me which
fork to use?'' he added with a wry grin.

It wasn't, of course, the question she'd hoped it would
be, but she didn't mind. ''A man who can run a restaurant
knows perfectly well which fork to use.''

''You know what I mean.'' He flexed his shoulders and
scowled. ''I don't really relish the idea of going at all. It's
not my thing.''

''So, why go?''

''Ben's my friend. And—'' there was a pause ''—I'll
look like a jerk if I don't.''

Diane would have said that it didn't matter what he
looked like, that whatever people thought didn't matter, because certainly to her it never would have mattered.

But she realized that to Nick it did. People would have
commented if he hadn't gone, they would have recognized
his insecurity for what it was. And, recognizing it, never
would have accepted him as their equal.

It was idiotic, in Diane's opinion. She also knew her opinion didn't matter. Nick, for all that he would never need to
count on these people for his future, still didn't want to
appear lacking in their eyes. He needed to show that he

could handle their world with aplomb before he went back to his own.

"I'd be delighted to go with you," Diane said and leaned forward to kiss him on the cheek.

Nick turned his head, catching the kiss on his mouth instead, surprising her with the eagerness of his lips and the fervency of his response. He rested his forehead against hers and squeezed her nape gently with his hand. "You're a good sport," he said, his voice rough.

A GOOD SPORT.

As accolades went, it didn't go far. But, Diane supposed as they sat side by side that Friday afternoon on the bus heading toward Newport, coming from Nick, it meant a lot.

Just asking her to go to Bennett Hamilton's affair with him meant a great deal. It was not, as it sometimes seemed to her, Nick against her background; now it was Nick enlisting her support as he took on the society she moved comfortably in.

She slanted a glance at him now. He was slumped against the window, sleeping. He'd been sleeping ever since they'd changed buses in Providence. He'd slept down from Boston before that.

She knew he'd spent the last forty-eight hours in sleepless effort, working up final case-study presentations for two of his classes, going over them with a fine-tooth comb, sounding them out on his study group, on Jared, on Annie, on her, on anyone who would listen.

And, having delivered them, he'd just had time to take a last-minute call from his father regarding something about herb farms and sources of fresh basil, before he propelled her to the bus terminal, onto the bus, then had sunk down beside her and given her a tired grin.

There, clasping her hand in his, he had fallen sound asleep.

But now they were pulling into Newport, people were rustling about gathering up shopping bags and cases, preparing to get off, and Diane knew she would have to wake him.

She leaned over and brushed her lips across his cheek. "Nick?"

Her breath stirred his lashes and he blinked, disoriented. Then he opened his eyes wider and a brief smile flickered across his face. It vanished a second later when he realized where they were.

He groaned. "Unfair."

Diane smiled. "What's unfair?"

"Being here with you."

"What's wrong with me?"

He shook his head. "Not you. Here." He scowled around the bus. "I can think of a million places I'd rather we were." He paused. "I was dreaming about one of them."

The look on his face gave her a pretty accurate idea of the place in his dreams. She blushed.

He laughed, then sighed and stretched mightily. "I'm embarrassing you." He was still grinning, enjoying her disconcerted look.

She ducked her head, then lifted it and met his gaze squarely. "You're not, you know," she said bluntly. "I'd like it, too."

She saw Nick swallow. He didn't speak, just looked at her, his blue eyes warm and worried.

Afraid she had said too much, she squeezed his hand and, as the bus slowed to a stop, moved to get up.

Nick held her fast. When she turned to look down at him, his gaze was compelling. "I'm glad," he said gruffly. Then he also got to his feet.

Bennett was waiting, and within moments had shepherded them from the crowded, noisy bus to the air-conditioned comfort of his black Jaguar XJ6 sedan.

"Not mine, actually," he apologized when they got in, Nick beside him in the front, Diane in the back. "My father's."

"It'll do." Nick grinned and put out a hand to Diane in the back seat. She took it in hers.

She'd been to Newport only twice. Once, when her grandmother had visited, they had driven down to visit a college chum of Gertrude's. Once she had come with her father when he had invited her along to crew with him on the sailboat of a man he knew.

Her grandmother's school chum had lived in a lovely old house not far from Hammersmith Farm on Narragansett Bay. But it couldn't compare to the opulence of the Hamilton "cottage" that overlooked First Beach and not the bay.

"What lovely gardens," she exclaimed as they turned into the private driveway and into the gates of the Hamilton estate.

"There's a maze, too," Bennett pointed out as the car purred along the curving driveway. "Tom and I used to play hide-and-seek there as kids."

"We had a small one at my grandparents' place." Diane said eagerly. "Aren't they great fun? I loved it, but my mother used to complain that she always got lost."

"Sounds like my aunt Lolly." Bennett laughed. "You'll meet her tonight. She's a stitch."

He proceeded to tell Aunt Lolly stories as he parked the car and led them up the broad marble stairway and into the palatial entryway of the house.

There a maid offered to show them to their rooms, but Bennett waved her off.

"Never mind. I'll take them up." He headed for the staircase that curved up to a second-floor balcony. "I'll introduce you to everyone else at dinner. Come along," he said blithely over his shoulder. "Scatter bread crumbs if you want, so you won't get lost."

Diane laughed. Nick managed a wan smile. She dropped back and fell into step beside him. "What's wrong?"

He shook his head. "Nothing. Just…tired."

He shifted his duffel bag to the other hand and smiled again. It was broader this time, determined, Diane would have said, but it didn't reach his eyes.

She squeezed his hand and pecked his cheek. "Come on. You must be exhausted. You can take a nap before dinner."

HE DIDN'T sleep. He was tired, all right. Exhausted, more like. But there was no point in lying down. He was far too keyed up for that. He might have slept on the way down. But that was before he'd caught sight of Bennett lounging against the fender of his Jag as the bus pulled up. Then he'd awakened in a hurry—to just how far from home he'd come.

This wasn't his scene. He didn't belong here, he told himself over and over as he paced the bedroom Bennett had stuck him in.

A major part of him wanted to cut and run, go home, back to the familiar, the comfortable, before he was discovered for the charlatan he was.

But he couldn't because he'd dragged Diane into this with him. If he vanished now he'd either have to take her with him or abandon her. Neither was an option. So he paced and sweated, glanced at his watch and chewed his lip.

"It doesn't matter," he told himself. But that was a lie; it mattered a hell of a lot.

Oh, not what the Hamiltons thought of him, or what their friends and acquaintances said. No, he didn't care about them in the least. He cared about Diane, about being the proper escort for her, about holding his own, about people not saying behind their hands or, worse, in front of them, "What on earth does she see in him?"

He wished he hadn't asked her. He wished he'd declined the invitation when it had come. Bennett wouldn't have cared, really. He was Nick's friend; he would have understood. Nick could have said he was too busy studying or he could even have told a partial truth, that renting the requisite tux was going to cost him far too much.

His father certainly thought it was a mistake. "What're you going there for?" Dominic had demanded when Nick had told him he'd be gone for the weekend. "You got studies, don't you?"

Nick had agreed he did.

"Then study. That's what you're there for. Next thing you know you'll be getting a swelled head," Dominic grumbled. "Try paying attention to my fresh basil problem if you have free time. We aren't going to have a restaurant if I don't get this solved."

Nick assured his father that he would give it consideration.

But when the invitation came, Diane had just told him she was going to stay in St. Louis. He had considered that, too, had mulled over its possibilities, and had known that he had a more pressing problem than fresh basil. In Diane Bauer he was dealing with more than a semester's fling.

He was dealing with something that might very well be called love.

In fact he had known it for some time, but he hadn't wanted to admit it. He admitted it then, admitted that she was going to come face-to-face with the Granatellis some time this summer. And it suddenly seemed imperative to show her that he could exist on her level of society, too.

Bennett's invitation, therefore, had seemed like a god-send.

Now it seemed like an invitation to doom.

He glanced at his watch again. Bennett had said drinks before dinner. Then dinner. Then port. Then dancing and celebration on the terrace. If he took it a step at a time, he might possibly make it. He'd start with a shower. The colder and more bracing the better.

AT PRECISELY five minutes to seven he presented himself outside Diane's door.

He didn't know if he was supposed to escort her down or not. He thought somewhat grimly that he should have spent less time on Lee Iacocca and more on Emily Post. Maybe they should have made etiquette part of the curriculum for those not to the manner born.

In any case, meeting her here seemed preferable. They'd have a couple of moments alone and Nick needed to see her alone, to reassure himself.

The sight, when she opened the door, was not reassuring.

She was a Diane he'd never met—an elegant, stunning Diane, wearing an off-one-shoulder floor-length peach silk that brought out the honey tones in her hair and in her skin.

She looked at him just as stunned.

His hand went to his tie. "Did I do it wrong?"

She shook her head quickly. "No! Not at all. You… you're beautiful."

He flushed, scowled, then shook his head again.

"I feel like an ass. The tie's too tight. I can't lift my arms in this jacket."

"You're not supposed to have to carry the furniture," Diane said, laughing.

He frowned, and eased his collar away from his neck,

grimacing as he did so. "I still don't like it. Hell of a price to pay for beauty, strangulation."

Diane grinned. "Smile. Even if you're strangling it will look good on you."

"If you say so," he muttered ungraciously, then remembered his manners. "You're gorgeous," he told her and meant it. "More than gorgeous."

Diane smiled. "You like the dress?"

How could he not? It was the perfect complement to Diane's coloring and a marvel of engineering. Everything hung, literally, from one tiny pearl button at her left shoulder. From there on down everything clung with just the right amount of cling, swirled with just the right amount of swirl.

"It's...impressive," he managed in a gruff tone, which seemed a polite way of saying he'd love to rip the dress off her right then and there.

"Annie says it's supposed to drive you mad with desire," Diane told him.

"Annie's dead right."

Whatever Diane might have replied was lost because Bennett came bounding up the stairs just then. "Oh, good, you're ready. Drinks are being served in the parlor." He offered Diane his arm. "Shall we?"

She held out her other arm to Nick. He hesitated briefly, feeling a sudden stab of panic. Then, when she still waited expectantly, he took her arm.

"Ready," Diane said to Bennett.

"As we'll ever be," Nick muttered under his breath.

Dinner was a family affair, only three forks and a like number of spoons. He had no problems. He didn't actually expect he would—as far as the silverware went anyway. It was something far less tangible that worried him—a sense of belonging or of being out of place.

But dinner at the Hamiltons, even black tie, wasn't as foreign as he'd thought.

Diane laughed and chatted with Bennett's uncle Ralph on her left, and his eccentric aunt Lolly on her right. Periodically she caught Nick's eye and slanted a smile at him across the table.

At first his answering smiles were forced. But as the dinner wore on, he was able to do so more naturally because his fears weren't materializing. Bennett's cousin James, in his last year at Phillips Exeter, seemed somewhat awed by a man who didn't have a Mayflower genealogy and yet was making good anyway. Far from being put off by Nick's declaration of his background, James thought he was heroic.

"You're doing it yourself," James said. "That takes guts."

Nick felt suddenly ashamed of his chip-on-the-shoulder attitude and ducked his head. "I had a lot of encouragement along the way," he said. "I didn't do it on my own. My family helped."

"Well, sure," James said. "Families do," as if it were a given no matter where one lived or what one's circumstances were.

Nick began to feel maybe he wasn't so different after all.

After dinner and before the first of the evening's guests began to arrive, Ben took them on a tour of the estate.

The house was palatial, but not as daunting as Nick had expected. Or perhaps it was because he was more comfortable now. In any case, it didn't unnerve him, and he was able to appreciate it for what it was—welcoming, airy, and, of course, polished to perfection. The grounds were immaculate, the plantings color coordinated, the view incredible.

Diane smiled up at him, her gaze expectant. And this time he took her hand with more assurance, feeling a burgeoning of hope, a tiny bud of promise beginning to develop some- where in the region of his heart.

By the time they walked back across the lawn the guests had begun to arrive. A string quartet was playing in the ballroom, and waiters were beginning to circulate there and on the terrace, offering trays with glasses of champagne and hors d'oeuvres.

Ben introduced them to one of his father's clients, the president of a stereo components company, apologized with a "Can you manage from here? I have to circulate," and gave them a grateful smile when they assured him they could.

As they stood there, the terrace filled with glittering groups of people, men in evening dress and women in gowns of every color and description. Before long even the cavernous ballroom seemed to be getting crowded.

He moved through the throng with Diane, making small talk with a few of his fellow students, answering the occa- sional question from one of Bennett's father's colleagues. Diane was in her element, talking and laughing, beautiful and poised in her peach-colored gown.

A starchy old man with a lot of brass on his uniform appeared and claimed her acquaintance. He was, he in- formed them, General Bachman, a friend of her grand- mother's. If Diane had ever met him before, Nick couldn't tell. She greeted him with enthusiasm, asked about his re- cent tour of duty, which happened to have been in the Far East. This led to a discussion about his interest in ivory, and Diane began to question him about poaching, endangerment of species and the ivory trade.

Nick listened, awed. He was almost certain she had no previous interest in or knowledge of ivory, elephants or game poaching, but he never would have known from her conversation. And when the music started up and the general danced her away, he stood there with his mouth open, slightly dazed.

By the time the music ended she was nowhere to be seen. Nick craned his neck, feeling for the first time since he had got his bearings, incomplete without her. But the crowd was large and he sought her without success until the music began again, and she was danced past him once more.

This time she was in the arms of Peck, who was in his management seminar. Peck nodded to him, smiled at him. Nick scowled. Then they turned and Diane twirled in his direction, saw him and smiled a smile that stilled his fears.

He wanted her now more than he'd ever wanted her. And she disappeared into the throng again.

He didn't see her after that dance, either. Or the next. She was, if not the belle of the ball, certainly one of its foremost lights. While he fidgeted on the sidelines, trying again to catch a glimpse of her, she twirled about the room in the arms of all and sundry. And when he finally did spy her, he was trapped next to a potted palm, captive to three lawyers discussing obscure points of constitutional law.

Nick took a hasty swallow of his still full glass of champagne, slipped out from behind the lawyers and moved in her direction.

He didn't know who her partner was. He was certainly distinguished, clearly handsome, and probably far more eligible than Nick himself. But all evening long his desire for her had been building. It was time to make his move.

He didn't know if Miss Manners or Emily Post or the CEOs in attendance tonight approved of cutting in on dancers. He didn't stop to find out.

He stepped forward and tapped her partner on the shoulder. He turned, his smile fading into puzzlement.

"This dance is mine," Nick said.

"But—"

"Believe me. I'll take good care of her," he promised, then swept her away in his arms.

She smiled up at him, equally starry-eyed and bemused. "I think you shocked Justice Hammond."

"Probably." He didn't care himself, but it occurred to him that Diane might. "Does it matter?" he asked her.

"Not to me. I'm flattered."

"He's more eligible than I am. So's Peck for that matter," Nick said gruffly, wanting to make sure she understood.

"That doesn't matter, either," she said looking straight into his eyes, shrinking the universe until it contained none but the two of them. "No one matters but you."

Chapter Five

Nick was a here-and-now man. A doer.

He'd never been much for fairy tales, and before tonight, even though he'd had hopes, he would have said that that was what this was.

But tonight, with Diane in his arms, with the cellos playing, the trees aglitter, and the rise and fall of cheerful conversation all around him, he finally believed.

Tonight had been the proving ground, the place in which fantasies were tested, and Nick—and his fantasy—had been proved.

He had faced his fears. He had lived through, even enjoyed, an evening in Diane's milieu. He had handled it with aplomb. He knew that whatever future events her society background threw at him, he always could.

Of course he couldn't have her yet. There was one more hurdle to jump. One more year and he would have his degree, the symbol of success that would make him her equal. One more year and he wouldn't feel inferior to Gertrude Hoffmann, to Cynthia Bauer, and to all the St. Louis blue bloods who would wonder at her marrying a man like Nick Granatelli.

He wanted her now. This minute. It had been all he could do this evening to take her up to her door, kiss her with a hunger that ate at his very innards, then leave her to go to his own solitary bed.

But he'd done it because he believed in a future for the two of them.

Even now, still wanting her, still aching for the fulfillment of his love for her, he stayed in bed instead of heading for her room.

He stayed because the future he envisioned with Diane was one he would do everything in his power to make perfect, even if it meant holding off on the fulfillment of his more immediate desires.

He closed his eyes and focused on some nebulous future date in which he stood outside a home just slightly less grand than this one, Diane at his side, smiling up at him, loving him, while a bevy of golden-haired children played at their feet, and a cadre of contented relatives, both his and hers, smiled benevolently in the background.

It didn't make his yearning for her go away, but it did make it bearable.

And, if he allowed himself a few more carnal fantasies before the night was over, well, no one ever said Nick Granatelli was a saint.

THE BRISK TAPPING on the door woke him not long after dawn. Nick groaned, stretched and scowled at the bedside clock. It wasn't even six.

He'd been having a marvelous dream, better—or at least more graphic—than his deliberate fantasies of the night before.

Diane had featured prominently in it. So had the queen-size bed in which he now lay. They had been lying there together, naked, loving, their bodies growing hot and eager for the fulfillment they had so far denied themselves.

The dream was fading rapidly, but the need in his body

was not. He hauled himself to a sitting position, waiting for another tap, wondering if he'd imagined it.

And if he hadn't…

It came again. Brisk. Impatient. But not loud.

Diane?

Could it possibly be Diane? No, he thought at once. But then a tiny voice inside him asked who else it could possibly be.

He closed his eyes in a moment of thankful prayer, then shifted the sheet to preserve his modesty, leaned back against the pillows, smiled and said, "Come in."

It was a maid he'd never seen before.

"Sorry to disturb you, sir," she said quickly, ducking her head. "You're Mr. Granatelli?"

Nick nodded, frowning.

"There's a phone call for you, sir. A Mr. Flynn."

Flynn? *Jared?* What the hell? Nick started to get up, remembered he was naked, and nodded. "I'll be right there."

"You can take it in Mr. Hamilton's study, sir. To the right at the foot of the stairs." She gave him a quick smile and left, shutting the door behind her.

Nick scrambled out of bed, snagged his jeans off the top of the bureau and pulled them on. Still zipping them he padded toward the door, opened it and headed down the hall.

Gardner Hamilton's study was right at the bottom of the marble staircase. Paneled in cherry, with glove-leather furniture and a thick Oriental rug, it seemed warm and welcoming on a still-chilly May morning. Nick curled his toes into the pile of the carpet and picked up the phone.

"Jared? What's wrong?"

"It's your father."

Nick groaned. "Cripes, what is it this time? More basil?"

"Basil?" Jared sounded doubtful. "I don't think so. He had a heart attack."

"IT'LL BE ALL RIGHT," Diane said. They were speeding back up the highway toward Boston in Bennett's Porsche. "I'm sure he'll be fine."

She wasn't sure at all. She was babbling and she knew it. She'd been babbling ever since Nick had banged on her door almost before it was light.

At first she'd thought Dominic Granatelli had died.

Nick, stunned into incoherence, had just kept saying, "He had a heart attack. My dad had a heart attack." His face had been chalky, his hands cold.

It had taken Diane several minutes to discover that, in fact, the senior Granatelli was still among the living. But just how bad he was, Nick didn't know.

"Do they want you to fly home?" she'd asked, putting her arms around him, holding him.

He had shaken his head. "I don't know."

"What hospital is he in?"

"I don't know that, either!" He pulled away, pacing irritably, slamming his hand down on the fireplace mantel. "I don't know what they want. I don't know what hospital he's in. I don't know how he is. I don't know anything at all, damn it!"

She put her hand on his bare arm. "I'll pack."

She had packed, first her things, then his. At her request the maid had awakened Ben who came hurrying from his own room wanting to know what he could do.

Nick, still pacing, didn't answer. Diane gave Ben a quick, grateful smile. "Just find out the quickest way for us to get back to Boston, will you?"

Nick raked his hand through his hair. "Find out the bus schedule," he snapped.

"Take my car," Ben said when he was told. "I'll have it brought around for you."

"I can't—" Nick began.

But Diane nodded. "Thanks."

Ben left hurriedly. Diane slid Nick's tux into the garment bag and zipped it up. "There. All set. Let's go."

She handed him the bag and his duffel, picked up her own and led the way downstairs. Numbly, Nick followed.

Ben's parents and brother were waiting at the bottom of the steps, all concerned and solicitous.

"If we can help…" Mr. Hamilton said.

"Do let us know." Mrs. Hamilton squeezed Nick's hand.

Tom clapped him on the shoulder. "Drive carefully."

But Nick didn't drive at all. He just stood there, dazed. It was Diane who stuffed the luggage into the back and then slipped behind the wheel of Ben's Porsche.

She looked up into Ben's family's faces. "Thank you all so much. I'll leave your car at your place," she told Ben.

"Don't worry about it. Here's a map in case you need it. Just see that he gets there." Ben's gaze went to Nick.

Diane smiled. "I will. Thanks again."

And without a backward glance, she set off.

Nick sat in silence beside her, his face still pale, a muscle working in his cheek. His hands clenched and unclenched against his thighs.

"Check the map for me, will you?" Diane said. "See if I'm on the right road for getting out of town."

Nick blinked at her. "Huh?"

"The map," Diane said patiently. "I don't know my way around."

Nick fumbled with the map, folded it open, stared at it blankly. "What if he dies?" he blurted.

Diane reached for his hand. "I don't think he's going to die," she said steadily. "He's what? Fifty-three?"

"Four," Nick said dully. "Fifty-four. He turned fifty-four in April, the thirtieth."

"He's a bull, then," Diane said. She gave his hand a squeeze. "A Taurus. They don't give up without a fight."

She wanted Nick to smile. She willed him to smile. But he didn't. He only clenched his jaw and shut his eyes against the world.

She groped her way out of Newport by dint of instinct and the occasional road sign. She couldn't read the map and drive at the same time, and Nick was no help at all.

"Jared said Frankie would call when they knew something," he said, staring blindly out the window as they sped through Fall River heading north. He pressed his palms against his eyes. "I wonder if they know something."

"Do you want to stop and call?"

"No. I'll wait." He gave a despairing laugh. "Who would I call? Where would I call them?"

Diane pressed harder on the accelerator. It was all she could do to help.

The traffic going into the city on Saturday morning was light and they made good time. Still there was no place near Nick's to park so Diane just pulled up at the curb.

"I'll let you off so you can see if they've called. I'll take Ben's car to his place and leave it, then come back. Okay?"

Nick was out of the car and heading up the steps without looking back.

IT WAS UNREAL. It all looked the same—his apartment with its mismatched lumpy and splintery furniture, its cache of unwashed dishes, its scattered books and papers, his final paper in Ethics still in rough form lying beside the computer, Jared's script on top of the refrigerator.

Yet it wasn't the same.

It was a whole new world, Nick thought as he punched

out the telephone number on the slip of paper that Jared had handed him.

It was a world in which by now his father might be dead.

Jared hadn't been able to tell him much. When Frankie had called, she'd been gabbling, frantic.

Dominic had awakened in the middle of the night with indigestion, she'd told him. But it became clear quite soon that it was far more than that. When baking soda didn't quell his discomfort, and walking the floor only seemed to make it worse, he'd finally let Teresa call the hospital.

"He got worse before the paramedics got there," Jared had told Nick when he came in. "She said they were using all sorts of stuff to keep him going while they took him to the hospital."

"What hospital?" Nick demanded.

"She called back later to give me this number."

The number Nick was calling now.

It was a direct line to the Intensive Care Unit, but once he got it, Nick could barely form the words.

When he did, there was a pause, a "one moment, please," dead silence, then a nurse saying, "Mr. Granatelli is doing as well as can be expected right now."

Which meant, Nick hoped, that he wasn't dead. At least he didn't think "as well as can be expected" covered that particular eventuality.

"But how is he?" he demanded.

"One moment. I'll let you speak with Mrs. Granatelli. The doctor just talked to her."

Nick waited what seemed an interminable time.

Finally, "It's Frankie. Ma's in with Dad now. They only let you in for a minute or two every half hour."

"What happened?"

Frankie repeated most of what she'd told Jared, the information he already knew. "He had a small heart attack before Mama called the doctor and a major one while they were at the house." She swallowed and Nick heard her voice break. "He was so white, Nick. It was bad. Scary. I've never seen him so..."

She stopped and gulped back a sob. "And Mama...oh, God, Nicky. I've never seen Mama so upset."

Nick could well imagine. Teresa Granatelli's sun rose and set on her husband. He was the center of her world. "What about now? How is he now?"

"Stable, I think. A little better."

"Is he...do they think he's..." But Nick couldn't even bring himself to ask.

"Going to make it?" Frankie said shakily into the silence. "I think so." She paused, then qualified. "I hope so. Who knows?" she almost wailed after a moment. "The doctors come out and tell you about his enzyme levels and his potassium. They do EKGs and have all these things that go bleep-bleep. But I don't know what it means. I don't know what any of it means! It's scaring the hell out of me!"

"I know." It was scaring the hell out of him, too.

Dominic Granatelli was invincible, unconquerable, the mainstay, the guiding light of his family's life, the rock on which the Granatelli fortress had been built.

Nick couldn't conceive of his father hurt, pained, laid low. He couldn't imagine a world in which Dominic Granatelli wasn't in control.

"What can I do?" he asked. There must be something. Damn it, there had to be!

Frankie didn't answer at once. It wasn't a question he'd ever asked her. It wasn't a question any of them had ever asked. They'd never had to; they'd always been told.

"I don't..." she began and her voice faded.

"I mean," Nick said hastily, realizing that she was no more used to making decisions than he was, "do you want

me to come home now or what? Shall I catch a plane today?''

"I—I'll ask Mama.''

"Then call me, will you? Call me right back.''

"I will.''

She hung up, but he didn't. He hung on to the receiver
as if, even with the connection broken, the phone itself
somehow linked him with his family. With his father.

"THANK GOD you're here,'' Jared said, hauling Diane un-
ceremoniously into the apartment.

She glimpsed Nick across the room with his back to her,
his ear to the phone. "What is it?'' she demanded. "Is
he—''

"He's talking to his sister now.'' Jared crossed his fingers. "I don't know the latest, but I've gotta run. We have
a matinee at one. I was supposed to be there by ten, but I
didn't want to leave him alone.''

"No.'' Diane squeezed Jared's arm. "He's not alone
now,'' she said. "I'll stay.''

"Right.'' Jared shot Nick one last worried glance and left.

Diane stayed, watching him, worrying herself.

She wanted to do something, fix something, comfort him,
make everything better. And she couldn't. It was out of her
hands.

He had stopped talking now. She supposed he was listening. But then, slowly, he put the receiver down and stood
motionless staring out the window.

She shifted from one foot to the other and the floor
creaked beneath her. The sound seemed to penetrate his
awareness. He turned, his face reflecting surprise at seeing
her there.

"Where's Jared?''

"He had a performance. He wanted to stay, but—''

Nick raked his fingers through his hair. "I know. I know." He sighed and shut his eyes. "The show must go on." He didn't sound bitter, just dazed.

Diane went to him then, taking his hands in hers and simply holding them. They were still icy, and she chafed them between hers, trying to warm them. "Did you talk to the doctor?"

He shook his head. "My sister." He told her briefly what Frankie had told him, then bit down on his lower lip. "All of which means basically nothing at this point. We don't know a damned thing." There was a frantic note in his voice.

Diane held his hands more tightly. "You know he's hanging in there."

Nick bent his head so his forehead touched hers. Then he took a deep breath, held it, and then, slowly and deliberately, let it out. "Yeah," he said. "We know that."

Diane laid her hand against the nape of his neck, massaging the tense cords, ruffling his hair with her fingers, wishing again that she didn't feel so helpless.

"God," Nick muttered. "I don't believe this. I mean, just last night... just this morning I was...we were..." His voice trailed off, achingly.

"I know," Diane said and pulled him down onto the couch beside her. "I know."

There was nothing to do but wait. There were papers to write, notes to go over, exams to study for, but Nick did none of them, only sat, staring into the distance, his mind, his heart, more than a thousand miles away.

And Diane, whose heart was right here with him in this very room, could sit beside him just so long. Then she got up to move around quietly, make him cups of tea, touch him in passing, and listen to him whenever he muttered. But she didn't leave him even when her own finals, her own papers, her own life beckoned. None of it mattered so much as Nick.

Finally at just past two Frankie called back. Nick talked to her briefly, then to his mother. When he got off the phone he still looked shaken.

"He's hanging in there. They're planning to do a heart catheterization tomorrow if he's still doing all right. Then they'll be able to assess the damage and know what they're going to do."

"What about you?"

"I'm flying out tonight. I have to be there. I have to," he repeated.

And, seeing the tightness in his jaw, the strain in his face and the haunted look in his eyes, Diane knew that he did.

"I'll pack for you," she told him. "You book a ticket, then call your profs."

Having a goal, knowing what he was going to do, seemed to help.

Nick booked a flight, called his ethics prof and arranged to send in his paper, then began gathering together the books and papers he'd need.

Diane finished packing, then made sandwiches which neither of them ate.

"I can't," Nick said after one bite, and got up to pace the room.

"You haven't had anything all day," Diane reminded him. "Who knows when you'll get another chance?"

Nick shrugged. "They'll serve dinner on the plane."

Diane feigned hurt. "You'd rather eat airplane food than mine?"

For the first time that day a faint smile flickered across Nick's face. He crossed the room and put his arms around her.

"No," he said and brushed his lips across her cheek,

leaning against her the warm, welcome weight of his body. "I'd rather have your peanut butter sandwiches than any airline's plastic shish kebab. I just...I just..." He sighed, and tried again, "I just can't."

And Diane held him in her arms, rested her head on his shoulder, rubbed her hands up and down his back, and loved him with all the love of which she was capable. "I know," she whispered. "I understand."

THE HOSPITAL was another alien world. A world of stainless steel and disposable plastic, of beepers and monitors, of leads and bags and tubes.

What mattered here was not the merger of Feinemann Plastics with ABC Chemical, was not the questionable ethical compromise when XYZ took over RST, was not the cost and quality of fresh basil or the best year for *Asti Spumante.*

What mattered—the only thing that mattered—was Dominic Granatelli's life.

All the way home on the plane Nick had told himself his father would be all right. His mother had said he was stable, that he was "doing well," that things were looking better.

He made himself believe it.

He wasn't aware, though, of how very much he'd wanted to believe it until he walked into the Intensive Care Unit and saw his father at the mercy of all those machines.

This was "stable"? This was "doing well"?

This was a man on the edge of death, a man held back from the brink by heaven knew what tenuous threads.

As he walked toward the immobile figure lying on the high, steel-edged bed, Nick felt as if someone had punched him in the gut.

"D-dad?"

Slowly his father's eyes opened, focused on him, blinked. His lips moved but no sound came out.

"I'm here," Nick said softly.

Dominic's hand moved, and Nick reached for it, feeling the rough fingers curl weakly around his. He swallowed against the tightening in his throat.

"Nick. Good." Dominic managed something resembling a smile. "Take care of…rest…restaurant."

Nick rubbed his father's hand. "I will. Don't worry. I'll take care of everything."

Dominic's lips worked again, but no words came out. The few that he said had exhausted him. He, however, managed another smile.

It was his father's smile that Nick clung to over the next twenty-four hours. It was the memory of that smile that helped him leave the hospital when everyone else was coming so that he could do what he knew his father wanted him to do—go to the restaurant and keep everything running the way it should.

Granatelli's restaurant was the family's livelihood, its security, the one sure thing that stood between the family and economic peril.

As such it had to be cared for at any cost, even if it meant that while Frankie and Carlo, Vinnie and Paula and Sophia took turns going in with Teresa to see Dominic every half hour, Nick wasn't there.

The supplies had to be logged in, the orders made, the laundry delivery received, the dirty linens sent out. Little things. Big things. Necessary things.

So when everyone else hovered around waiting while Dominic went down for his heart catheterization the following day, when everyone else paced the hallways waiting for the doctor's verdict, when everyone else conferred about Dominic's scheduled surgery, Nick wasn't there.

SHE'D ASKED him to call.

He did. Once.

He sounded distant, vague. Not like Nick at all.

Diane worried, fretted, stewed. She finished her own papers, took her last finals, paid her library fines, picked up her cap and gown for Saturday's commencement exercise. But all the while, she worried about Nick.

She hesitated to call him. She didn't want to intrude, didn't want to distract him, didn't want to create pressure in a situation where there was clearly already more than enough.

But she did want to know. She cared what happened to Dominic Granatelli.

She loved Nick.

It was Jared who finally got some news and Annie who passed it on to Diane.

"He's on his way," Annie said without preamble, walking into the apartment.

Diane, who'd been trying to decide if she dared call her father and invite him to her graduation the next morning, thereby risking a confrontation between her father and her mother and stepfather or, worse, one between her father and grandmother, suddenly forgot them all. "Who?"

"Your one true love."

All her worries fled in the face of the news. "Nick? He's coming? Now?"

Annie nodded. "Jared said he called this morning."

For a moment Diane wondered why he hadn't called her. But then she realized she'd been gone all morning, spending one last tutoring session with her French students, so she wouldn't have been here even if he had.

"What else did he say?"

"Not much. His dad came through the surgery all right.

Quintuple bypass, Jared said.'' Annie grimaced. ''Sounds pretty rough to me.''

It sounded rough to Diane, too. The one time Nick had called her, he had just found out that his father was going to have surgery. At the time he hadn't known when or how extensive it would be.

Still, Dominic must be doing well now if Nick was returning. For the first time since Nick had told her the news, she felt as if a weight had been lifted off her chest.

She smiled. She grinned. She closed her eyes, breathed deeply and then opened them again to a brighter, newer world.

''Thank God,'' she said.

She called Jared. ''How's he getting home? When's he coming in?''

''He said he'd take a taxi. He should be getting here about ten.''

''I'll meet him.''

''You can't,'' Annie reminded her. ''It's dinner at the Ritz tonight. Remember?''

Diane hadn't. In fact she'd totally forgotten her graduation dinner. At ten she would be in her parents' hotel suite visiting with Cynthia and Matthew and Gertrude who had come for her graduation.

There was no tactful way to get out of it. They didn't even know Nick existed, and the logistics of the family celebration dinner before her graduation had all been planned for months.

Matthew had, with his customary consideration, called her clear back in February to find out where she wanted to go to celebrate.

''I just want to be with all of you,'' she told him.

''Then we'll eat in the suite,'' he replied. ''I think that's a fine idea. Easier on your grandmother, too.''

Gertrude cultivated the notion that things should be made easier for her. She was, after all, she told them frequently, "not as young as she used to be."

Privately Diane didn't think age was slowing her grandmother down at all. But if she wanted to propagate the image of herself as a doddering septuagenarian, who was her granddaughter to oppose her?

"Sounds fine," she'd said to her stepfather. "I'm looking forward to it."

Since Nick had left, though, she'd all but forgotten it.

Now she groaned as the mantle of family obligation settled on her shoulders.

"Tell Nick…" She cast about for something appropriate and could think of nothing. She wanted to tell Jared to tell Nick she loved him. But so far she hadn't even told it to him herself.

"Tell him I'll call him in the morning or he should call me. All right? Tell him I wanted to be there, but…" She trailed off, helpless.

"I'll tell him," Jared assured her. "He'll understand."

Diane hoped so.

SHE HADN'T SEEN her parents or grandmother since Christmas. Five whole months. It seemed a lifetime. Yet her first impression, when her mother opened the hotel suite door that evening, was that none of them had changed a bit.

Diane had.

At Christmas she had been a child, smiling, blissful, innocent, unaware. Now she had awakened to the potential of her womanhood. She had fallen in love.

She stood motionless in the doorway wondering if they could tell.

Was her love of Nick written as clearly on her face as it was rooted in the depths of her soul?

Whatever showed on her face, Cynthia Bauer was obviously overjoyed to see it. She flung her arms around her daughter, hugging Diane for all she was worth.

Then, stepping back, she held Diane at arm's length, her blue eyes shining as she looked her over from head to toe.

Diane found that she was looking at her mother with new eyes, too. Though she was aware of having her mother's honey-blond hair and figure, she knew that her features were her father's. She had Russell Shaw's wide brown eyes, his slightly shy smile.

Did her mother see those things? Diane wondered. Did she ever think about him?

Had she loved him once the way Diane loved Nick?

And what about her love of Matthew?

They were questions she'd never really dwelt on before. Adult questions. She couldn't ask. At least not now. But seeing her mother and Matthew again, receiving their embraces, their love, made her wonder.

It also settled her debate about asking her father to her graduation.

She had learned to like the man who'd fathered her. She was, in a way, coming to love him. But she wasn't going to call him.

It would please her if he came to her graduation. But loving Nick had sensitized her more than ever to the feelings of others, and she knew that chances were too great that either he or Cynthia—possibly even Matthew—could be hurt.

She looked into her mother's face now, then her gaze shifted to Matthew who was smiling at her with equal love and pride.

"I think graduation is making a woman of our girl, Cynthia," he said to his wife.

Cynthia hugged her once more. "I think you're right."

Diane could have told them what had really done it. But she didn't—not then. That would come later, when the time was right.

She answered Matthew's questions about the ceremony, her mother's about where Annie was and if her parents had arrived. She crossed the room to where her grandmother sat in regal elegance, bent down and kissed Gertrude's lightly rouged cheek.

"You look wonderful," she told her grandmother.

"Ought to," Gertrude said tartly. "I work hard enough at it."

Diane smiled and sat down next to her when Gertrude patted the seat of the couch. The conversation became easy and general.

Diane, for the most part, contributed little. She sat back after the meal and listened while Gertrude held forth, while Cynthia added the occasional tidbit, while Matthew interposed a comment here and there.

Most of the time she thought about Nick, wondered if he was back yet, wondered how he was, how his father was doing.

Only when Gertrude raised her voice, did she attend carefully to the conversation.

"Flo's a scatterhead, if you ask me," Gertrude said now. "I know she's your sister, Matthew, but that's no excuse. It's outrageous. One never knows what she's going to do next."

"But she's wonderful with Diane, Mother," Cynthia said quietly. "And it's so kind of her to ask Diane to spend the summer with her."

"Probably wants her to carry the luggage," Gertrude sniffed. "Don't know why I let you talk me into it."

"It will be good for Diane," Matthew said with gentle firmness. "She needs a chance to spread her wings."

Gertrude fiddled with her glasses. "In my day girls didn't need to spread their wings," she said. "Did what they were told."

"Diane always does what she's told," Cynthia reminded her mother in a light tone.

Gertrude looked down her considerable nose. "Better than some, I suppose," she agreed shortly.

Diane saw her mother stiffen, but she didn't reply.

"Anyway, it's settled," Matthew said briskly, stepping between his wife and her mother, ending the discussion right there.

He was so good at that, Diane thought. Matthew could always diffuse the tensions that built up between the Hoffmann women. He never raised his voice, never argued, never fought. He just spoke, clearly and forthrightly, and even Gertrude didn't dare disagree with him.

Under the circumstances Diane didn't think that now was the time to tell them she'd changed her mind about spending the summer with Flo.

She would talk to them later, first Matthew, then her mother and, if necessary, her grandmother. Matthew would help her handle whatever problems arose.

She straightened her dress and stood up. "I really need to go," she told them. "I have a big day tomorrow."

Cynthia laughed. "Indeed you do. Are you sure you won't stay here?"

Diane shook her head. "Thanks, but it's sort of special, really. My last night with Annie as an undergrad. We've been together four years."

"I'll see you home, then," Matthew said.

"I'll be fine in a taxi," Diane assured him. "You stay here. You're tired. I know you are."

It was an indication of how very tired he was that her

stepfather let her persuade him. But he did accompany her down and saw her into the taxi.

"Will we see you for breakfast?" He bent down and peered into the taxi.

"I don't think so. We've got to get ready." *And I've got to see Nick.* She gave Matthew an apologetic shrug and a quick smile.

He leaned down and pecked her cheek. "Then we'll see you at graduation, sweetheart."

The taxi pulled away, and Diane, already thinking about seeing Nick in the morning, already anticipating the feel of his arms around her and the touch of his lips on hers, didn't even look back as the cab turned the corner and drove out of sight.

Chapter Six

He had it all figured out.

He would dash over to Professor Riggs's office first thing, drop off the last case-study evaluation, which he'd been allowed to write up, then swing by his other professors' offices, get their comments, check his grades.

Not because it mattered now. Not even the paper mattered now.

But for purely academic reasons and just a bit of personal satisfaction, he wanted to know.

Then he'd come back and finish packing, say goodbye to Jared, hope to catch Diane and Annie and wish them well. Then he would head back for the airport and take off.

It was simple.

Organized.

The way he'd done everything lately.

The way he was running his life.

He did well, too, making the stop at Riggs's brief and perfunctory. His explanation about his situation was brief, too. If Riggs didn't understand, well, it couldn't be helped. Nick was simply doing what had to be done.

He did the same with Edmonds and Cooper. Their comments were favorable. His grades were good. They would, he knew, have served him well. He felt a momentary satisfaction. The regrets he wouldn't dwell on now.

He got back to the apartment just as Jared was waking up.

His roommate rolled over in bed and regarded him and then all the gear lined up by the door with one half-opened eye.

"You've already packed?" His tone was incredulous, and as they really hadn't had a chance to talk the day before, Nick couldn't blame him.

He consulted his watch. "Got to." He grimaced. "Flight's at one."

"Flight?" Jared sat up, rubbing his fists against his eyes. "You'll be leaving?"

"I'm leaving."

"Your father? Is he worse, then?"

Nick's smile was grim. "He's recovering. But it will be a long, long haul, and even then we don't know how much he'll be able to do." He shrugged and stuck out his hand. "I've left my share of the rent with Mrs. Patchin. I wish I could've hung on a bit longer, but—" He shrugged again.

Jared inclined his head briefly, then shook Nick's hand. "You do what you have to do," he said simply.

Their eyes met in complete understanding.

Nick nodded. "Yeah. That's it."

The last thing he had to do before he left was stop to see Diane and Annie.

He supposed he could have gone without taking the time. In the end, of course, it would make no difference.

Something else that didn't matter now, he thought as he lugged his gear down the stairs and left it by the front door.

But it was the right thing to do—the polite thing to do. So he would stop by, explain his plans and say goodbye before going.

It would be brief. Ten minutes. No more.

He opened the door and saw Diane coming up the walk.

She was smiling, her long hair streaming out behind her, her arms opening to him as she came.

Nick felt something twist in his heart.

And then she had her arms around him, her hair in his face. And he was drowning in the lemon scent of her shampoo and the soft, flowery freshness that was Diane alone. Automatic and unbidden, his arms came up to hold her close.

"I'm sorry I wasn't there last night. I wanted to come. I missed you so much. I— Oh, Nick!" And she kissed him full on the lips.

And whatever was twisting inside him tore then, as, for one desperate moment, he kissed her back.

Then he pulled away, looked down into her welcoming eyes, steeled himself, and forced a smile.

"I was just coming to see you."

She beamed. "I beat you to it."

A moment of silence, of expectation, hung between them. Then Diane took his hands in hers. "Your father? Is he better?"

"Some."

"I thought he must be since you're here." She smiled up at him again. "I'm so glad you're back. I don't begrudge them wanting you there, but I—"

"I...came to get my gear."

His words halted hers. A tiny frown appeared between Diane's brows as she looked at him. "What do you mean?"

"I'm going back."

"Back? To St. Louis?"

He nodded.

"When?"

"Today. I have a flight at one."

There was another pause while she digested that. "For the end of the year," she said. "You finished your paper? Turned it in?"

"Yes."

Traffic hummed past them as they stood on the sidewalk. Pedestrians pushed past them. A bus, chugging away from the corner, choked them with diesel fumes.

"Well, good," Diane said, mustering a smile. "Then you've finished everything up."

He nodded.

Now, he told himself. *Tell her now.* But he couldn't say it. Couldn't form the words.

He let go of her hands and stuffed his own in the pockets of his jeans. He studied the toes of his shoes, watched a gum wrapper blow past down the street.

"I'll be coming home in a week," Diane told him. Unable to take his hand, she laid hers on his arm. "I'll come and see you then. Maybe I can meet your father. I—"

"No."

Her eyes jerked up to meet his. "Only if he's well enough," she said hastily. "I won't intrude. I just—"

Nick shook his head quickly, desperately. "No. No, it's not that. It's—" He stopped, casting about for a way to express the inexpressible. He thought wryly of all those management classes, all the glib verbal footwork he'd been so good at in class. "Golden-tongued Granatelli," Ben used to call him.

But now—when it mattered—he couldn't say a word.

Diane was looking at him, her eyes wide and almost frightened now. There was a bewildered innocence in her face that made him ache.

But it was just exactly that innocence that made him press on with what he had to say.

He took a breath and began. "I'm not coming back next year."

"Not…"

"I can't! It isn't that I don't want to. I can't. I have to work now, full-time, at the restaurant. It's on my shoulders. All of it."

"Your father…"

"Is in for a long recovery. He's doing all right. But the doctor isn't making any promises about when or if he'll be back at work. He's got to live a whole new life-style. New diet, new behavior. No stress. And for him no stress means no restaurant." He met her gaze steadily, determinedly, almost defiantly.

For a long while Diane didn't speak. She bit down on her lip, obviously weighing his words.

"That doesn't mean we—" she began finally.

Knowing what was coming, he moved to cut it off. "It means, there is no 'we.'" He said the words harshly, with every ounce of determination he could muster.

And he meant them.

He'd done a lot of thinking during the last week in the wee hours of the night, which was just about the only time he had to think anymore. And the conclusion he had come to was that a future with Diane Bauer was a pipe dream.

Once it might have seemed remotely possible. Once, when an MBA was a probability, when a privileged future was a possibility, he had the right to consider it.

He couldn't consider it now.

She couldn't consider it now.

He thought about the night they'd gone to Jared's play, how astonished he'd been at gifts his roommate had that he hadn't even suspected, that hadn't had a chance to be revealed until Jared was given the opportunity.

It was the same with Diane. He thought how she'd blossomed the night of the Hamiltons' party, how she'd charmed every person she'd met. She belonged in an environment like that. She deserved opportunities like that.

He couldn't promise her any.

On the contrary, all he could promise her was a future on The Hill. It was all right for him. He'd been groomed for it. He understood it. It would simply stifle her.

"To love someone is to want what's the best for them," his grandfather had once told him.

Nick knew what was best.

"Forget me," he said gruffly when she didn't speak.

"Forget you?" Diane looked at him, aghast.

He shrugged negligently. "There are bound to be plenty of men willing to come along and take my place."

She looked stricken. "But I don't want any other man!"

Oh, hell. Nick's fists clenched in his pockets. His toes curled inside his shoes. He held himself rigid, controlled. "Don't be stupid," he said.

Diane's eyes widened. She opened her mouth, but no sound came out.

"Look," Nick said, desperate. "I'm not coming back. I'm not getting my MBA I'm going home to St. Louis and I'm going to be there the rest of my freakin' life. I have a family there and they need me! I have to go!"

She didn't even hesitate. She lifted her chin and looked right at him. "I'll come with you," she said.

For a split second he wanted to say yes. He wanted to grab her offer with both hands and hold it tight. He wanted to hold her tight, to close his eyes and believe that dreams might come true, that good might prevail, that a future for the two of them together might go on happily ever after.

He wasn't that much of a fool.

"Marry me, you mean?" he asked her now with gentle mockery.

There was a stricken pause, as if she had just realized what she was offering, as if she'd just noticed that, standing in the middle of a crowded sidewalk, she might actually have made a proposal of marriage. She hesitated, color rioting on her cheeks.

Nick wanted to reach out and brush his thumbs across them. His nails bit into the palms of his hands. He allowed himself a small smile as he said simply, lightly, "It wouldn't work."

Diane, obviously deciding that yes, she had proposed and meant it, lifted her chin. "Why not?"

"Think about it. Really think about it. Think about a future with me there. Would you be happy on The Hill for the rest of your life?"

"If you're—"

"Don't say, if you're there. It won't wash." He made his voice deliberately hard. "You're kidding yourself. You don't know what my life is like. You've had it easy, Diane. Anything you wanted, you got."

"That's not fair, Nick!"

He shrugged. "Life isn't fair. I wouldn't be quitting school if life was fair. But it isn't and I am. I have a job to do, a family to support, a life already laid out for me."

"Nick—"

"Listen to me. You don't even know who you are yet. You're only twenty-two years old. You've got your whole life ahead of you. You can do anything, go anywhere, meet anyone. You don't know what you want. And I'm damned if I'm going to wake up some morning with a discontented wife, a wife who thinks the world has passed her by because she's stuck with a guy running a restaurant for a living. I have enough on my plate without that."

She stared at him, her jaw slack.

"It was fun while it lasted," he said, moving in for the kill. "You're a nice kid. But it won't work. It would never work. I have my life all cut out for me. You don't fit."

Chapter Seven

New York City, September 1990

"Ma, no. Ma!" Annie could say it in her sleep now. "No, forget it." Pause. "I don't believe this."

This last, muttered to herself, wasn't true. Lucia D'Angelo's matchmaking attempts had become the one constant in Annie's otherwise unpredictable life. Still, it didn't mean she welcomed them.

"Ma..."

But Ma went on. And on.

Annie considered strangling herself with the phone cord, then wished her mother were closer so she could strangle her instead.

"Ma, I don't—" But it didn't matter what she didn't because Lucia D'Angelo was in full spate again. Annie glowered out at the brief summer thunderstorm that was making the rain sluice down the windows of her West Side apartment. Her mother's voice rose and fell on the other end of the line.

There was another pause. "No," Annie said into it. "How many times? How many men? I don't want you to send me any more men, Mother! I'm through with men!"

More cajoling. More plaintive guilt-inspiring lamentations emanated from her mother.

"I don't care if he's handsome, Ma." Annie banged her head softly against the windowpane. "I don't care if he's Italian. I don't—"

There was a sudden *brrrring* from the buzzer at her door. Annie frowned. Nobody had buzzed to be let in downstairs.

But then, she thought, when did that make a difference? With eight apartments in the brownstone where she lived, somebody was always letting somebody else's guests in.

Lucia, having taken her daughter's pause for the opportunity to get in more of her current hopeful's qualifications, rattled on.

There was a second ring. Sharp and insistent.

Annie crossed the room and peeked through the spyhole. Startled, she pulled back, frowned, then peeked again. Shaking her head, she hurriedly unlocked and jerked open the door. She stopped dead and stared.

Lucia kept on talking.

"Ma, I don't care. I don't want to know. Ma," Annie interrupted her, "I'm not interested in your handsome Italian hunks. Right here on the doorstep I've got one of my own."

And she hung up before Lucia could say another word.

"Nick."

It wasn't a question. There *was* no question.

It was definitely Nick, as large as life and as handsome as ever—if you discounted the several days' stubble on his cheeks—standing in the doorway looking back at her.

He wore holey sneakers, faded jeans and a St. Louis University sweatshirt with the sleeves cut short and the neck ripped out. And as much as he looked gorgeous, he also looked exhausted and rumpled. On the floor behind him were two navy duffel bags.

"Can I come in?"

There was a hesitancy in his voice that surprised her. Nick had never been short on self-confidence.

Of course, she hadn't seen him for a year and a half since cousin Mario's wedding. People changed, she thought grimly. She, of all people, should know that.

But she stepped back and waved him in, then shut the door behind him. "What are you doing here?"

"I'm running away from home."

HE KNEW IT SOUNDED melodramatic. Childish. Idiotic.

But he didn't know what else you could call it, really.

He had, in truth, run away from home.

And if he hadn't exactly stolen away in the dark of night or tied up all his worldly belongings in a bandanna and hitched a freight train north, he had still taken everything that mattered to him, loaded it silently and deliberately in the back of his '88 Toyota and, with his mother looking on in anguish, his brothers and sisters staring in amazement and his father caught in the middle of banging on the fender, he had driven off without looking back.

He hadn't said where he was going. He hadn't said when he'd be back. He hadn't said *if* he'd be back.

He wasn't sure he would be. Not at any time in the foreseeable future, at any rate.

"Does this mean you want me to hide you?" Annie asked him now, her expression curious and slightly bemused.

Nick flushed. "I don't think you'll have to, actually." His mouth twisted. "I doubt they're looking."

Annie's brows lifted. "You are Nick Granatelli, aren't you? Hotshot entrepreneur? Heir apparent? The whiz kid from Harvard who turned Granatelli's into the 'hottest spot on The Hill'? That's according to the *St. Louis Post-Dispatch*. The—"

"Stuff it," Nick said gruffly. He scowled and dug his toe into the worn carpet.

Annie gave him a quick smile and patted his arm. "Sorry. Just my flaky sense of humor getting the better of me." She slanted him a sideways glance. "You weren't kidding about running away?"

Nick sighed and shook his head.

She weighed that, then nodded. "So, you need a place to stay and you've come to Auntie Annie?"

He grimaced, then scratched the back of his head, feeling again like an idiot. He shouldn't have bothered Annie. He didn't know why he had. He'd been thinking of Jared when he'd headed this way. The summer he'd left Cambridge and returned to St. Louis, Annie and Jared had moved together to New York.

"You'll get lost there," Nick had warned them.

But Annie and Jared had shrugged happily. "It's a great city to get lost in," they'd told him. Besides, they had each other.

They were friends, Jared had told him. Colleagues. Yeah, sure, Nick had said, unable to believe that Jared's interest was only collegial. But all his speculation seemed to have been wrong.

Jared and Annie had, indeed, shared the apartment for a year. Then Jared had got a fantastic offer from Hollywood to star in a weekly adventure series about an Interpol investigator.

Nick had expected both he and Annie would go. It was a surprise, then, when Jared called him one day to talk about his new career and Nick had asked how Annie was.

"I haven't a clue," Jared had said.

"She isn't with you?"

"She isn't with me."

"But I thought—"

"Think again, my lad. Annie's an actress, remember? She has her own career in New York." If there was bitterness in Jared's voice, Nick wasn't quick enough to detect it. And as Jared had gone right on to talk about something else, that was the last overt reference either of them had made to Annie.

So they had been just good friends after all, Nick concluded. When Nick had seen Annie at her cousin Mario's wedding a year and a half ago, she'd confirmed it.

"Do you miss Jared?" Nick had asked her while they were dancing together.

She'd shrugged. "I have my work. And there's plenty to keep me busy in New York."

Perhaps it was the notion that there was plenty to keep one busy in New York that had drawn him to the city. Or maybe it was because, as he had told Annie and Jared earlier, one could get lost there.

Or maybe it was because Annie was the closest he could get right now to the person he suddenly found himself thinking about more than anyone.

The person he lay awake at night remembering.

Maybe he hadn't intended to come to New York at all. Maybe he'd just been passing through on his way to Cambridge when he came to his senses. Because, heaven knew, a part of him wanted to go back to Cambridge, to try to rethink things, to discover where he had gone wrong.

But there was no point in going on to Cambridge, he realized sometime on the third day of his wanderings.

You couldn't go back. You couldn't change things.

You simply had to go on.

"I—I drove around for a few days," he said when it became clear that Annie was waiting for an explanation. "I wasn't heading anywhere really. I...just ended up here. If you want me to leave—"

Annie rolled her eyes. "Don't be a fool. Put your gear in the bedroom. You can sleep on the sofa. You're welcome to stay as long as you want."

He hesitated, not having thought it would be that easy. But when Annie just waited expectantly, he nodded, picking up his duffel bags again and heading toward the bedroom. "Thanks, Annie. You're a pal."

"Oh, yes," Annie said dryly. "Oh, yes."

DIANE HAD BEEN STANDING in front of the restaurant for twenty minutes. Another five and she'd have to give up on Annie and head down to the Village lunchless. She never should have agreed to meet her given her schedule today, but when Annie insisted, one didn't say no.

At least Diane never had.

"Lunch?" she'd said when Annie had called her at eight in the morning jolting her out of a sound sleep. "You want to 'do' lunch?"

"Doing lunch" was not an Annie D'Angelo thing. Annie was a pizza-after-the-matinee, BBQ-after-the-night-show sort of person.

"Yeah, lunch," Annie said. "What's wrong with that? We've got to eat, don't we?"

"Well, yes, but..."

"I'll meet you at Fernando's at twelve."

"Make it eleven-thirty," Diane had said. "I've got a tour at one."

But it was now nearly twelve and Annie was nowhere to be seen.

Pacing up and down in front of Fernando's was a questionable activity at the best of times. A Chelsea dive whose only redeeming feature was its Tex Mex dim sum, Fernando's was not the best place for a single woman to hang out. Diane glanced at her watch once more before she moved toward the bus stop.

"Whoa! Wait! I'm here!"

Diane spun around to see Annie hurtling down the sidewalk toward her, waving madly. She stopped, looked at her watch, arched an eyebrow, tapped her foot.

Annie shrugged unrepentantly. "Sorry. I got caught in traffic. Should've taken the subway."

"I only have forty minutes," Diane told her as they went into the restaurant. "I have to be at Washington Square at one."

"What is it this time?"

"Writers' Paradise: lives, loves and landmarks of Village Literati," Diane recited as they slid into opposite sides of a cramped vinyl booth.

Annie grinned. "Very poetic. They ought to eat it up."

"They do."

"Business is booming?"

Diane nodded. She had been developing her own business in the last year—giving walking and bus tours to out-of-towners, in her case mostly non-English speaking tourists or business people.

She'd discovered the need during her work as a night concierge at a luxurious midtown hotel. She'd moved slowly at first, done some research, talked to people in the business—both the hotel and the tour business. Then, last April, when the walking tour season had begun again in earnest, so had Diane. She kept her concierge job for security for the time being. But Manhattan Meanderings was becoming an increasing success.

The waiter appeared with menus.

Annie waved him away. "Dim sum for both of us."

The waiter nodded and reappeared moments later with a

cart laden with a variety of house specialties, half of them Chinese, half of them Mexican.

Annie made her choices with her usual rapid-fire intensity. Diane pondered a bit, then picked two.

"That's all?" Annie scowled.

"I'm not very hungry. I'm trying to think." Diane poked at her cheese enchilada, then broke off a piece with her fork. "I've got to come up with a way to make Greenwich Village writers relevant to Japanese teenagers. I'm distracted, I guess."

"You'll be even more distracted when I tell you the news."

The fork paused halfway to Diane's mouth. "What news?"

"Nick's here."

Normally Fernando's at lunchtime was a place in which a person had to shout to hear himself think. It seemed to Diane that at that moment a drop of water hitting the ocean might have easily been heard.

It was her imagination, of course. The noise level was just what it always was. Only in her head was there this pool of unending silence.

Annie speared a wonton, dipped it in salsa and waved it on the end of her fork. "He's in my apartment this very minute."

Diane's enchilada fell unnoticed to her plate. She set her fork down and knotted her fingers together in her lap. "Nick," she said, as if the word were in a foreign language, incomprehensible, difficult to get her tongue around.

"Nick," Annie repeated. "Granatelli," she added helpfully in case there was some mistake.

But Diane hadn't made a mistake. For her there was only one Nick in all the world.

"Oh," she said after a long moment.

What else was there to say?

Nick Granatelli was part of her past. A memorable part, to be sure. But not a part she dwelt on often. Not a part she wanted to dwell on now.

In actual fact she felt acute discomfort whenever she thought about him very much. It was far better to gloss over the months when she had been a naive young idiot who thought that all she had to do was wait and the world—and a husband—would drop comfortably into her lap.

Deliberately she picked up her fork again and speared the piece of enchilada she had dropped, putting it into her mouth, chewing slowly, concentrating on the bustle of humanity swirling through Fernando's, on the talk she was going to have to give in less than an hour, on the date she was going to have with Carter MacKenzie tonight.

"He's run away from home."

Diane choked, then spluttered.

Annie grinned. "Truly. That's what he said."

Diane gave her a skeptical look. "What does it mean?"

"That he isn't working at Granatelli's anymore, apparently. That his father is back running things. That he just…left."

Diane didn't think that sounded very likely. Granatelli's was in Nick's blood. Sometimes she'd doubted he had blood at all, suspecting that it was perhaps spaghetti sauce that ran through his veins.

No, that was unfair, she chastised herself. He was simply committed to the family enterprise. She'd known that, had accepted it, had wanted to be a part of it.

Had been turned down.

Not enough spaghetti sauce in the Shaw-Hoffmann veins apparently.

Annie seemed to be waiting for some further response, so Diane shrugged. "I hope he's happy," she said, then deliberately finished off her enchilada and began picking her way through her refried beans and cashews.

"Is that all you can say?"

"What am I supposed to say?"

Annie gave her an impatient glower. "Once you wanted to marry him."

"Yes," Diane said, proud of how indifferent she sounded. "But, as you'll recall, he didn't want to marry me."

She shoved her plate away, glanced at her watch and slid out of the booth. "Got to run," she said. "Tours wait for no one." She pulled her wallet out of her purse.

"This one's on me," Annie said.

"But—"

"You've fed me often enough. The least I can do is treat you to a couple of refried beans." Annie was smiling up at her, her expression compassionate, understanding.

Diane felt unaccountably like slapping her. She didn't want compassion. She didn't want understanding. She was past both where Nick Granatelli was concerned. She just wanted to forget him and have everyone else forget him, too.

"See you Tuesday at softball," she said over her shoulder. "Thanks for lunch."

"Don't mention it."

Diane wouldn't. She wished Nick Granatelli hadn't been mentioned, either.

IT WAS ONE THING to refuse to go for the bait. It was quite another to deny that the bait had been offered.

And if Diane hadn't asked Annie any questions about Nick, it didn't mean she wasn't interested in the answers.

She took her fifteen Japanese university students on a brisk Village walk, pointing out the former homes of writers

like John Dos Passos, Sherwood Anderson, Henry James,
Mark Twain, Edna St. Vincent Millay, e.e. cummings, Mari-
anne Moore, Theodore Dreiser, and John Reed. She talked
knowledgeably about their works, their lives, their loves, but
her mouth was on automatic. Her mind was preoccupied
with Nick.

It was curiosity, of course. Nothing more.

She hadn't seen him or heard from him in over two years.
He had gone back to St. Louis and she had gone to spend
the summer with Auntie Flo in Provence.

From there she had gone to the Sorbonne for a term, to
Tokyo for a term, and then she'd come to New York. Nick,
she presumed, had stayed in St. Louis. He had, he'd been
at pains to assure her, intended to remain in St. Louis for
the rest of his life.

So she couldn't help but be curious. She wanted to know
about this "running away from home" business. It didn't
sound like the Nick she knew at all.

But then, she asked herself in a moment of honesty, had
she really known Nick Granatelli?

And the answer was, probably not.

Certainly she'd thought she had. In her youthful naiveté
she had imagined that she had known his deepest desires
just the way she had imagined he'd known hers.

He was right, she thought, when he'd intimated that she
was a child. He was right when he had said she didn't know
her own mind.

She ought to be grateful to him, she supposed.

Perhaps she even was.

But she certainly didn't want to see him again.

It was one thing to feel begrudging gratitude toward the
man who had forced her to grow up. It was another to find
oneself in a situation in which one felt one might be obliged
to acknowledge it.

Well, she needn't worry, she told herself. In a city of eight million people, it was highly unlikely that their paths might cross.

Besides, she reminded herself, given the way they parted, given Nick's disparaging attitude toward her, it was unlikely he would want to see her any more than she wanted to see him.

The tour was not one of her best. She didn't add her usual crop of anecdotes as she led her gaggle of tourists through the narrow Village streets. Nor did she try to relate the writings of her selected Villagers to the sorts of writings her group might be familiar with.

For once she simply did the best she could with half a mind on the topic, then bowed and smiled them on their way, and sought refuge in her own apartment, intent on reordering her thoughts and keeping her mind on the present, not the past.

She should have known better.

ON HIS EIGHTH GRADE report card Sister Benedicta had written, "Dominic has purpose enough for two."

She should see him now, Nick thought. He didn't have any.

He was lost. At sea. Adrift.

Everything he'd been aiming for all his life had suddenly ceased to matter. Sometimes he wondered if it ever had.

"You're really not going back?" Annie asked him after a week during which he alternately stared out the window and pounded the pavement looking for work.

She hadn't asked before. It was as if she knew he wasn't ready to talk about it, as if she was giving him time to come to terms with life, to heal.

He marveled at her patience. It wasn't one of Annie's

more notable attributes. But now, after a week of mooching off her, he owed her an answer.

"I'm really not," he said.

She was hemming a skirt, sitting in front of the window that faced the tiny garden four floors below, basking in the early-afternoon sun. Now and then she looked at him as he sat hunched over the newspaper, which was spread out on the bar between the kitchen and the living room. He had spent the last hour plowing his way through the want ads circling anything that looked remotely feasible.

"Did you hate it?" she asked him. "The restaurant business, I mean?"

He looked up, thinking back, trying to decide when everything began to go sour. "No. Not really. At least, I didn't at first. I wanted to get my hand in, to *do* something."

"According to my mother and dad you really made things hum."

Nick shrugged. "I did a few things."

"Picnic lunches," Annie said. "Ball game suppers. Pasta to go. Family reunion dinners. I'll say you did."

"You heard a lot."

"My mother is a great news source," Annie said dryly. "If a single Italian-American man accomplishes anything, I hear about it."

"Yeah." His mouth twisted. "Your mother isn't a lot different from mine."

"She's trying to find you single Italian-American men, too?" Annie grinned.

But Nick didn't smile. He shut his eyes and saw before him the future his mother had planned. "Not men. Women. One woman, in fact. Virginia Perpetti."

Annie's brows drew together momentarily, then her expression lightened. "I've met her. She was at Mario's wedding, too. Tall, slim, clouds of black hair and a Betty Boop voice. Porcelain complexion. Very ethereal looking.''

Nick grunted. ''Sounds like her. Frankie calls her Virginia Perpetua.''

Annie laughed. ''It's got to be the same girl. Your family wanted you to marry her?''

Nick shifted uncomfortably. ''Mmm.''

''And that's why you left?''

''Not...entirely.''

She stopped hemming and looked at him. ''Why, then? Entirely.''

Nick chewed on his lower lip. His tongue traced a circle inside his cheek. ''It's a long story.''

''This is a long hem.''

He smiled wryly. ''All right. I guess I owe it to you.''

''You do,'' Annie assured him.

But it was still hard to find the right place to start. With Ginny? With the restaurant? With his father and the rest of the Granatellis?

Finally he just plunged in. ''You know how you were always fighting your family, trying to be your own person?''

''*Am* fighting my family,'' Annie corrected.

Nick shoved his fingers through his hair. ''Yeah, I guess so. Well, I never did. I mean, I was a classic believer in 'Father Knows Best.' I bought it all—hook, line and sinker. I was Daddy's boy from the word go.''

Annie didn't say anything, just nodded and kept poking the needle in and out of the fabric.

''I was the oldest son. The best student. The best athlete. You name it, I could do it better than any Granatelli born.''

''Didn't your brothers and sisters hate you? I'd have hated you.''

He shook his head. ''No, oddly enough, they didn't. In a way I made it easier for them. Because I filled all the folks' expectations, they were pretty much free to do what they wanted. Sophia, my oldest sister, might've caught a bit of flak if she hadn't fallen in with the party line. But she and Aldo were going steady from ninth grade on. They were a sure thing. So the younger kids didn't have to toe the line the way we did.''

"I thought Frankie once told me your father wasn't exactly thrilled about her hat shop."

"He wasn't. But she has the hat shop, doesn't she? He wasn't exactly thrilled about Carlo going into the seminary, either. But Carlo's there. And Vinnie—God Almighty—the old man sure hasn't controlled him. But he didn't need to. He had me." He paused, then corrected, "He used to have me."

He'd never been able to understand his brothers and sisters' reluctance to conform. He'd always wanted what his father did.

"I wanted him to be proud of me. I was proud of myself. We had it all figured out, how I would go to college, play baseball, go on for a business degree, then come back and set the restaurant world of St. Louis on its ear."

"SuperSon?"

Nick sighed and rested his chin on his hands. "You got it."

Annie cocked her head. "My father would have loved you."

"*My* father loved me. Past tense."

Annie's eyes widened.. "Oh, come now."

Nick grimaced. "Oh, in an emotional sense I'm sure he does still. But in another emotional sense, I drove a dagger into his heart. I stopped being the son I'd always been."

"But how? Why?"

He sighed. "It was weird, really. His heart attack devastated me. I couldn't imagine functioning without him tell-

ing me what to do. He always had, you see. Even when he
wasn't there, he was there. In spirit, even when I was at
Harvard, I had him with me. Every case study I ever worked
on, I used to do a separate accounting in which I'd apply it
to Granatelli's. I lived and breathed that damned place.''

"And obviously you did it very well."

Nick grunted. "I tried. But even with all that book learning, I was terrified when I got back there. Everybody was
depending on me. My mom, my sisters and brothers. Aunts,
uncles, cousins. My dad had always been the rallying point
for the family. With him out of commission, they all turned
to me."

Annie gave him a sympathetic smile. "You had your
work cut out for you."

"I didn't have time to worry if I was doing things right
or wrong. Decisions came so fast and furious it was all I
could do to make them. I was lucky most of the big ones
worked. And that made it easier in the beginning for my
father. Once he was on the road to recovery, he didn't have
to worry about providing for everyone else, so he had a shot
at getting well."

"Which he did," Annie put in.

"With a vengeance," Nick agreed. He didn't smile.

Her gaze was quizzical.

"He wasn't the best of all possible patients. The doctor
told him he had to take it easy, change his diet, his life-
style. He did, but he grumbled about it constantly. He drove
my mother nuts. She kept trying to get him into some bridge
group or some bocce league. After a year he was a basket
case. So was she. The doctor said that perhaps, for five or
six hours a week, he could go back to work." Nick made
a face.

"Too many cooks?"

"Amen. Five or six hours wasn't enough. He wanted

more. He wanted the decisions back. He wanted to be the big cheese.''

''And you were the big cheese.''

A corner of his mouth lifted. ''The biggest. Suffice to say, it didn't work.''

''What did you do?''

''Damned near had a heart attack myself.'' He shook his head. ''No, not really. But as time went on he spent more and more hours there, with the doctor's blessing. It was his 'lease on life,' the doctor said. The one thing he really cared about, that he could get his teeth into. But I couldn't work with him, and he sure as hell couldn't work with me.''

Even now the memories of their confrontations made his fists clench, his jaw tighten.

''Everything I did, he had a better way, an older way, a more tried-and-true way. *His* way. And while he liked to get my suggestions when I was in Boston, he didn't want anything to do with them once I was working in *his* restaurant.''

''So what happened?''

''He decided it was time for me to go back to school.''

''What?''

Nick shrugged. ''I hadn't finished my MBA. He thought it was time for me to do it. And he and my mother both thought it was time for me to settle down with a family. I was twenty-nine. High time I got married, they said.''

''I understand,'' Annie said with the voice of long experience.

It shouldn't have been a shock, for heaven's sake. He'd known three years earlier that Ginny Perpetti was on his parents' ''short list'' for potential daughters-in-law. At the time it hadn't mattered to him. At the time he'd been indifferent to all women as marriage material.

Afterward he compared them all to Diane Bauer.

But since he'd left her in Boston, he hadn't let himself think about her. For the better part of the past two years he hadn't had time to think about anything at all. It was only when his father came back, he'd had more time.

"Time for a wife," his mother had said.

"Time for a wife," his father said.

"Remember Ginny," Sophia said.

Everybody had. It was only a matter of time until they were fixing her up with Nick.

"It was like it was a given," Nick said now, still marveling at the events of the summer. "One minute I was taking her to her cousin Leo's kid's confirmation, and the next we were engaged to be married."

Annie stared. "You're kidding."

He shook his head. "There were a few intermediate steps. Not many. It just…happened. They had it all worked out. Nicky'd done his duty, saved the business, pulled the fat out of the fire, and now they didn't need him for a while. So they were going to set him up with a proper wife and send him back to Harvard until they needed him again."

"I doubt they were quite so calculating," Annie began.

But Nick slammed a fist down on the bar. "They damned well were! And I was stupid enough to go along with it!"

Annie had stopped hemming. She sat staring at him as if she'd never seen him before. "So why aren't you married? You didn't leave her at the altar, for heaven's sake?"

"Not quite. Ginny picked a date, a dress, a florist, colors, menus. All that rot. And…I guess it was the menus that did it."

He raked his fingers through his hair and gave a shaky laugh. "When I think about it, it terrifies me. Do you realize that I would right now be an unhappily married man, if it hadn't been for my allegiance to my grandmother's recipe for risotto milanese?"

"Say what?"

"I wanted it included on the reception menu. Nobody else did."

Annie just looked at him, mystified.

"Not a big deal, huh? But for me a very big deal indeed. I mean, I was going to be the groom, right? This was going to be *my* wedding. So I wanted my grandmother's risotto on the menu. I liked it. When I was growing up it was my favorite thing that she cooked. My mother has the recipe." He bounced off the bar stool and began pacing the floor.

"My sister Sophia said it was too hard to make. My father said we should have polenta instead. My brother Carlo said he thought any kind of risotto was unsuitable, too messy. My mother suggested potato salad! Even Ginny said she didn't want it. She wanted some pasta dish. I said, 'Let's have both. Let's have potato salad, too.' Hell, I didn't care." He reached the end of the room and turned and glared at her. "I was overruled."

"They said no?"

"They said no. So I said no, too. To the whole thing."

He did another complete circle of the living room, raking his hands through his hair.

"It wasn't the risotto, of course. It was what the risotto meant. It was that I didn't matter. Not me. Not Nick. Not the person I was. I only mattered when I was doing what they wanted in the way they wanted me to. And they were bound and determined I was going to fit in." He gave a bitter laugh. "When the risotto hit the fan, I started to think."

"And what you thought was that you'd pack it all in," Annie said quietly.

"I said I was quitting the restaurant. I said I wasn't going back to school. I told Ginny I wasn't ready to get married. And I left."

"What did they say?"

"A lot of things I don't want to repeat."

"They do sound a lot like my family." Annie plied her needle again. She waited until he settled back on the stool, then turned to look at him.

"So, setting aside all the things you thought you wanted and don't, what *do* you want for yourself, Nick?"

He gave her a faint smile. "That's what I have to find out."

Chapter Eight

Three days later he got a job managing a restaurant on Third Avenue in the upper seventies. The owner aspired to make Lazlo's to Hungarian cuisine in New York what Granatelli's already was to Italian dining in St. Louis.

Nick understood. He dug right in.

He studied the operation, checked the ordering system, visited all the suppliers, went over the books. He did all the things he'd done at Granatelli's. He worked himself to exhaustion and hoped it would bring him the satisfaction he was looking for.

It didn't.

Annie seemed to feel better once he had a job. She stopped looking at him worriedly all the time. She smiled more.

"You're looking a lot better," she told him after he'd been at Lazlo's two weeks.

It was a Monday, the only day Annie didn't have to work, and they were sharing a rare leisurely supper. Nick was going over to Lazlo's to supervise the new chef he'd hired, but he didn't have to be there until seven, and Annie had an hour until she had to leave for her ballet class.

Nick wished he could say he felt a lot better. He didn't feel much of anything. He worked, he ate, he slept. But a part of him was always outside looking in. And that part knew he was just going through the motions.

"You need a date," Annie said.

Nick rolled his eyes. "Yes, Mother."

"I'm not trying to marry you off," Annie protested. "I'm just trying to broaden your horizons."

"Broad being the operative word?" Nick grinned.

Annie flipped a strand of spaghetti at him. "I know a really nice girl who works at Zabar's. You'd have something in common right off the bat."

"I don't think so."

"Zabar's deals in food."

"I mean, I don't think I want to meet her."

"Well, you don't know what you're missing. Laurie's really sweet. I have another friend, who works in midtown. Very intense corporate type. A climber."

Nick grinned. "What am I, a trellis?"

"A pain in the rear, more like," Annie told him. "Her name is Wendy, and—"

"No."

Annie pushed away from the table and went over to the desk, picking up her Rolodex, flipping through it. "What about Daphne? She's got a litter of puppies and an apartment in Soho. I wouldn't think you two would—"

Nick laughed. "No. No, no, no."

Annie looked at him, offended. "Picky, picky, picky. I don't have a limitless supply of unattached women friends, you know. How will you know which one's right for you if you don't meet them?"

"What if I already have?"

Annie's eyes narrowed. "What?"

He shoved the spaghetti around on his plate, debating the wisdom of what he'd said, then deciding he couldn't deny

it any longer. He lifted his eyes and met her gaze. "Wha
if I already have met her?"

Annie's frown deepened. "Her who?"

"Diane."

She stared at him. "Diane…*Bauer?*"

Nick nodded.

Annie shook her head quickly and firmly. She pointed her
fork at him. "You dumped Diane Bauer," she reminded
him.

"I had obligations. She was a kid. It wouldn't have
worked. She wouldn't have been happy."

Annie just looked at him.

"Could you see her stuck in St. Louis the rest of her life
living with me and the entire Granatelli clan on The Hill?
Forget The Hill, cripes, she didn't even come back to St
Louis at all. I don't even know where she is!"

"Just as well," Annie muttered.

It was Nick's turn to frown. "What did you say?"

"Nothing. Listen, Nick." Annie perched on the edge of
her stool. "Forget Diane. You can't go back. You can't
change things."

"I know that, but—"

She shoved the Rolodex under his nose and riffled
through the cards. "Pick one. Any one. And forget Diane
Bauer."

DIANE BAUER wished she could forget him.

Some days she damned Annie for telling her he was in
the city. Other days she was extremely glad Annie had. It
kept her from appearing at Annie's unannounced the way
she used to. It kept her from calling Annie on the phone.

In fact, the only time she saw her friend now was when
they played softball on Tuesday or Thursday afternoons.

The first time she'd seen Annie again after their dim sum lunch she'd asked cautiously if Nick was still with her.

Annie had said he was. She hadn't said more than that, and Diane hadn't asked. If perverse curiosity wanted to know, common sense did not.

At subsequent ball games, she never mentioned his name. Nor did Annie.

After four weeks of silence and of never running into him even though her own apartment was only eight blocks from Annie's, Diane began to breathe easy again.

Then she looked in from her position at second base that hot afternoon in late September, and there he was.

THE FIRST TIME Nick heard about Annie's softball league was when some guy called Bruno phoned and left a message that the rain-out date had been changed to Friday.

"Rain-out date for what?" Nick had asked her when he delivered the message.

"Softball," Annie said absently. She was doing sit-ups a mile a minute, her feet tucked under the sofa, a hot pink leotard outlining her curves.

"You play softball?"

She stopped mid-sit-up. "What's wrong with that?"

"Nothing." He was still grinning. "It just doesn't go with my image of you."

"What is your image of me?"

"Oh, you know. Intense, committed, artistic type. No sense of humor."

"That's me," Annie said. "And I play to win." She began her regimen again.

Nick laughed. "I'll bet you do. Can I come watch?"

She jerked to a stop. "No!"

He scowled at her vehemence. "Why not?"

"Because I don't like an audience."

"You play in Central Park."

"So?"

"So, people must watch you."

"Not people I know." She was exercising again now, but she wasn't going as fast, and she had a frown on her face.

"I won't tell anyone I know you," Nick offered.

She stopped moving entirely. "No. Please, Nick. Just don't come, okay?"

"But—"

"I'm very self-conscious."

"You're an actress."

"I'm a *good* actress. I'm a lousy softball player." Her look implored him. "Please."

So he hadn't. Not at the rain date. Nor at the next three games she played.

She was, after all, doing him an enormous favor letting him stay with her. He was helping with the rent now, but that didn't give him the right to ignore her request. It wasn't as if it was important.

He never would have stopped at all if he hadn't been walking across the park midafternoon that Thursday, coming back from a morning of working on the books at Lazlo's.

Through the trees he glimpsed a game in progress, and the uniforms looked a great deal like the one that turned up in the laundry every week.

Curious he angled his path through the trees, wanting only to catch a glimpse, to see if Annie was really there.

He didn't know what position she played. And so he stood scanning the entire field, trying to pick out the ones with long dark hair, the ones that might be Annie.

But the women had their hair pulled back or stuffed under their caps and it was hard to tell.

He moved closer, squinting against the bright sunlight,

watching as the woman at bat hit a grounder through the infield. He followed its progress, saw the right fielder practically throw herself on it, her enthusiasm knocking her hat off.

He smiled. Annie.

She didn't so much field the ball as smother it. But at least, he thought, still smiling as his eyes followed the ball, she threw it to the right base.

And that was when he saw Diane.

HE SHOULD HAVE KNOWN better than to follow her.

He probably should have known better than to stand and watch, let alone shadow the second baseperson home.

But, damn it, he wanted to see her.

He *had* to see her.

One tiny part of him—the part that dreamed impossible dreams—believed that the past two and a half years had been nothing more than a bad dream that seeing Diane again would banish.

He had to know. He had to try.

He still couldn't believe that she'd been right there under his nose the whole time. But there was no mistaking her, even with her honey-colored hair obscured under a cap.

"Diane?" He'd said her name aloud. But his voice was breathless. He sounded stricken.

Not surprising. He was.

He was torn between joy and fury. Joy at having found her here of all places. Fury at Annie for having never told him that she was.

When he'd left her in Boston he told himself it was best not to know anything more. It was over, after all. What could come of it but pain?

Still, she'd been nagging at the back of his mind for the

last two and a half years. Always there when he'd slowed down long enough to let himself think.

It hadn't taken long for his resolve never to look for her to die.

After all, it wasn't as if he was going to go after her, he told himself.

He was simply curious. He wanted to know what had happened to an old friend.

At first he assumed she'd returned to St. Louis. So when the bug first bit him, he scoured the society pages, looking for some mention of her. He found nothing.

Periodically, holding his breath, he checked the wedding announcements. He breathed again only when he was sure he wasn't reading hers.

He'd even asked Annie when they danced at Mario's wedding, but the music was loud and there were people everywhere. She hadn't heard his question.

For two and a half years, he'd heard nothing.

From society deb to vanished woman, Diane Bauer was nowhere to be found. He felt as if she'd dropped off the face of the earth.

She certainly hadn't dropped out of his dreams.

In fact during the last few months, especially since his engagement to Ginny, she seemed to appear nightly, smiling at him, taunting him silently, reproaching him for his foolishness.

He'd tried to ignore the dreams; he'd tried to forget her. He'd focused desperately on the life he'd chosen.

It hadn't worked.

It had taken him some time to realize it, of course. He was not, Nick thought wryly as she hurried away from him down the street, a quick study.

One might call him a lot of things—many people, not least, Ginny Perpetti had—but a quick study he wasn't.

He stayed in the shadow of the pizzeria on the corner, watching as Diane ran up the steps of a brownstone midway down the block. She'd taken off from the game as if all the devils in hell were behind her. He'd tried to catch her then, but it hadn't worked.

He'd shot a glare at Annie. She glared right back at him.

"Why didn't you tell me?"

"I told *her*," Annie said. "Don't you think if she'd wanted to see you, she'd have come by?"

"She's going to see me," he said flatly and started after her.

Annie called after him, "Nick?"

He glanced over his shoulder. "What?"

"Think about someone else for a change." Then she turned her back and was gone.

Think about someone else for a change? As if he hadn't, two and a half years before! Damn her, anyway.

He practically ran after Diane's fast-disappearing form, then decided against catching up with her on the street. He didn't want their meeting to be a momentary encounter. He slowed his pace and followed her discreetly.

He hung back now, watching until she went inside. Then, taking a deep breath, he followed.

There was a tall, bespectacled man coming out of the brownstone as he went in. Nick smiled his most disarming smile. "I'm going to Diane's," he said.

He didn't know whether to be glad or not when the man gave him a knowledgeable shrug and held the door for him.

According to the mailbox she was in apartment three. He headed up the steps. It was three flights up, and that he was winded had nothing to do with the climb. He took a deep breath and pressed the bell.

The door opened almost at once.

"You're early," she began, then stopped dead, the color

draining from her face. "Oh," she said tonelessly. "It's you."

Not precisely the reaction he'd hoped for.

Nick swallowed, then wiped suddenly damp palms on the sides of his jeans. He had rehearsed a few little opening speeches on the way over here. One for every occasion, he'd told himself. From the one where she threw the lamp at him to the one where she threw herself at him.

Words deserted him now.

She was still wearing her softball uniform. Her hair, no longer covered by the cap, lay damp and golden against her shoulders. Her face was devoid of makeup, and yet the exertion of the ball game had given it a radiance that other women spent hours trying to duplicate. She was not smiling.

She was still the most beautiful woman he'd ever seen.

He licked his lips, cleared his throat, offered her a hopeful smile. "Diane. Hello."

Still unsmiling, Diane nodded. "Nick." It was an acknowledgment, nothing more.

Silence rose around them like a rapidly rising flood. Nick raked a hand through his hair, shifted from one foot to the other, groped for something—anything—to say. "I—I'm visiting Annie. I saw you at the game. I—I thought I'd say hi."

In his worst nightmares, he'd never ever thought he'd come face-to-face with Diane Bauer and there would be nothing to say.

It was inconceivable.

The night they met they'd spent hours talking nonstop. Subsequent dates had been the same. There had never seemed time enough for them to get it all said.

It wasn't that way now.

Nick scratched the back of his head. "It's…been a long time."

"What do you want?"

To start over? To take back all the stupid things he'd ever said? To make her love him now the way she'd loved him then? Given an ounce of encouragement, he might have said such things. But her stolid, unwelcoming stance precluded any such confessions.

He shrugged awkwardly, managed a smile. "I checked out the society pages now and then. I expected to see you in there—that you'd gone to a party or—" his voice roughened "—got married or something."

"No."

"No," he repeated. Then with false heartiness, he asked, "So, what have you been doing?"

"Finding out who I am."

The words came at him like an unexpected body-blow. He winced, remembering all too well when he'd suggested just that to her. He rubbed a hand across his eyes. "I was an ass. I never should have said—"

"On the contrary," Diane cut across his apology. "You were right. Absolutely right. I'm very grateful."

She didn't sound grateful. She sounded as if she'd like his head on a plate.

"That's…great," he said hollowly. And then, because she didn't volunteer anything else, he asked, "What did you do? I mean, how…" He felt like an even bigger ass asking.

Diane hesitated a moment, as if she were debating what to reply. "I looked around and decided I had to make some decisions of my own."

"You didn't come back to St. Louis at all?"

"No."

"You went to Provence?" It was what he expected.

"I went to Provence, then to Paris. Then I went to Tokyo."

"Tokyo?" Nick's eyes widened.

Diane's chin lifted. "Why not? I'm good with languages. I wanted to be better. I studied Japanese language and culture there for six months."

That he hadn't expected. "Good for you."

"It was. I learned a lot. I'm my own person now," she told him, confirming his thoughts. She met his gaze almost belligerently.

Nick was the first to look away. He tucked his hands into the pockets of his jeans. A corner of his mouth lifted in an ironic smile. Her own person, huh? More than he could say for himself. "You're lucky."

Diane frowned. She didn't speak for a moment, then opened the door a little wider. "I need a shower, but it can wait. You might as well come in for a few minutes as long as you're here."

As invitations went, it wasn't the most welcoming he'd ever received. But under the circumstances it was more than he had any right to expect.

"Thanks."

Her apartment was larger than Annie's, in a slightly better block. It was a floor-through up three flights in a brownstone not far from the Park. The furnishings were Crate and Barrel modern. Piles of gaily colored pillows on the floor and on the brown-and-white striped sofa softened the atmosphere. Diane herself softened it even more.

"Sit down." She gestured politely toward the sofa. "Would you like something to drink? Tea, milk, soda, or cranberry juice? Or I could give you a glass of wine."

"No wine," Nick said quickly. But he needed something to assuage the dryness in his mouth. "How about juice?"

"I'll be right back." She disappeared through the doorway to the kitchen in the center of the apartment. Nick could hear her taking out glasses and opening the refrigerator. He wished he could follow her. Instead he sat down on the sofa and tried to figure out what he was doing here.

Diane reappeared moments later carrying a tray with juice, napkins and a plate of cookies. Homemade oatmeal with nuts and raisins.

Nick's brows lifted. "Did you make them?"

Diane shook her head and sat down at the opposite end of the sofa. "I have a friend who owns a health food store. He keeps giving them to me. They're very good for you." She smiled. "That's what he tells me, anyway. I don't know how he'd know. He never eats them."

He.

He, he, he. Four *he*'s in the space of five seconds. And a smile to boot.

Nick felt a primitive twisting deep in his gut. Had he really expected she wouldn't have male friends?

Had he actually imagined that she had spent the last two and a half years pining away for a man who had thrown her love back in her face?

She set the tray on the coffee table, then handed him the glass of cranberry juice and offered him a cookie. He took one. Sawdust had more flavor.

Diane nibbled on one, too. Then she smiled reflectively. "I can see why he doesn't eat them now," she said. "You don't have to finish it."

"It's fine." Nick took another bite. It was penance. A small price to pay for all his years of being a fool.

"So," Diane said. "What are you doing in New York?"

He was glad he had his mouth full. It gave him a chance to think. Not to Diane was he going to offer the glib "I've run away from home," though she, more than anyone perhaps, deserved to hear it.

He couldn't. It sounded too childish, too foolish. God

knew it was, of course. *He* was. But there was a limit to a guy's humility, for heaven's sake.

"I'm on vacation." It was, in its way, true. It was the first vacation he'd had in his life—the first time since he was eleven that he hadn't had school or work or family hanging over his head, determining his every move.

"How's your father? Well, I imagine, or you wouldn't be on vacation."

"He's fine. Better than fine. He's fantastic. Back at work."

"Full-time?"

"And then some." He gave a harsh laugh.

"So, if he's running things, what are you doing?"

The question of the year.

So much for dissembling, Nick thought.

"That's what I'm trying to figure out."

For the first time he thought he detected a flicker of concern on her face. She started to say something else when the doorbell rang. "Oh, heavens!" She glanced at her watch, then looked in dismay at the uniform she still wore. "Excuse me," she said to Nick and got up to answer the door.

It was not the sort of scene a guy wanted to witness.

The man—whoever he was—grabbed Diane up in a bone-crushing hug, then spun her around once and kissed her soundly before settling her back on her feet. "Early for once," he said smugly. "How about that?"

"Amazing," Diane said. "As you can see, I'm not. I have a visitor."

She took his hand and drew him further into the living room so that his gaze collided with Nick's.

He was a little taller than Nick with shaggy dark auburn hair and the most truly patrician nose that Nick had ever encountered. He wanted to break it on sight.

"This is Nick Granatelli," she said to The Nose. "He's an old...friend. From school."

Nick saw her link her fingers with The Nose's before she added, still smiling. "Nick, I'd like you to meet Carter MacKenzie."

She didn't have to explain who Carter MacKenzie was. It was all too obvious.

IT WAS OVER.

It was over. She said it again and again like a mantra. Over. Over.

She had seen him. She had talked to him. He was gone.

It was over.

"...with me tomorrow?" Carter said.

She didn't reply. She stood in the middle of Central Park and stared at him dumbly.

He bent and peered intently into her face, a whimsical grin teasing the corners of his mouth. "You are in there somewhere, aren't you, Di?"

Diane gave herself a mental shake and managed a wan smile. "Sorry. I was...thinking about...work."

"Work," Carter grumbled, beginning to scuff along the path again. He squeezed her fingers gently. "The bane of my existence."

Diane laughed. "Why don't you quit then? Live off the family millions?"

Carter frowned and pushed his hair off his forehead. "Can't," he said.

"Why not?"

"If I did, Daddy would think he could tell me what to do."

"No one could ever tell you what to do, Carter," Diane told him with absolute certainty. If ever she had met an absolutely dedicated free spirit, it was Carter William MacKenzie, IV.

"Try telling him that," Carter said. He shook his head and laughed. "No, don't. I don't even want you to meet the old man." He paused, considered, then changed his mind. "On second thought, maybe I do."

Diane stopped where she was. Surely he couldn't be serious. Carter MacKenzie had told her the first time she met him that theirs would be a frivolous relationship.

"Fun and games, how about that?" he'd promised her the night of Auntie Flo's party, when he had followed her out onto the balcony of Flo's apartment and tried to charm the serious, unsmiling young woman she'd been then.

She had rebuffed him at once, still unwilling to get involved with anyone, even though she'd last seen Nick Granatelli a year and a half before.

When he'd persisted, she'd said flat out, "I don't want a boyfriend. I don't even want a date. I want to be left alone."

He'd feigned horror. "Forever? Well, in that case, I have the name of an absolutely delightful Mother Superior."

She couldn't help smiling then. And his continued gentle teasing had nudged her into a conversation. From there it was a small step to agreeing to meet him for a walk in the park, then a hot dog from a street vendor, then a tram ride to Roosevelt Island.

He didn't come on to her again. He simply smiled at her and tried to get her to smile at him.

They had been smiling at each other for almost a year now. But this was the first time he had intimated that he might want to take her home to meet his family.

It was a serious step. It didn't help that he thought of it the very day she'd confronted Nick.

Nick.

Even now, faced with Carter's hint of something deeper, something stronger, she was thinking about Nick.

She wanted to say he hadn't changed. And in some ways, of course, he hadn't. He was still ruggedly handsome. His thick brown, sun-streaked hair still made her want to twist her fingers in it. His firm jaw still made her want to reach out and touch it.

But in other ways she sensed a difference in him. She couldn't put her finger on it, but it was a mood more than anything else.

If she'd had to describe the Nick Granatelli she knew in Cambridge in five words or less, she would have picked *intense, determined, committed, purposeful.* Also *sexy.* Only the last still seemed to apply.

But, she reminded herself, what did she know? She'd seen him for less than an hour. They had barely begun to talk when Carter had appeared.

There had been little talking after that.

She, who could make small talk with the best, found herself floundering in a sea of surly stares and monosyllabic mutterings.

"You're not listening again," Carter chided her.

"I know. I'm sorry. I—"

"Is it really work bothering you?" Carter asked. "Or is it your 'old friend' Nick?" He put a twist on the words that made them spin in the air.

Diane scuffed at the dirt underfoot. She'd never lied to Carter, never pretended with him. She sighed. "It's Nick."

Carter nodded glumly. "Figures."

Diane gave him a sidelong glance. "Why do you say that?"

"Always happens."

"What do you mean?"

"Me and women. I spook 'em." He shrugged philosophically and hunched his shoulders against the wind.

Diane caught his arm. "It has nothing to do with you."

"Oh? I could have sworn I was the one in the room with you and friend Nick today."

"Of course, you were. But it goes back a long way. A very long way."

"Ah."

It was an all-knowing "ah." An all-seeing "ah." It made Diane nervous.

"What do you mean by that?"

"You have a 'past.'"

Carter could invest a word with more meaning simply by his tone of voice than anyone Diane had ever met. He made "past" sound deep and mysterious, intriguing. Not the way Diane remembered it at all.

"*We* have a past," she agreed flatly. "I was in love with him and he told me to go away and grow up."

"The more fool he," Carter said promptly. He towed her over to a bench and pulled her down next to him.

Diane shook her head. "Not really. I was a naive little jerk in those days. I thought the world was my oyster. And he was the pearl in it, just sitting there waiting for me to come along."

"I wouldn't mind being your pearl," Carter told her.

She smiled at him and brushed a lock of hair off his forehead. "Shows what you know," she said, but she smiled.

"See? You're brushing me off."

"I'm not!"

"No? Sounds like it to me. And believe me—" He grimaced "I'm an expert on it."

"Then you pick the wrong women."

He sighed, stretched his feet out in front of him and

crossed them at the ankle. He contemplated his toes. Then he raised his head and looked sideways at her. "Have I this time?"

Diane didn't know.

SO PENANCE was going to be more than an oatmeal cookie that tasted like sawdust.

Somehow Nick wasn't surprised.

It would have been too much to hope for, just as it had been too much to hope that his interest in Diane Bauer had died when he cut her out of his life three years ago. He'd told himself he'd quickly forget her. And if she'd stayed a girl, he might have done so.

She had become quite a woman.

Even in her dirt-streaked softball uniform she was beautiful. Obviously she was successful, too.

He hadn't stayed long once Carter had arrived, but in the course of what conversation they'd had, her job as a concierge had come up. So had her fledgling tour business. She didn't make a big deal of it. She didn't have to. She was clearly a person in her own right, just as she had said.

She had taken his words seriously.

It was odd, really, because even though the words were true enough when he'd said them, he'd meant them more as self-defense than as a condemnation of her.

He'd wanted her, and yet he'd been afraid of what the future might have brought the two of them. It was too uncertain. He had too little confidence in her—in himself.

He didn't know, at the time, what else he could have done.

So now he had to live with it.

Diane Bauer had a full, successful, self-determined life. And a boyfriend.

He had zilch.

Annie was at the apartment when he got back. She was eating macaroni and cheese and a lettuce salad, and though he knew she was dying to say something else, what she said was, "There's enough for two."

"I'm not hungry."

Annie looked at him critically. "You're getting too skinny. Women won't drool over your manly bod if you don't eat."

Nick threw himself down on the sofa and folded his arms behind his head. "I don't want them drooling over me."

Annie's eyes widened. "No? None of them?"

Nick scowled and made a disparaging noise.

There was a pause. Then, "Did you see her?"

"Yes."

"And?"

"She wasn't thrilled."

Annie had the grace not to say, "I told you so." She gave him a sympathetic look and went on eating.

"Who's her friend?"

Annie frowned. "Friend?"

"Carter somebody. God's gift to women." Nick cracked his knuckles irritably.

Annie laughed. "I'm sure he'd be delighted to hear you say so. His name is Carter MacKenzie. I can't believe Diane didn't introduce you."

Nick scowled. "She did. I wasn't listening."

"You should," Annie said. "Carter is worth knowing about."

Nick gave her a doubtful look. "So, who is he?"

"Carter William MacKenzie IV, heir to the MacKenzie Metal fortune, also to the Blalock Oil Conglomerate, also to Taft Chemicals." A pause. "Proprietor of Jack Sprat's Health and Wellness Store."

Nick blinked. "Jack Sprat's...?"

Annie shrugged. "Carter is his own man. He's also been many women's man. But never for more than a month. He dumps them or they dump him."

Nick brightened. "Then he must be on his way out with Diane."

"Don't count on it."

"Why?"

"It's a funny thing about Carter and Diane. At first no one thought they were a couple. When Carter has a woman, it is generally a very high-profile affair. But he was never high profile with Diane." She stood up and carried her plate to the sink to run it under the tap. "They went for walks together, they cooked pancakes together. Once, she told me, they walked across the Brooklyn Bridge together."

Annie laughed, saw Nick's face and stopped at once. She shrugged awkwardly. "Anyway, I don't think you could say he's on his way out with Diane. On the contrary, what they have seems really different than anything Carter's ever had with anyone. You might say they're just getting started."

Nick sat up. "She's serious about him?"

Annie lifted one shoulder. "I don't know." She fixed him with a level stare. "Why?"

He hunched his shoulders. "I...just want to know."

"Why?"

"Because I care," he said irritably.

"Why?"

"Damn it, Annie, because once she loved me."

"Loved," Annie repeated firmly. "Past tense. For all the good it did her."

Nick winced. "I know." He shut his eyes.

"You hurt her."

"I hurt us both."

"And you're not going to hurt her this time?"

"I don't want to!"

"But will you, Nick? That's the question."

Nick sat with his head bent. He studied his toes, flexed them, watched as they pushed against the rubber tips of his sneakers. He sighed and shook his head slowly, recognizing the justice of the question at the same time that he recognized his inability to answer it.

He lifted his gaze to meet Annie's. "I don't know."

Chapter Nine

When he was little, Nick had had a guardian angel. His Nonna had told him so. It hovered somewhere right behind the headboard of the bunk beds he and Carlo shared.

He'd wanted to know if they shared the angel, too. But Nonna said no. Nick was surprised; they shared clothes, toys, bats, balls, books, friends and everything else. Still, it was a good thing, he'd thought.

He couldn't imagine any angel being energetic enough to be able to keep both of them out of trouble, let alone see that anything good came their way.

In recent years he hadn't given a lot of thought to guardian angels. The theology courses he'd taken at St. Louis University didn't focus on them. At Harvard he hadn't had time for one. And since then, it seemed, his family had determinedly taken over all the angel's duties. For the last two and a half years the Granatellis had definitely overseen his life.

But in New York he was on his own.

He hadn't thought a lot about guardian angels there, either, until the Sunday afternoon four days after he had seen Diane at the softball game.

He was in the midst of helping the bartender restock the

bar at Lazlo's right after the Sunday brunch rush was over, and the door opened.

In walked Diane and her tour walkers.

Nonna would have said, "You see, I'm telling you. You got to trust and you got to wait. Your angel, he knows what you need, Nicky."

Nick needed this.

Diane didn't see him at first. The bar was in the shadows on the far side of the room, and she was busy talking to her group, telling them a bit about the history of the Yorkville area while she herded them toward Carla, the hostess.

"I'm Diane Bauer, Manhattan Meanderings. I called earlier about bringing my tour by."

The hostess beamed. "Of course. Come right this way."

Nick didn't move. He vaguely remembered Carla saying something to him about a group coming in this afternoon for a taste of *konyakos meggy,* a Hungarian dark chocolate, sour cherry and cognac specialty. He'd never imagined it might be Diane's.

Now he sent a prayer of thanksgiving winging heavenward. *Nonna* would have been pleased.

Diane's back was to him when she sat down, and she was still speaking to her group. There were twelve of them, men and women ranging in age from twenty to seventy, all listening intently. Nick moved closer and discovered she was speaking German.

His German was basically nonexistent. And he was relieved a few moments later when she switched to English, detailing the history of the Hungarian community that had settled on the Upper East Side after 1905. Nick edged slightly closer so he could listen, too.

Using anecdotes to illustrate the history as she talked, Diane had no trouble capturing his attention. And only the arrival of the promised treat and cups of steaming coffee with whipped cream distracted her listeners, even those whose English was not the best.

Fascinated by her talk, Nick had to remind himself that he was a fool if he didn't take advantage of the chance.

He waited until they were eating before he made his move. And then he simply walked up alongside her and asked politely, "How is everything today?"

Startled, Diane spluttered into her coffee.

"Wunderbar," the lady seated next to her said when Diane couldn't seem to catch her breath.

"Delicious," seconded the man at the end of the table. "Just like my mother used to make."

Nick smiled at him. "I'm glad. Can I bring you more coffee?" He addressed the question to the table in general, nodded as they made their replies, then dropped his gaze to meet Diane's.

"And you, miss?"

She wiped the crumbs off her mouth and gave him a wary look as she struggled for composure. "Er, I don't think so, thank you." She glanced at her watch. "We really shouldn't be spending too much longer here. We have quite a lot more to cover in the next hour and a half." She looked as if she might bolt right then.

"I'll be right back with the coffee," Nick said and returned to pour it before she could mobilize her troops.

The coffee poured, he left them alone. For the moment it was enough to let her know he was there. He busied himself behind the bar again, straightening the bottles on the shelves, putting the new stock away.

She ignored him, concentrating with great determination on the questions her tourists asked her, charming them, Nick could tell.

When they were about to leave he slipped up beside her again. "May I come along?"

She frowned at him. "You're at work."

He shrugged. "It's Sunday. I'm just helping out."

"You don't want—"

"I do want," he cut in. "That's why I'm asking."

"You want to learn about the history and development of Yorkville?" The look she gave him was scornful.

But Nick nodded. "Yes, I do. Lazlo's developed out of the culture in Yorkville. I don't know much about it, and that means I'm at a disadvantage marketing it."

"And you think following me around will help you?"

"It's worth a try." He gave her a guileless smile.

She still looked doubtful. "Suit yourself."

Nick would have liked to have walked alongside her but instead he hung back. He knew he made her nervous, could tell from the swift little glances she darted his way. He managed to look politely interested, not obsessed. It wasn't easy.

In fact, he was studying her every move, analyzing the ways in which she had changed and the ways in which she hadn't changed at all.

She still had the ready smile and look of fresh-faced innocence he had seen the first time he had met her. But her eyes were knowledgeable, her poise even greater than before, her maturity evident.

She knew her stuff and didn't hesitate to show it.

As they walked, she spoke in German, then repeated herself in English. There were several third- and fourth-generation Hungarian-Americans in the group as well, all asking questions about the culture and how their grandparents and great-grandparents had coped with American ways.

She was as comfortable with the German-American history of Yorkville as she was with the language, expounding on their history as she led her charges up Third Avenue.

She talked about the changes in the neighborhood,

pointed out the new high-rise developments and those establishments that had been in the neighborhood for years.

"A neighborhood is a living thing," she told them at the end as they stood on the corner of Eighty-sixth and First Avenue. "It is born, it grows, and if it isn't infused periodically with new blood, with new businesses, with new people, it dies. What you see around you is a neighborhood in the process of revitalization. Appreciate it. Enjoy it. Walk through it with your eyes and your ears open. You will be amazed at what you discover. And if you find any particularly fascinating spots, I'd love to hear about them so I can pass the word to others. A tour has to develop and grow, too."

Then she handed them each a list of a number of local businesses and restaurants in the neighborhood whom she had personally dealt with.

"And I don't get a kickback," she promised them with a smile. "I just think you might enjoy some further contact with the local people and the local businesses, and these are all establishments I deal with myself."

Nick, scanning the sheet, discovered that Lazlo's was on it. He raised his brows.

"I've been there several times," she said in answer to his unspoken question. "It's improved enormously of late, so I just included it."

She turned then, making a point of answering the question of one of the tourists who was waiting.

The others were wandering off, studying the sheets Diane had given them and looking around the neighborhood with new eyes.

The middle-aged woman, who had asked Diane a question about Yorkville during the Second World War, smiled her thanks and moved off. Nick waited patiently until she was finished.

Diane looked at him standing there. "Was it useful?"

"Very."

She nodded. "I'm glad." She started to leave.

"Wait." He caught up with her. "Have coffee with me."

Her fingers knotted around the strap of her purse. She seemed about to shake her head.

"One cup of coffee...to say thanks for the plug."

"I said, 'no kickbacks.'"

He rolled his eyes. "All right. Not for the plug." His eyes met her, compelling her. "For old times' sake, then."

Still she hesitated.

"Please."

She sighed. "One cup of coffee."

He didn't take her back to Lazlo's though they were only a few blocks away. Lazlo's would distract, and he needed no distractions.

He had one cup of coffee's worth of conversation promised; he wasn't about to waste it solving kitchen problems or helping fold napkins before the dinner crowd came in.

He steered her into a hamburger joint on Second Avenue. It was noisy, culturally insignificant, and had just the right nonthreatening atmosphere Nick was looking for. He would have preferred someplace dark and intimate and full of tiny discreet tables for two. The sight of one, he knew, would send Diane Bauer heading in the other direction so fast he probably wouldn't be able to see her move.

So he opted for bright awnings and plate glass, an old-fashioned soda fountain and a flashy black-and-white checkerboard linoleum floor.

"Do you want anything else?" he asked her when they'd taken a table by the windows.

Diane shook her head. "I'm still full."

"Two coffees," he said to the waitress, then turned back to Diane. "I've never seen you at Lazlo's."

"I never saw you, either," she said quickly.

"You mean you didn't put it on your list because of me?"

Diane gave him a long-suffering sigh.

It reminded him of the sorts of sighs he used to provoke when he teased her. He grinned. "Somehow I didn't think you had."

A faint blush touched her cheeks. She folded her hands primly. "How long have you been there?"

"Three weeks."

"Are you the new manager?" she asked, and when he nodded, she said. "I knew there was a difference recently. I try to check places out fairly frequently. There's been a big improvement in three weeks. But then, I suppose you're very good at that."

He shrugged. "It's a job." The server brought the coffee and Nick stirred a bit of milk into his.

But he didn't want to talk about his job. It was just that, nothing more. He wanted to know more about Diane. "So, tell me more about your tours. How long have you been doing it?"

"I'm just starting out really. It's a seat-of-the-pants operation, not a Harvard Business School sort of project."

Nick snorted.

Diane shrugged. "It's not. It just fills a need I saw. I mean, I know there are other, doubtless more qualified, tour guides in New York. There are people who have made it their life's goal to know as much about the history and the development of the city as they possibly can. I've gone on a lot of their tours and, believe me, they know what they're talking about. But mine are usually tailored to specific needs—very often language needs. I do the French, Italian and German ones myself. And I can give a sort of basic Japanese tour if I have to. But I try to farm those out. I have several students and other free-lance guides who help me.''

Nick was impressed. ''How'd you get started?''

She sipped her coffee. ''When I came back from Japan, instead of going home to St. Louis, I came to New York to stay with my Aunt Flo. You remember me telling you about Aunt Flo?''

He nodded. ''The Bauers' black sheep?'' He grinned, recalling her description of her renegade aunt.

Diane laughed and she looked again like the Diane he remembered. His heart ached.

''The one and only,'' she said. ''But Flo is terribly respectable in terms of society, you see. She 'married well.''' Diane gave the phrase all the dignity it deserved. ''And to my grandmother that is a paramount consideration. So she could hardly object when Flo offered me a chance to live with her. After all—'' Diane grinned, too ''—Who knew? Flo might've found me a baron, too.''

She'd done just as well with the heir to every damned company in America, Nick thought grimly. He didn't say it, of course, but he felt it there, looming in the back of his head.

''I got a job fairly quickly working as a night concierge at the hotel where my aunt and uncle used to stay when they just visited New York. It's sort of European. The baron liked that.''

Annie, when grilled, had told him the name of the hotel. It was an expensive one on the Upper East Side, very elegant and cosmopolitan in fact as well as in reputation.

''It was family connections that got me the job,'' Diane admitted. ''The 'old baron's network,' I guess. But it was a trial only, and they made sure I knew it. That was all right with me. I didn't want it if I couldn't handle it. I thought I could, though, and I worked like crazy because I loved what I was doing.''

"And they were pleased?''

"Yes, they were. They liked my languages and my willingness to learn, I guess.'' She gave a blithe shrug. "Anyway, they seemed happy with me. And the first Christmas I was there, they sent me to Munich for a month to work in a hotel there while I practiced my German.''

"It's very good,'' Nick told her.

"Better than it used to be, that's for sure. The second Christmas they sent me back to Japan because they'd been getting lots of Japanese business and I was the only one who could talk to them.''

"Lucky woman.''

"Good business for them, too. You'd be amazed how much return business they get because they have someone who can speak the language of the guests. They've found, too, that guests bring their families if they feel someone is looking out for them. That's my job.'' She smiled at him then. A confident smile. A proud smile.

And Nick, looking at her, saw how much she'd changed, how much she'd grown.

It made him glad, in a way, that he'd walked away from her. It had been the right thing to do.

So why, he asked himself, did it have to hurt so much?

"And what about the tours?'' he asked. "That's your own, not the hotel's right?''

"Right. But they're the reason I got going in the tours,'' Diane went on. "Families that came along wanted to know about different areas of New York. So I started to learn about various neighborhoods, different parts of the city or life-styles. I took guests on tours of neighborhoods, first as a part of the hotel's services. Then, with the management's encouragement, I went out on my own.''

"And you like it?"

"I love it."

Nick managed a smile. "Sounds like you've done well for yourself."

"I'm happy," Diane told him. She looked him squarely in the eyes as if daring him to dispute it.

He didn't. He couldn't. His gaze slid away.

The waitress came and poured more coffee into their cups, then drifted away.

"Do you see your family much?" Nick asked.

"I go home once or twice a year. My mother comes here now and then. Matthew, my stepfather, died almost two years ago."

"I'm sorry."

Diane nodded. "I still miss him. So does my mother, naturally. I wish she'd find someone else. But I don't suppose she ever will."

"What about your father?"

"He comes into the city every few months and we have dinner." She smiled. "I like him more and more."

Nick remembered her telling him about Russell Shaw, the poor boy who'd swept Cynthia Hoffmann off her feet, married her and given her a daughter, and then, a few months later, unable to give them what he thought they needed, had disappeared.

Two and a half years ago Nick had taken Russell Shaw as an object lesson and had refused to do the same thing to Russell's daughter.

"So everything's worked out swell, familywise and workwise," Nick said, summing it up for both of them.

For a moment a shadow seemed to pass across Diane's face. But then she smiled. "I guess you could say that, yes." She shoved her hair back away from her face and met his gaze squarely.

"What about you, Nick?"

Nick was afraid they'd come to that.

Indeed, what about him?

For a man who'd had everything going for him, who'd had enough purpose to lead an army, Nick didn't think he'd accomplished much. In fact, compared to Diane, he'd accomplished damned little.

He shrugged. "I worked at my folks until my father was back in harness, then I left."

It summed things up, of course. It told nothing of the pain, of the sense of desperation he'd felt, of his increasing despair at the tangled mess his life had become.

But those were things he couldn't tell Diane. Not now. Not under circumstances like these. Once he might've. Now he had no right.

"Well," she said brightly after a pause, "you seem to be doing fine. Your taking the job at Lazlo's must mean you've decided to stay."

"I guess."

"Are you enjoying it?"

"Could be worse."

"You don't sound very enthusiastic."

"I'm not, especially."

"I thought restaurants were in your blood."

"Once I thought so, too. Now I wonder. Sometimes at night when I'm sitting there with all the damned orders and the invoices and the columns of figures it feels like I'm going to drown in them. And instead of digging in, I just start to daydream." He slanted her a glance and saw her smile.

He shoved his fingers through his hair. "I remember things that happened when I was a kid. The good times, you know? The baseball games. The days we played hooky and

went fishing. Those times I used to work with my grandfather.

"Do you know, sometimes I'd be sitting there, trying to
make sense of these damned orders and I'd be rubbing my
thumb along the side of my other hand, and all of a sudden
I'd realize what I was doing—in my mind I was sanding
wood." He gave a self-mocking half laugh. "Maybe it's
sawdust, not restaurants I've got in my blood."

Diane smiled.

"But it doesn't matter, either way," Nick said heavily.
There was no workshop now. His grandfather's tools were
stored away. There was nothing left but the memories that
crept up on him when he sat, unsuspecting, and made him
want to run his fingers through his hair.

"I don't know what I want anymore." He smiled wryly,
then sighed and pushed back his chair so he could stretch
out his legs. His eyes met Diane's. He remembered so many
other times in the past when their gazes had caught, when
they had looked at each other with perfect understanding,
with sympathy. With love.

He wanted that now, wanted it desperately. And knew he
had no right to it.

He saw concern in her eyes. Even a vague sort of sympathy, which only made him feel worse. But he didn't see
love. Where love had been, there was a wall now. A wall
that Nick himself had built.

He hadn't expected it to fall at once, of course.

But right now it seemed the height of presumptuousness
to expect it to fall at all.

He felt suddenly at sea, swamped with a depression he'd
never known before. When he had worked, he'd had purpose; when he'd left, he'd had anger, determination.

Now, for the first time, he felt he had nothing.

It had seemed so simple days ago—even minutes ago—

to get to know Diane again, find his place in her life again, start over again.

Yet now it didn't seem simple at all.

What was he doing walking back into her life, expecting her to accept him back?

Why should she?

If he'd had little to offer her three years ago, he had, as Jared would have said, "damn all" to offer her now.

And if he had nothing, Conrad—or Carpenter or whatever his name was—had everything on earth. Hell.

"What *is* his name?" he asked her irritably.

Diane blinked. "Whose name?"

He scowled. "That guy. The one in your apartment." His fingers clenched against his thigh.

"Oh. Carter."

"Yeah," Nick said grimly. "Carter."

Diane's eyes widened at his tone. "He's a good friend."

Her assurance did nothing to make him feel better. A good friend? Nick bet he was. He didn't want to think how good.

"Mmm."

Diane gave him a challenging look. He knew what it meant. He knew she dared him to object. He knew he couldn't. He, of all people, had no right to voice any objection whatsoever.

He closed his eyes, suddenly wanting to get out of there, to live the life of a hermit, to forget the past, the present, the future.

What future? he asked himself.

There was no future—not, at least, like the one he once had hoped for.

You can't go back.

And of course he knew that, had always known it.

It had been folly to ask her to join him for a cup of coffee. Folly to have followed her back to her apartment last week.

Folly to dream. Folly to hope.

He shoved his cup away decisively and stood up. "Thanks for joining me," he said. "Don't let me keep you."

Diane looked up at him startled, then scrambled to her feet. "No, that's fine. You're right. I really should be going," she said hastily.

Nick dropped some money on the table and stood back to let her precede him out the door. He held it for her, then stood on the sidewalk outside and shoved his hands into his pockets.

Diane looked at him, at the ground, then at him again. He didn't know what she was thinking now. She looked distant. Remote.

Passersby jostled them as they surged past. A bus rumbled away from a stop, spewing exhaust.

Nick pulled a hand out of his pocket and held it out to her. He managed a smile. "It was nice to see you again."

She took his hand. Her touch made him burn and he steeled himself against it.

"Yes," she said. She gave him a smile that he was certain her grandmother Hoffmann would have been proud of. "I enjoyed it, Nick. I'll be sure to bring my tours by Lazlo's again, too."

Nick kept smiling. "You do that," he said and let go of her hand.

He had been going to stand there and watch her as she left. But he couldn't do it. He turned abruptly, even before she did, and walked quickly down the street.

"HOW'S NICK?"

Annie stopped midway down in a plié. "What?"

Diane, who kept right on going up and down with a grace owed to long years of apprenticeship at St. Louis Youth Ballet, repeated the question.

It had been haunting her—*he* had been haunting her—for the past two weeks, ever since she had run into him that Sunday on her tour of Yorkville. It had been an afternoon she'd dissected over and over.

At first their meeting had disconcerted her. She'd been embarrassed to show up in what was clearly his territory. She didn't want him to think she'd planned it. And she'd been reluctant to allow him to come along. But short of being rude, she hadn't seen how to stop him.

But then, when he had come, and when he'd followed her every move with such interest, she'd been determined to show him just how good at her job she was.

She'd been the consummate professional. And she'd been a warm, caring, effective guide at the same time. She hoped she had impressed him. She sure as heck impressed herself.

His invitation to join him for a cup of coffee hadn't been much of a surprise. What had been was the way their time together ended.

He'd been rapt in his attention. He'd listened when she'd talked just as he always had. And Diane had had to be careful not to allow herself to bask in his approval the way she had done in the past. Nick's approval didn't matter now, she reminded herself. She was her own person, not his.

She was sure she'd made that point, too.

She had even dared to ask about him. That was when the mixed signals had started coming her way.

It surprised her. Nick had always been so straightforward, so focused. Now he seemed—was it possible?—lost.

Certainly he'd given her little to go on. ''My father came back to work, so I left.'' That was it in a nutshell.

But there was plenty there between the lines—unhappiness, aimlessness, melancholy. All emotions she'd never in her life associated with Nick Granatelli.

And no matter how much she tried, she couldn't seem to stop thinking about him.

She'd have thought that Lazlo's would have given him the perfect chance to do what he'd been training for, what he'd been doing, what he wanted to do.

And yet he seemed to show little interest in it at all. "It was a job," he'd said.

That wasn't Nick, either.

She sensed a hesitation in him, a doubt.

And, at the end of the conversation, when he had asked her about Carter, she sensed something else. Anger? No. Maybe that was putting it too strongly. But irritation for sure.

Was he jealous?

It didn't seem likely. Nick had had a great deal more of her three years ago than Carter had now. He could have had all of her, and he hadn't wanted her.

It was Nick, not she who had walked away. He wouldn't be regretting that. Why should he?

No, he wasn't jealous.

He probably, she thought, had just decided that they'd dawdled long enough over their cups of coffee, that there was nothing much else they had to say to each other, that he had spent quite enough time catching up with a woman he must simply count among his old friends.

Still, she worried. Sometimes, when she took a group of people around Yorkville, she considered dropping in for *konyakos meggy*.

But she didn't want him to think she was chasing him. She wasn't.

But she did, heaven help her, care.

She wondered how he was doing, if he was any happier

than he'd seemed that day, if he had made his peace with whatever had driven him away from Granatelli's, if he'd come to terms with New York.

She didn't want to ask him, of course.

Finally she asked Annie.

Since softball had ended, she and Annie met at a health club equidistant from their apartments. They ran laps around an indoor running track on Mondays. They did ballet on Wednesdays.

Diane never had enough breath left on Mondays to do more than gasp.

On Wednesday, two weeks and two days after she'd run into Nick at the restaurant, she found the courage to ask.

"He's okay," Annie said now, midcrouch. She gave Diane a searching look.

"We had coffee together a couple of weeks ago."

Annie frowned. "You did?"

Diane extended her leg along the barre, then leaned toward her pointed toes. "I was taking a tour around Yorkville." She gave Annie a brief rundown of their encounter, ending it by saying, "He didn't seem very happy."

"He's not."

"Because of leaving Granatelli's, you mean?"

Annie considered that for a moment. "I guess," she said at last.

"It's too bad."

Annie nodded. "It is."

"Maybe he just needs some time to adjust."

"Maybe."

"And a few friends."

"Mmm."

"You don't sound too sure?" Diane gave Annie a quick searching look.

Annie brushed her hair out of her face. "No. I agree," she said quickly. "He probably does need friends. Heaven knows, I'm certainly not enough. I'm gone so much."

"Maybe I'll call him."

Chapter Ten

Paprika was to Lazlo's what basil was to Granatelli's. And if basil had caused his father's problems, paprika, it seemed to Nick, was going to do him in.

There was Hungarian paprika and there was Bulgarian paprika. There was Spanish paprika and Moroccan. There were paprikas in varying shades of red and brown. There were paprikas that were sweet and paprikas that were pungent. There was paprika that suited one recipe and paprika that suited another.

Most of all there was paprika that his chef liked and paprika that he loathed.

It wasn't immediately apparent from an order form which paprika, the likable or the loathable, Nick was dealing with.

He never knew until it got here, and then he heard loud and clear. The diners unlucky enough to be eating in Lazlo's at the time, heard, too. There had been another outburst yesterday evening. It made him want to tear his hair.

It wasn't that he didn't appreciate his chef's problems. He knew what happened when you used oregano in a recipe that called for thyme. He knew the difference between poplar and cherry, chestnut and oak.

He could sympathize with the creative process, damn it. It was trying to come up with the materials sight unseen that was the problem. It was so tedious, so thankless, so bloody boring. Some people, he conceded, might consider it a challenge. Not him.

It was his day off and he'd been in the office since seven. It was one now, and he still had plenty of work to do. He pored again over the order sheets, trying to decipher the codes and descriptions, forcing himself to concentrate, to finish up so sometime today he could go home.

But when the phone rang, he grabbed it. Any distraction would do.

"Want to play hooky and go fishing?"

His eyes widened. He dropped his pencil. "D-Diane?"

"Yes. Remember what you said about daydreaming you were fishing? Well, a bunch of us are going on Saturday, staying the weekend, actually. And I…wondered if you'd like to come along?"

He thought she sounded slightly breathless. He felt as if she'd knocked the breath right out of him.

Diane calling him? To go fishing?

"Er, yeah, sure," he managed, impulse setting in before common sense reared its ugly head.

"Great. We'll pick you up at seven-thirty, okay?" And she hung up before he knew what hit him.

"Do you suppose I could build a casket?" Annie asked when he got home.

"Mmm?" Nick's mind was miles away. Fishing.

"I've tried everything," Annie went on. "No undertaker will part with one for less than four hundred dollars. Four hundred dollars we don't have, naturally. And I don't know what else to do. So, do you?"

Nick, smiling, still turning over in his mind the invitation that had come out of the blue, blinked at her. "Do I what?"

Annie rolled her eyes. "Think I can make a casket?"

What she was asking registered for the first time. "What in hell do you want to do that for?"

"For my play," Annie explained patiently. "We're doing a wake simulation this month. *The Wake of Archie O'Leary*. And we had a perfect one. Unfortunately the director's uncle died and got himself buried in it this morning."

Nick nodded dutifully, not even thinking it was strange. He'd lived with Annie long enough now to know she acted in some pretty far-out things. But her recent spate of simulated dinner parties, wakes and weddings was proving to be popular with theatergoers, so who was he to say?

"Have you ever built anything?"

"A paper-towel holder in seventh grade."

He grinned. "I think you might need a bit more expertise than that."

Annie looked glum. "Maybe Jack could help me," she said. "Or Frances."

Her downstairs neighbors, she meant. Nick had met Jack Neillands and his wife on the stairs a couple of times. Jack was a model and Frances, a writer.

Nick said he didn't see how either occupation qualified them for making a casket.

Annie shrugged. "Well, maybe Jack has a saw at least."

"You get a saw and I'll build you a casket."

"You?" Annie goggled at him.

"Of course, me." Damn right, me, he wanted to tell her. He found that his fingers tingled at the prospect.

"What is there about being a restaurant manager that qualifies you to build a casket?"

"Not a thing," Nick admitted. "But being the grandson of Vittorio Cardona qualifies me for a lot."

Of course he needed more than a saw. He needed a plane, a level, a miter box, and more. Not to mention wood. But even offering made something spark to life within him. He wanted to do it, wanted the challenge. Paprika be damned.

Annie, galvanized by the possible solution to her problem, was already on the phone. Minutes later she turned to him. "The wood will be here in an hour."

Jack, serendipitously, turned out to have some of the things he needed in the basement workshop he and Malcolm, the owner of the brownstone, shared.

And when Nick walked into the narrow, low-ceilinged shop with its long, broad workbench and its wall hung with clamps and tools, and breathed in the smells of sawdust, turpentine, varnish and linseed oil, even though he'd never been there before, he had the oddest sense of belonging.

"You don't mind if I work down here?" he asked Jack, who had brought him down.

Jack shook his head. "It's Malcolm's really. But he and Julie have gone to Europe for a month. Before he left he was helping me work on a cradle for our coming addition." He grinned at his very pregnant wife who had followed them downstairs. "But now I'm on my own. I'm not all thumbs, but I've got maybe six of them, so if you want to offer some advice, it's welcome."

Nick, spotting a cradle lying against the far wall, went over to crouch down and look at it with interest. He ran his fingers along the curving oak. And as he did so, it was almost as if he could feel his grandfather's presence in the room.

He felt calmer, safer, more settled. He felt as if he'd come home.

"I'll take a look," he promised.

The casket didn't have to be professional quality, Annie had told him. It only had to look as if it were. To Nick, once he started, it was the same thing.

He measured, he mitered, he joined, he sawed. Things he

dn't thought about in years occurred to him. Memories he
dn't known he had, resurfaced, sometimes making him
ile, sometimes causing a lump in his throat. Things his
nd wasn't sure of, his fingers knew.

And always, there was the wood.

He forgot about Lazlo's, about the books and the orders,
out the price of paprika, Hungarian or otherwise. He for-
t the fumble-fingered waitress and the cashier with the
cky hands.

He forgot about what had led him to Lazlo's in the first
ace—about Granatelli's, about his parents and Sophia and
nny Perpetti.

He even forgot about going fishing with Diane.

He became wholly consumed with his work, with the
ood beneath his fingers, with the precision of the tools in
s hands.

"A simple pine coffin," Annie asked him for.

A simple pine coffin was what she got. But for all that it
as simple, it was beautifully made.

Its corners were true, its top was level. He had sanded it
til it was as smooth as glass. And when he lifted the lid
d lowered it, the hidden hinges moved without a whisper.
It was a job Vittorio Cardona would have been proud of.

He worked the rest of the day, into the evening. Into the
ght. And when Annie came down after she got home from
r performance, she stopped on the bottom step and stared,
iazed.

Nick looked up from the stool where he sat. He had fin-
ied half an hour before. But he hadn't left. He hadn't
inted to leave.

The smell of the sawdust soothed him. The feel of the
ood under his fingers was as seductive and enticing as a
oman's flesh. Not as exciting, of course. But as he sat and
obed his fingers again and again along the wood he held,

tracing the grain of the piece of scrap pine in his hand, he felt for the first time in nearly two and a half years a sense of peace.

"Nick?" Annie's voice was almost a whisper.

He looked up and brushed his hair off his forehead, then gave her a rueful smile. "Oh, hi. Back already?"

She glanced at her watch. "It's almost two."

"Is it?" He'd lost all track of time. He shrugged. "Well, I finished it. What do you think?"

She came all the way into the room and walked around the casket, which sat in the center. She touched it gently, running her fingers along the edge of the lid.

"Open it," Nick said.

She lifted the lid. It went up soundlessly. She slowly lowered it back down. "You did all this today?"

He nodded.

"You're amazing."

"I was possessed." And saying it, he knew it was true.

She looked at him, still marveling. "Your grandfather taught you all that?"

"Yeah. It's all right, then?"

"It's marvelous," Annie assured him. "I'll stain it tomorrow. One of the costumes girls can do the liner on Saturday. It'll be perfect." She threw her arms around him. "You saved my life."

"Yours, maybe," Nick agreed, giving a sidelong glance at the casket. "Not Archie's."

Annie grinned. "Archie won't mind in the least."

Nor did he. The director was equally pleased.

"D'you suppose your friend would look at that table we've got that keeps cracking?" he asked Annie.

"Sure," Nick said when she asked him. "When?"

"Oh, sometime next week. No hurry. Besides, you're busy this weekend, aren't you?"

He had forgotten about that.

Had he really said he'd go fishing with Carter and Diane?

 E HAD. He did.

Diane wondered at first if it had been a mistake to invite
m. Carter was, to be sure, less than thrilled.

"You what?" he demanded with as much asperity as she
 d ever heard from him when she told him she'd asked
 ick to spend the weekend with them.

"Why not?" she said with more confidence than she felt.
You asked Jack and Frances."

"That's different. They're friends."

"Nick's a friend."

"Is he?" Carter looked at her doubtfully.

Diane steeled herself against his doubt, against her own.
Yes," she said. "And he needs friends right now. He
 ems so...I don't know...lost."

Carter still looked doubtful, but he only said, "He went
 Harvard Business School, right?"

Diane nodded.

"Then he's got more direction than a compass. I know
 e type. Runs in my family."

"He's not like your family," Diane said.

"We'll see," was all Carter promised.

But however unenthusiastic he was, Carter had had a
 ildhood of proper manners drilled into him, and he was
 r too much of a gentleman to show any reservations at all
 hen they picked Nick up Saturday morning.

It was an hour-and-a-half drive to Carter's family home
 northern New Jersey. In the past it had always seemed
 laxing to Diane.

Now, even with Carter behaving impeccably, it seemed
 aught with peril. For one thing, she found that her desire

to be friends with Nick might be academically sound. Emo
tionally it had more cracks than a three-egg omelet.

Her panache seemed nonexistent. Her savoir fair
n'existait pas. She couldn't think of a thing to say beyon
the mundane, and when she managed even that, Carter'
contributions were polite platitudes and Nick seemed dis
inclined to do more than mumble.

Why had she bothered? It wasn't as if Nick wanted he
to. It was obvious he couldn't have cared less.

He wasn't rude. But she could feel a distance betwee
them, a wall that kept him apart from her now. It was as
he wasn't the Nick she had once known at all.

She should have left well enough alone. She should hav
accepted his abrupt departure the day they'd had coffee fc
what it was—a dismissal, a desire to have nothing more t
do with her.

Heaven knew she didn't need any more to do with him

Still, she had done it and he had accepted.

So they were stuck with each other—and Carter was stuc
with both of them for the next two days.

Please God, the time would pass quickly.

"How's your family?" she asked finally as they spe
along the highway heading west. They had already talke
about the weather, about softball, about walking tours, abou
Carter's health food store.

She turned toward the back seat and caught Nick's gaz
momentarily. He shrugged, unsmiling. "I got a letter fror
Frankie last week. She's the one with the hat shop."

"How's she doing?"

"Fine. She got what she wanted and she's making some
thing of it."

"Good for her," Diane said.

Nick's mouth twisted. "Yeah. Good for her."

His gaze shifted abruptly and he lapsed into silence, turning once more to stare out the window.

So much for conversation.

Diane didn't think she wanted to try again.

Carter's family owned a colonial mansion, a stately brick ile with a curving driveway leading up through manicured rounds. If it looked as if it could have graced the cover of *rchitectural Digest,* it was only because it had. Diane ensed Nick's skepticism at once.

"You *fish* here?" he said as they pulled up in front and iled out. He looked around disbelieving, as if the catches f the day could only be caviar, lobster and fillets of sole.

Carter laughed. "Just wait."

Diane knew what he meant.

The immaculate order of the house and its front grounds ave way to totally uncontrolled woods behind. She waited, o, for Nick's reaction.

His amazement was obvious when they led him through e subdued elegance of the house to the back and pointed it the dense foliage not twenty yards from the porch.

"Voilà," Carter said. "The forest primeval." He waved 1 expansive arm. "Nobody's been there since Washingn's troops in 1778." At Nick's astonished look, he rinned. "Just kidding. The stream is about a hundred yards wn that path." He nodded his head toward a narrow break the foliage.

Nick looked from Carter toward the woods and back gain. He also looked as if he might finally believe it. "Did u fish here as a kid?"

Carter gave a shake of his head. "My folks didn't buy is place until '83. They used to have a country house in Iassachusetts, but my dad wanted to be close to the city. hey come out a lot during the summer, but now they head Florida every chance they get."

"Nice work if you can get it," Nick said dryly.

"I never thought so," Carter said.

Nick's brows rose.

"Carter is the family black sheep," Diane said.

"Not wholly black," Carter grinned. "Just sort of a dirt gray. Diane's working on reforming me."

"I am not," she protested at once when Nick's gaz sharpened.

Carter laughed and gave her a quick hug. "You couldn even if you tried." He dropped a kiss on her forehead befor turning to Nick. "Jack and Frances will be along late You've met them?"

Nick frowned. "You know them?"

"I went to college with Jack. We go back a long way," Carter said. "And I'll be damned if I want Jack to catch th biggest trout. I'd like to get a jump on him if I can. Ar you game?" He gave Nick a conspiratorial grin. It was th first offer of friendship he'd made. Diane prayed it woul be reciprocated.

She saw Nick hesitate. His eyes flickered from Carter t Diane and back again. Then, at last, he nodded. "Sure. Wh not?"

And for the first time that day Diane heard a flicker c enthusiasm in his voice.

JACK CAUGHT the biggest trout and several more beside: Nick caught three medium ones and a carp.

Carter caught an old boot.

"It's my father's, too, wouldn't you know?" he grumble as he tossed it back. "Too bad the old man isn't in it."

Nick, who'd had similar thoughts about his own fathe over the past few months, shot him a sympathetic grin.

It was well past midday now. The sun was shining, bath ing the woods and the river in a warm Indian summer glow

ey'd been fishing for most of the day, first he and Carter,
en later with Jack.

Every once in a while he told himself he would wake up
d find himself back at Lazlo's going over invoices. But
far he hadn't. He was beginning to believe his where-
outs might be real.

They sat in the silence of the woods, and far from being
agued with doubts about the wisdom of his decision, Nick
und that he was enjoying himself.

Diane had walked down to the river with them, but had
clined to fish. "Frances won't," she said. "I'll just keep
u company till Jack comes."

She stayed a little more than an hour, sitting quietly, her
ck against a tree, her face tilted upward to catch the gentle
tumn sun. Nick looked at her from time to time with
nger, with regret, with resignation.

Carter caught him staring once and he felt unaccountably
ilty. But the other man didn't speak, just tugged a little
his fishing line and shifted his feet.

When Diane left to go wait for Jack and Frances, Nick
aced himself, expecting Carter to warn him off. But Carter
st watched her go, his own gaze a little wistful. He didn't
eak.

He lay back against a tree trunk, letting his line drift, his
es closed, content merely to fish.

When Jack came he stirred himself to be a genial host.
e joked with Jack, scowled at the almost immediate suc-
ss of his friend who caught a trout within minutes of ar-
val. Nick, watching them, was reminded of his own rela-
nship with Jared, with his brothers. Something he missed.
nd when Carter made a point of including him in the con-
rsation, he roused himself to make an effort.

That was when Carter caught the boot.

"Wouldn't you know," he said. "The old man is dete
mined to get me."

"You have trouble with him?" Nick asked.

Carter shrugged, his mouth twisting into a parody of
smile. "We get along," he said. "As long as he goes h
way and lets me go mine. I can't work with him, that's f
sure." His eyes met Nick's, frank and open.

Nick nodded. "I understand."

Whatever differences they had, whatever competiti
they felt over Diane, they were in complete accord on th

"Right," Carter said.

"My old man's a peach," Jack said bluntly. "When
grow up, I'm going to be just like him."

Carter turned a baleful stare on him. "Go soak yo
head."

Jack just laughed, hoisted his full string of trout, stoc
and stretched, then thumped his chest in a modest Tarz
imitation. "Let's go back. Maybe supper will be ready."

"Dreamer," Frances said when he got there. "Supp
will be ready when you cook it." She smiled seraphical
up at him from a chintz-covered armchair.

Nick thought she looked cozy and maternal and extreme
well loved.

"Like that, is it?" Jack growled as he bent over her.

She giggled and reached up to pull his head down so th
their lips met. "Just like that."

And Nick, watching them kiss, felt a sudden ache cours
through him. His gaze went at once to Diane. Their ey
met, their minds remembered. Whether their hearts bo
jolted or only his did, Nick couldn't have said. But Diane
eyes flickered away and a flush stained her cheeks. Sh
moved quickly to Carter's side and hooked her arm throug
his.

"Come on," she said, looking up at him. "Let's you an

I put the meal on.'' She was already drawing him away with her. ''What do you have in the kitchen?''

''Trout,'' Carter said equably, allowing himself to be drawn. ''Acorn squash. Salad fixings. An old boot.''

''A what?''

He grinned and tugged at her ponytail. ''Come on. I'll show you.''

Nick watched them go, the ache still there. It took a determined effort to refocus, to remember that there wasn't anything left between Diane and him anymore.

Still, even concentrating on the present didn't completely solve his problem. He hovered in the doorway, unsure where he'd be more superfluous—in the kitchen being the third wheel between Diane and Carter or in the den where Jack and Frances hardly needed a chaperon.

Before he could decide, Frances pulled Jack down so he sat on the arm of the chair beside her, while she asked Nick, ''How did you know Diane?''

''When I was at Harvard,'' he said and, at Frances's encouraging smile, he came into the room and sat down. ''I went out with her roommate once.''

He gave them an abbreviated and not entirely accurate account of their friendship at Cambridge. He played up the camaraderie. He played down the passion. He forced himself to sound cheerful and hail-fellow-well-met. And by the time Diane reappeared to say that dinner was served, he felt reasonably comfortable with the story he'd told.

Diane's behavior certainly corroborated it. She was a wonderful hostess, making sure that everyone had everything they needed. She was solicitous of Frances, teasing with Jack, and she treated Nick with the genial concern of an old friend.

She occasionally reminisced about something that happened back during their year at Harvard. And when she did, if he caught her eye, she gave him a conspiratorial smile.

"Nick remembers, don't you?" she'd say.

Nick always did.

After supper he and Jack washed the dishes while Frances, Diane and Carter ate chocolate cake. Then, as he and Jack finished and joined them in the living room, Carter got up to add a log to the fire and the discussion turned to firewood.

Diane beckoned the two of them, a smile on her face. "Come sit down," she said to both of them, but her eyes were on Nick. "Surely you have an opinion about the relative merits of various types of wood."

Nick shook his head. "Not for burning, I don't. Only for working with."

"Building with, you mean? As in houses?"

"No, furniture."

Carter turned. "You build furniture?"

Jack grinned. "Does he build furniture!"

Nick shrugged, embarrassed by Jack's enthusiasm, yet still enthusiastic himself. Even lying on the riverbank today, he'd found himself thinking how much he'd enjoyed building Annie's casket. "I built a casket for Annie."

Diane looked horrified. "A casket? For Annie?"

Nick laughed. "For the theater company."

"You should have seen it when he finished," Jack said. "It'd be a privilege to be buried in it."

"Jack!" It was Frances's turn to sound horrified.

Jack shrugged negligently. "It would."

Carter looked up from the fire. "Do you do other stuff? Do you do bookcases?" he asked.

Nick hadn't, but he found the idea appealed. "What sort of bookcases?"

"I want some built into my living room." Carter finished

with the fire and got to his feet. "It's a great barn of a place, all wall, no storage. And I have a lot of books." He shrugged, looking embarrassed almost. "No big deal. I just wondered. I mean, if you don't—"

"Can I look at it?" Nick asked.

"You would?"

Nick nodded, unable to mask his eagerness.

Carter grinned and stuck out his hand. "As soon as we get back."

"It's a deal." Nick grinned, too.

"There are some upstairs in the library that I really like," Carter said now. "Want to see them?"

Nick said sure.

Later, when he had time to think about it, as he lay awake, but not sleepy, in the high mahogany bed that lay like a brocade-covered whale in the bedroom he'd been assigned, he was amazed.

The day had turned out quite differently than he'd imagined.

When he'd contemplated coming along with Diane and Carter, he'd thought it would be tense. Carter was her boyfriend, after all. He'd be making claims by the minute and Nick would be there to watch.

But, having agreed, even though he'd told himself he was crazy, he had also told himself it would be an exercise in discipline, in getting his head on straight once and for all.

Instead it had been great fun.

He had relaxed and enjoyed himself as he hadn't done in ages.

Being around Diane had gradually become easier. The wall between them seemed to have crumbled a bit. She had treated him casually, comfortably, just as she might an old friend.

They were old friends, Nick reminded himself.

And he had tried to treat her the same way.

Carter had made it easy by not trying overtly to lay a claim to her. He hadn't behaved jealously or proprietarily. After an initial coolness, he'd been warm and mellow and funny, treating Diane more like a kid sister than an impassioned lover. Nick couldn't have disliked him even if he'd wanted to.

He found he didn't want to.

Carter might have the woman Nick had once loved, but he hadn't taken her away. He'd been there to pick up the pieces.

And, Nick thought ruefully, who could blame him?

No, there was nothing about Carter Nick disliked. In fact, the more he saw of him, the more he found he wanted Carter for a friend.

He found, as well, that he had stopped looking forward to the weekend being over. He was looking forward to morning, to sharing the cooking duties with Frances, to going for a drive through the small northern New Jersey towns, as Diane had suggested, to looking through the shops, buying some apple cider, then enjoying a bit more fishing before they left for home.

He thought about the bookcases Carter had shown him. He thought about the living room Carter had described, about finding some walnut to work with, about maybe buying a few tools of his own.

He hopped out of the bed and paced around the room, stood by the window, stared out into the moonlit night and smiled.

For the first time since he had slammed out of his parents' house, thrown his bags in the car and headed east, he felt as if the knotted skein of his life was beginning to sort itself out.

For the first time since he had told his father he didn't

want to be part of Granatelli's anymore, he had found something that gave him a sense of satisfaction.

For the first time since that night back in Newport before
his father's heart attack, Nick went to bed again with a smile
on his face.

It was ironic, he thought, that he owed it to Diane.

Chapter Eleven

Against all odds, they became friends.

The three of them. Diane. And Nick. And Carter.

"The three musketeers," Annie called them.

It wasn't far from the truth.

Where one was, the other two weren't far behind. They jogged together, they swam together, they fished together. They cooked and talked and played cards together.

Nick built Carter's bookcases, and while he did, Carter and Diane offered moral support, meals and a bountiful supply of St. Louis beer. They also offered praise and congratulations when the job was complete and well-done.

When Diane needed a tour guide through Little Italy for a group of Italian tourists, it was Nick who found himself reading up on the neighborhood's history until three in the morning, then spouting it all forth the next afternoon in the Italian he hadn't used in four years.

"They loved it," Diane told him afterward. "They loved *you*. Do you want a job permanently?"

She was kidding, of course, but Nick was pleased.

"I liked doing it," he told Diane as they sat together in her living room while Carter made mulled wine in the kitchen. "It opened my eyes."

She rested her head against her arm, which was propped

on the back of the sofa. Her eyes were wide and warm and watchful as she smiled at him. "How?"

He felt the stirrings of desire and promptly squelched them. She was his friend now, that was all. Deliberately he focused on answering her question. "I don't know if I can explain it really. It just made me recognize the pressures my folks were under, the ones they put me under..." He gave an awkward shrug. "It helped," he said simply.

Diane nodded. "I'm glad."

There was a look in her eyes that warmed him. It made him want to kiss her, to touch her, to feel once more the closeness that long ago they had shared together. But she was on the couch, he was in the chair, and before another moment passed Carter reappeared bearing a tray with glasses and pitcher, pungent and steaming, filled with wine.

"All hardworking men and women deserve a brew like this," he said, setting the tray on the table and sitting down next to Diane. He leaned over and casually kissed her on the mouth, then turned back with equal casualness and began to pour.

Nick sucked in a careful breath and let it out slowly.

That was the way it was, he reminded himself. They were friends, yes. But if there was more than friendship here, it was between Diane and Carter now. They were the ones who had the future.

He had no part in it—deserved no part in it, he told himself forcefully. He'd had his chance.

Still, sometimes the present mingled with the memories and somewhere deep inside he hurt.

BECOMING FRIENDS with Nick Granatelli was turning out to be the easiest—and the hardest—thing Diane had ever done.

It was easy because once she'd loved him, and all the many things she loved about him were still there.

It was hard for exactly the same reasons.

Still, she couldn't regret it happening. She thrived on the afternoons they spent playing touch football in Central Park, the evenings Carter would invite them both over for a meal and they would play Monopoly after. Both Nick and Carter battled to the death over their various monopolies, while Diane, with the luck of the indifferent, seemed more often than not to win.

She liked watching Nick work with wood. Sometimes, in the mornings when she didn't have a tour to prepare for, she would stop by Annie's to see if he was there. More and more frequently she found him in the basement workshop, humming softly to himself while he worked on whatever project was current.

He did fantastic work. She remembered him mentioning his grandfather's workshop while they were at Harvard. She hadn't given it a lot of thought until she saw him in one of his own.

There was a sense of peace about him when he was there. He exuded a purposefulness that made her simply enjoy watching him. It was quite different when she watched him at Lazlo's.

Of course, it was a different type of work. He never sat still when he was at Lazlo's, unless he was trying to sort through orders or balance the books. He was dealing with people and crises and everything was in flux. He handled it well, unflappably, she would have said.

But he didn't smile much.

And whenever she asked him how things were going at work, he never did more than shrug.

Sometimes, when he wasn't in the workshop, she'd catch him sitting in the apartment, his feet on the coffee table, a pile of Lazlo's papers spread out on his lap, his eyes shut, an expression of stark weariness on his face.

She wanted to ask him if he was all right. But once she
d, and his eyes snapped open and he said, "Of course I'm
right," in such a gruff tone that she backed off at once.

"I just thought you looked…unhappy."

"I'm tired," he said sharply. "My bloody maître d' quit
thout notice. I have a cashier I think has her hand in the
l, and half my suppliers don't seem to give a damn
nether they get their stuff there when I need it or not. I
ve a right to be tired."

"Of course you do," Diane agreed soothingly.

But privately she thought he was more than tired. She
arned not to speak of it, though. Their friendship didn't
em to allow for that.

Another thing their friendship didn't allow for was dis-
ssing his family.

When they were at Harvard he'd been full of stories about
s father and mother. Though she'd never met Dominic and
eresa Granatelli in person, she had a very clear idea of the
bust, determined man and the strong, capable woman who
ere Nick's parents. She also had a pretty clear picture of
s brothers and sisters, from the managing Sophia to the
ghtly flaky Vinnie.

But whenever she asked about any of them, he shrugged
r off. He might offer a tidbit of information, but nothing
ore. It didn't even seem to Diane as if he knew much
ore. She found herself wondering if his "running away"
eant that he wasn't even communicating much with them.
But when veiled, curious hints aimed in that direction
oduced nothing but curt, monosyllabic responses, once
ain she backed off.

She wished he would share with her the way he used to.
But, she reminded herself, things were not the way they
ed to be.

They were friends now.

She wasn't asking for more.

But she wondered just exactly when it occurred to he that sometime she might.

IT HAPPENED—she could actually put her finger on it—th day Frances and Jack invited everyone up to their place i Vermont for the Thanksgiving weekend.

Without even stopping to think, she found herself askin Frances at once, "What about Nick?"

"He's invited," Frances assured her, knitting needle clicking away, most of the already-finished blanket drape across her increasing belly.

The happiness Diane felt at hearing it was far beyon what it should have been if Nick had been only her frienc She felt a great burst of joy deep inside her.

Then, aware of how intense she sounded, she looke away quickly, staring out the window as if the Federal E press truck double-parked in the street below was of all consuming interest.

"Did you think I wouldn't ask him?" Frances asked he "I like Nick a lot."

"Yes."

There was a pause. Then Frances asked, "What do yo think about him and Annie? As a couple, I mean."

Diane's head jerked around, all pretense gone. "Nick an Annie?" She shook her head. "No way."

Frances's needles slowed down. "Why not? They're li ing together. He came to her when he left St. Louis."

"They're friends," Diane said firmly. "Just friends. The have been for years. Besides, matchmaking between the has already been tried."

Frances gave her a skeptical look. "If you say so," sh replied after a moment, her knitting picking up speed agai

You aren't, perhaps, protesting just a bit too much, are ou?'' she asked with a sly smile.

Diane knew her cheeks were reddening, but she shook er head anyway, unwilling to admit to anyone else what ne only dared to hint at to herself.

''I dated Nick for a while,'' she admitted after a moment. But that was a long time ago. A very long time ago.''

Whatever finality there was in her voice must have been onvincing, for Frances shifted the blanket on her lap, then odded. ''All right. Anyway,'' she said hopefully, ''now nere's Carter.''

Diane managed a smile. ''Yes. Now there's Carter.''

But nothing was likely to happen between herself and arter, she thought. If anyone was just friends, they were. ood friends, dear friends. They loved each other in their ay, but not the way she and Nick once had.

Or, she amended, touching reality tentatively, she'd nought they had.

''I'm really glad about you and Carter,'' Frances went on ow. ''You're the best thing that's happened to him since ve known him.''

She was looking so pleased that Diane felt unaccountably uilty. ''I don't think...I mean, it's not...Carter's a friend, nat's all,'' she said quickly.

''Carter needs a friend,'' Frances said and smiled an enig- natic smile.

Diane wondered if perhaps, in Frances's eyes, she'd also rotested a bit too much about that.

HE DIDN'T WONDER too long, however. She spent most of er time when she wasn't consumed with work, walking round smiling, pleased at the notion of spending a holiday eekend with Nick.

It didn't seem to matter if other people were going to be

at Frances and Jack's—even if she loved them dearly. I only mattered that Nick was.

Perhaps, she found herself thinking, it would reawaken the feelings they'd once shared. Perhaps it would be the start of something new. Perhaps...

She had a million "perhaps"; they all came to naught. Nick wasn't going to Vermont.

He had to stay in New York, he told her, and work at Lazlo's instead.

She wanted to protest, to say he should forget Lazlo's, that he should quit Lazlo's since he didn't like it anyway, that he should please, *please* just come.

She didn't, of course, say a word.

Instead she bit her tongue, smiled and said, "Enjoy yourself here, then," as brightly as she could when he waved them off the Wednesday afternoon before the holiday.

Nick smiled. "Sure."

She looked at him closely to see if she might find a few signs of regret, some slight hint that he wished he were coming along. He was giving nothing away at all.

Sighing inwardly, Diane gave him another smile and a blithe wave as Carter bore her off in his baby-blue '56 Thunderbird.

"We'll bring you some turkey," Carter said.

Nick nodded. "Do that."

Her last glimpse of him was of him standing on the sidewalk, the brisk November wind ruffling his hair as he stared after them. His hands were tucked into the pockets of his jeans, his shoulders were hunched, but he wore a perfectly bland, have-a-nice-time smile on his face.

She had, in fact, a terrible time.

Not that anyone knew.

If there was one thing Diane knew how to do, it was be a good guest. She was a lovely guest. She walked through

he hills with Carter, helped Frances stuff the turkey, and
layed backgammon with Jack.

She helped out when she was asked and sometimes when
he wasn't. But just as she wasn't reticent, she wasn't pushy,
ither. She participated when it was required and disap-
eared when privacy seemed the order of the hour. But
herever she was, whatever she was doing, her heart was
ith Nick.

She wondered what he was doing every hour of every
ay.

She wished she were back in New York, eating Hungar-
n goulash at Lazlo's, watching Nick fret over his invoices,
nterview his candidates for maître d', charm his guests.

And even though everyone else bemoaned their return to
e hustle and bustle of the city, she was delighted when
unday evening rolled around and they were finally on their
ay home.

HE FIRST WEEK in December Frances had her baby. Jack,
ormally the most relaxed of men and reputedly the best
ach in Wednesday night Lamaze, panicked and promptly
rgot everything he'd learned.

"It's happening," he blurted the moment Nick opened
e door to his middle-of-the-night pounding.

He was a Jack Nick barely recognized, his chest still bare,
s hair disheveled, his jeans half-zipped. There was a light
f desperation in his eyes as his gaze darted about the room.

"*What's* happening?" Nick asked him, fairly certain, but
anting a moment to get his bearings.

He'd been in the midst of a dream he had no business
aving and he needed to readjust, to get his feet back on
e ground.

He'd told himself it was a good thing he had to work at

Lazlo's over the holiday. He'd tried to convince himself that not spending time with Diane was the right thing to do.

And he might be right; but it didn't help him get through the day with fewer thoughts of her.

Nor, as witness the dream just interrupted, was he sleeping any better than he had been.

"It's Frances!" Jack said now. "She's having it! The baby!"

Nick yawned and rubbed his eyes. "Now?"

"Now!"

Annie, peeking out from the bedroom, saw Jack and echoed his panic, her face turning white. "Oh, my God."

Nick gave her a withering look. "How far along is she?" he asked Jack.

Jack shook his head. "I don't know. She woke me up a few minutes ago. She just rolled over in bed, poked me and said to go get the car. What should I do?"

"Go get the car."

Jack raked his fingers through his hair. "But I can't leave her. I—" He stopped, looking at Nick helplessly.

It was a look Nick had seen before. His brother-in-law Aldo, the sanest and most mellow of men most times, fell apart whenever Sophia went into labor.

"It's sympathy," he'd told Nick.

"It's idiocy," Nick had countered. But he understood. There was always the worry, the helplessness, the sense of having set in motion something that was now out of one's control. He knew deep in his gut that if it were Diane, he'd feel the same way.

"Never mind," he said, holding out his hand. "Give me the keys. I'll get the car. You bring Frances downstairs when I pull up in front."

"What about me?" Annie demanded as Jack departed.

What shall I do?'' She was stuffing her left foot into her
ght shoe even as she spoke.

Nick took one look at her and said, ''Go back to bed.''

When he drove up out front fifteen minutes later, Jack
as there, ready to bundle Frances into the car. Frances,
niling, her face flushed, was far calmer than Jack.

''You're a dear to be doing this,'' she said as she eased
er considerable bulk into the seat. ''Isn't he, Jack?''

''Dear,'' Jack muttered, tucking her in solicitously, shut-
ıg the door gently, then clambering into the back and
amming that door. ''Step on it,'' he said tersely.

Nick did.

At the hospital it didn't matter what Jack did, it was out
˙his hands. ''I'm coming with her,'' Nick heard him in-
sting to a doubtful nurse.

''He is,'' Frances agreed. ''He helps me breathe. He
˙eps me calm.''

The nurse snorted. ''Him?''

Frances smiled, her fingers tightening around Jack's as
ıother contraction began. ''Very definitely him.''

And Nick watched almost wistfully as the skeptical nurse
d them through the swinging doors and toward the elevator
˙maternity. When they had disappeared, he sat down to
ait.

It was odd sitting there, waiting. It was like being on
ıother planet, another plane of reality altogether. People
urried to and fro, all purposeful and intent. They walked
ıst him, deep in conversation, unseeing. He might as well
ɔt have existed. He certainly didn't matter.

Would he ever matter to anyone? he wondered.

He remembered the hours he'd spent sitting at the hospital
˙St. Louis, fretting over his father.

He had mattered then, of course, but not in the way he
ınted to. He'd mattered because he was the one who could

keep things going, who could keep the family on an eve
keel, who could make the restaurant work. Nick Granatell
the person, hadn't mattered a whit.

And now?

Now everything had changed.

No, not true, he corrected himself. The Granatellis hadn
changed.

But he had. He'd changed a lot.

"There you are." He heard a voice and turned to se
Carter and Diane coming toward him. They looked cor
cerned, but rumpled, as if they'd staggered out of bed to g
here.

Had they been in bed together?

Nick shoved the unwelcome question away as quickly a
he thought it. It wasn't his business, he told himself. H
didn't want to know.

Determinedly he dredged up a smile. "Did Annie ca
you?"

Diane nodded, sitting down beside him. "And then wer
back to sleep. She has a matinee today, but she said to ca
as soon as we heard. How's Frances?"

"Doing fine. I think it's Jack we should be worryin
about."

Diane rolled her eyes. "Jack will just have to cope."

"He will," Carter said. "He always does." There was
split second's pause, then he shook his head as if he'd ju
remembered evidence to the contrary. "No, not true. N
when it comes to Frances."

"They'll both be fine," Nick said firmly. "And so wi
the baby."

"Please God," Diane breathed, and before Nick realize
it, she had taken his hand in hers and was holding on.

Nick's mouth twisted at the bittersweet sensation of he

and in his. He shut his eyes briefly. "Please God," he muttered.

But it wasn't simply Frances and the baby he was praying for. Though what it was for, he couldn't have said.

JASON DANIEL NEILLANDS was born at 6:37 a.m., dark-haired and robust with a healthy set of lungs.

"The spitting image of his father," Frances told Nick, Diane and Carter from her bed shortly thereafter.

She was smiling and pale as she looked up at them. Her freckles stood out against her ivory complexion and her gingery hair was curly with sweat, but Nick didn't think he'd ever seen her look lovelier.

"His mother's son," Jack said, his voice breaking. His hair was still tousled, his eyes red. And though he couldn't stop grinning at his friends, he didn't even for a second, let go of his wife's hand.

"Have you seen him yet?" Frances asked them.

They shook their heads. "He wasn't ready for visitors yet," Diane told her. "They said to come back in a few minutes."

"He's lovely. Beautiful, just like his father," Frances said. "Of course, I'm prejudiced."

"Just a bit." Carter grinned. "I'm ready to be prejudiced too though, since I'm going to be his godfather."

That, Nick remembered, was something they'd asked Carter last week. Carter had seemed a bit doubtful at the time, questioning their good sense.

"What kind of role model are you looking for?" Carter had asked them.

"You only have to be yourself," Frances had assured him.

Carter grinned. "Foolish of you," he said. But he'd looked extraordinarily pleased.

Nick wondered if they'd ask Diane to be godmother, but Frances had said almost at once that an old friend of hers from Vermont was going to be godmother. Nick had looked at Diane, curious to see if she was miffed.

She didn't seem to be. She had smiled brightly. "Good idea."

Nick thought so, too. And if it had anything to do with jealousy, he wasn't ready to admit it.

"I hope you don't mind," Frances had said to her a bit worriedly.

Diane had shaken her head emphatically. "Not at all."

Now she looked at Frances and Jack—at the way they were looking at each other—and turned to Carter and Nick, taking them each by an arm. "Come on, guys. Let's leave these two alone."

Jason Daniel was both the spitting image of his father and his mother. He was beautiful. He had Jack's features in newborn form, but he had Frances's long, elegant fingers and, when he opened his eyes, though they might not focus yet, Nick definitely got the feeling that when they did, they would look at everything with the same curiosity and intensity that Frances's eyes did.

But it wasn't Jason who captured the bulk of Nick's attention.

It was Diane's reaction to this tiny newborn child.

She stood there, transfixed, absolutely silent and unmoving, her attention wholly caught by the child before her. Behind them breakfast carts rattled by, telephones rang, the intercom called for Dr. Washington to come to Emergency.

Diane, it seemed, heard nothing, saw nothing, beyond the child in the bassinet. She stood, her forehead pressed to the glass, and stared.

Finally she blinked, then swallowed. Her eyes went from

he baby sucking his fist, first to Carter, then to Nick, silent
ears rolling down her cheeks.

"Are you all right?" he asked her softly.

Biting her lip, she nodded her head helplessly and turned
ack to the child.

Nick, smitten with an ache he couldn't put a name to,
idn't ask anything else.

In the face of the miracle of new life, what, after all, was
here to say?

NOTHING MADE Diane regret more the loss of her love with
Nick than the birth of Jack and Frances's son.

She thought she'd reached the depths of pain years be-
ore. She thought she'd come to terms with it. She thought,
ven as she began to hope they might get back together
again, that she hoped in moderation.

She found out differently when she stood in the nursery
and looked at Jason and then at Nick.

All the "might have beens" came rushing back, inun-
ating her, swamping her, destroying her hard-won equilib-
ium. All she could think was how much she would have
oved a child with Nick, how, had things worked out be-
ween them three years ago, they might have had one—or
ven two—by now.

Instead they stood side by side and looked down at the
ign of another couple's love for each other. And when their
yes met, it was in silent pain; with words they could say
othing at all.

But it wasn't just the two of them, she realized. Even
Carter, normally voluble, seemed struck dumb in the face
of the child before them. He stared at Jason, swallowed
ard, then leaned his forehead against the glass and stared
ome more.

Finally, dazed and disoriented in a way that Diane had never seen him, he shook his head.

"Holy cow," he muttered. "A baby."

"You were expecting maybe a rhinoceros," Jack said, coming up behind them.

"I wasn't expecting anything," Carter said with complete honesty. "I never really thought about it. I mean, Frances kept getting fatter, but I never thought…" His voice trailed off and he stared once more with awe at the newborn child. "Amazing."

"Yes," Jack said simply, and he sounded no less awed than Carter. He looked down at the child again, a smile lighting his face. "My son."

"A big responsibility," Carter said gravely.

Jack cast him a sidelong glance, a furrow deepening between his brows, as if Carter's words surprised him. "It is," he agreed after a moment.

"You'd better do a damned good job," Carter continued.

"I'll try." Jack was smiling, but Carter wasn't. His gaze was fixed on his best friend.

Diane watched them both, curious at the interchange, amused at Carter's unsuspected gravity. Her gaze flickered to Nick, wanting to share the amusement. His face was just as grave.

"He might be your son," Nick said suddenly, "but he's his own person, too. Don't forget that."

Jack's gaze met his as if he heard the unspoken message in Nick's words. "No," he promised. "I won't."

Diane, seeing Carter about ready to extract another promise, leaped to Jack's defense.

"I'm sure he'll do fine," she said. "Let's give the man a chance." She gave Jack a quick hug, then turned to Carter and Nick. "I think we should be going," she said. "I have to give a tour of Yorkville at ten."

They followed her willingly enough. Both still seemed slightly dazed. They caught a cab in front of the hospital, and for the better part of thirty blocks not one of the three said a word.

Carter got off at 72nd, mumbling something about walking the rest of the way to the health food store, needing the air to clear his head. Nick and Diane continued on across the park toward the Upper East Side, she to her office, Nick to Lazlo's.

When Carter left them it seemed as if the silence grew to fill the space.

Diane looked at Nick, sitting there hard against the opposite side of the cab, staring out the window, his eyes focusing on heaven knew what, and she had to say what was in her heart.

"He's lovely, isn't he?" she asked. "Jason, I mean."

"Hmm?" Nick seemed to struggle back to her from far away. When at last he had, he attempted a smile. "Oh, yeah. He is."

"Makes me envious," Diane ventured.

Nick's eyes met her's briefly, then skated away. "Yeah."

"Do you ever wonder..." she began, then faltered. Should she do this? Did she dare? "I mean, if we...I mean, it could have been..." She stopped, panicked, then threw caution to the wind and plunged ahead. "Have you ever thought...we might have had a child by now?"

Their gazes collided again, hers frightened at her audacity, his surprised, at first bleak, then changing to— To what? Diane wasn't quite sure.

But he didn't look away. And even when the cabdriver pulled up in front of Lazlo's, he didn't move. Blue eyes searched her brown ones, and what he saw she wasn't certain. But finally he nodded his head, a smile more wistful than bitter on his face.

"Yeah," he said, his voice heavy. "I have."

Chapter Twelve

I have.

It wasn't much, granted, but it was enough to give Diane fantasies that wouldn't quit.

She sat at her desk at the hotel late into the night and remembered the fathomless look in Nick's eyes, the slightly rueful curve of his mouth when he had said those two words, acknowledging the present that might have existed had things been different.

What if…

What if, indeed? she chided herself. That was then; this was now.

But still, she couldn't seem to help it. She couldn't stop imagining that things might change now, that their friendship might turn to something more, that they might come together again.

She didn't know what Nick thought.

In the beginning, she admitted to herself somewhat ruefully now, he had been still interested in her. His following her home from the softball game had proved it.

But back then she'd been terrified. She'd shrunken from any contact with him at all. Nick reminded her of all her inadequacies, recalled all too well for her the innocent child she had been.

But once she'd got over her initial panic, once she realized that she did in fact have some feelings left for him, she took stock. Three years had passed, and she had changed. Part of her reason for becoming friends with him again was to gain an opportunity to prove it.

She thought, in fact, that she had proved it.

But to what end?

The more she had proven herself competent, talented, a woman to be reckoned with, the more it seemed Nick had withdrawn into himself.

If he still felt passion for her, she couldn't tell. If he had been interested in her in September, he didn't seem to be now. Except as a friend.

He seemed, she thought grimly, quite content to be her friend.

Yet now and then there was still that something in his expression—a longing she saw once in a while when she caught him looking at her, that wistfulness she hadn't experienced alone at the sight of Jack and Frances's son—that made her think there might still be something there.

An ember. A tiny, weak, flickering flame.

God, how she wanted to fan it to life again.

But how? *How?*

"St. Louis?" Nick strove to keep the dismay out of his voice as he echoed Diane's words. His fingers tightened around the rung of cherry he'd been sanding. He'd thought he was simply going to have to endure another session of being near her while she watched him work. He didn't realize he was going to have even deeper issues to cope with.

Her words shouldn't have been surprising, of course. Where else, he asked himself glumly, would she be spending Christmas?

He guessed he'd been hoping she'd spend it here. He

guessed he'd been hoping she'd spend it with him. Or at least with him and Carter.

But no. He'd dropped it into the conversation quite without thinking, saying something about the holidays, and she'd looked momentarily baffled, then said rather hesitantly that she wouldn't be here.

"No?" He'd paused in his work and looked up at her. "Why not?"

Her brown eyes widened and she said, "I'm going to St. Louis."

Then, even before he got over hearing that, she'd added, "Aren't you?"

The question stopped him cold. Him spend Christmas in St. Louis? He hadn't even considered it. Didn't *want* to consider it. He didn't want to think about St. Louis at all.

Diane, apparently seeing all those thoughts writ large on his face, said quickly, "I just assumed...I mean, I didn't..." She flushed. "I'm sorry."

Nick shook his head quickly. "No need." He gave a wry grimace. "It's just that it wouldn't be a very happy holiday for anybody if I did."

"But your folks—"

"My folks have plenty of other kids and grandkids to keep them busy," he said, trying to sound nonchalant.

"It's not the same."

"It'll have to be," he said shortly. Because he certainly wasn't going, though he had to admit that only part of the reason now had to do with the rift between himself and his parents. The rest had to do with Diane.

The more time he spent with her, the less he could imagine himself in St. Louis with her now. Before there had been economic issues, even class issues, if you would. But now there was, he thought grimly, the success issue.

Diane was. He wasn't.

It was as simple as that.

Hell, yes, he'd thought about the fact that they might have
a child by now. The thought could, if he dwelt on it,
most kill him with pain.

So he tried not to think about it. He tried to get by, day
day. And it wasn't getting any easier.

"I wouldn't be going, either," she told him, "except one
my friends is getting married." She sighed and smiled.
Actually she's more the granddaughter of one of my
grandmother's friends, but—" she gave an expressive shrug
—you know how those things go."

Nick did and he didn't. He knew about family obligations,
he knew. He had enough of his own.

But he didn't know about blue-blood society weddings,
if Diane's grandmother had anything to do with it, that's
what this one would be.

He gave a noncommittal shrug. "Sure," then bent his
head and concentrated again on the chair rung he was sand-
.

He expected she'd leave then, but she didn't. She stood
watching him wordlessly, unmoving. It unnerved him.

The first time she'd come he'd thought it was a whim,
but she'd been curious. He'd shown her around, told her
what he was working on, then had thought she'd leave.

She hadn't. She'd just said. "Do you mind if I watch?"
And he'd looked at her so blankly that she'd colored and
said, "I won't disturb you, I promise."

Nick didn't see how she could promise any such thing,
since her mere presence did incredible things to his mind,
his heart, his loins. But he'd shrugged, saying, "Suit yourself." And while he tried to concentrate on sawing a straight
line, Diane had stood and watched.

He'd been aware of her every breath, had wondered what
she found so fascinating, had not been able to ask. He'd

been unable to even formulate a sensible question for th
rest of her visit, and he'd breathed a sigh of relief whe
she'd left.

He was astonished when she showed up to watch y
another day. And another.

At first he'd offered to stop, but she'd shaken her heac
"No. Don't mind me," she'd say. "I won't bother you."

She had, of course. Sometimes, like now, he found h
presence distinctly unnerving and felt as if he ought to sa
something to fill in the silence, to justify her being ther
But at other times he became absorbed in his work, di
cussed what he was doing with her, and without realizing
at first, found that he liked having her there, moving abo
quietly, reading, watching, making the occasional commer
or asking a question.

It gave him hope where, as far as he was concerned, ther
was damned little reason for any.

"Is this for Carter's father?" she asked now. Carter'
father had seen the bookcases Nick had recently finishe
and had commissioned a project of his own.

Nick nodded. "A whole set of dining-room chair
Twelve of them. Solid cherry."

"You must be pleased."

"Yeah."

"But you're still going to hang on at Lazlo's?"

He scowled at the censure in her voice. "What's it t
you?"

"You're my friend."

"And friends find fault with their friends?"

"No." She paused, then apparently reconsidere
"Maybe they do. Maybe when they see their friends wastin
their lives doing things they don't like, walking around lik
they're half-dead all the time because they have no enthu

sm about their work when they could be doing something
out it—''

''Yeah? What?''

'Quit!''

Did she think he hadn't considered it? Ever since their
k before Thanksgiving, he'd toyed with the idea, tossed
and turned it in his mind while he did his own tossing
l turning in bed at night.

But the conclusion he came to was always the same.
'here's the little matter of eating. You want to support
?''

''I will,'' she said without missing a beat.

'The hell you will!''

'I'm successful enough.''

'Too damned successful,'' Nick muttered, his head bent.

''*What?*'' She stared at him, aghast.

He twisted the chair rung, strangling it. ''Nothing.''

But Diane had heard what he'd said. ''Does it bother you
t my aunt knew the people who gave me the concierge
?''

''No, of course not!''

''Then what does bother you?''

But he couldn't tell her that. It was buried too deeply, it
ttered too much.

''Nobody handed me my tour job,'' she went right on.

''I know that!'' Nick gritted his teeth. ''We can't all be
successful as you are, I guess,'' he said bitterly and
ned back to the wood he was sanding.

Damn her, anyway. *Quit Lazlo's,* she said. Just like that.
t as if other jobs were there for the taking that would
ke him her equal. Once he'd had that chance. Not any-
re.

God knew he thought about it. He couldn't help himself.
entertained the hope almost every night when he lay in

bed and stared at the lights in the high-rise apartments i
the next block.

If only he could quit Lazlo's…. If only he could get son
jobs lined up…. If only he could feel secure enough abou
getting something steady with the woodworking, the
maybe, too, he and Diane could—

He blotted the thought out now as he did then.

Once he'd been a dreamer. Once he had dared. Neve
again.

He could feel Diane's eyes boring into him. He hardene
his resistance to the needs they evoked. "Have a nice tin
in St. Louis," he made himself say.

"I will," she said flatly. There was a moment's paus
and she added, "Too bad you won't come."

"Can't," Nick corrected, flicking her a glance.

Diane gave a small snort.

Nick glared at her, then shifted uncomfortably under he
unblinking stare. "Maybe next year," he muttered.

"You're afraid."

His head jerked up sharply. "The hell I am!"

"What would you call it?" Her eyes flashed fire.

He'd never seen her like this, combative, irritated. "I'
call it doing what *I* want for a change instead of what m
family expects me to do!"

"And you want to stay in New York?" she mocked.

"Yes," he said, tightly.

"Work all day at Lazlo's? You love it so much." Sh
was smiling, infuriating him.

"It's my job, damn it! It's what I have to do!"

"Is it?" Her voice changed suddenly and she sounde
almost sad.

It was the hint of pity that undid him. "You don't hav
to feel sorry for me, damn it!" he said harshly.

Whatever sadness he'd heard vanished in an instant. D

he bristled like a hedgehog right before his eyes. She tossed
er hair and lifted her chin, then looked at him down her
ersion of the Hoffmann nose. Her brown eyes glinted.

"I wouldn't dream of it," she said with biting scorn.
"You're feeling sorry enough for yourself."

JENNIFER'S HAVING ten bridesmaids, you know," Gertrude
Hoffmann said, stirring sugar into her tea.

"Ten bridesmaids?" Diane, who'd been staring blindly
out at a pre-Christmas snowfall, looked at her grandmother,
aghast.

Gertrude Hoffmann calmly sipped her tea and ignored her
granddaughter's outburst. It was the way she handled everything, ignoring what she didn't want to see or hear, plowing straight on, determined to make the world over in her
own image of it.

"All in blue silk, Minna says," she went on as if Diane
had never interrupted. Minna, Jennifer's grandmother, was
quoted frequently these days.

Gertrude had been nattering on for the better part of an
hour now about Jennifer Naylor's wedding, and Diane had
been half listening, making what she hoped were coherent
noncommittal responses—always the best kind where
grandmother Gertrude was concerned.

But she'd been preoccupied then, as she had been ever
since she'd come home, with thoughts of Nick.

She anguished about the angry accusation she'd flung at
him. She fretted that it might be the last she'd ever see of
him. Yet more than once she stopped her fretting and her
anguish to tell herself it might be good riddance if it were.

It was true, what she'd said about him feeling sorry for
himself. It was true that he was hanging on to a job he hated
for the least sensible of reasons. He was so much happier

when he was making furniture or refinishing woodwork. He
was more like Nick.

Try telling him that, she told herself.

And, of course, she had. For all the good it did her. He
had taken her flaring accusation with stony silence, never
even looking up when she'd stamped her foot and flung
herself across the room and up the basement stairs.

He didn't call her after her outburst, either. And he hadn'
been at Carter's the next evening when they strung popcorn
and cranberries. He didn't even call her to say goodbye.

And now it was Christmas Eve, and though she knew
better, she couldn't help wondering in spite of herself how
he was and what he was doing today.

It was her preoccupation with Nick that had caused her
to express her honest astonishment at what seemed an ex-
cessive number of bridesmaids. Normally she wouldn't have
said a word.

But it didn't matter anyway as Gertrude, as usual, chose
not to acknowledge it. "Graduated shades from ice to in-
digo," her grandmother went on. "Stunning, I should think
Pity you couldn't have been one of them."

"I don't know Jennifer that well," Diane reminded her.

Gertrude looked down her nose. "Pish."

Diane shrugged helplessly, "We were only at cotillion
together one year."

"She could have asked you, regardless," Gertrude maintained. "Matthew was one of her father's dearest friends."

"Perhaps Jennifer wanted her own friends."

Gertrude gave an elegant snort. "What does that have to
do with it."

It wasn't a question. It was a statement. In Gertrude Hoffmann's world friendship had little to do with such things.
Social obligation was all.

"You'll like her brother," Gertrude continued. "He's fin-

hing a residency at Johns Hopkins this year, Minna says.
ardiology.''

"Mmm.''

"A fine field, cardiology,'' Gertrude said. "And he'll
oon be wanting a wife. A man like that needs a wife.'' She
ightened as if the idea she'd been leading up to for the
st half hour had suddenly, miraculously occurred to her.
Derek would be absolutely perfect for you, dear. And vice
ersa, of course.''

That demanded more than a noncommittal response. "I
on't think—''

"Of course you don't think,'' Gertrude snapped. "You
ever think! And you never meet anyone appropriate in that
diculous job of yours! That's why I arranged for you to
ance with him. I—''

"Grandmother!''

Gertrude gave her a look of purest innocence. "What
ear?''

"You asked this man to dance with me?''

"I mentioned it to Minna. Heaven knows, he needs you
badly as you need him.''

"I don't need—''

"*I* know what you need, my dear. And you would do
ell to pay attention. I haven't gotten to be seventy-four
rough sheer stupidity.''

"I know that, but—''

"So you will dance with him. Smile at him. Talk to him.
nd who knows?'' Gertrude smiled her cat-eating-canary
mile. "Maybe next Christmas you'll have ten bridesmaids,
o.''

It was no secret that Gertrude would like her married
ff—and married off well. She had been parading eligible
en in front of Diane since she'd graduated from eighth
rade.

Cynthia had objected, of course.

"She's a child, Mother," Diane had often heard her say

"One can never start introducing one's child to the righ people at too early an age," Gertrude said flatly. There wa: a pause, then, "I clearly should have started earlier witl you."

What her mother answered to that Diane never heard. She did hear, moments later, the slam of a door.

"Oh, Mom," she'd whispered, and she'd felt the hollow aching sensation in the pit of her stomach that she alway: felt when she confronted the memory of her mother's ill fated marriage to the man who had fathered her.

Gertrude was determined not to let such a mismatch hap pen again. She would do everything she could to prevent it

Diane smiled as she wondered what Gertrude would have thought if she'd married Nick.

And there she was…right back at Nick again.

She had to stop thinking about him. There was no point The next move—if there was a next move—would have to be up to him.

"Tell me about this cardiologist," she said to her grand mother. And she settled back against the sofa and pretended once again to listen.

CHRISTMAS in New York. In the minds of most it conjured up the leg-kicking Rockettes at Radio City Music Hall, the sight of skaters whizzing past the brightly lit tree in Rocke feller Center, the smell of roasting chestnuts and pine trees and the sound of Salvation Army bell ringers.

For Nick it conjured up the legs of a hundred Chicken Paprikas, the sight of thirty *Dobosh Tortes*, the smells o: dilled zucchini and roast duck and goose, and the sound o: five waitresses calling in sick so they could spend the hol iday with their families.

He nearly went berserk.

He got to the restaurant at seven on Christmas Eve morning, he didn't leave until eleven in the evening.

When he finally dragged himself back to Annie's empty apartment—even she had gone home for the holiday—he was exhausted.

He stumbled up the stairs, and fell onto the sofa face-down.

He had given up St. Louis for this?

Even the thought of confronting his family, armed as they would undoubtedly be, with a dozen rounds of guilt, didn't seem as bad as going through the day he'd just experienced. He rolled over, kicked off his shoes and loosened his tie.

"Come have a drink with us. Or even better, dinner," Carter had said to him. "My family's quite tolerable on state occasions. They rise to them."

But Nick couldn't rise to it, and he knew it.

He knew where he wanted to go. He knew whom he wanted to be with. It wasn't on the Upper East Side and it wasn't the seasonally well-behaved MacKenzies.

His gaze lit on the reindeer Christmas card propped up on the desk. The one that had come yesterday morning with a St. Louis postmark. The one with no other message than a signature.

"Diane," he muttered, closed his eyes and pulled the pillow over his face.

WHEN THE PHONE RANG it was well past midnight. He'd fallen asleep on the couch, the pillow still on his face. He groaned and groped for the receiver only because one tiny molecule in his brain wouldn't believe she'd given up on him.

But it was a gruff, masculine voice demanding, "Where's

Annie?'' on the other end of the line. Nick frowned, disconcerted, then recognizing the accent, amazed.

"Jared?''

There was a moment's pause, then, ''Nick?''

In spite of his weariness, Nick found he was smiling.
''Damn right.''

If it wasn't Diane—and had he really expected it would
be?—to hear from Jared Flynn on Christmas was the next
best thing.

No one had ever been as good a friend to him as Jared.

So he was a little surprised at Jared's fierce ''What in
hell are you doing there? Are you—'' There was a pause,
then, ''Where's Annie?''

There was a wealth of sudden suspicion and irritation in
his tone. Nick could hear it. And once more he wondered
just how platonic this relationship between Annie and Jared
had been.

He didn't ask.

Instead he said quickly, ''Annie isn't here. She went
home for the holidays.''

Jared breathed what sounded rather like a sigh of relief.
''Ah, well, that's a surprise. They closed down for the holiday, then?'' His suspicion was gone, but there was an edge
to his voice and a tone Nick couldn't quite put a name to.

''Just for today. But she won't be back till the weekend.
Director's orders. He thought she needed a break.''

''Ah.'' It was a weary, all-knowing sound.

''Do you want her number?'' Nick asked.

''Doesn't matter,'' Jared said brusquely. ''I…only
thought, since it's Christmas, you know, and us having been
friends and all…''

''Friends?'' Nick couldn't help querying.

''Drop it,'' Jared said.

And Nick, with pains of his own along those lines, did.

"So, how are you? What are you doing in New York, then?" Jared asked. "There's a story behind it, to be sure."

"A long story," Nick said wearily. "Have you got a while?"

"As it happens, I have," Jared replied, and there was a kindred weariness in his tone that made Nick wish his friend weren't a continent away.

"I've the whole bloody night," Jared said. "Tell all."

So Nick did.

He didn't intend to, really. He didn't want to burden his friend. But he'd forgotten how much he and Jared had once shared, how close they once were, how they'd bolstered and supported each other when their dreams and their hopes had once been all either of them had had.

And so when he began talking, he couldn't seem to stop.

He told Jared about his father, about the family's expectations, about his increasing dissatisfaction with it all. He told him about Ginny, about her expectations, about his inability to be the man everyone wanted him to become.

"So I split," he finished hotly. "I got tired of fulfilling everyone else's expectations. I wanted, for once, to do what I want to do!"

"And are you?" Jared asked him quietly.

And are you?

Three simple words. So simple they caught him off guard. So blunt they made all his arguments and rationalizations meaningless. So direct that for once they elicited an honest answer.

"No," Nick said. "I'm not."

And as he spoke, the angry heat that had been building up within him seeped from his voice. In its place the weariness crept back.

And with it came the pain, the loneliness and all the other

emotions he fought, like tigers, day and night. Most of the time he vanquished them. Not tonight.

"You have to," Jared said.

Nick didn't say anything. He remembered Diane telling him he ought to quit. He remembered her telling him he was afraid. He remembered her scornful dismissal of his qualms, her accusation that he was feeling sorry for himself.

And he knew she was right.

Just as Jared was right.

What he enjoyed was working with wood.

He was good at it. He liked it. It gave him a personal peace and satisfaction that even Granatelli's never had.

Diane said he should try it professionally.

And he'd dismissed it out of hand.

Why?

Because, and here she was also correct, he was afraid. Afraid of failing.

He never had. In his whole life Nick Granatelli had never failed. He'd never even worried about it. Life had always been, if not easy, then at least quite manageable. He was clever, capable, a good student, a good athlete, and he had all the Granatellis behind him, cheering him on.

Nothing he set his hand to ever crumbled under it. Nothing he'd set his mind to ever slipped away.

"My son, the success," Dominic used to call him and clap him on the back.

And while Nick had laughed, he'd always known the pride that had come with his father's approbation. He'd basked in it, in fact.

If his natural abilities had given him a head start on success, family approval had always been his safety net.

But he didn't have that approval anymore.

If he tried woodworking, he was trying it on his own.

It was scary. It wasn't by any means a sure thing. But if

he didn't do it, he knew now with certainty he'd regret it all his life.

And if he did risk it?

A faint smile began to dawn on his face. If he did risk it, he could take other risks—like trying to get back together with Diane.

"I will," he said to Jared now.

"I'm a fine one to be telling you." Jared sounded almost sheepish.

Nick didn't know what he meant. It seemed to him that Jared had every right to tell him. He had pursued his own dream in the face of obstacles Nick couldn't even imagine. Now a big-time Hollywood actor, he'd succeeded beyond his wildest dreams. But even as he thought it, Nick realized something else.

"Didn't matter who else told me," he said with sudden insight. "It only mattered when I told myself."

CARTER CALLED on Christmas morning. Annie called. Jack and Frances called. There was no call from Nick.

Was she surprised? Diane asked herself.

No.

Disappointed?

Oh, yes. Because for all the pep talks she gave herself reiterating how not seeing him was for the best, she couldn't control her fantasy life. She couldn't forget. And she couldn't squelch entirely the fledgling hope that somewhere inside the unhappy man she knew now was the Nick he'd once been, the Nick who had been her soulmate, her friend. The man who had come closer than anyone to being her lover.

She knew she'd made him angry that last day in New York when she'd come to his workshop. She hoped she'd

made him think. At first she'd worried about it, regretted it.
Now she wished she'd said more, not less.

She was almost sure she hadn't been wrong about the
way he'd looked at her the day Jason was born. She was
almost certain he still felt something for her. Perhaps if
she'd goaded him, challenged him, told him how she still
felt…

But she hadn't.

And he hadn't written or called.

Yet even in the face of silence, she clung to a hope.
Maybe, with patience he could be brought around. Maybe,
she told herself with inveterate optimism, he was already.

But so far she'd had no sign.

She got through the day on social grace alone. She smiled
when required, said thank-you when appropriate, and passed
the turkey on cue.

She didn't feel much of anything until late Christmas evening when the phone rang and Cynthia answered, then held
it out and said, "It's for you."

It was Carter. Again.

"I'm missing you," he told her.

She missed him, too, but not the way he meant. That
worried her, too, the little hints Carter seemed to be dropping lately, the way he looked at her, the sense that to him
there was getting to be more than friendship here.

"Did you have a good Christmas?" she asked him.

"Not bad. The old man didn't even show up."

"What about your mother?"

"Oh, she was there. Hanging in. She ought to dump the
bastard," he said with as much savageness as she'd ever
heard from Carter.

"That's for her to decide," Diane said gently and heard
him sigh.

"I suppose. Anyway, it isn't much of a Christmas topic. How was yours?"

"Fine. Everyone showed up at least."

He told her about calling Frances and Jack. She told him about talking to Annie. And then she had to ask.

"Did Nick come for dinner?"

"No. I don't know where he is."

"He didn't even stop by?"

"Nope. I tried to reach him. He's not at work. He's not at Annie's. Or Jack's. Maybe he went home for Christmas, after all."

"Do you think?" But even as she voiced the question, Diane felt the hope inside her burst into flower.

Of course he had. He was a Granatelli, wasn't he?

A man like Nick, even one who'd run away, wouldn't let a holiday keep him away. He'd come back. She was sure he would.

And if he'd come to St. Louis to see them...

She smiled all over her face.

He'd made a move.

WHEN GERTRUDE had suggested—no, demanded—she get a new dress and hat for Jennifer's wedding, Diane had been indifferent. When Minna suggested a little hat shop called The Mad Hatter not far from Neiman-Marcus she'd manufactured several reasons why she couldn't go.

But now all her reasons had vanished. She not only went to The Mad Hatter, Francesca Granatelli, Prop., she was smiling as she walked in the door.

Up until this moment she'd only thought of the Granatellis in the abstract. She had known the remarkable influence they'd had on Nick, but she'd never encountered any of them.

Suddenly she wanted to.

The smiling blond woman who waited on her had Nick's eyes, Nick's smile. She was so friendly, so welcoming, so correct in her assessment of just what Diane would need for Jennifer's wedding, that Diane liked her at once.

And as the woman wrapped her purchase, Diane found herself asking with as much casualness as she could muster, "Are you by any chance related to Nick Granatelli?"

She might as well have dropped a bomb. The woman's head jerked up and her words, which had been flowing so easily, dried up. Her mouth formed a silent O, and for a moment there was only silence.

Then slowly she nodded, her expression, once merely friendly, was now intently curious. "His sister."

"Frankie?"

The woman shook her head. "No. I'm Sophia. It's Frankie's shop, but sometimes I take over so she can work on her hats and I can get out of the house." She gave Diane a cautious, still curious, smile. "Where do you know Nick from?"

"I…live near him in New York." That seemed enough to say for now.

"You're not from St. Louis?"

"Yes, but I live in New York now. I'm home for Christmas." She paused a millisecond, then dared to ask, "Is he?"

"Home?" Sophia snorted. "Not Nick."

Diane frowned. "But I thought…I must've been mistaken."

"Must've." Sophia concentrated on wrapping the hatbox, then sighed and asked, "Have you seen him recently?"

"About a week and a half ago."

"How is he?"

Diane wasn't sure how to answer that. She'd obviously

isread one sign. She wondered about the others. "He's…
l right," she said finally. "Working hard."

"At what?"

Surprised that he hadn't even told his family, she
rugged. "He's managing a little Hungarian restaurant on
e Upper East side."

"He could be managing *our* restaurant," Sophia said
uffly.

Diane didn't know what to reply to that. She shifted from
e foot to the other, wishing she hadn't come.

"He'd better come to his senses pretty quick," grumbled
phia. "Ginny isn't going to wait forever."

"Ginny? Who's Ginny?"

Sophia blinked. "Ginny? Ginny Perpetti. Why, she's
ick's fiancée, of course."

It came out of the blue, the fatal left jab when you had
e wrong side covered. Diane felt her mind reel. "His…
fiancée?"

"For the moment anyway," Sophia said grimly. "She's
saint, Ginny is. But I don't know how much longer she'll
t around waiting for him. Stupid man."

Stupid man? No stupider than she was, Diane thought
zedly, her dreams evaporating even as she stood there.
Nick Granatelli? Engaged? Oh, God.

"I…d-didn't realize," Diane stammered. "He never
id."

Sophia looked disgusted. "Figures. Just goes to show
w crazy he's behaving. Arguing with Papa. Fighting. Caring on. Acting like an idiot. I couldn't believe it when he
ok off. It doesn't make sense. He's got everything—*ev-
ything*—going for him—the restaurant, Ginny, the folks'
use even, if he wants it—and he acts like it's a disaster!"

A disaster, Diane thought, was exactly what it was.
r her.

"It's a good thing Ginny is so understanding. Not many women would wait," Sophia went on.

"I guess not," Diane said hollowly. She took one last stab. "Is she…sure? That he's coming back, I mean?"

Sophia stared, then rolled her eyes. "Of course he's coming back! It's a momentary aberration, that's all. He's a Granatelli, isn't he?"

He's a Granatelli, isn't he? Diane had asked herself the same question last night. She knew the answer.

She held on to the edge of the counter for support. Her mind tested the "momentary aberration" idea and found it all too likely. She felt sick.

"There've been a lot of demands on him these past few years," Sophia said. "Papa's heart attack, his having to leave school. He took over too soon, I suppose. He never really got to sow any wild oats, I guess." She smiled and shrugged, as if the explanation were that simple.

Perhaps, Diane thought grimly, it was.

She'd never thought of herself as a wild oat before. The idea wasn't comforting. It was, however, probable.

Sophia finished tying a red bow on the hatbox. "He'll come around," she went on. "It's just a matter of time. It's all here waiting for him. The family, the restaurant, Ginny. Papa knows he had good ideas. He's ready to make some concessions. And Ginny will, too. Did he tell you about that business with the menu?"

"No, he—"

"I knew it. I knew he'd regret it. Probably embarrassed to even mention it. Imagine throwing away a life over a little bit of risotto." Sophia laughed and shook her head. "No. He's a loyal guy, our Nick. He won't let us down."

Diane took the hatbox wordlessly and smiled a bleak smile. "No, I suppose he won't," she said in a voice that

unded to her own ears as hollow as a drum. "Thank you
ry much."

"You're quite welcome." Sophia walked her to the door.
Are you going back to New York soon?"

"Right after New Year's."

"And you'll see Nick?"

"Probably." Though she'd love to avoid it.

Sophia smiled. "Good. When you see him tell him Papa's
aiting. Tell him Ginny's waiting. Tell him a June wedding
ould be nice."

Chapter Thirteen

He handed in his resignation at Lazlo's the day after Christmas. It wasn't much; but it was a start.

He owed them two weeks' notice and he'd give them that. But the die was cast. He was out of the restaurant business forever.

He was now Nick Granatelli, woodworker and furniture restorer, pure and simple. He was also, for all intents and purposes, unemployed.

As he walked out into the lead-gray afternoon, he felt a moment's panic, a throat-choking fear of the unknown, and then, quite suddenly, the sharpest surge of exhilaration he'd ever known.

He felt, for the first time, as if he were truly his own man.

He took a deep, cleansing breath, not even caring that it was ten parts car exhaust. Then he headed back across the park, feeling expansive, liberated, alive.

His only regret was that Diane was still in St. Louis, that he would have to wait until she came back to tell her of his decision.

He could have called her, but he knew he wouldn't. He was on the right track now and he knew it. He wanted to see her face when she knew it, too.

He did go to tell Carter. He stopped at Jack Sprat's o

is way home, needing to tell someone, to share his good news.

Carter was in the back room, sitting at his desk, scratching his signature across a stack of invoices in front of him while a lullaby played in the background and he rocked a baby buggy with his foot.

Nick halted in the doorway and stared.

Carter kept right on flipping through the invoices, unaware that he was being watched, unaware of any outside interference at all until the lullaby ended and there was a tiny whimper from the buggy.

Then he was on his feet in an instant, bending over the buggy and crooning softly to the child within.

Nick shifted from one foot to the other, then, finally and loudly, cleared his throat.

Carter looked up startled. "Oh, hi." His gaze flickered from Nick to the baby buggy and back again. "I'm babysitting," he said unnecessarily and with none of the sheepishness Nick might have expected from him.

The whimper turned into a hesitant wail, then a full-throated yell. There was no hesitation on Carter's part. He picked up the baby at once, cradling Jason in his arms with an ease of familiarity, rocking him gently as he swayed back and forth, humming in tune with the melody as he did so.

Nick watched them, amazed.

Jason hiccuped, let out one more tentative whimper, then managed to focus on the man holding him. Nick thought he might as well not have been there. They saw only each other.

Finally he cleared his throat. "Where're Jack and Frances?"

"Jack had an assignment this morning and Frances had a meeting with her editor. Brief, but necessary, she said. I don't think she trusts me with him for too long.'' Carter gave him a rueful grin.

''She should,'' Nick said. ''You're a natural.''

''You think so?'' Carter looked inordinately pleased.

A corner of Nick's mouth lifted. He rocked back on his heels, considering man and child. ''Yeah,'' he said. ''I do.''

Carter dropped a kiss on the baby's forehead. ''So do I.'' He looked down at Jason again, then lifted his eyes to meet Nick's. ''What brings you here in the middle of the day? Run out of paprika?''

Nick shook his head. ''I quit.''

Carter's eyes widened. ''At Lazlo's? Why?''

''I talked to a friend of mine in California the other night. A guy I knew when I was in Boston. A guy who had even fewer possibilities to do what he really wanted than I did. But he didn't give up. And now he's doing it—with a vengeance. It made me think.''

''Thinking can be dangerous,'' Carter said softly, his eyes drifting once more to regard the child in his arms.

''I know.''

''It makes you want to take risks.''

''Yes.''

''And do things you never dared think of doing.''

''Exactly,'' Nick said.

It was uncanny how Carter's words were reflecting his thoughts, his dreams.

''It's funny the way things work out,'' he said slowly, groping his way, looking for the right words in which to tell Carter how he felt about his future now, about his past. About his love of Diane.

''Sometimes,'' he said carefully, ''you know you'd like to, it's just that the time isn't right. Or the circumstances. For what you want, I mean. For woodworking, for example.''

"Or getting married."

Nick stared at him, amazed. Carter had really picked up is drift. "Yeah, right, or getting married. Sometimes, you now, the right person can be there under your nose for ges but you're…afraid to take the risk."

"I know."

"Afraid to make the commitment, afraid to ask her to ommit to you…" He looked at the other man hopefully, nd was relieved to see Carter nod vigorously. It was the ne thing he'd dreaded, telling Carter how he felt about)iane.

"I know exactly what you mean," Carter said. He looked own at Jason again, still smiling. He touched the baby's heek.

"And then something wakes you up, makes you look round," Nick went on. "And you realize what you should ave done a long time ago."

Carter nodded. "Uh-huh."

"You understand?" Nick couldn't mask the hope he felt. t would make things so much easier if Carter understood bout the past, understood about the circumstances, under-tood that even though he and Diane were friends, Nick was ne one who loved her, who wanted her to be his wife.

"Of course I understand," Carter told him. "Didn't I just ay so?"

"Yeah, but—"

"And I owe it all to him." Carter nodded at the baby in is arms. "He woke me up. Made me take a look at where ny life was going. Who I wanted to spend it with. Made ne realize what I really wanted." He was looking at Nick ow, his gaze steady, his eyes smiling.

"What's that?" Nick asked.

"To marry Diane."

JENNIFER Amelia Naylor married Anthony Ward Beecher II with all due pomp and ceremony two days before the New Year. Diane Bauer and six hundred and twelve more of their closest friends were witnesses to the marriage.

They were wed at the new cathedral, attended by a veritable regiment of beautifully dressed attendants, feted at LaClede's Landing, and, after champagne toasts, a sit-down supper and a night of dancing, whisked off in Jennifer's father's private jet to their Bermuda honeymoon destination.

It was, according to Gertrude, the most perfect wedding she had ever seen, even more beautiful than Cynthia and Matthew's. It set a standard to strive for. To outdo if possible.

"When you get married…" she started every third sentence she said to Diane. "When you get married…"

Diane wasn't listening.

Diane didn't give a damn.

She was mulling over Carter's marriage proposal.

IT HAD HAPPENED last night. She'd been sitting there in quiet misery, watching the evening news with her mother, pretending vast interest in the state of the world, when the phone rang.

When Cynthia handed it to her, Diane had answered almost absently.

"Oh, hi, Carter," she'd said when she'd discovered who it was.

"Hi." Just the one word sounded different, as if there was a suppressed excitement in him—a newer, more enthusiastic Carter, struggling to get out.

"What's new?" she asked.

"My goal in life."

It was an answer designed at least to attract her attention. As far as Diane knew, Carter had never *had* a goal in life.

eyond, perhaps, annoying his family by his free-spirited ursuit of irresponsibility with regard to the family fortunes nd expectations. "Say what?"

"You asked me what was new, and I said—"

"I heard you. I'm just surprised. What is it?"

"I want to get married."

"Married?" God, Carter, too? Her knot of misery twisted ghter.

"Married," he confirmed. She could definitely hear it ow, the excitement threading through his tone.

She curled her feet under her and found herself smiling 1 spite of her own unhappiness. "What brought this on?"

"Jason. He made me realize what I've been missing out n. Fatherhood. Family. Marriage. It's a long story."

"I guess it is." She'd hear it sometime. She couldn't bear now. "Well, I'd say it's an admirable goal, Carter."

"I'm glad you think so."

"Oh, I do. I do."

He laughed. "That's what I hope you'll say."

"What? When?"

"At the wedding. Will you marry me?"

HE SHOULD HAVE been expecting it. She'd seen it coming, fter all.

She'd seen the way he'd been changing recently, the way e'd stopped teasing Jack for his devotion to his wife, the vay he'd sought opportunities to be around them, especially ince the baby had been born.

But she'd just said to herself, "Isn't that nice? Carter's nellowing in his old age. How about that?"

She hadn't thought beyond that because she hadn't vanted to. She'd been too busy thinking about Nick.

And now what?

What in God's name was she going to say?

No?

It wasn't that easy. They'd been friends—close friend,
dear friends—too long. Maybe, she thought wryly, it wa
all those damnable social graces she'd been endowed with
No matter what she felt, she couldn't turn him down fla
Not without some compassion, not without gentleness, no
without, however difficult, some explanation.

So she'd laughed, hemmed, hawed, stuttered, mumbled
She'd hedged and stammered.

And finally Carter said quietly, "I know. It was rotten o
me. I never should've sprung it on you over the phone."

"It doesn't—"

"I'm a jerk."

"You're not a jerk, Carter. You're just…impetuous."

"And in love."

"No."

"Oh, yes, I am. We've been friends for a long time, D
More than friends. And we've even been heading in thi
direction for a long time, too, haven't we?"

"Well…" But she couldn't absolutely deny it. She re
membered the kisses, the warm, comfortable embraces a
too well. And if they hadn't had the passion of Nick's, sti
there had been something there.

"You're just as slow as I was. Maybe even slower," h
said, shaking his head. "It's because we've been conten
with the status quo. We've never really thought how muc
more there could be."

"I—"

"But I, for one, have been thinking lately. And I've de
cided: I want to marry you."

She hadn't said no.

She'd let him ramble on. She'd let him excuse her from
answering right then. She'd let him tell her he'd see her a

ne airport when her plane landed and ask her in person. he'd let him hang up after he'd said, ''I love you.''

And she hadn't said no.

She'd sat through the rest of the newscast. She'd eaten a ght supper with her mother. She'd dropped by her grand-nother's for a quick visit.

And she hadn't heard a word.

She was busy turning over and over the predicament her ife had become. Nick was going to marry someone else. Carter wanted to marry her.

She went to Jennifer and Anthony's wedding the next ay, her mind still spinning, still trying to make sense of he upheaval of the past two days.

She looked stunning. She acted charming. It just went to how, she thought grimly, how deeply ingrained her social races were.

She watched Jennifer and Anthony, saw them look at ach other with tenderness, saw them laugh, saw them kiss. And she thought, *I will never do that with Nick. Carter vants to do that with me.*

And for just one instant, she let the pain of it surface, •linked her eyes furiously, sucked in a deep breath, and vent back to smiling as if she were the prototype Wedding Guest Of The Year.

Jennifer and Anthony certainly never noticed her lapse. Nor did her grandmother or six hundred and ten of the other •eople who were present at the wedding.

The only one who noticed was her mother.

Cynthia didn't comment. Not then. She did her own fair hare of smiling, hand-shaking, cheek-kissing and platitude-•rattling.

Diane didn't even know her faux pas had been detected intil late that night when she was getting ready for bed. She was removing the last of her makeup when there was discreet tap on her door.

Answering it, she found Cynthia, already in her robe standing there with a tray bearing a pot of tea and two cups

"I thought we'd toast the bride and groom," she said and stepped into the room.

Diane hovered by the door uncertainly. The last thing she wanted tonight was to think about happy wedding couples

"Come sit down, darling." Cynthia set the tray on Diane's dressing table, then sat down and patted the bed.

Smiling halfheartedly, Diane did. But she sat where she could see the mirror and continued removing her eye shadow, not wanting her mother's scrutiny. Cynthia very often saw too much.

Cynthia poured out the tea, added sugar to hers and milk to Diane's.

Diane concentrated on dabbing at her eyelids, steeled for whatever platitude served as the toast.

But Cynthia didn't speak until Diane's eyes met hers in the mirror. Then she raised her cup, a poignant smile on her face as she said, "To Jennifer and Anthony, may their good times be many and their bad times be few. And may they always be there for each other no matter what."

Then, blinking several times very rapidly, Cynthia bent her head and took a long sip from her cup.

Diane, shutting out the thought that it would never be that way for her and Nick, did the same.

I should drink to Nick and Ginny-Whoever-She-Is, she thought.

But nothing in her could make her do it.

"You were sad today." Cynthia was watching her, a gentle smile on her face.

It could have been a question, a guess, but Diane knew it wasn't.

She gave a tiny shrug. "Weddings sometimes do that to me."

Cynthia's mouth lifted at one corner. "Wishing?"

Diane finished removing her eyeliner, then sighed. "Maybe."

"Someone special?"

"Mmm."

"The man who called last night?"

"Carter?" Diane couldn't keep the surprise out of her voice. "Not...exactly."

"He's been very attentive," Cynthia commented. "He's called you several times."

"Yes."

"Is he the one you met at Aunt Flo's?"

"Yes."

"But he's not the one who matters." That wasn't a question, either.

Diane smiled sadly. "He matters a lot," she said, but without any real force.

Cynthia's smile was gentle. "I'm sure he does. But he's not the right one."

"I don't feel for him what I feel for—" Diane broke off suddenly. She'd never talked about Nick to anyone in the family, had never even mentioned his name except as a friend she'd met through Annie. At first it had been too special, later it had hurt too much.

She didn't imagine she was fooling Cynthia into thinking there wasn't a man responsible for some of her irritability three years ago. Her mother was far too astute. She was also circumspect, and she didn't pry. Unlike her own mother, Cynthia never demanded her daughter's confidences. Diane was grateful for that.

And she was discovering gratitude again tonight when

faced with her mother's gentle perception and the comfort she so delicately offered.

"You don't feel for Carter what you feel for…" Cynthia prompted softly after a moment.

Nick. She would never feel for any man what she felt for Nick.

Had it been the same for Cynthia?

Diane looked at her mother and saw not simply the woman who had raised her, who had bandaged her cuts and scrapes, kissed away her petty hurts, baked her birthday cakes and attended more mother-daughter functions than anyone should have had to.

She saw as well a woman who understood the joys and pains of relationships—a woman who had had two marriages. And two losses.

She saw a woman who would understand.

She took a deep breath and began. "For Nick," she said. "Nick Granatelli."

And once she said his name, she couldn't stop. She needed to talk to someone about Nick.

She told her mother about their time together three years before, about how he'd seemed like a gift from God, the perfect man to fulfill her fantasy.

She saw Cynthia smile, a painful smile, as if perfect men were something her mother, too, had thought about.

She told Cynthia about Nick's father's heart attack, about Nick dropping out of Harvard and returning to St. Louis. She even, swallowing gamely, told her mother that she had volunteered to come with him.

"He said no," she admitted in a tiny voice. "He said I hadn't grown up yet. That I wouldn't…fit."

Even now it hurt to say the words, and she ducked her head, dug her toes into the thick ivory-colored carpet, twisting a tissue in her fingers.

"Oh, Di—"

Diane shook her head. "He was right."

"Was he?" Cynthia said, surprising her.

Diane's gaze lifted and met her mother's, saw there compassion and understanding and heaps of love.

"I had nothing to offer him," she said. "I *was* a child."

"You were," Cynthia agreed. "But I think you did have something to offer him. You had a great deal of love—all for him."

"He didn't think love was enough."

Cynthia's gentle smile twisted slightly. "No—" her voice was a bare whisper "—sometimes men don't."

There was something in her voice—some deep, terrible pain—that Diane couldn't ignore. "My father, you mean?"

She rarely spoke of her father to Cynthia. When it came to speaking of Russell Shaw, Diane could never get beyond her mother's reserve.

It wasn't that she hadn't told Diane about him. When Diane had thought he was dead, she had always simply accepted the praise and the generalities that had made her father a shadowy benevolent figure in her past. She had hoped, after she'd discovered he was alive, that she would learn more about him, about his relationship with her mother.

It hadn't happened. Russ had been forthcoming enough about his own recent past. He'd even told her quite a bit about his growing-up years. But all he had said about his relationship with her mother was that, except for Diane, it had been a mistake.

"She's a wonderful woman, your mother," he'd said to Diane. "She deserved better than me." And that was all he'd said.

Cynthia had said little more about him.

But now she nodded, chewed briefly on her upper lip, then nodded again. "Yes, dear. Like your father."

"You…really did love him, then? It wasn't just…" But how did you ask your beloved mother if you were simply the product of a brief infatuation, a terrible mistake.

But she didn't have to say it. Cynthia understood.

"I loved your father more than anyone on earth," she said with a fierceness that left no room for doubt. "Don't you ever, *ever* believe otherwise!"

Diane couldn't help smiling. "My mother, the tigress."

Cynthia flushed. "I loved your father," she said. "And you'd better believe it."

"I do."

"He was good, and kind, and loving," Cynthia went on firmly. Her gaze drifted away and she stared unseeing across the room. "And when he left—" her voice broke "—he left because he was all those things."

"What do you mean?"

"He didn't want to be selfish. He wanted for us what he could never provide. He tried. God, how he tried. But it was too much for him."

"He could have loved us," Diane said, her voice thin, aching almost as much as her mother's.

"He did," Cynthia said quietly. "Never doubt that, either. And I loved him." She closed her eyes and added in a voice Diane could scarcely hear. "For all the good it did me."

"At least," Diane said, reaching for her mother's hand, "you had him for a while."

She had never had Nick. Except in her heart.

"I did," Cynthia agreed. "And I had you."

Their fingers squeezed and their eyes met with a warmth and a solidarity that made Diane sorry only that her father had missed out on sharing it.

"Also," Cynthia went on quietly, but firmly. "I had Mat-
w."

Matthew. Matthew Bauer. Kind and loving Matthew. The
id support on which both Diane and her mother had de-
nded. The man who had shared in what Russell Shaw had
t.

"Did you...love Matthew?"

Diane had always loved Matthew dearly herself. She
ld never have asked for a more wonderful father. And
'd always assumed her mother had loved him, too. But
 fierceness of Cynthia's answer to her question about
ether or not she had loved Russ suddenly gave her reason
 wonder.

"Absolutely." There was no hesitation in Cynthia's re-
. She smiled. "Matthew was the finest man I have ever
own. He taught me that there was more to love than pas-
nate yearning. He showed me how many various, won-
ful facets of it there were. He was there for me when I
ded him. He loved me as selflessly as ever a man could
e."

It was true. Diane believed it. She knew that Matthew,
, had been married before and that his first wife had died.
 couldn't help asking, "So...passion isn't necessary?"
 didn't know if she felt more doubtful or hopeful.

Cynthia smiled. "Passion is...wonderful. Marvelous.
autiful. But it is not everything. It is a part, not the whole,
 love."

"And you were happy with Matthew?"

"I was happy with Matthew."

"And...my father? Are you sorry—?"

Cynthia smiled. "I will always be sorry we don't live in
erfect world, a world in which mad and impetuous love
ds a safe haven. But I'm an adult now. I learned a long
e ago I couldn't have everything the way I wanted it.

Sometimes—'' and here she smiled at her daught
"—sometimes I think I am a far luckier woman than I ev
deserved to be.''

She set her teacup down on the tray, got up and came
stand behind Diane's chair. She laid her hands on her daug
ter's shoulders, meeting her eyes in the mirror.

"I consider myself a very fortunate woman,'' she sa
and dropped a kiss on Diane's hair. "I have been blesse
I wish the same for you.''

I LEARNED a long time ago I couldn't have everything th
way I wanted it.

Some of us, Diane thought ruefully as she snuggled bac
into the airline seat and shut her eyes, are not such quic
studies.

Some of us rail against fate far too long. Our expectatio
are unrealistic. Our demands too great.

We need to make adjustments, to compromise. We nee
to be grateful for what life offers us, not bemoan the lo
of what we can't have.

We need to learn to love the men who love us.

And not, Diane thought as the plane hurtled down th
runway, taking off toward New York and La Guardia an
Carter, the men we can never have.

CARTER had been whistling the whole damned afternoo
Tapping his feet. Humming little snatches of love song
Driving Nick to distraction without even trying.

"What is it with you?" he snarled finally, glowering
Carter from where he sat in the dining room, sanding th
door to the built-in buffet. It was his latest project, refinish
ing all Carter's woodwork to match the bookcases he
built.

'I'm in love,'' Carter said through a mouthful of corn
ps. ''Love makes everyone happy.''

'Does it?'' Nick muttered and rubbed the sandpaper even
der against the wood.

'You're just jealous.'' Carter grinned.

Nick bent his head over the door. ''Yeah.'' Trust Carter
nail him right where it hurt and not even realize it. He
hed and wiped a hand across his face.

'Her plane is due in an hour,'' Carter said now. ''You
nt to come to the airport with me?''

'No, I don't want to come to the airport with you.''

'Hey, I just asked. No need to get sharpish. What's the
tter? Worried about work? I'm sure some will come
ough. My uncle said—''

'No, I'm not worried about work.'' Work was the least
his problems. The biggest was how he was going to get
ough the rest of his life with one of his best friends mar-
d to another best friend who just happened to be the
man he loved.

Carter raised his hands defensively. ''Right. Work isn't a
oblem.'' A pause. ''Then what is?''

Nick shrugged irritably. ''I don't know. The weather
ybe?''

'It's a nice night,'' Carter said. ''Clear. Cold. No storms
sight.''

Nick scowled. ''So maybe it's not the weather.''

He wished Carter would leave, would take his cheerful
untenance and his tapping feet and get the hell out.

'Well,'' Carter said, ''it sounds to me as if you've got a
g up your butt about something. But if you don't want to
k about it, it's all right with me.''

'I don't want to talk about it,'' Nick said tersely. He
rted sanding again. Out of the corner of his eye he could
 Carter's Topsiders flex.

Then the heels hit the floor and Carter said, "Right. We suit yourself. You will anyway. See you when I get back

Nick shut his eyes. "Yeah."

Carter rummaged in the closet for his jacket, slipped on, then opened the door and stopped, looking back ov his shoulder. "You sure you're all right?"

"I'm all right."

Carter still looked doubtful.

"I'm fine," Nick said more forcefully. "Go on. And he added rashly, "bring her back here afterward. I'll buy bottle of champagne. We can celebrate."

It was a stupid thing to say. Stupider even to do, Ni thought. But for all that he cursed his idiocy, it did make perverse sort of sense.

It was called facing your worst possible nightmare. H grandfather had been a great believer in it.

Nick remembered well the afternoon he sat there in h grandfather's workshop telling him about Wally Tompkir the hotshot from a rival high school who had struck him c four times—the last one with the bases loaded—when th had played that spring.

"He'll do it again," Nick remembered saying fatalis cally. "He'll do it again."

His grandfather puffed on his pipe, considered the b hunched on the stool next to him, then laid a hand on Nick shoulder. "And if he does, so?" he said finally.

"Well..." Nick groped to reply. "I'll look like an id again."

"Are you an idiot?"

"No!"

"So what more?"

"I'll let down my team."

"There's only one way to help a team?"

"Well, no, but—"

"What more?"

The quizzing went on until Nick began to realize that
even if he struck out, it wasn't the end of the world. He was
capable, competent, worthy, only at times fallible.

So he had gone out there and faced Wally Tompkins.
He'd struck out. He'd survived.

Next time up he'd hit a homer.

So tonight he'd face Carter and Diane in the afterglow of
their engagement. He'd smile and offer them champagne.
He'd survive.

But he knew he'd never ever get another at bat, let alone
a homer.

HER PLANE ARRIVED at seven. At least that's when it was
scheduled.

Nick imagined the whole scene: Carter waiting, scooping
her into his arms, grinning like a fool, popping the question
yet again, and being told yes—here Nick shut his eyes—
then sweeping her into his car, and within the hour arriving
back at his place where Nick, steeled, would be waiting with
his duty bottle of champagne.

By nine o'clock Nick had revised the scenario to include
a quiet candlelit dinner for two at The Sign of the Dove or
some other posh Upper East Side place.

By eleven he had added a nightcap at the top of the World
Trade Center.

By midnight he had tacked on dancing at the little Soho
nightclub that he knew Carter was fond of.

By two he'd imagined them taking in the last set at the
jazz club right around the corner.

By four he was frantic.

By six he admitted the truth: Carter and Diane were not
coming back here, had no intention of coming back here.

They had undoubtedly gone from the airport to Diane's

apartment (with or without any intermediate stops) and wer
at this very moment—his eyes shut again—consummatin
their engagement in Diane's wide, welcoming bed.

And that was a worse nightmare than he'd ever let himse
imagine.

He drank the champagne by himself—the whole bottle of
it—then went into the bathroom and was thoroughly an
disgustingly sick.

THE DOOR OPENED shortly past noon. Nick was lying o
Carter's sofa, his face buried in the cushions. Slowly, wit
the utmost care, he turned his head.

Carter's Topsiders stood still before him.

He drew a careful breath, clamping his teeth against th
nausea that threatened. Then, just as carefully, he levere
himself up and swung around sideways, dredging up a pair
ful smile from somewhere, expecting happy faces to smil
down on him.

Carter was alone.

It was easier this way, Nick told himself. Easier to fac
Carter first. Then Diane.

His eye caught the champagne bottle, which lay on it
side under the coffee table. He noticed Carter looking at i
too. He gave a rueful shrug.

"I...decided not to wait," he said. "You didn't come
after all." He tried to make his words sound light and care
free, but his voice was rusty, as if he hadn't used it in year

Carter didn't say anything. He looked, Nick decided, a
if he'd had a hard night. His eyes were bloodshot, his shi
creased, his hair rumpled and his tie askew.

"But..." Nick said when he could form the words, "
suppose that's the way it goes." Then he made himself as
because, after all, Diane didn't have the corner on the soci
skills market, "Did you have a good time?"

Carter turned his head. He stared away out the window across Central Park and beyond. The words, when they came, fell tonelessly from his lips.

"She turned me down."

 WAS CRAZY to hope.

It was worse not to know.

Nick was sure Diane's refusal to marry Carter would have nothing to do with him; he was sure he was making an idiot of himself by seeking her out and asking.

But he couldn't stay away.

He'd done his best by Carter. He'd squelched his natural inclination, which had been to shout hallelujahs from the rooftop, and made himself and Carter a pot of strong black coffee. When they'd drunk in silence, he made another.

It was over the second pot of coffee that he had ventured his first question. "Did she...say...why?"

"Probably." Carter stared moodily into the murky black liquid. His fingers knotted around the mug. His hair drooped across his forehead, looking as lifeless and unhappy as he did. He shoved it back, but when it fell forward again almost immediately, he ignored it.

"So...why?" Nick felt like a heel asking. He couldn't help himself.

Carter's dark eyes met his squarely. "It was long and complicated and sincere and every bit what you'd expect from Diane." He flexed his shoulders, then hunched them again. "The gist of it was, she doesn't love me."

Did she love *him?* The question filled Nick's throat as if he'd swallowed a stone.

He could still feel it now as he made his way up the front steps to Diane's brownstone. He made no immediate move to ring the bell, hoping someone would come out instead. He wasn't sure he wanted her to know he was coming.

If he was going to be rejected, too, he wanted it to b
face-to-face.

But no one came out and no one went in. And afte
twenty minutes of shifting from one foot to the other, alter
nately cursing and praying, he rang the bell.

There was no response for quite some time. Then h
heard a faint, "Who is it?"

"Nick."

"I don't—"

"Please! I just want to talk to you!"

"It isn't necessary. You don't—"

"I do! Please, Diane!"

He didn't know why he was bothering. He had his an
swer, didn't he? There was certainly no enthusiasm her
No joy. No expectation.

But at the moment his shoulders sagged and he was read
to turn around and go away, the buzzer sounded and Dian
said flatly. "All right. Come up."

The door was shut against him when he got there. Sh
wasn't making it easy for him, he thought grimly as h
raised his hand to knock.

The door opened slowly and Diane stood before him, he
hair pinned back, her expression drawn. She looked pale bu
composed, not loving in the least.

He licked his lips, tucked his hands into the pockets c
his jeans, shifted from one foot to the other and regrette
once again his decision to come.

In the top two of people Diane Bauer least wanted to se
at that moment, Nick Granatelli was the only one higher o
the list than the man whose proposal she had just turne
down.

It wasn't fair, she thought. How dare he?

Had he come to tell her about his own bride-to-be? sh

ondered. Probably, she thought, tasting irony. They were
ich good friends.

"What do you want?"

"I…you…" Oh, hell, what was the point? He shoved a
and through his hair. His head ached abominably. "Car-
rsaysyouturnedhimdown."

Diane gave a jerky little nod as she stepped back to let
im in. Then she pressed her lips together in a tight line.
er eyes were as hard as stones. "You're not here to do a
ohn Alden for him, are you?"

Nick frowned. "Huh?"

"To talk me into marrying him?"

He shook his head and immediately regretted it. "No. No,
m not."

"Then why are you here?"

"I just wondered…why. Why you're not going to marry
m, I mean."

"What business is it of yours?"

He shrugged awkwardly. "I suppose it isn't, but…" He
altered, groping for words that would make it all right or
least get it over with. "I love you," he said.

He couldn't imagine why he'd said it.

He couldn't think of a worse thing to say. Yet he couldn't
ave retracted it if he'd tried.

Diane stared at him. Her mouth opened as if she might
spond, then closed as if no response were possible.

"I'm sorry," he muttered. "I shouldn't have—I don't
ean to—" He shook his head, defeated, dismayed.

Diane was now looking equally dismayed at him. Were
ose tears welling up in her eyes? They couldn't be, he
ought at the same time she began blinking furiously and
wiping a hand across her eyes.

"Damn you," she said, and her voice broke. "Oh, damn

you, Nick Granatelli! Why in God's name would you com
and tell me that? I could have survived without that!''

Nick frowned, confused. What the hell right did she hav
to talk about surviving? That was his problem!

"Why did you come?" she demanded angrily. "Did yo
want my blessing maybe?"

"Blessing?" Nick stared at her, baffled.

"On your wedding. You and Virginia Perpetti!"

"Ginny?" Nick croaked. "What about Ginny?"

"Don't give me that. You don't have to play dumb wit
me. I know."

Nick didn't. Nick felt as if he'd slipped out of his ow
reality into someone else's. "What in the hell are you talk
ing about?"

"I just came back from St. Louis, remember?" Diane'
voice was icy.

He nodded. "I remember. But—"

"Actually I just came back from a wedding. A weddin
for which I was required to buy a new dress and a hat. *
hat that I bought at the Mad Hatter." She gave Nick a sig
nificant look.

"You went to Frankie's?"

"I did."

"And she told you I was marrying Ginny Perpetti?" H
couldn't believe that.

"Not Frankie. Your other sister. Sophia."

That he could believe. Didn't want to, but could.

Sophia was a chip off the Granatelli block. If his fathe
said something was going to happen, it did. Sophia share
that same view of reality. But to think she was still hangin
on to that ridiculous idea after all this time!

"No," he said.

Diane just looked at him.

Outside a siren wailed. Someone was pounding down th

airs. A door slammed. A horn honked. "No?" she re-
ated in a barely audible tone. It was still disbelieving, but
t quite as forceful.

Nick shook his head slowly, adamantly. "No. I am not
arrying Virginia Perpetti. No, I am not going back to run
ranatelli's. No, I am not even in the restaurant business
ymore. I quit at Lazlo's the day after Christmas."

His mouth was dry. His knees felt weak.

Her mouth was dry. Her knees felt weak. What was he
ying? What did he mean? Why, she asked herself again,
d he come?

He'd said he loved her. Yet he didn't look loving. His
pression was unreadable and his blue eyes were clouded
ith an emotion she didn't understand. She waited, not
owing for what.

"Why," Nick asked her again, "did you turn Carter
wn?" There was a gentleness in the question this time, a
nt of hope. Diane could have been imagining it; she didn't
ink she was. Her fingers knotted together.

"Why did you come?" she asked him.

"Because I love you," Nick answered, and Diane said
e words along with him.

Their gazes met, locked. Their souls touched.

And Nick, shutting his eyes and holding on to the mo-
ent, bent his head. "Yes."

E HAD LOVED her for years. But never like this.

Never with the fullness of heart and soul, mind and body
at existed between them now. He had never before given
r all of himself; he had never had all of her.

It was everything he could have wished for. The warm,
elcoming bed he had envisioned her sharing with Carter,
knew she had only shared with him. The arms that drew

him into her embrace had held no one else the way the
held him.

And his own love of her was all the more wonderful fo
having been so long in its realization.

At first there were no words, only touches. At the la
there were pounding hearts and sounds of love.

And in the aftermath, with nothing but their love settle
between them, he dared to ask, "Will you marry me?"

And he held his breath until he saw her smile and he fe
the word "Yes" whispered against his lips.

She snuggled against him, feeling both shattered an
whole. The world as she had known it, in the space of
few hours, had spun like a kaleidoscope, arranging and r
arranging itself in myriad patterns—promises. But none (
them equaled the beauty of the one in which she foun
herself now.

She turned her head slightly and kissed Nick's bare ches
She felt his lips graze her forehead, felt his shoulder sol:
and warm beneath her head, then closed her eyes and drar
in the pure, perfect happiness of it all.

"Sleepy?" Nick asked her, his voice tender.

She shook her head and opened her eyes. "No." Sl
looked up at him, smiling. "I just keep closing my eyes an
opening them again, daring you to vanish. Am I temptir
fate?"

"I'm not going to vanish," Nick promised her. "You':
stuck with me for life."

"Thank God."

"Amen," Nick agreed. "I thought you would marry Ca
ter."

Diane pushed herself up on her elbows so she could loc
down into his dear face and thought how close she'd con
to doing just that. "I nearly did," she told him.

Her mother's relationship with Matthew had almost cor

inced her it would make perfect sense. It was only when he realized how strong Carter's feelings were and how one-ided their love would be that she'd found the courage to ay no.

Nick's expression grew grave. "He could give you a amn sight more than I can. He's got a successful business, penthouse on Columbus Avenue, and a trust fund worth iillions. Maybe you should reconsider."

Diane eyed him carefully, pondering his words. "Maybe should," she said.

Nick's expression was startled. "You'd better not!" he iuttered, grabbing her as her mouth swooped down to nip t his nose.

"You idiot!" she chided. "Do you really think millions iatter to me, or penthouses?"

"No, but—"

"Carter is a wonderful person. He'll make some woman great husband, but not me. When I thought you were mar-ying your Virginia—"

"She's not my Virginia," Nick protested. "She's *never* een my Virginia. We were engaged once, by default."

Diane laughed, amazed that she could even find such a ling funny. "As I was saying, when I thought you were iarrying her, I considered marrying Carter. My mother, af-er all, had married Matthew and they had a wonderful mar-iage."

"So why didn't you?" Nick felt almost safe asking the uestion now.

"For Carter's sake."

Nick scowled. "What's that mean?"

"I had known passion," Diane said simply. "I had nown deep love, just as my mother had. So had Matthew riefly, years ago. His first wife died in childbirth when iey'd been married only a year. But Carter—" she shook

her head "—as far as I know Carter only recently woke up
to the fact that love exists. What we shared was not a deep
abiding, passionate love."

Nick smiled his relief. He stroked her arm, her hip, bask
ing in the light of love in her eyes.

"Someday the right woman will come along," Diane
went on. "And I didn't want Carter to find her when he
was married to me!"

Nick grinned. "Thoughtful of you." And damned lucky
for him, he thought, aware of how close his escape had
been.

"Careful of me," Diane said. "Marrying Carter wouldn'
have worked for that reason, but mostly for another one.'
She leaned over and kissed him soundly. "I've neve
stopped loving you."

Nick shook his head, believing now, grateful to God fo
Diane's wisdom, still bemoaning his own lack of it. "
walked away from you," he reminded her.

"I remember," she said dryly.

He winced. "I didn't want to. It was the hardest thing
ever did. But I couldn't drag you into the mess my life wa
about to become."

"Noble Nick Granatelli."

He flushed. "I try."

"You're very trying," she agreed. She kissed him again
Then again. "I must be making up for lost time," she mum
bled.

Nick grinned. "Go right ahead."

So she did, and he helped her. And it was another hou
before they began talking seriously about the problems tha
lay ahead.

"What will your sister say?" Diane asked him when onc
more they were lying snuggled together under the comforter

"Sophia? She'll say congratulations, what else?" Nick

plied firmly, then sighed. "She'll come around, really.
on't worry. She's not a bad sort, just a bit bossy. But if
ou know your own mind, she doesn't feel she has to make
up for you."

"I hope they like me."

"I like you," he said. "I love you." He rolled onto his
de and looked at her. "More to the point, what about your
other? Your grandmother? I can't imagine that Gertrude
offmann will think I'm the catch of the year."

"She doesn't have to as long as I think you are."

"You're prejudiced."

"I am," she agreed. "My mother, I predict, will be ec-
atic. She believes very deeply in true love. And my grand-
other...well, let's just say she and your sister Sophia
ight find they have a lot in common."

Nick grinned. "Can't you just see it? Gertrude and the
ranatellis?"

"Sounds like a geriatric rock group," Diane said.

"I'll bet it'll rock St. Louis to the ground." He groaned.
Imagine what they'll do with our wedding."

Diane smiled. "It will undoubtedly be the Wedding Of
e Century."

"If they don't kill each other in the process."

"They'll behave," Diane assured him.

Nick lifted a skeptical brow. "Oh, why?"

Diane smiled. "Because if they don't we can always
reaten to elope!"

. *Louis, Missouri, June 1991*

WAS OVER.
The Wedding Of The Century had been accomplished,
e champagne had been drunk, the toasts had been made,

the dances had been danced, and the bride and groom had
at long last, made good their escape.

"Thank God," Nick said, falling on the hotel room bed
closing his eyes and undoing his tie even as he fell. "I neve
want to go through that again."

Diane, standing over him, looked quizzical. "Do yo
think you might have to?"

His eyes flicked open. He saw her smile and reached ou
a hand to drag her down on top of him.

"I'm never going to have to," he growled. "I told yo
that today. Vowed it, as a matter of fact, in front of Go
and most of the western civilized world."

"So you did," Diane said primly, though what she wa
doing, wiggling against his body like this, wasn't prim i
the least.

"Stop that," Nick muttered. "Or at least let me get un
dressed first."

Diane sat up and folded her hands, still smiling, waitin
expectantly. There was a warm wickedness in her gaze. "B
all means, undress."

And Nick, burning under her gaze, began fumbling wit
his cuff links. "You're full of it, you know that?" he grum
bled as she took over the job for him, undoing them wit
ease, then turning her attention to the studs on his shirtfron

"Me?" She was innocence personified.

"You, oh, Deb Of The Universe. You've been tormentin
me for the past week," he accused. "A touch here, a kis
there. And that's all!"

She grinned, unrepentant. "I suppose you wanted me t
wrestle you to the ground in front of my mother and gran
mother and your fifty thousand relatives?"

Nick grimaced, then shivered as she trailed her finger
down his chest, over his ribs, past his navel, then unbuckle

belt. "We haven't had a lot of time to ourselves, have
?"

Diane slid down the zipper of his black trousers. "Not a
, no."

Her hands urged him up, and he stood and stepped out
them. Then, as she held out her arms to him, he wrapped
in his, pulling her close, reveling in the beat of her heart
ainst his.

"But we do now," he whispered and thanked God for
:ond chances, for first loves, and for a future in which he
uld experience the wonder of both. "We have a lifetime,
love, starting now."

Diane kissed his chin, his cheek, his ears, his lips. "Prove

She brought sunlight into his darkness...but
could a man who had lost everything hope
to reclaim his heart?

Award-winning author

MYRNA MACKENZIE

MORNING BEAUTY, MIDNIGHT BEAST

Seth was a reporter who
fiercely guarded his
privacy. He'd seen what
love could do and wanted
no part of it ever again.
But Molly just might
change all that....

**Available in
September 2004.**